Jo

R. M. Dorn

© R. M. Dorn 2015

R. M. Dorn has asserted her rights under the Copyright, Design and Patents Act, 1988, to be identified as the author of this work.

First published in 2015 as Jorn, and Juncture by Acorn Independent Press Ltd.

This edition published in 2017 by Venture Press, an imprint of Endeavour Press Ltd.

Table of Contents

Prologue	5
Chapter 1	7
Chapter 2	21
Chapter 3	36
Chapter 4	51
Chapter 5	70
Chapter 6	85
Chapter 7	95
Chapter 8	103
Chapter 9	109
Chapter 10	119
Chapter 11	136
Chapter 12	154
Chapter 13	172
Chapter 14	186
Chapter 15	205
Chapter 16	222
Chapter 17	228
Chapter 18	246

Chapter 19	264
Chapter 20	279
Chapter 21	294
Chapter 22	309
Chapter 23	324
Chapter 24	338
Chapter 25	354
Chapter 26	371
Chapter 27	390
Chapter 28	411
Epilogue	429
A BRIEF GUIDE TO THE WORLDS	430
GLOSSARY	432
SHIAN DICTIONARY	438

Prologue

On hard-packed earth, under a cloudless sky, a vast military encampment spread in all directions, covering the dusty ochre scrubland to the north of the city. Greyish tents formed long lines, arranged with military precision, not a tent peg out of place, not a guy rope sagging. It was a ghost town right now, empty except for menial slaves and a few guards facing the dishonour of punishment duty instead of parade.

The 180,000 troops in the raash army had been assembled for review. They had stood since dawn, silent, immobile, at ease in perfect, square formations, rank upon rank, battalion by battalion. Sergeants had checked their men with hawk eyes, alert for the slightest fault. Every weapon and piece of kit was in place, uniforms immaculate, helmets bright, armour flashing in the rising sun. Today, Darric, Lord of All Vard, would inspect his invasion force. Only perfection would do.

The sun rose. Trumpets blared. Orders were barked, and the entire first division came to attention as one with a clash and stamp, which shook the ground. The Mage-Lord and his Sister Consort rode slowly out. They were both armed and armoured, escorted by their generals and a detachment of their personal honour guards.

The rulers of Vard and their entourage paced sedately along the massed ranks, with the rippling tide of sharply executed salutes preceding them. They rode past the green uniforms of the elite Foragers with their thunderbolt standard, on past the engineers, pausing for a moment by the crews that operated the new style of immensely powerful wrecking catapults, and the dart-throwers that sent out a barrage of a thousand armour-piercing missiles at a time.

The couple moved steadily on down the second row of battalions, eyeing the archers, grenadiers, incinerators and spears. Behind the regiments of purebred raash, another five divisions of halfer troops waited for their Lord's attention.

Unseen on the edge of the marshalling ground, a slave in the dusty-blue tunic of a domestic moved silently away and faded into the background. Mordant had seen all she needed to, and far too much for her peace of mind. The Mage-Lord's army was prepared. Now was the time to leave, when everyone's whole attention was fixed on Darric and his inspection.

Chapter 1

The High Master of Mage Hall was used to problems; his entire life was devoted to dealing with them in one shape or another, and he had the worry lines and wrinkles to prove it, but today, Kayman felt the weight of it all pressing down on him. It was all a question of time, or rather the desperate lack of it.

The corpulent mage sat back in his solid desk chair, steepled his fingers, and stared out of the window, remembering. It was almost 19 years since a young half-raash mage named Mordant had made her perilous escape from Vard to bring him the news that Darric, Lord of the Raash, planned to invade Earth, but not quite yet, not for, perhaps, another 20 years.

Back then, 20 years had sounded like a long time. Time enough to prepare. And now, the final few fingers-widths of sand were steadily trickling out of the glass, and he was no nearer to knowing how to stop the disaster than he had been then.

There was a light tap on the door. Kayman sent, *"Come in Mordant"* in mind-speech, and stood to welcome her. The slim mage took his hand warmly, and then folded wearily into the armchair he had waved her to. Her tightly-sculpted alien features never revealed much, but he could tell she was exhausted, her bald head, brow crests and shabby blue tunic were brown with dust. He smiled.

"I was just remembering our first meeting."

She reached up to untie the thong that bound her blond hair into a tight slave dock on the nape of her neck and shook it free with a sigh of relief.

"Powers, that's going back a bit, Kayman."

"You look just as young as you ever did. I wish I could say the same. But every time I look in a mirror, it reminds me that time has passed and Darric has been preparing all the while. I'm glad to see you back. Thank you for coming straight here to see me. I fret every time you take the risk of a spying mission. So, what's the bad news from Vard this time?"

Her expression remained impossible to read, but her human eyes conveyed grim frustration.

"I'll write you a full report as usual, but there's no longer any shred of doubt. Darric has his army. I've seen it this morning, turned out for a mass inspection, and very impressive it was too. It's not as large as he wanted, or quite at peak readiness, despite all the show his generals put on for him, but as close to it that it makes no difference. He has put the war sector of the city onto intensive production of arms and military supplies. The question now is not 'Is he ready?' but 'What is he waiting for?'"

Kayman blew out a heavy sigh. "Did you pick up any rumours concerning where they might attack first?"

"You're joking! Darric keeps those thoughts so close I doubt if his own shadow knows. But he can't delay for long. The army must be fed, and the farms are struggling to do that. The water situation is critical too. But field slaves eat and drink; it's a fine balance. And the supply of metal ores and coal for the blast furnaces is all but exhausted. You know, Kayman, I heard that they are using children as miners now, because the seams are too narrow for adults to work. The conditions underground are terrible and the death and accident rates are appalling."

Kayman looked grim. "I don't even want to think about it."

"Darric must know how bad things are. It will make him even more determined to get off his dying planet before everything falls apart. It has to be in the next 12 moons."

The High Master nodded. "The hit and run raids on Earth have started to increase again. I don't know why, and I don't like things I don't understand. We've not had anything like this for almost 15 years. It's not just slaving any longer; usually they kill everyone they find. But we can't stop them like you and Brett used to, because they no longer mark their targets with tags, at least we are not finding any. There is no way of knowing where they will strike next."

"There may be a pattern. Do you want me to look into it?"

"Yes, thank you, if you would, once you've had a rest. Though I get the feeling it's more about keeping Darric's troops busy and practising translocations to Earth than anything else."

"Where have these new raids been happening?"

"Mostly it's in Pain, Daunce, and Norlond, and the little kingdoms along the south of the Inner Sea. They're avoiding the Andrean Empire; Darric doesn't want to risk facing the might of the largest army on Earth just yet. He'll likely want to get himself a stronghold or two and mop up round the edges before he confronts the Emperor."

"Surely the local governors or kings, or whoever, must be getting worried?"

"Well, you'd think so, but on the whole, they are not. It's the old story. Lords like Barrass who really care about their people and protect them are rare, and so far, the raash have not attacked Dart for that reason. These new raids are not frequent enough to be seriously alarming. Each one terrifies the locals, and spreads stories of phantom beings with faces like skull masks, but the raash never hit the same region often enough to get the authorities seriously worried. Just a few peasants are killed, and their steadings or hamlets burnt. Most of the rulers believe it's the work of brigands, or at least that's what they say in public. They think it's annoying, but not much more. Humans have a great capacity for ignoring inconveniently inexplicable events."

Mordant shook her head. "You've had no success in convincing the Emperor that there really is a threat?"

Kayman snorted crossly. "I've long given up! Emperor Malchious distrusts mages and he simply doesn't believe in an alien invasion from another dimension. Andrea is a vast country, and well-defended, with the best professional army in the Western world. Darric has been careful to avoid alarming Malchious. As far as the Emperor is concerned, Earth is not at risk of an alien invasion, and not likely to be." He sighed in frustration. "Mordant, I once tried to rally the leaders of the major countries in a grand military alliance. Those hopes foundered years ago, sunk without trace on the rocks of disbelief, mutual distrust and political inertia. It's hopeless; I'm a lone voice. People will only understand the danger when Lord Darric and his sister arrive in person."

"By which time it will, of course, be much too late."

"Exactly. Even the High Council of Mages thinks I'm exaggerating the capabilities of Darric and Ajina. Even though they know that Darric has both the Knife and the Chain, they refuse to believe that these Tools can significantly augment his Power. That's Professor Turner's influence, of course. He simply won't accept that the Tools can be used as weapons. I will tell them your latest news, but I suspect they will sit back and do nothing, as usual."

Mordant shook her head. "I'm glad I'm not sitting in your chair, my friend. This would be a very good time to have our Master of Nine ready and waiting. But I guess there is no news?"

"None. From what Rolf last told me, Jorn is a perfectly normal young human. He shows no sign of Power. He's 18 now; his colours should have started to become active years ago."

Jorn

"Maybe Idris got it wrong; it's very hard to see a new-born's Spectrum." Mordant stood up and stretched to ease her tension. "But worrying about it won't help. Right now, I just can't wait to get the smell of dust and pigs out of my hair, and eat a meal that does not contain pork that has to be chewed for 10 minutes."

When the door had closed, Kayman got up and paced his study in restless thought. The disinterest and disbelief of his colleagues was infuriating. The only action he could take at present was to protect Mage Hall and the store of ancient knowledge that it contained, and he already had that in hand.

The Master of the Hall sat again, ran his hands across his rapidly balding head and sighed, feeling suddenly old and tired. Mordant was right. What they needed right now was overmastering Power. Something stronger than Darric could ever muster. But his own strange fore-seeing before Jorn's birth, and the hope that he and his closest friends had cherished in secret for the past 18 years, had so far come to nothing. He must speak to Rolf.

*

Jorn stood at the worktable in the storeroom next to his weaving loft, totally absorbed in his selection of colours for his apprentice piece. The complex tapestry depended on getting the subtle shades exactly right, graded so that he was almost painting with the fine yarns, and then using the bright flashes of contrast to make the whole thing sing. He could see the design so clearly in his imagination, where all the colours glowed with life, but turning it into reality, given the restrictions of the dyers' art, was another matter.

The small boy sitting on the floor near his feet was not, as he fondly imagined, helping, but Jorn had not the heart to make him leave. Red looked up at him, his face intent and serious.

"Did I get it right?" He held up a length of simple braiding for examination. It had got rather grubby.

Jorn squatted down and took a look. "That's great Red, yes you did, well almost; look, it's gone a bit wobbly just there. But I guess it won't show in Fern's mane."

Red frowned. "No, I'll do it again. A weaver doesn't make mistakes. Dad's always saying that. And our pony and trap is going to be the very, very best at the Summer Festival."

"You'll be a good weaver, Red, if you start out thinking like that. The Festival is still almost three moons away; there's plenty of time for you to make Fern's new trappings and get them just right. You could do some for

Warp and Weft too; we are going to enter our big cart in the parade. Now, look, let's find you some more colours from my scrap bin, and then you can go and sit out in the sunshine and do some real work, eh? I must start my weaving."

Red bounced up. "Can I have some scarlet?"

"Just a bit. But be careful with it, it costs a lot. I can only give you short pieces. But you could put it into some tassels like I showed you the other day."

The six-year-old skipped away happily with his loot. Jorn gave a fond grin as he picked his first set of yarns and took them through to his loom. His foster-brother was actually very dexterous for his age. Weaving was definitely in his blood.

Jorn stretched, looked longingly out of the wide window where the sunshine was gilding the stone buildings round the cobbled yard, and sighed. He enjoyed his work, and he really wanted to start his tapestry, but it was so hard to concentrate when it was spring and every part of him was yearning to be out in the forest, watching the first leaves burst out of the bondage of their buds. *Later*, he promised himself, *when I've done the first few rows.*

*

Kayman and Rolf portalled out from Mage Hall to the Horse Transit Point, and from thence to the Shian Realm. Arden's mild climate produced an earlier spring. The forest was already lush with soft green. Polished golden celandines glittered at the roots of the big trees, and buttery clumps of primroses dotted the edges of the broad, grassy glade. Stiff tips of the first bluebell shoots poked up through last winter's bronze leaf-litter. J'Louth's magnificent beech was bursting into fresh leaf.

J'Louth's *shi* slid from their home-tree in a stream of shimmering energy. The mage's muscular, naked body took form, and Rolf was struck by how much Jorn resembled his father, now he was nearing manhood. The shian greeted his old friend, Rolf, with pleasure, but then turned to Kayman with a questioning look.

"We are delighted to see you, but you are such an old storm crow that we cannot help but wonder what ill wind has blown you here to Arden?"

Kayman smiled at the good-looking, auburn-haired male. "We need your advice, and Idris' too, assuming he is home, not off on one of his long wanderings?"

"He is at home. I have already called him. Sit down my friends, though I fear the ground is somewhat damp. We had a heavy dew this morning."

A drift of rapidly moving mist came through the glade and then took the form of a pale-skinned male whose glimmering scales marked him as a shian of the water.

"Good to see you Idris," said Rolf. "It's been too long *tantar-alta*. Though you make me feel my age! You don't look a day older than when we first met, more decades ago than I care to remember, and here's me with grey in my beard and wrinkles round my eyes."

Idris gave his old friend a welcoming smile. "That's the advantage of being able to shape a new body every time one needs it." He became serious. "I can sense questions," he said with typical shian directness. "So what is the problem?"

"Jorn," said Kayman succinctly. He turned to the boy's parents. "J'Louth, your son is 18. His colours should have emerged by now, restless and ready to be mastered, but he gives no sign that he is even aware of them. We need to know what to do. Why isn't he ready? Is our hope in vain? If ever we needed a Master of Nine, it's now. Mordant has just returned from Vard, and she says that Darric's army is ready for action."

"That is the news we expected soon, but did not want to hear. As for Jorn, I'll need to see him before I can answer your question. Is he well? No sign of any problems?" asked Idris.

"None," said Rolf, "at least not last time I saw him, but that was six months ago. Then he looked just like any human boy of his age, except for his height, and of course, the auburn hair and green eyes." He grinned at J'Louth. "There is no mistaking his parentage."

J'Louth looked thoughtful. "For a human, 18 is on the threshold of manhood; for a shian, it is still childhood. A shian male does not become an adult until he is past 40. It is rare for a shian's Gift to show much before 30. It may be that our son's shian side is holding back the development of the Gift."

"Perhaps," agreed Idris. "I will find an opportunity to observe him in the next few days, and let you know what his aura tells me. He is bound to come by that lake in the deep-wood sooner or later, he loves that spot."

"Thank you old friend. I'll go and see him myself first thing tomorrow. I wanted to get your views first."

*

Jorn blinked at the light filtering through his window. He shrugged off the lingering memory of his familiar dream about numberless and nameless colours, stretched, yawned, and got up. He swore quietly as he banged his head on the rafters. He kept forgetting his recently acquired need to duck where the beamed ceiling sloped over his bed. If he got any more bruises, he was likely to remember the hard way.

He pulled the curtains back from the dormer window and opened the catch to let in the scents of early morning air and the sound of bird song. In the distance, the crowns of the forest trees showed the first faint mist of green. He simply had to go for a long walk today. He'd work all the better after that.

Jorn sloshed his face in cold water from his ewer, and dressed rapidly in his pants, stockings, knee britches and loose linen shirt, topping it off with a long-belted waistcoat, fronted by panels of floral brocade. As he ran a comb through the dark red tangles, he happily scrutinised his reflection in the small mirror, pleased to greet the image of the young man he was fast turning into, instead of the boy he had been. The change was still a novelty.

No spots! But no sign of a beard yet. He touched his bare upper lip. The tantalising smell of baking wafted up the stairs and his reflection grinned back with anticipation. He left his room, his feet rattling down the wooden treads.

Hot griddle scones! And yesterday, Mary churned new butter. There's still some honey.

His stomach rumbled expectantly. These days he was always hungry, desperate for sweet things. But breakfast had to wait until he had finished his morning chore of chopping wood. Aldrick did not believe in letting the servants do all the heavy jobs.

In the still morning air, the sound of Jorn's axe raised echoes from the stone walls. He took a smaller hatchet and, with steady work, reduced some of the logs to kindling with practiced ease. As he stacked the piles of wood neatly by the wall, he muttered his foster-father's favourite saying: *"Method, my boy, organisation and method. Attention to detail, that's the weavers' way."*

Jorn straightened his back, docked the axes, and made quickly for the pump to rinse his hands and face. He was starving. Last one to the table was likely to find less than his share. He hurriedly pulled on his shirt and waistcoat, careered round the corner of the house, and nearly crashed into a very short, dark-skinned man.

"Hey, lad, is that any way to greet a person?" the visitor demanded, his twinkling black eyes taking the sting out of his gruff voice.

"Uncle Rolf!" Jorn exclaimed with delight. "It's been ages! You missed my birthday. Where have you been?"

Rolf smiled, his luxuriant beard jutting as he tipped his head back to peer up at the tall, deep-voiced, young man. "Oh, here and there, lad, as usual, here and there; making an almost honest living. Sorry I couldn't get back in time for your birthday. Eighteen already! My, but you've grown again. I'd give you a hug but I can only reach your knees!" It was an exaggeration, but Jorn already topped his very short guardian by around four spans.

"It's not me growing; I think you've shrunk! Come on, Anna has baked griddle scones, and there's bacon, and if we don't hurry, the kids will wolf the lot!"

"That sounds good. I've already put Tricky in the stable."

They went together towards the back door, down a stone-flagged passage and into the big kitchen. Aldrick was seated in his chair at the head of the long deal table, with Rob and young Red wriggling on benches beside him and Polly in her high chair. Mary was busy at the range, and a delicious aroma of frying bacon made Jorn's mouth water. Rolf's unexpected arrival was greeted with shouts of delight.

"Well, you are the early bird! You're very welcome, Master Rolf," said Aldrick warmly, rising to greet his visitor. He surveyed the little man with shrewd eyes that took in the expensive fabric of his well-cut jacket under the generously-caped travel cloak, and the hint of gold on his belt. "Life has been treating you well, I see."

"Stories, stories!" clamoured Rob and Red.

"P'esents!" insisted Polly, waving a spoon with enthusiasm.

"Just you ignore these greedy brats, they're spoilt enough without you adding to it!" laughed Anna, waving Rolf to sit at table, and shushing a chorus of loud questions.

Rolf raised a hand in protest. "Whoa there; breakfast first. And I can't stay long enough for stories this time." There was a chorus of disappointment.

Mary confirmed, "Breakfast first" in one of her 'don't mess with me' voices. "Who wants bacon?"

"Meee!" chorused the children, including Jorn who slid onto the bench opposite Rolf. As the family ate, with the usual snatch and grab and gentle bickering, Rolf unobtrusively took a good look at his guard-child. *Eating enough for three.* He raised his eyebrows in comic disbelief as Jorn devoured yet another hunk of bread, smothered with butter and honey.

Anna caught the look and cast eyes to heaven. "Growing pains!" she said, shaking her head.

"And hollow legs," added Aldrick, "shooting up like a sapling."

Rolf grinned, his merry eyes shielding his thoughts.

He looks normal enough. And that's the problem; if he's a Nine, surely something ought to show by now?

Jorn wiped the last buttery crumbs from around his mouth with a questing tongue and transferred his full attention to Rolf. "Come on, now, where have you been? We haven't seen you for almost half a year."

The little man waved his arms in an expansive gesture. "Away east, a long way, across the Narrows to Tamor and over the edge of the Great Sands to Karth and Utiskan. I shall tell you all the tall tales another time. But first things first: I have left my pack outside; let's see if there just might be something in it for all of you."

There was, of course; Rolf produced silver buttons for Aldrick, lace for Anna, wooden toys for the little boys, and a doll for Polly.

Anna bent to hug him. "You are too generous, my dear friend."

"Making up for missed birthdays, and Longest Night," he beamed.

The clock chimed eight. Aldrick got up from the table and left for work. Jorn gently cuffed Rob, who was already fiddling with his intricate wooden puzzle.

"Come on, young man, that can wait, you have to walk to school." The reluctant boy was chivvied from the table, despite his predictable protests. Red went into the yard intent on play, and Mary took Polly off to the nursery. Anna started to tidy up.

"And now, Jorn, something for you." Rolf held out a cloth-wrapped parcel, which turned out to be a superb knife with a bright pattern-welded blade and a handle covered in sharkskin. There was a finely-worked leather sheath to go with it.

"Wow, Rolf! That's really special. Thank you very much." Rolf held up his clenched hand for a trader's knuckle touch to seal the deal. Jorn glanced at the wall clock. "Oh my! Dad will have my guts to warp a loom if I'm late. I must do at least four hours work on my tapestry today. But

Jorn

Mum, it's a perfect day and I want to take a long walk in the woods later, so I'll miss lunch. Any chance of a bite to take with me?"

Anna gave him raised eyebrows. "One bite? Oh, I am sure I could find you *one*."

Jorn grinned and gave her a peck. "You know very well what I mean!"

"I must see this tapestry of yours," Rolf told him.

"Come on up to the weaving loft then, not that there's much to see yet, except the warp. But you can see the cartoon, which shows the design. And we must talk a bit before you go. Light's good, must dash!" He rushed out, remembering just in time to duck under the lintel.

Anna's eyes were soft as she watched him leave. She turned to Rolf and smiled. "He's a good lad, and very talented. A bit on the solitary side, but then he always has been. Still spends most of his spare time in the woods. But anyway, the local youths of his age boast and swagger and snigger as girls go by, and sneak cider to drink in the old barn when they think no one is looking. I'm not sorry he doesn't go with that crowd."

"Better no friends than the wrong ones. But, my word, he's grown again! I can remember when I found him abandoned in the snow, a premature baby, so tiny that he fitted in my two hands."

"He was lucky. Both that he was found, and that he was found by you. You have been a wonderful guardian for him Rolf."

"And you have been a great foster-mother; I'd like to have raised him myself, but that would have been quite impossible. He needed a real family."

"And I needed a son. Aldrick and I thought we might never have children; we'd tried so hard with no luck. And then seven years after Jorn came into our lives, Red arrived, and then Rob and Polly, so we did get a family after all. The boys dote on Jorn, and he's very good with them. He'll be a fine man, Rolf."

"What about girls? With his good looks, he must surely be fluttering a few female hearts?"

"You should see how the lasses stare at him in Borthwick on market day, huddling in corners and giggling! But Jorn never seems to notice. Heaven knows there is time enough for that, and I've no doubt he'll break a few hearts soon enough."

"He's bound to start noticing one day!"

Rolf chatted with Anna for a while, asking about the children and the business. It was always good to have this glimpse of family life. With his constant travel and dangerous missions, the mage was unlikely to have one of his own.

Finally, he got up and stretched. "Well, Anna, mustn't keep you chatting all day. And I can't stay too long myself. Must go and see Jorn's work before I go."

"He's putting his heart and soul into it. Really wants to impress his dad. Not that he has to try. His way with the wools is already exceptional."

Rolf went out of the warm kitchen into the fresh sunshine and crossed the yard to the weaving lofts. The weavers and their families lived on the ground floor of the long, stone buildings. The first storey workrooms had skylights and wide south-facing windows for maximum light. Rolf walked quietly up the stairs and halted, watching Jorn from a distance, intrigued as always by the complex techniques involved in weaving a tapestry.

It was a very slow process. Even a skilled weaver could produce no more than one or two fingers width in a day. Because Jorn was using a high warp loom, he had to weave with the back of the tapestry facing him. He could glimpse the finished work by using a mirror placed behind the weft. He would only be certain that it was exactly right when the completed tapestry was removed from the loom. His cartoon, the drawing which depicted the design in exact detail and full colour, hung as a reference behind his weaving bench, but he scarcely looked at it, because the image was so clear in his mind.

Rolf went softly across the boarded floor and stood close to Jorn, but the young weaver was so lost in his work that he seemed unaware. Finally, Jorn caught sight of him in the mirror, turned on his bench and smiled.

"I only started on the weft a few days ago. So, as I said, there really isn't much to see." He gestured towards his cartoon. "It's going to have a border of forest flowers and leaves, and then the middle is a stag with his hinds caught in a shaft of sunlight. Not that original, I know, but Aldrick said it had to be something that would sell easily."

The mage looked at the well-drawn design. "I love your choice of colours."

"That's probably the bit I like most. Choosing the right ones and getting them to work together. They change, you know, Rolf. The colours look different, depending on how you combine them; that's the challenge, to make it look as if there are more shades in the work than there really are. I collect colours you know, all the time, I'm always looking for new ones. I'm so wrapped up in it all, I even dream about colours."

Jorn

Rolf's sense tweaked. "Do you now? So what do you dream?"

"Oh, I don't know; I've usually forgotten as soon as I wake up. Just something about having hundreds of them to sort out; silly really."

"Doesn't bother you?"

"Heaven's no!"

"Well, lad, I must go. But I'll be back to see the finished product. How long will it take do you think?"

"At least three months."

"My, you have more patience than I could muster! Well, good luck with it. I'm sure it will be excellent."

Jorn got up to give his guardian a parting hug and see him off. "Thanks for the knife, Rolf. Don't leave it so long before your next visit."

"I won't," Rolf assured him. *No, indeed I won't. I can sense a change in him. But it's plain he has no idea about his Gift as yet. I wonder what Idris will make of him?*

*

At noon, Jorn went to the kitchen to collect his lunch bag, took a peek inside, gave his mother a pleased hug, hooked his sheepskin-lined coat off the peg, and set out. His work at the loom kept him away from the forest more than he liked, and now the soft sounds and smells of spring called to him, stirring needs in some deeper part of himself that he hardly understood.

To Jorn, the whole forest was beautiful, but of course, there were places that he especially enjoyed.

I'll head for the lake and say hello to my favourite trees as they wake up. The frogs might still be mating; they are so funny to watch, all that noisy desperation. There'll be nesting birds too, maybe the first mallard ducklings. I can have lunch there and just sit and listen, and feel the greenness.

After a brisk two-hour walk, Jorn reached his destination and found his usual seat on a fallen willow trunk where the long strands of new leaves were already tossing in the soft breeze, like kite-tails tied with green bows.

The young weaver unpacked his treats and munched happily. The frogs had almost completed their job; the shallows were blobbed with grey spawn. He could still hear some croaks, and the harsh squawks of the herons squabbling over their high nest sites. The calls of ducks, moorhens, coots and grebes came loudly as they dabbled busily across the lake and fetched beakfuls of weeds and twigs. The sun was warm and bright, pulling sparkles off the water. He automatically analysed the colours of the reflections, greens, golds and azures, silver and indigo, matching them to the ones in his memory, placing new ones into his mental storeroom.

Idris watched from the water, invisible in his *shi*. The mage concentrated on Jorn's aura, looking for the spectrum that defined his Gift, scanning for any sign of a blockage on his Power. His own ability to Read auras was extremely unusual and highly valued by Kayman. An aura never lied, and revealed much. What this extraordinary aura was telling him was amazing, but then, a shian-human halfer was unique, and a mage with the Power of Nine was way outside his experience, or that of anyone's in the past thousand years.

Jorn shifted, a little uncomfortably, and looked round him, brushing his forehead as if getting rid of a strand of cobweb. Idris broke off his scan at once; the lad had sensed his presence. That in itself was significant. The shian mage watched until Jorn had finished his meal, thrown a few crusts to a noisily grateful group of mallards, and finally left for home.

Idris portalled out to the Dolphin Transit Point, where the resident mage could translocate him to Mage Hall in the Dwarran Realm.

When he arrived, Idris went to his old base, the grotto pool with its ornate fountains and refreshing waterfall. He stood beneath the fall for a while, remembering. It was many years since he had been to the Hall, and the place held mixed memories. Refreshed, he made a mind call to Kayman and Rolf to announce his arrival. The two mages hastened down to his pond and he took form to bespeak them.

"*Let's get the big question out of the way. There is no shadow of doubt. We do have a potential Mage of Nine.*" Both mages blew breaths of relief. "*But that is where it gets very strange. I have never seen an aura quite like Jorn's. It flames with Power, and at times, it seems to double, like a rainbow with its own shadow. But he shows no sign of knowing that he has his colours, nor are they seething around in his mind, as they usually do when Power awakes and has not yet been mastered. If I did not think it impossible, I would have said he already has Mastery. But how can an untaught mage achieve that? It is surely impossible without the Quincunx.*"

"*And even more improbable that he should do so and not know it,*" said Kayman. "*This young man is an enigma in every way. Can you understand this, Rolf?*"

The mage shook his head, his brow furrowed in thought. *"I don't know. In the far distant past, before mages used the Quincunx, they must have had some other system for controlling the colours, so I suppose it is possible. We have to throw away the textbook here, I think. But I was talking to Jorn about his work and one thing did strike me: he has a passion for the colours he uses in his weaving. His day is spent handling coloured threads, making decisions about which to use, how to blend them. When I first sought a foster family for him, Aldrick came to mind partly for that very reason. A weaver's seemed an apt environment for a child with the Gift. He has handled colours all his life. I wonder if this has had some effect."*

"You mean it may have given him a kind of control?"

"It's a theory. But that aside, what do we do now? He must be told and soon, for both his own sake and ours."

"And he must be watched," said Kayman, *"for his protection. Until we can bring him here and let him train in safety."*

"But Kayman, as usual you are making the assumption that Jorn will accept his Gift. It must be freely chosen. We must not put him under undue pressure. What if he does not want to be a mage?" Idris looked at his friends with real concern.

"Let that water flow, Idris, we'll bridge it if we must," responded Rolf.

"I will tell J'Louth of course. Between us, we will watch him as closely as we can."

Rolf sighed. *"Thank you Idris. Power or no Power he is almost a man, and he has the right to know his true parentage. I think the time has come, though it will grieve me to disturb his happiness. Yet that may be the key to the other thing. Meeting J'Louth will be life-changing. Who knows what it will do to his colours?"*

*

Rolf spent most of the next three days trying to decide how and when to tell Jorn the truth. He talked it over with Kayman, seeking the best words, the right way to begin. He was used to breaking the shattering news to young humans who had no idea they possessed the Gift, and it was never easy. The emotional realisation could trigger a lethal eruption of ungoverned Power. That could be devastating with an ordinary Eight, and must be far more lethal in a Nine; Rolf was far from sure his own Power would be able to contain the explosion. And, at worst, Jorn might reject his Gift, and Rolf would have to deal with that too.

Chapter 2

Rolf finally braced himself and made the translocation to his usual hook near Aldrick's premises, covered himself with a never-mind, and went to his fateful meeting with his guard-child. When he reached the weaving loft, the mage stood in the doorway, watching Jorn's deft movements, still finding it hard to begin, still half uncertain whether he should.

The young apprentice was working at his loom, deep in concentration on a particularly difficult part of his design. He absent-mindedly stretched out his hand for a new colour, which was just out of reach. The small shuttle rose and landed in his hand. Jorn was so wrapped up in his work that he never even noticed. But his visitor did. When he saw the spontaneous apport, Rolf's mind was instantly made up. He shed his never-mind and made his voice deliberately cheerful.

"Well now, lad, you have made progress haven't you?"

Jorn's whole body started in surprise and then he turned and sprang to his feet with a broad smile of welcome.

"Rolf! Sneaking up on me like that! You made me jump! I didn't expect to see you again so soon. I thought you were off on another of your long journeys?"

"Something came up to delay me. And my last visit here has set me thinking. It made me see that you are not a boy anymore; you're a young man and there are things you have to know. Jorn, I need to have a serious talk with you. Can we go somewhere more private, in case one of the weaving assistants comes in?"

Jorn's anxious frown reflected his tense incomprehension of any possible reason for his guardian's request.

"It's lunch time so no one is likely to come up here, but we can sit in the wool store right through there, if you like. There's a bench."

The stocky mage led the way and they sat surrounded by the pigeonholes, filled with boxes holding hanks of wool, graded in every possible shade of every colour ever dyed. The irony of that was not lost on Rolf. His opening was a deliberate gamble, but his sense told him to try it.

"I'm going to start with a question. Where do you keep the colours you have inside your mind?"

Jorn's eyebrows shot up in surprise. His hand indicated the storeroom. "In boxes. A bit like this. Isn't that what everyone does?"

Rolf kept his face neutral and interested, but inwardly he was jubilant. His long-shot had paid off.

He said, "Sometimes. Those of us who have the colours. But not everyone does."

"Don't they? That's odd. I guess I just assumed we all do. I mean, it's normal isn't it? Just the way our minds work?"

Rolf had to snort a laugh. "Jorn, I have to tell you, there is nothing normal about the way your mind works. Or indeed mine. The colours show you've the potential to work magic."

"I've *what*?" Jorn goggled at his guardian as if he had lost his senses. "You can't be serious! There's no such thing as magic."

Rolf regarded him with some amusement. *"Oh yes, there is! You are looking a real, live magician, although I prefer the word mage."*

Jorn flinched as he heard Rolf's words inside his head. His guardian had not moved his lips. This was beyond scary.

Rolf had established that Jorn could bespeak. And there had been no explosion — yet. He switched to plain speech to get back to safer ground, deliberately trying to seem relaxed, keeping his voice casual.

"I can assure you that I don't spend my time pretending to pull ribbons and doves out of thin air!" He paused and placed his hand on Jorn's arm, giving a quick, reassuring squeeze, his dark face serious. "Now take a deep breath and listen lad, because what I have to say next is going to be a shock. There is no easy way to tell you this. You are not only a mage; you are also not entirely human."

"Not human? But Rolf of course I am. What else could I possibly be?" Jorn's green eyes narrowed with total bewilderment, desperate to understand, his body taut with expectation and uncertainty. Had his guardian gone totally mad? Or was this a dream? If it was, he wanted very much to wake up.

"There's a very long answer to that question, and that will have to wait, but the short version is easily said. You are a halfer; part human and, in your case, part shian. J'Louth, your father, is a shian of the wood; your mother, Jelda, was human. I am also a halfer, but in my case half-human and half-dwarran."

"Halfer? Shian? Dwarran? What on earth are you taking about, Rolf?" Jorn's face was a picture of bewilderment.

"It's confusing, I know. I'll try to explain. A halfer is a mixed-race being. The shians are spirits of wood and water who inhabit Arden."

"Where's that?"

"Another earth located in a different universe. J'Louth is a shian, a kind of spirit of the trees."

"Whoa!" Jorn shook his head. "This is all totally mad. Let me get this straight. My real father is a tree spirit? And he lives in another universe?"

Rolf nodded. There was a long pause as Jorn wrestled with the implications. His guardian seemed absolutely serious. *He's always told me the truth. He wouldn't joke about something as important as this. However impossible it all seems, I have to trust him.*

"So that's why..." he muttered eventually.

"Why what?"

"Oh, you know, the thing I have with trees, the way I love the forest. No one else I know feels quite like I do, and now I guess I know why." He shook his head as the other thing Rolf had said hit home. "And you aren't fully human either? What the hell are you then?"

"As I just said, a halfer. The dwarrans are a race of black dwarves, who live on a different duplicate earth. My father was human; my mother was dwarran, hence my dark skin and lack of height." Rolf continued rapidly before Jorn could interrupt again. "And, as I just said, I am a mage, and so is J'Louth. And so, if you decide to train, are you. So now you know. That's the big surprises out of the way." He gave the stunned young man another pat on his shoulder. "I think you should breathe a bit now!"

Jorn was hardly aware of holding his breath, but he blew it out in a gust of dismay. He was shaken to his core. He latched onto the one thing that he had fully understood, grasping it like a straw of hope.

"Do you mean that my real father is alive?"

"Yes, he is."

His emerald eyes were suddenly bright with need. "Can I meet him?"

"Yes, but I'm afraid that to do so, you have to face up to a hard choice." Rolf sat up straighter, preparing for the most difficult part of his life-changing news. Jorn shook his head in denial; he'd already had more than enough to cope with.

"A choice? Oh my! What choice? Rolf, right now I'm totally confused."

Rolf sighed and his voice was filled with understanding. "Of course you are, and I'm truly sorry, but sometimes there are two paths in the wood and you cannot take them both. I can take you to meet J'Louth, answer all your questions, and help you to become a mage. But if you choose to do those things, you must give up your present life, and very probably, you will never be able to return to it."

"But…"

Rolf held up his hands again and shook his head to forestall another predictable rush of questions. "Just listen. Your mage Gift will soon become dangerous, liable to spontaneous outbreaks of potentially lethal Power. You must either master it, or lose it. If you do not want to become a mage, I will use my Power to lock your colours deep, beyond your use. As far as you will be aware, all this will never have happened."

Jorn's forehead furrowed in his battle to understand. He looked intently at Rolf. "Let me get this straight. I have to choose between finding my father, and becoming a mage, or leaving everything just as it is, and not even remembering we ever had this conversation?"

"Yes. That is the choice. You can't have both."

Rolf gave that a few moments to sink in. He could see Jorn reel as the weight of it hit him. He was silent for a long minute. "Do I have to decide at once?" he asked in a low voice.

Rolf nodded, his face still serious. "Yes, you do. Or at least, very soon."

Jorn shook his head, overwhelmed again by the enormity of the decision, and then exploded in a mixture of anger and distress. "But that's just too cruel, too unfair, especially at this moment when things are going so well, feeling so right."

He surged off the bench, tight-lipped, took a few steps away and back again, and heaved in a deep breath, making a huge effort to control his emotions. Rolf watched him with a calm expression that masked his intensely anxious concern. This was the critical moment; his sense told him that Jorn's colours were primed to explode at any moment. He had a mind-fetter hung ready, but he fervently hoped he would not have to use it.

Jorn became still, staring down at his guardian, fighting for control. His next words carried a quiet desperation. "And what about my foster parents? They have been so good to me; they love me, and I love them. Weaving is my life." He looked towards the weaving loft and spread his hands in frustrated indecision. "How can I just walk out on everything?"

"I'm not asking you to. I'll find an acceptable excuse for you to go away with me. And it's not forever. In a few years, when you've become a mage and your colours won't put you or anyone else in danger, you can come back and visit. At least, I hope you can. Before you decide, I need to tell you one more thing that may affect what you choose to do."

Jorn nodded, still looking distressed, too agitated to sit down again. "I'll try and concentrate, but my brain is mush right now."

Rolf allowed himself to relax a little; the explosion of ungoverned Power seemed to have been averted, for the moment.

"You imagine a settled future here. That may be so, but only if there is peace. Right now there isn't, only the illusion of it. I have spoken of other earths in other universes. There is another such, named Vard. In a short time, unless we can stop them, its inhabitants, the raash, intend to invade our Earth. They are utterly ruthless. They will enslave every human they do not kill and take the planet for their own. Nowhere will be safe. Even here. If you choose to accept your Gift, you could help us to fight them. We need every mage we can get."

Jorn sighed, shook his head, and went to lean on the windowsill, silently staring out at the distant trees, his hunched shoulders mirroring his confused misery. Rolf watched him in mute sympathy, twining his fingers through his beard, trying to leave his guard-child some space to consider his decision. He could hear the unshielded thoughts as clearly as if Jorn was bespeaking.

Alien races, other universes; it's beyond belief! Two paths in the wood; impossible choices; my whole life changed in less time than it takes to put one row of weft on the loom. Two paths. One leading to my real father and an unknown future, the other to the life I know and love, except Rolf says even that is threatened. And I can only take one. This is too much. How can I decide when I don't even understand half of what he's told me? Then he braced himself, clearly trying to find a way to cope with the shattering discoveries. *Things are as things are. Deal with it. You have to choose. But how?*

Rolf knew that Jorn was battling with his indecision, balanced on the edge, torn between his destinies. Right now, it could go either way. He stood and bespoke quietly, his words chosen with care to tip the balance. He was aware that Idris would probably not approve of his deliberate manipulation.

"Ask yourself one important question, Jorn, how would it feel if you never met your real father?"

"I don't think I could bear that."

"Then you have already made your choice, haven't you?"

The truth of that cleared the fog from his mind. Jorn straightened up, squared his shoulders and turned. He looked down at his guardian, no longer uncertain, but still troubled.

"Yes, I guess I have. But that doesn't make it any easier. I want to meet my father, of course I do, but I'm not sure that I want to be a mage. I'm not even sure what that means. But I can't have one without the other, can I?"

"No, I'm afraid you can't. It just wouldn't work."

"I have to finish my apprentice piece. I can't just walk away with it half-done. I may never have another opportunity to do work like this. I can't get my head round that right now."

Rolf sensed that Jorn needed to find a familiar reality to hold onto after such intense emotion. He led the way back into the weaving loft and stood in front of the tapestry. The trader in Rolf knew tapestries and, even in this unfinished state, he could see that this one was exceptional.

"This is going to be wonderful Jorn. How long will it take to complete it?"

"About another 30 days." Jorn ran his hand gently across the weft.

"Well, make sure it is exactly that. I'll come back then and persuade Aldrick to let you come away with me. I'll take you to meet your father, and we can start your training."

Jorn plumped down onto his weaving bench, suddenly uncertain again, feeling his future in front of him like the mouth of a dark tunnel.

"The thought scares the hell out of me, Rolf. I'd like a bit more time here, if it's possible."

There was no way right now that he could tell the young weaver that there was no time, no time at all. Even another two moons was too long, but he could not press him any harder. He smiled reassuringly.

"Firstly, finish your tapestry. Secondly, make quite sure in your own mind that you have made the right decision. Meanwhile, and this is important, try hard not to let the colours start forming into braids or knots or nets in your mind — you could end up in all sorts of trouble. And, Jorn, you can't talk to anyone else about the colours and our mage-craft; you do understand that? Even though they have known me for over 20 years, Aldrick and Anna have no idea that I'm anything more than a travelling trader. And they do not know the full truth about you either. They believe you are just a foundling I picked up."

Jorn nodded. Rolf monitored his churning thoughts, still so near to the surface of his mind that the mage could read them easily. He was feeling stunned; the idea of leaving his loom and his family was frightening, but staying put and rejecting his true heritage was simply impossible. Underneath the fear, a new determination was building, and a pressing curiosity. He would find his father. And he would learn to use his Power, and help to fight the raash. But he didn't feel ready to face any of that right now.

Rolf gave Jorn's arm a final reassuring squeeze, left the weaving loft, and hung a never-mind to ensure that he passed through the yard unnoticed. He was relieved that Jorn had taken the shattering news as well as he had, but that had not made the telling of it any easier. He shook his head. *A cruel decision for one so young. But it went as well as I could have hoped. And there was no explosion of Power, thank the Nine.*

Rolf strode briskly towards the forest, heading for the glade that Jorn had once shown him. As arranged, J'Louth was waiting for him there. Shians show little emotion, but Rolf could sense his old friend's anxiety.

"How did he take it?"

"Bravely, I am pleased to say, and with good sense, once he got past the shock. It's astonishing; the lad has managed to store his colours so that they do not cause chaos in his mind. He says he has hundreds of them! He had no idea that it was anything unusual. I believe he will accept his Gift. He just needs time to get used to the idea. And, of course, he can't wait to meet you, though to be frank, the truth of that will come as another blow."

"I know."

*

Rolf portalled back to the Hall to tell Kayman and Mordant what had happened.

"My instinct was right. Working as a weaver, using colours in his daily life, has somehow enabled him to gain a degree of natural mastery. It's most unusual."

The High Master nodded and pulled a wry face. "I suspect we are going to have to get used to saying that where Jorn is concerned."

Rolf turned to Mordant. "If he does accept his Gift, you'll help to train him, won't you? You have great skill with glamours, and your attacking constructs are awesome."

"Train a Nine! I'm only a Mage of Six. Powers, what a terrifying thought! But of course I will. I just hope he's a fast learner."

"And so say all of us," said Kayman grimly. "I know we can't push him too fast, but we are running out of time."

Jorn

*

Over the following days, Jorn worked at his loom from dawn to dusk. It soothed him, and stopped the useless round of questions and worries. And, in any case, he really wanted to see his tapestry completed. He was trained to be a perfectionist, and he knew it was good. The colours were superbly blended, the picture crisp, the tension exactly right, the edges perfectly straight. People started to make excuses to drop by and take a look.

He was unaware that Rolf also paid visits, invisible under the cover of a pass-me-by, to observe his guard-child with anxious care, and monitor his progress.

The fine spring weather had brought out a rush of potential customers, all suddenly enthusiastically planning to redecorate their best rooms in the latest style; most of them would be disappointed. There was a waiting list for Aldrick's finest bespoke work that ran into years. But he did keep a selection of fine hangings, brocades, damasks and cut velvets for sale, for those with deep enough pockets to pay for this specialised work.

When quality customers arrived, the master weaver often called Jorn down to assist him. The tall, handsome apprentice was expert at showing the samples, while Aldrick himself did the sales pitch. The experience of listening to trade-talk, and learning how to deal with the ultra-fussy, ultra-rich, was valuable.

Today there were newcomers; agents for some rich, but anonymous patron who required a very large order of fine window and bed hangings, and who was also interested in tapestries. Aldrick privately doubted if he could meet their demands in full, but he was certainly not going to pass up the lucrative trade without trying for at least a part of it.

The two men were well-mounted, well-dressed, well-spoken, and Jorn thought, not from anywhere near Dart, or even Arun. Their Basic was almost too good, spoken with pedantic precision, like some foreign ambassador, not like any of the gentry or rich merchants who were their usual buyers. One did the dealing. The other watched and seemed uninterested in what he was being shown, but let his eyes wander around, missing little, and finally walked out of the display room and wandered idly round in the yard.

The potential buyer was picky, and apparently unimpressed, despite the quality of Aldrick's stock. He made some comments, took a few details, and finally left without promising to come back.

The master weaver watched them depart and shook his head. "We'll get no sale there. And frankly, I'm not sorry. Clients like that have trouble written all over them. What was your impression Jorn?"

"Can't say I liked them. But as we often say, liking one's customers is an optional extra. What matters is whether they choose well and pay promptly."

"And I suspect those two will do neither. Ah well, thanks for your help lad. Back to your loft, now. No slacking!"

Jorn grinned, knowing his foster-father was joking. "I'm determined to get it done by the Summer Festival. Then I can really enjoy the holiday. Red has been driving me mad all spring with making new trappings for Fern and the carthorses. We have to use them, Dad, or he'll be so upset. He's actually done really well now he's got the hang of braiding and making flights and cockades."

*

On the day he finished his apprentice piece, Jorn carefully removed the tapestry from the loom and spread it out across the work-table, at last being able to see it the right way round. He stood for a long time, scrutinising it minutely for any imperfections. Then he went to tell Aldrick that his weaving was completed, bar the final hand-finishing and stretching.

Jorn waited anxiously as his foster-father carefully examined the texture and tension, back and front, looking for every tiny error and snag. Finally, he stepped back, his face giving nothing away.

"Well, now. Perhaps that flower could have been a brighter blue? The turn of foliage there is a bit clumsy. There are too many butterflies in the border. You've made the novice's mistake and thrown all your good ideas into the one design. Next time, make it simpler." Then, unable to maintain the pretence of being critical, Aldrick's face beamed and he gave Jorn a firm hug and held out his hand. "Welcome, journeyman. I hate to say it, but you will be a better tapestry weaver than I ever could be. But don't go getting big ideas. You are not a master yet."

Jorn shook his head, and went pink. "Don't I know it!"

"A celebration supper is due, I think! A nice steak, eh? And mother's famous strawberry meringue, with whipped cream?"

"Great!" But it was all he could do to keep smiling. Aldrick left the room and Jorn turned back to survey his work again with a critical eye. The master weaver had been kind, but Jorn knew his weaving was not totally faultless. *But there won't be a next time, will there? Or at least, not for a long, long while. I do so hope I'm doing the right thing. It's going to be so very hard to leave, but I just have to find out who I really am. And I can feel my colours getting restive.*

*

Rolf arrived with perfect timing just before supper. He sat down at the table, which had been placed outside in the garden and made a great fuss of his guard-child. The late-spring evening sped by on a tide of laughter, favourite food and family banter. Rolf produced pretty boxes filled with candies and crystallised fruits, which had everyone greedily picking a share, despite their large suppers. For Jorn, he had a special present — a set of pearl buttons. Darkness fell, lamps were lit, and they all relaxed in the warm evening air.

Anna eventually persuaded Rob and Red to get ready for bed; Polly had already been carried up, sleepy and stuffed into silence. Aldrick, Rolf and Jorn were left in peace.

Rolf stretched and said casually, "I want to see this famous apprentice piece of yours, Jorn. Come and show me, will you?"

Jorn took a lantern and led the way to the weaving loft. Rolf examined his work with professional appraisal.

"I could get 500 in gold for that in the right market."

Jorn was astonished. "Really? But it's quite small as tapestries go. Perhaps I had better stay here and get rich!"

Rolf looked at him with raised eyebrows. "Do you mean that?"

Jorn sighed and shook his head. "Not really. I have to meet my father. And I know I can't put off learning how to control my colours. Since you explained about them, I'm starting to feel them in my mind, kind of wriggling in their boxes, wanting to be used. But, Rolf I am still torn in half by all this. I want to have my cake and eat it, but I know I can't."

"I must ask your foster parents about you going away with me. It doesn't have to be at once, though it must be soon."

Jorn was silent for a long while. Then he looked at Rolf, puckered his forehead in concentration and sent, *"YES, PLEASE; do ask them."*

Rolf greeted his first attempt at mind-speech with a slight wince. *"There is no need to shout! Let's go downstairs again."*

They rejoined Aldrick in the garden. Finally, Anna came back with a smile.

"The young ones have settled; now I can relax a bit."

Rolf scoffed a final sweetmeat and announced, "I have a business proposition."

"Heavens!" exclaimed Aldrick, "I never talk business on a full stomach!"

"I always do," chuckled Rolf. "Never hurts to have the opposition softened up! But this is important and it concerns Jorn, so I thought it best to have a family conference. I've talked to the lad about this some time ago, but I knew he had to finish his apprentice piece, so I said I'd wait before I spoke to you. I'm shortly going on another of my long journeys and I want to take Jorn with me."

Aldrick frowned and Anna looked concerned. Jorn felt as if his whole life depended on the next few words, and he was half-way to interrupting, but Rolf said quickly, "Let me finish. Aldrick, you have taught him weaving skills, but I can teach him trading skills and how to deal with people. One day, Jorn will have his own business to run, and he won't learn how to do that by spending all his time in the woods or sitting at his loom. He's reached the standard of journeyman a good two years ahead of most. He has time, and he still has a lot of growing up to do. There's a big world out there and he needs to learn how to survive in it. And he's earned a bit of fun, too, hasn't he? Give the lad to me for a couple of years, and I'll bring you back a man. There, I've said my piece. What do you think?"

Aldrick looked at his foster-son uncertainly. "Do you really want to do this Jorn? I was looking forward to taking you out with me when I go buying stock."

Jorn did not have to pretend enthusiasm. His eyes shone. "I can do that later, Dad, and I'll probably do it better for having spent time with Uncle Rolf. Please say yes. It's not that I want to leave you all, but I'd love to see more of the world while I can. I'll be really careful, and do what Rolf says and…" he turned to his foster-mother with a big grin, "I'll clean my teeth, and change my underwear, and keep out of fights, and eat my greens and…" Anna held up her hands in mock surrender to stem the flow.

"I think we need to talk this through a bit more carefully before we say anything more," said Aldrick, firmly. "Jorn, you leave us to speak to your guardian in private now, and we'll tell you our decision in the morning."

Jorn got up and gave his foster-mother a kiss and a big hug. "Thanks, Mum. And thanks for that wonderful meal too. This is a day I'm going to remember forever!" He hugged his father and Rolf, "Goodnight then."

He met Rolf's eyes, who responded; *"Leave it to me now, lad. They'll agree."*

Jorn left quickly, resisting the temptation to lurk in the shadows to hear what was being said. He went to bed, but sleep plainly wasn't coming with him. He was still tossing and thumping his pillows when he heard the stairs creak.

"*Still awake, Jorn?*"

"*Need you ask?*"

"*Don't trouble to get up and let me in. Your foster parents have agreed. I've persuaded them to give you at least a year out.*"

"*When do we go?*"

"*Well, I don't want it too look as if there's any great rush. How about seven days after the Festival? You'll want to spend one final holiday with everyone.*"

"*I don't know what to say.*"

"*Then don't say it.*"

Jorn heard the mage clump down the steep treads. The decision had been made, but his mind was still churning with conflicting emotions. *I really want to meet J'Louth; I wonder what he's like. I meant to ask Rolf. A tree spirit? What does that mean? What can I say to him? Why didn't he want to have me living with him? So many questions and no answers. And this other place Rolf's going to take me to, not even in this world. How do we get there? At least there will be trees; that will be comforting. And then I have to train as a mage. Rolf hasn't told me much about that either, except that it will take time.*

He could feel the colours in his storeroom, shifting in their boxes, wanting to be used. He had to keep the door inside his mind locked now. Some of the brightest colours were trying hard to get out.

And then I have to fight these — what did Rolf call them — raash — and stop them invading Earth. That sounds pretty frightening. I can't even imagine a war on that scale. Dart always seems so safe, a place where you can live quietly and not worry. I guess that's worth fighting for.

He got out of bed and stared out of his window, across the weaving yard and out towards the forest; everything was silvered under the full moon. *I'm leaving all this behind; my whole life, my family, my weaving, the places that mean so much to me. I've never been away for more than a few days before. It's going to be a wrench. But at least Rolf says I can come back one day, when I've done what I have to do. But Rob and Red could be teenagers by then, and I would have missed seeing them growing up. And Polly won't be a baby anymore. And Anna and Aldrick will have changed, and so will I. I wonder if I'll even remember how to weave. It's like cutting a chunk out of my life that I'll never get back. But I really don't have a choice, do I?*

Eventually he got back into bed again, and finally fell asleep. His dreams were filled with tangled threads.

*

Jorn was officially a journeyman. He had finished his apprenticeship in just five years instead of the usual seven, and had his own commission to work on. He should have been proud and pleased, but instead he was tormented by conflicting desires. He wanted to be a weaver. He wanted to be a mage. He wanted to stay with his foster kin, near to his beloved forest. He wanted to meet his real father. The tension made him moody and irritable. He did his best to concentrate on his job and found it very difficult.

When Anna asked if he was certain that he really did want to go away with Rolf, he nearly snapped her head off, and had to go back later to apologise.

"I do understand, love," she told him. "It's all very unsettling. But you know I'm here for you if you want to talk about it."

He did know that, and it only made him feel worse, because the last thing he could do was to tell her what was really going on.

*

The Summer Festival arrived, a full seven days' holiday from work, and Jorn was determined to enjoy it and take his mind off his future. The fair at Borthwick was a big local event. The preceding afternoon, he helped Rob and Red to dress the trap and the two covered wagons with ribbons and swags of greenery. The posies would be added fresh in the morning. The brass bright-work on the harnesses was already gleaming.

The boys were up at dawn to make sure that Fern, the pony, and Warp and Weft, the two heavy horses, had their manes, tails and harnesses properly dressed with their carefully-made plaits, flights, cockades and tassels. Rob was old enough to be allowed to do some of the combing and grooming himself, and Red watched enviously as he tackled the tails, while Jorn plaited the heavy horses' manes into fancy patterns, incorporating the coloured braids and the stiff, fan-shaped flights along the arches of their necks, without even needing to stand on a box to reach.

"You can help more next year," Jorn told him.

Red looked at him accusingly. "But you won't be here next year, will you? Mum says you are going away with Uncle Rolf. Is that really true?"

Jorn knelt down. "Yes Red, I'm afraid it is really true. And I'm going to miss you and Rob lots. But I don't want to think about anything sad today. We are going to win best turnout. You just see if we don't."

Red grinned, easily distracted. "Sure, we will!"

The whole family, together with the servants and the weavers and their assistants, changed into their best clothes and put on hats, bright with ribbons and fresh flowers. It was perfect weather. Usually it only took 20 minutes to drive into the town, but today, the roads were already thronged and the horses had to keep stopping. Finally, they were directed into the large fields set aside for the transport and found a place to park. The servants drew lots to see who had to take first session of minding the carts, and the family moved off in noisy high spirits. Polly went with Mary, clutching the servant's hand, wide-eyed with a mixture of excitement and fear.

Aldrick headed for the market; it might be a holiday for everyone else, but as far as he was concerned, this was also an important business opportunity. Borthwick Fair was the largest in the area and attracted big crowds. His own stall had been set out the previous night, and his senior staff had been busy since dawn, laying out samples of his more affordable fabrics and the intricately-patterned ribbons, which Anna and the other women spent most of the year making just for this occasion.

Music drifted from the showground, and the smoke from the cook-stalls and hog roast was already full of tasty promise. Anna saw Jorn's nose twitching and cast her eyes to heaven. In the main field, a parade of impressive bulls were being judged, but Rob and Red pulled Jorn urgently in the direction of the rides and fair booths.

"So what's first boys? Juggler? Acrobats? The man with the dancing pig?"

"I want a go on those big boat swings that go really high, and the slide ride," Rob told him, loudly. "And I want to see the fire-eater and the sword swallower. And the calf with two heads."

"Toffee. And syrup pancakes. And the roundabouts," demanded Red. "And the puppet show with the funny man who hits people."

"All right. I've got coins in my purse and we are going to spend it all! Just stay with me and don't go running off now. And we have to watch the time. Mustn't miss the parade; the carts go first, and they keep the trade wagons back until last, because that's always the best bit."

Jorn won three toys at the turnip shy, and another two at the horseshoe toss, so the boys were loaded with loot. The sun shone, no one was sick, and they did win the red rosette for the best pony and trap, and the cup for the best turnout of a commercial vehicle.

Rob declared, as Fern trotted her way home, rosette in place, "That was the best fair ever!"

Jorn, with Red asleep on his shoulder agreed, "Yes, it was."

He watched the familiar fields and hedges vanishing down the road behind them and wondered for the hundredth time if he was making the right decision, and if he could actually bring himself to say goodbye to his foster kin, his loom and his forest. But, for the hundredth time, he decided that he had no choice. He was a mage who had to master his Power. His real father was in another universe waiting to meet him. There was an alien enemy to fight. It was frightening, but also immensely exciting. He had chosen his path and there was no going back.

Chapter 3

Jorn awoke with a start, his sleep abruptly banished by the sound of shouts, screams, an ominous crackling and the smell of smoke. It was still dark and a red flickering came from behind his curtain.

Fire! Shit, the weaving lofts are on fire! It'll spread like crazy. Jolted into urgent action, he leapt out of bed, fumbling for his britches in the dimness, dragged them on, slipped on his clogs, and clattered down the stairs at top speed, mentally checking the location of buckets.

He dashed to the front door, which was already open, and froze as he realised that something else was terribly wrong. The leaping flames illuminated armed figures. He saw one quite close. Beneath his crested helmet, his lower face resembled a skull. Jorn's body stiffened with shock. The yard was in chaos, the buildings ablaze, weavers and their families were being beaten into submission or lying in bloodied heaps. He pressed back against the passage wall, fighting against panic.

Two soldiers rushed past, dragging Mary between them; the young servant screamed and struggled. Behind her came two more, carrying terrified children: Rob and Red. Burning with helpless fury, his heart hammering, Jorn turned back and ran through the kitchen, grabbing a big knife as he went.

That won't do much against fully-armed soldiers. An axe would be better.

He made for the back door, but the kitchen yard was already full of fighting. He saw Aldrick using the big axe to defend himself against two sword-wielding attackers. He was smashed to the ground in seconds. Jorn wanted to vomit. Icy dread drowned his rage. The killers looked round, seeking their next targets, and quickly found them. Behind Aldrick's fallen body, Anna cowered in the shadows of the wood pile, clutching Polly. They had nowhere to run. His foster-mother was too frightened to scream when they dragged her out. Jorn drew back into the dark kitchen, knowing he could do nothing, unable to watch, but hearing the sickening sounds of violent death.

Escape, his mind told him, sharply breaking past the numbing horror and grief; *I can't fight these things. They've must have killed everyone by now. I must escape or I'll be next. Mustn't see me; have to hide. Get to the forest.* Jorn slipped out of the door and slid round the side of the building, sticking to the shadows, pulling them around him like a cloak, willing himself to be unseen. He had to get away. He kicked off his clogs and sprinted out of cover, past the storage sheds, towards the darkness, all his instincts making him head for the trees. But when he heard shouts, he knew he had been spotted.

He gasped for breath as his long legs took him fast down the familiar track. He couldn't keep this up for long. He gripped his knife; he would try to go down fighting. Then an arm grabbed his own and hauled him off the path to one side with irresistible force. In a moment, he was securely pinioned and held tightly against an unyielding body. Jorn could not use his knife. He back-elbowed viciously and grunted with pain. He might as well have hit a tree trunk.

"Be still Jorn." The urgent mind-voice brought him up short. *"We are trying to help you. Stop flailing around. You cannot outrun the raash. Trust us. Be still and silent. We have covered us with a pass-me-by. They will not find us."*

Jorn made himself stand still, shuddering with reaction, leaning against the solid strength of his rescuer and trying desperately not to breathe too loudly. Stunned and shaken by what he had just seen, expecting discovery at any moment, his heart pounded like a trip hammer, as if it was trying to break out of his chest. The booted feet of his pursuers slammed on down the path. After some time, they came back again, more slowly. There was a harsh comment in a foreign language, followed by a short, expletive answer. Then they moved back towards the burning buildings.

The person who was holding him remained still and silent. Jorn felt icy with shock. Nausea rose in his throat. He could not fathom what had happened. His thoughts spiralled. *They're gone, Aldrick, Anna, everyone I love, murdered, smashed down, even little Polly, and I couldn't do a thing to stop it. They took Rob and Red; are they dead too? Why did they attack us? What the hell are they? Who is this? How does he know my name? He used mind-speech so he must be a mage. He said "we"; does that mean someone else is here?*

It seemed a long time before his rescuer released his hold, although it was probably only minutes. Jorn whispered shakily, "Thank you. You saved my life." He looked back towards the remains of his home. Smoke billowed; there was a distant flicker of fire. It was horribly silent. "I must go back, there might be something I can do. Maybe someone is alive and needs help." He started to move down the track.

"Jorn, there is nothing left that you or anyone can do. The raash do not leave survivors. They have done what they came to do and they have gone. It is nothing short of a miracle that they did not find you. You must come with us now."

Jorn had taken a few steps back down the path, driven by the urgent need to go and see what had happened, to confront the reality of the impossible nightmare. He hesitated and turned back to get a view of the man who had helped him.

Dawn was lightening the smoke-stained sky. He saw a very tall, strong-looking, youngish man with dark auburn hair and bright emerald eyes, dressed like a forester in shades of green. Jorn's heart seemed to stop for a beat. He felt an extraordinary sensation deep inside himself, a kind of reaching out, an incredulous recognition.

"Father?"

"It is rather obvious isn't it? This is not the meeting we had planned for us, my son." J'Louth held out his arms. *"We are so very sorry for your loss."*

Jorn ran to his father, propelled by a tide of conflicting emotions, and was enfolded in a firm hug. After a moment, J'Louth released him and he stepped back, regarding this improbably young parent with embarrassed bewilderment.

"I don't understand," he muttered, his voice desperate with his need to do so. "I don't understand anything."

"We know. And this is not the place for long explanations. We are going to form a portal to take you to our home in Arden. Then we can answer all the questions we can hear buzzing in your brain like bees in a honey-tree."

The portal materialised as a mist-filled doorway. J'Louth said, "Just walk through. You may feel a bit dizzy on the other side, but it will quickly pass."

Jorn took a deep breath and entered the swirling, rainbow-tinted mist. His body instantly felt as if it was being pulled somewhere much too fast, in tiny pieces and then reassembled. The next moment, he was on his knees. The dizziness did ease off after a moment, and he looked around.

He was in a forest clearing with a giant beech tree at its head. For a disorientating moment, he thought it was his own wood, but then he saw that the trees were much larger. The air tasted different somehow, the light was greener.

J'Louth stood beside him, patiently waiting for him to recover. When Jorn scrambled to his feet, his father pointed to the big beech.

"Welcome to our home-tree. Let us sit down so that we can talk properly."

Jorn followed J'Louth and they both sat beside the grey-green trunk. He hardly dared to take his eyes off this stranger who was his father. His heart was still thudding with the terror of the past hour. His hands quivered. He needed so desperately to know the answers to his questions. J'Louth sat beside him.

"How did you know I was in danger?"

"We have been nearby, watching, in case you had need of us. Rolf had to go away for a while, so he asked me to stay close. Rolf feared that your Power might start to get out of your control before he could take you away. It can happen. Neither of us expected anything like this. The raash have not conducted such raids in Dart for many years. Our mage sense gave us urgent warning that all was not well with you. Luckily, we were in time to save you, but not the others. We are sorry."

Jorn ignored the confusing plurals. "At least I have you. I grew up thinking that you were dead."

"But we are very much alive."

Jorn looked at his father, his face puzzled, and then illuminated by fervent hope. "We? Do you mean... you can't mean... is my mother alive as well?"

"Yes she is."

"Can I see her?" he asked eagerly.

J'Louth shook his head. "No Jorn, you cannot. Or to be more exact, you already have. This is going to be very difficult to explain, and even harder to understand. We are both your father and your mother. Our essences are bonded to each other in the shian way, two who are one."

Jorn felt as bewildered as if the shian was speaking a foreign language; his oddly precise Basic was clear enough, but it made no sense. "You're right. I don't understand. I haven't a clue what you mean."

"Of course not. Let us tell it as simply as if it is a tale in a storybook. Once upon a time, there was a very beautiful, young noble-woman named Jelda who was married to an elderly, rich, powerful man. He treated her with great cruelty. One day she came riding through the woods near their mansion, very unhappy, and she met a young forester who was kind to her. They met again, but then she told him that her husband had forbidden her to ride in the woods anymore. The forester found out where she lived and he went and waited for her, by a great oak tree in the park. She came to him there. Little by little, they began to fall in love. Then, one day, in the middle of a wild summer storm, she ran to the oak tree in great distress. Her husband had hurt her badly. She was terrified; she had nowhere to escape to, she dared not return. And so the forester, who was also a mage, comforted her, and healed her. And then, because they loved each other so passionately, beyond fear or caution, and wanted that love to last forever, he took her mind and spirit from her body and joined it with his own. And they both lived happily ever after."

Jorn was stunned and totally horrified. He had found his father, and he was some kind of weird alien monster. J'Louth appeared totally calm, his face expressionless.

"We warned you this would be difficult."

"But, but... you killed her. You consumed her. How could you do that to someone you say you loved?"

J'Louth sighed at his horrified incomprehension. "Jorn, it was not as you imagine. Yes, Jelda's body died, eventually, empty as it was of mind and essence. But that essential, precious part of her is safe within me. Once I was Louth. Now we are J'Louth. When you hugged our form, you hugged your mother too. Our union was made from a love so deep that we could not bear to part from each other. Now we never will. Look." The shian mage held out his hands. "Imagine that this hand holds a spoonful of fine yellow powder, and this hand holds a spoonful of blue." He mimed pouring the contents of his hands together and mixing them. "Now there is a heap of green powder. But where have the yellow and blue powders gone?"

"They are still there, I guess."

"Yes. But they cannot be separated." J'Louth's green eyes were deep and strange. "Jorn, can you be brave again, just for a moment, as you were when the raash went by?"

"I wasn't feeling brave then, I was terrified!"

"Yes, but you mastered your fear. We think you should meet us as we really are, our essences, not this human-seeming form. Will you trust us and let us make mind contact with you?"

Jorn nodded, trying hard not to show how frightened he was. This was so very far from what he expected. J'Louth's form blurred and was gone.

Where he had sat, the air shimmered with an energy, which Jorn could sense more than see. That was alarming enough. Then Jorn felt a presence reach out and enter his mind. He encountered a being who was intelligent, caring, but very large, complicated, and totally unhuman. Interwoven with this enormity was the sense of a second person swimming within it, as if in a familiar sea.

Shock at the contact rippled through him, and yet at the same time, another feeling welled up. From deep within himself, something reached out, urgently yearning to be closer, wanting to understand. In answer, a vivid sensation pulsed through his mind. For a few seconds, his awareness of his own body faded and he became an intricate latticework of energy flowing through the cellular interstices of roots and shoots and leaves, seeking sweet fluids, stretching to the life-giving sun. It was at once terrifying, strange and wonderful. Driven by a desire beyond his understanding, the shian part of his own essence surged outwards, urgently seeking.

However, J'Louth gently but firmly blocked his questing. The link with his mind snapped shut and J'Louth reappeared, standing nearby, quite naked except for a leaf-shaped loincloth.

"Oh my, but you are so… huge, so… complicated." Jorn had no words to express what he had just experienced.

"I am shian. And so, to our surprise, are you, deep down. Your essence responded much more strongly than we had expected." J'Louth's emerald eyes were thoughtful as they studied their son. "We believe that it may be possible to teach you how to shift into your *shi*. But not yet; you have many other things to learn first, and your human body must finish growing. Meanwhile, never attempt to send your shi out of your body; you could seriously harm your human self. But now, there is an old friend we want you to meet. He will go and fetch Rolf, who can explain the rest of your story rather better than we can. We will call him."

A few moments later, a shimmering coil of mist swept rapidly across the glade, and then coalesced into a shape. A handsome, naked man stood in front of them, marble-pale. His back, shoulders and lower legs glittered with iridescent scales. His silver-blond hair was as short as an otter pelt, and his dark blue irises, ringed with silver, sparkled.

The newcomer gave an elegant formal gesture of greeting and smiled. "Welcome, Jorn, it is good to meet you. My name is Idris. *Salla-leashta-te.* May the waters sustain you."

Jorn

He turned to J'Louth, already knowing from the disturbances in Jorn's aura that something both unexpected and deeply evil had happened. His colours boiled like a storm-lashed sea.

"But I did not expect him here so soon. I sense violence and death."

J'Louth explained tersely about the raash raiders. "Please fetch Rolf for us. I hope he is back at Mage Hall by now. He must know about this as soon as possible, and Jorn needs his support right now. He is coping with more shocks in a small space of time than anyone of his age should have to manage. If Rolf is not there, bring Kayman."

Idris nodded. With swift efficiency, he constructed a portal and vanished through it. J'Louth stretched wearily.

"Jorn, we are sorry, we know you are deeply distressed and in great need of comfort, but we have to leave you. We are very weary and we cannot sustain form any longer. We must return to our tree and rest. Wait here and Rolf will be with you shortly." The shian's shape wavered and vanished. The shimmering stream of energy flowed into the beech tree and disappeared.

The traumatic events of the last hour seemed totally unreal. Jorn sat and stared at the tree, unable to imagine that J'Louth was somehow inside. He looked round the glade, feeling numb. *Aldrick and Anna are dead. Poor little Polly also. Red and Rob were snatched away to some ghastly fate. Everyone I knew is dead and gone. My home is reduced to ashes.* The appalling truth was too much to take in. It wasn't real, couldn't be real. *So I guess that my apprentice piece was probably burnt to a cinder as well.* That was the last drip into the tank of grief that unlocked the flood. He buried his head in his hands and wept.

Jorn had no idea how much time had passed when he became dimly aware that Rolf had arrived. The mage quickly draped a warm cloak round his bare shoulders and then put his arm round his guard-child's back, and waited in silence until he grew quiet.

Jorn felt a handkerchief pushed into his hand, and he blew his nose and mopped up. "Hell, Rolf, what a bloody mess. I'm so worn out, I can't think straight."

"I know. And I'm not going to give you any platitudes. You have cause for grief, and the hurt will take a long time to heal. I am stunned myself; your foster parents were my good friends. Here, now, Idris told me you need some clothes. You are chilled." He handed Jorn a shirt, jerkin, and a pair of thick socks. "Best I could do in a hurry. No shoes though. But now you need to rest and have something to eat." Jorn shook his head and pulled on his socks. "Yes, I know, you think food would choke you right now, but you need something to steady you. I purloined some sweet things from the kitchen before I left. Come with me and I'll take you to my hut."

Jorn shrugged and nodded; he was still finding words difficult. He stood with awkward stiffness. Rolf looked up at the tall youth who so much resembled his father.

"And when you've eaten and feel a little more settled, I'll answer all the other questions that are piling up in your mind. Here, you can carry the food. It's not far."

Jorn took the pack, and followed Rolf through the pathless wood, wondering uneasily if any of the trees they passed were inhabited. 'Hut', he thought, was rather a fancy name for a small, triangular shelter made from two big hurdles thatched with earth and bracken, and floored with close-packed logs. A log served as a bench and a flat stone supported on more logs made an adequate table.

Rolf collected some wood from a stack and set about making a cooking fire, which he lit without doing anything visible. He was feeling shocked and seriously worried but he had to hide that for Jorn's sake. He had to keep the young man calm.

"Be a good lad, and go and fill my kettle for me. There is a small stream a short way over there."

His guardian's matter-of-fact normality was comforting. Jorn went off to find the water and, when he returned, Rolf got him to sit down and gave him some honey cake to nibble.

"The shelter keeps out the wind and rain and that's all I need. I only use it occasionally in the summer for a few days when I come to spend time with Idris and J'Louth. I like to keep up with my old friends, but I so seldom find the time for leisure. We'll need to cut fresh leaves for bedding."

Rolf set about preparing his favourite lemon balm tea. He let the silence drift on until the water boiled.

"Now try some tea." Jorn did not much like the taste, but he had to admit that the hot, sweet drink was refreshing.

Rolf sipped and watched his guard-child carefully over the rim of his mug, knowing that an emotional upheaval on this scale was bound to have disturbed his colours. He could sense how they churned in response to Jorn's grief and anger, and it was a wonder that Jorn's control had held. He

Jorn

had the mind-fetter hung ready in case, but he was far from sure that he could deal with an ungoverned explosion of Nine. He had to reduce the emotional pressure if he could.

"Can you bring yourself to tell me what happened, Jorn? I know it must have been terrifying. Sometimes it helps to talk about such things, but if you don't feel ready, just leave it for now."

"It doesn't feel real yet. Just a nightmare. I'll wake up soon and find it never happened. Only, of course I know I won't." His grief was still raw. "They're all dead, Rolf, everyone I love, except Red and Rob. They may be too, by now. I saw them carried off. Where did the raash take them?"

"To Vard. I don't know what will happen to them there. What happened next?"

"The buildings were all on fire and the raash were killing everyone. I saw Aldrick die. He was trying to defend Anna and Polly. The raash got them next; I couldn't watch. At least it was quick, I think. And then I ran for the forest. And J'Louth saved me and brought me here."

"So you finally met your parents. But not in circumstances any of us could possibly have foreseen. How did it go, Jorn? I would have warned you what to expect, but instead you had to find out the hard way."

Jorn looked tense and uncomfortable as he remembered. "J'Louth certainly isn't what I was expecting. He looks almost human, but he's anything but. He makes me uneasy. I can't get my head around two people being inside one body — if you can call it a body when it can just dissolve at will. And how does he make his clothes appear and disappear?"

"To a shian of the wood, clothes are like the leaves of a tree. They are a part of their form, put on or shed as needed. Mostly they go naked, except for the flap, or *kiri*, which only the males have. And you have to get used to saying 'they', not 'he'."

"They said something about a shi; I didn't really understand what they meant."

"That is the energy form of a shian. Shians of the wood are shifters; they can adopt solid forms when they are out of their trees."

"Weird! And to think that I'm their son is even weirder. I mean, how could that happen? How on earth was it possible for a shian and a human to produce a child?"

"Are you sure you are up to this right now, lad? It's not altogether a pleasant story."

"I think I'd better know. It's eating away at me."

"Well, shian couples conceive their first child when they merge their essences to become one entity with a single *shi*."

"Essence; that's another word I didn't understand," interrupted Jorn. "J'Louth made contact with me, somehow inside my mind, only deeper. He touched me with his essence. He... I mean they... were so very strange."

"Essence is a difficult concept. Humans might think of it as the soul, but it's more complex than that; it's a combination of mind and individuality and spirit that animates the *shi*."

Jorn shook his head in bewildered incomprehension. "Well, I guess I'll get used to all that eventually. But I interrupted. You were telling me about shian children."

"Well, as I said, conception takes place when two shians merge their essences, but their process of gestation and giving birth is not anything like that of humans. All of it happens inside a tree. But in your case, of course, that wasn't possible. Louth was in form when he and Jelda made union, which is unusual. He thinks that you were conceived in the shian way, but embodied in a human way. So far as we know, that has never happened before, and it is most unlikely to ever happen again. You are unique!"

"But that's another thing I don't understand. My mother's essence, her spirit or whatever, left her body. Surely that meant that her body died, so the baby would too?"

"Well, of course you are right; left exposed, empty of a guiding mind and spirit, with only the most basic, automated responses maintaining life, the physical shell wouldn't have lasted long. But we can thank the possessive nature of her husband, Arnori Sarn Sardi, for her survival. As soon as he realised his wife had run away, he sent out search parties. She was quickly found and taken back to his mansion. The doctors were puzzled. They thought she must be in some kind of coma."

"But it's amazing that she didn't die soon afterwards."

"Sarn Sardi had already had two wives die, and he could not afford gossip saying that he had allowed a third one to wither away, so she was given every care. Then more so because, after a while, it became very obvious that she was pregnant. A Sardi heir was no small matter. So Jelda's body was fed and nurtured until, in mid-winter, they could delay no longer; the time had come to make her give birth. Jorn, they were faced with a terrible choice. Her body being so very thin and weak by then, and lacking any will to assist the process, it was soon clear that the baby would not be born by normal means. To Sarn Sardi, Jelda was now nothing but a useless encumbrance; death in childbirth was not unusual and no one would question it. It was his child that mattered. He ordered that the doctor should cut you from your mother's womb."

"Oh Rolf, how dreadful. I've heard of such births. But her body could not survive that."

"No. It finally gave up what remained of life. But despite all the extraordinary circumstances, and being more than a moon early, you were fine; tiny, of course, but alive and well. Except that it was glaringly obvious that you were not the son of Sarn Sardi, not with those green eyes and a fluff of auburn hair."

"You make it sound as if you were there?"

"I was. Not that anyone knew that. I was determined to keep you safe."

"I guess Sarn Sardi was furious when he saw that the baby wasn't his?"

"Furious enough to commit murder. He called you a bastard changeling, a devil's brat. As soon as the doctors and midwife had left, he ordered that you should be taken out and left exposed in the snow to die."

"And you saved me?"

"Yes. Sarn Sardi just made it easy for me. As soon as his hired killer left you, I picked you up and took you to Mage Hall."

"But why didn't J'Louth look after me? Didn't they want to?"

"Of course they did. J'Louth held you and loved you, and named you Jorn, which means acorn, by the way. But look around you. Is this any place to rear a tiny human infant? No comfort, no milk, no shelter or warmth? It was impossible. My cousin, Florrie, took you to her home in the Dwarran Realm and cared for you until you were strong and old enough to be fostered. The rest you have always known. I didn't lie to you Jorn, I just couldn't tell you the whole truth. We always made it clear that you were fostered. When you were old enough to ask me where you came from, I explained how I found you abandoned in the snow and took on the role of your guardian; I always intended to tell you the rest once you became a man."

Jorn was silent for quite a while, and Rolf deliberately avoided listening to his thoughts. Finally he got up and stretched and said quietly. "Rolf, I need to go for a long walk and let all this settle down a bit."

"Good idea. Don't get lost, though."

Jorn snorted. "I've not got lost in a wood yet."

He spent several hours wandering around the forest, trying not to think too much, just sitting and looking when he came to an outstanding tree or vista. Arden was astonishingly beautiful, as if every leaf was somehow special and more real than those in his own world. He could feel the subtle energies of spring surging up to green the canopy, where a medley of birdsong proclaimed exuberant possession.

Gradually he felt calmer. He knew he could have done nothing to save his foster family. He couldn't change the extraordinary circumstances of his birth, and, hard though it was to accept, he was glad to know the truth. He was, for better or worse, a unique being of mixed parentage, with a Gift of magic that he did not understand, and had never even wanted, but must accept. He could feel his colours surging in the place he had made to keep them. He felt their anger. There was no room in his mind now for indecision. He would learn to use this magical power, whatever it was, and when he did, the raash would pay. That, at least, was a good thought.

As the sun began to set, he made his way back to Rolf's hut, where the mage was busy cooking over his fire. His keen brown eyes took in the changes in Jorn's posture, the new glint in his eyes. He didn't need to ask now if the Gift would be accepted. It already was.

"I'm glad you're back. Tonight there will be a *corun-i-lashulann*, a Gathering for Music. The shians have been told about the loss of your foster-kin, and also that you have returned to find your true parents. Shian mages have high status in their Clan. The whole Clan will assemble to rejoice with you, and mourn with you, in the shian way. Idris will sing."

Jorn looked at his ill-assorted clothes. "My, Rolf, I'm not dressed for that kind of thing."

"That will not disturb them. The cloak will hide the worst. You simply need to be there. But first, have some bacon and trail bread, and I've got cheese and apple pie for afters."

The savoury aroma of the frying bacon made Jorn unexpectedly hungry. He squatted down by the fire and warmed his hands.

"I've been thinking about the raash. I don't really know anything about them. You told me they want to take over Earth? I need to know more about that."

Rolf nodded. "Yes, you do. I'll explain after supper. The bacon's hot and I'm not going to let Darric spoil our appetites!"

After supper, Jorn listened to Rolf's grim account of Darric's territorial ambitions with close attention. It all sounded so huge and menacing that

Jorn felt overwhelmed. He couldn't begin to imagine how he could make any difference, but he was even more determined to do his best to be part of the action.

"So there isn't much time, is there? How soon can I start training, Rolf?" he asked, when his guardian drew his summary to a close.

"Tomorrow sound good?"

Jorn nodded, and stared into the fire in silence, and Rolf let him be. He wondered how quickly Jorn would gain control of his colours, and if he did, what it would be like to teach a Nine, and whether the old tales about the power of a Master of Nine could possibly be true.

As evening approached, they made their way to the twilit glade. J'Louth was waiting for them, naked, crowned with beech leaves and ivy. Other shians began to filter silently into the clearing. The pale shians of the water went unadorned. The shians of the wood had smooth, hairless skins, varying from pale greenish-bronze and copper through to gold and dark brown. The long hair on their heads was brown or red, worn loose and garlanded with leaves and berries. Females had tiny breasts, and lovely slim figures. Jorn hardly knew where to look. Rolf noticed this, but said nothing; it was high time the boy extended his education.

"I don't see any young children? Are they not allowed to attend?"

"A shian child stays within his host tree until he is some 10 summers old. Only then is the shi mature enough to leave the host tree and be taught to take form. A young shian cannot sustain form for more than a short time until he is a teenager. Even adults can only manage an hour or two. Mages like J'Louth and Idris are the exception, and even they have to retreat to tree or water at regular intervals," Rolf explained.

J'Louth began to speak in a complex language, full of long liquid sounds interspersed with clicks. He gestured and a group gathered to form a half-circle under the beech, bringing wooden percussion instruments, hollow drums of various sizes, rattles and tuned wooden keys to be struck by a hammer. Others had pipes made from reeds and hollow stems.

"This is the only form of craft in the Shian Realm, and these objects are greatly valued." Rolf told him. *"J'Louth says that for shians, making music is the only real justification for taking solid form; if it were not for that, probably very few would bother to do so, except when obliged to communicate with other races who like to see the person they are speaking to. But, to be perfectly honest, shian music usually sends me to sleep after*

the first 10 minutes. Except for the drums — ah, the drums are a different matter!"

The music began quietly enough. The complicated rhythm was strangely uneven and tuneless to human ears. Voices sighed and hummed in ebbs and flows, which made Jorn think of wind in the branches, leaves under rain.

"This is Unmelli-Diaklana, the song of earth and sky," J'Louth's mind-voice was softly joyful. "It comes from the sounds made by a living tree; when the limbs move, when the sap rises and leaves unfold in spring, this is what you hear. This welcomes you to our clan."

"It's wonderful!"

"It pulses within your essence, even though you have never heard it yourself. Next comes the Tataka-Deshuka, the drumming dance. This celebrates our meeting today, and your rescue."

The beat became faster and insistent, drumming out complex, syncopated rhythms that were unpredictable and irregular, yet with sequenced structures that defied analysis. The assembled shians began to clap and stamp, making the ground vibrate.

Without even thinking about it, Jorn found that he had risen to his feet and was joining in. His body throbbed with the music. Finally, the drumming reached a thunderous climax and ceased. He sat down, his heart pounding as if he'd just won a race.

"No human would respond to the drums as you have done. Our essence is strong within you." J'Louth's mind-voice rang with quiet pride. "And now you will hear the music of the water. Idris will sing for us. This is for the humans who died, a song of loss and leaving, and hope that one day your essences will meet again."

The moon had risen now, and Idris gleamed with silver. He sang alone, and Jorn was certain that he had never heard a more beautiful voice, soaring from tenor into counter tenor, and then even sinking to baritone. It did not matter that he could not understand the words; the sad and lovely melody enraptured his ears and captured his heart.

Suddenly, he was aware of a movement in the trees near him. He froze, hardly daring to breathe. An extraordinary animal stood looking at him, framed in the moonlight. The head was delicate — more deer than horse — and his body was slim, yet strong, poised on long legs, as if any sudden movement might send him into flight. His white coat glimmered like frost; his twisted horn shimmered with soft rainbow colours.

The beast walked towards them. Jorn suddenly realised that its mane and tail were white feathers, not hair. For a moment, the animal's intelligent dark eyes looked intently at him. Then it turned away and vanished into the trees.

Idris let his song drift softly into silence and came over. J'Louth joined him.

"Jorn, you were exceptionally lucky to see that. The unicorns come, sometimes, when we sing. They seem to be drawn to the music."

Jorn was still looking awed. "That was true magic. That and the music. Thank you for it. But I hope it wouldn't be rude if I go back to the hut now. I'd like to be alone for a while."

"Of course," said J'Louth. "We understand. Come to see us tomorrow, to say goodbye before you leave for your mage training."

The trio of mages watched the tall lad stride away.

"When I shifted my essence a little way into his mind to make contact with his own, I was astonished," J'Louth told friends. *"He is shian in his core. It is as if his shian essence is just living inside his human body, not properly integrated with it. But that part of him is still undeveloped."*

Idris nodded. *"His aura is strong, despite the shocks he has received; strong and angry, which is no surprise. But he has his emotions under control for the moment. However, you are right, J'Louth. Jorn's human body is aging faster than his shian essence, and that may cause problems for him. If, that is, he accepts his Gift. Will he do so, Rolf?"*

"We no longer need to be concerned about that, he already has. The raash left him no option. But by the Powers, why did they target the weavers, and why now? Was it just a coincidence or did they somehow know about Jorn? That seems impossible. At least he survived, and he is safe. We have our Nine."

"But has he come in time?" asked Idris. *"We have a race to win now."*

Chapter 4

A bed of springy twigs and bracken and a long day full of danger, torn emotions and unsettling revelations is not a recipe for sleep, but Jorn was so worn out that the next thing he knew after settling down was the chorus of birdsong heralding the dawn. He lay still as memories flooded back in an unwelcome series of disturbing images of fire and death. His grief was renewed, and hard on its heels came the anger.

He was at once aware of his colours, urgent and disturbed, thrusting at the lids of their boxes behind their locked door. *Calm down*, he told them severely. He tried to push all the emotion to the back of his mind. The urgent thing now was to learn how to use this power he had been born with. He got up, brushed himself down, and went out to face the morning.

"How do you feel?" Rolf was already up and seeing to breakfast.

"I'm all right, I guess. Still can't quite believe what happened. My colours are restless."

"Hardly surprising. The sooner we can sort your head out the better."

Jorn was not too sure that he liked the sound of that. He went to the stream and rinsed his face and hands, and then returned to the camp and munched on the rather dry bread left over from supper. *I could do with one of Mary's ample breakfasts right now.* The thought brought another agonising pang of loss. He pushed that away and raised enquiring eyebrows, trying to keep his voice level.

"So, where next? Mage Hall, I think you said. How do we get there?"

"We need to translocate to the Dwarran Realm. But we're presently in Arden. One can't form a portal directly between one Realm and another, so we have to go via Earth. I'll take us through to an Earth Transit Point, where another mage can form the second portal to Mage Hall for us." He saw Jorn on the brink of another round of questions and shook his head. "I'll explain all that later. Let's just get you there."

"Must say goodbye to J'Louth before I go. I wish I could get to know him — them — better. Oh mercy, Rolf, I can't get my head round this plural thing."

"It is confusing. Partly it's because we're speaking Basic. We just don't have enough pronouns and the plurals don't always work because the identity seems singular. In shian, there isn't this problem, of course. Louth is still himself, in some ways. He is the mage, not Jelda. And he is my old friend, so I can use the singular there, if I wish. When he's in form, he is male in appearance, and his body is, naturally, a single entity, so we can in some contexts, say 'he'. But when J'Louth are in their *shi*, or when you are speaking to both of them, then you must use the plural. And most of the time he will say 'we'. You'll get used to it. And J'Louth understands how odd it is for a fixed form. There, you see, a good example; I really can't say 'J'Louth understand', even though it would be more correct. Just do the best you can."

"Fixed form? Is that how they see us? I suppose it would be. We must seem as strange to them as they do to us. I suppose I'll get used to it in time, but I guess I have to deal with being a mage first."

"Indeed. Let's pack up and leave things tidy. We'll go to J'Louth's home-tree and then I can portal out from the glade."

Jorn pulled his borrowed cloak round him to hide his dishevelled appearance and shouldered the nearly empty pack. He felt as if eyes followed him, but no shian was in sight. When they reached the beech, Rolf stood and waited, and after a few moments, Jorn half saw, half sensed the shimmering energy of his parents' *shi* emerge from the tree, and J'Louth took form, not bothering to dress.

J'Louth regarded their son a little sadly. "We have hardly met and now we must say goodbye. Not, I think, what either of us wish."

"It's not. But I have to master my colours. I'm not going to let those raash bastards get away with this. I mean to fight them with every skill I can learn."

"That is right. Nothing else is important now. We will have time to get to know each other later."

Jorn nodded, tongue-tied, not sure what to say, or how to handle the moment. J'Louth solved that by coming to give him a firm embrace, and then he stepped back and smiled.

"We are already proud of you. Never forget that you are shian in your essence; it will give you strength in time. Now go. We shians do not waste words when feelings are already plain. Come back to us as soon as you can."

"Yes, yes I will. Um… J'Louth, what can I call you? I can't say 'mother-father' all the time."

"You can call us '*bibba*'; it is the word that our children use for their parents." The shian shed form and shifted back into the tree.

Jorn smiled. *"Thank you bibba. I'll come back as soon as I can."*

"Ovrassedea, Jorn-issa (tuk) e dol fullissara pella do lorga se (tuk). Your first lesson in shian; blessed be your days, young Acorn, and may the sun shine kindly on your tree."

Rolf sent, *"Ovrassedea, tantar-altar. And don't worry, I'll keep a close eye on him."*

Rolf then became still, his eyes closed, concentrating on the complex working for the Earth portal. Jorn watched the mist-filled gateway form. Rolf made a gesture towards it. Jorn now knew what to expect. He walked into the mist and was instantly yanked elsewhere.

As before, he gasped and suddenly felt very dizzy. They arrived in a nondescript yard, with a magnificent bronze sculpture of a rearing horse at its centre. Rolf saw Jorn looking at it.

"That is the hook. It gives one something to aim for. Each Transit Point has something different, a kind of visual target."

A tall, dark-haired man hurried out of a doorway and smiled. "Good morning, Master Rolf. Mage Hall, as usual?"

"If you would be so kind, Master Philip. But give us a few minutes. Jorn here is unused to translocations and he needs a while to recover." Jorn sat on the plinth of the statue until he felt better. Rolf spoke briefly to Philip, tersely explaining about the raash attack. The Transit-Master looked grave and troubled.

"I am sorry for your loss," he told Jorn.

Rolf looked at his guard-child. "Ready for one more translocation?" Jorn rose and nodded.

Philip formed a new portal. Rolf went through first and then Jorn followed. The dizziness took a bit longer to clear this time, and he was glad of Rolf's steadying hand. When he opened his eyes, he saw the flagged courtyard of an old, rambling, human-style mansion. Long, mullioned windows punctuated mellow stone walls. There was a carved arch over the oak doorway, and gargoyles and grotesques leered from the guttering.

A short, dark-skinned woman and a tall man passed and nodded at Rolf, unfazed by his sudden appearance. In a sunny corner, a person dressed in black sat reading a book. He looked up for a moment and raised a hand in greeting before returning to his text. Jorn felt a kick of shock. He recognised the mask-like lower face and now saw that it was topped by a bare forehead with prominent, bony crests above the eyes and extending back across the skull. It was a raash! Rolf saw his horrified dismay and sent quickly, *"Relax Jorn, Mordant is a friend."*

He had no time to ask about that. An elderly, rotund, balding man bustled out of the door, holding out a welcoming hand. "Rolf! Good to have you back! And this must be Jorn?"

"Indeed. Jorn, this is Kayman, High Master of Mage Hall."

The mage nodded at the tall youth, his face serious. "Idris has told me what happened to your foster family. You have my sincere condolences. But now we have to think about you. A shock of that kind is bound to unsettle your colours, so the sooner you can put them in a safe place, the better. Come inside."

Jorn followed the two mages. They led him through a panelled hallway and up a wide staircase with carved banisters, along a landing, up a further staircase. He had never been inside a house so large. Portraits peered down at him, tapestries rippled, but he had no time to examine them.

Finally, Kayman opened a door. "Come in, young man. This is my study. Now, don't be alarmed," he said, as he walked across the comfortably cluttered room to his large desk, "for I can feel your concern, which is only natural. I'm not going to do anything unpleasant, quite the reverse. I will help you to use your colours when you want to and not when you don't intend to. Does that sound all right?"

"I suppose so. I know I have to do something to keep them in better order."

"You soon will," said Rolf, kindly. "Now sit quiet for a while because I need to bring the High Master up to date, and tell him what I know about your Power."

Jorn sat in a large leather armchair whilst the mages bespoke. Neither let any emotion show on their faces, but Kayman looked intently at him a couple of times.

Finally, Rolf turned back to Jorn. "When we first talked about your colours, you told me that you had boxes to keep them in. Can you tell us a bit more about that? You have a place for them, inside your head, right?"

Jorn frowned, searching for the words. "Yes, I guess so. I don't really think about it. It just seems natural; I thought that everyone did the same. There is..." he paused and corrected himself with a slight catch to his voice, "was, this big store next to the weaving loft." He looked at Rolf, who nodded his understanding. "It was one of my favourite places, right from when I was small. So when I started to find colours swirling around in my mind, I thought I'd better make a place to keep them, so I copied the storeroom with all its neat pigeon-holes and boxes. Weavers have to be tidy. Whenever I found a new colour, I put it in a box inside the storeroom in my mind. And then, when I created a design for a tapestry, I could find the colours I wanted, waiting in my memory."

"Amazing," breathed Kayman, unable to keep his expression free from wonder. "And how many colours do you think you have in that mental storeroom of yours?"

"Heavens, I never counted them! Hundreds and hundreds." He looked round and spread his hands in an all-encompassing gesture. "All the colours you can see, all the tints and tones and shades, colours that don't even have names. I'm always adding more."

Kayman shook his head in stunned disbelief and exchanged another silent message with Rolf.

"Well Jorn, I can now understand why your colours have not troubled you before. You are probably not going to find this next thing as hard as most mages do, because you are more than halfway there already. But, at this stage, you do not need all those colours; they will just confuse you. Maybe you will need them later, but for now, you only need the primary colours of magic. I think it is best if you make a new place to keep these. A mage is a craftsman and, like any worker, he needs tools, materials and place to work. The difference is that the mage works inside his own head, so he needs a space there that becomes, in effect, his workroom."

Jorn nodded. "Just like my weaving loft. That makes sense."

"You already have an image of a storeroom, but now you need your workroom. You will make this yourself," said Kayman. "I will simply guide you. You'll feel a light contact with me in a moment."

Jorn blinked as he felt Kayman's presence in his mind, but oddly, it was not frightening. More like having a hand to hold.

The High Master switched to mind-speech. *"Now, Jorn, I want you to close your eyes and imagine your workroom. It must be somewhere you feel completely at home. Do not forget a door! You can have a window too, if you like. Don't make it too complicated — you can add things later. I suggest a table and a comfortable chair, and a big cupboard with a lock on it where you can keep the main colours separated from the rest."*

Jorn had no problem with that. Plainly, it had to be based on his weaving loft. There was his drawing table and chair, his big loom, and the window with a view of distant trees. It felt so real that his awareness of his external surroundings faded. He was in his own inner space. Kayman's presence seemed to hover behind him, looking over his shoulder.

"Now, connect that to your storeroom, but keep the door shut for now. That's ideal," approved the mage. "Now, are you happy with that?"

"Yes."

"Good. Now open your workroom door and leave the room. Open your eyes."

Kayman's study came back into focus, and Jorn blinked and looked round.

"That's really strange. When I was inside my head just then, it was totally real, just as real as this room is now."

Kayman was watching him intently. "Good. Now, close your eyes again, imagine the door to that room. Open it and go through." Jorn did so, and was once more inside his weaving loft.

"Now, Jorn, we don't want all your other colours getting in the way right now, so I want you to make sure that they are all safely inside their boxes and the door to your storeroom is firmly shut."

Jorn did that, still amazed at how real this inner space seemed to be. He sat by the table in his workroom and waited for Kayman's next instructions.

"Now comes the hard bit. In a moment, I want you to imagine all the colours of the rainbow, plus pink and a silvery, creamy-grey. Each colour should be clear and bright. The most scarlet red; the brightest green, you understand?"

"Yes. You mean the ones that I call the name colours; the purest and most perfect, the ones in the centre of their shade clusters."

"Exactly. Now imagine that there are nine empty boxes inside your cupboard. Collect them and put them on the table. Then sit in the chair."

He obeyed, making two trips to the store and then settling down with the boxes open in front of him.

"Good. You may not fill all the boxes, but it is traditional to have all nine in front of you to start with. Relax for a moment and clear your mind. Now bring one colour at a time into your mind. Make the colour real, and place it ready on the table. You can have the colours in any form you like, but as you are a weaver, I guess that hanks of yarn might be easiest. You want to stick to things that are familiar. You don't need to touch them, just see them arriving there and they will."

Jorn focussed his attention. He made a huge effort of will and summoned red. The colour arrived in a hurry, a tangle of threads, swirling with energy, anxious to be used. *Not yet,* he told it firmly. *I want you here, and tidy.* The threads began to separate, straightened out, and formed a neat hank on the table in front of him. He repeated the effort with orange, and worked steadily through the Spectrum. It got a little easier as he went on. Finally, he had nine hanks in front of him: rose pink, cream with a touch of grey, azure, rich blue, emerald, yellow, orange, scarlet, and violet. A wonderful exhilaration flooded through him, followed by a deep satisfaction, coupled with a sense of enormous possibilities.

"Now put each colour into a box. Then close each lid."

Jorn did so. The closed boxes lined up across the table-top.

"Open each one again, see what is inside, and then close the lid once more. When you have done that, put the boxes back into the cupboard and lock the door. Finally, leave your workroom and return to us."

Jorn opened each box and confirmed that each contained hanks of yarn of the same colour, neatly wound and ready for use. He stored them tidily, secured the cupboard door, and then left his workroom, shutting that door behind him. When he finally opened his eyes, he was beaming with amazed delight.

"How do you feel, lad?" asked Rolf in a controlled, neutral voice.

"Wonderful! The colours are all in order. I know how to find them when I need them." He got up and turned to the High Master. "Thank you, Kayman." He became aware that both mages were regarding him with strange expressions that might almost be awe. "What is it? Is something wrong?"

"Not wrong." said Kayman. "In fact, you could say, very, very right. We are looking a bit shaken because something extraordinary just happened. Something we hoped to see, but were not quite sure if we would. You filled all the boxes, didn't you?" Jorn nodded. "And of course you have no idea that what you have just done, with apparent ease, has not been managed by any mage for over a thousand years!"

The young mage looked totally bemused. "You need to explain that!"

"Jorn, you have just put nine colours in their boxes. No one has done that since Myron, the founder of the first Mage School! You are not just an ordinary mage who can weave a few colours using natural talent, and with much practice, may master one or two more. You have all nine colours in their clearest and most powerful forms. If you can learn to control your

Spectrum, you will be a Master of Nine. Which is not just like being a Mage of Eight plus a bit extra, but a totally different level of Power with awesome potential."

Jorn sat down again, abruptly. He took a deep breath. "Oh my word! Then it's just as well my colours are in their boxes for now. I guess that isn't going to be a five-minute job."

Rolf smiled. "You're right. But the main point is that your colours are safe now, and they won't start to come into use without you meaning them to. And for that, you'll have all the help we can give you. And now, we three must do our best to pretend that you are simply another novice who has come to train with us. It would not do to announce your Power until you have full Mastery, and that isn't yet guaranteed. The only people who know about this are us, J'Louth, Idris and Mordant. And now, unless I am much mistaken, you will be feeling tired, thirsty and very hungry?"

"Ravenous!"

"And there's another lesson learnt. Using Power drains you of physical energy, and exhausts your mind. 'No Power without price,' as we mages say. There is a limit to what you can work at any one time. If you overstretch yourself, you may damage your mind, or weaken your body. In an extreme case, you will die. You have to learn when to stop, and you need to eat well and rest after a complex working. So now, we'll go off to the refectory and refill that rumbling stomach. I am quite peckish again myself after portalling so many times across time and space."

On the way to the dining hall, Rolf insisted they went into the library. Jorn looked round the long room, flooded with light from generous windows and lined with bookshelves. It reminded him rather too much of his old school, but the so-called library there had no more than a few dozen textbooks, and here they must run into thousands.

The refectory was much more to his liking, food being plentiful and tasty. Rolf introduced him to a few mages, most of whose names he instantly forgot. But he remembered one. Mordant, the raash who had been sitting in the courtyard when they arrived, was finishing his meal at a table by the window. He looked young, but after yesterday morning, his skull-like, alien features raised goose-bumps on Jorn's arms. Now that he was close, Jorn could see that his head was bald, except for a heavy fall of blond hair around the back. The undulating ridges of bone extended above his eyes, forming a semicircle across his forehead, almost like a coronet, and joined to form a crest that swept back over his crown. There was an indefinable aura of danger about the slim, black-clad mage, who wore a silver-hilted sword with casual ease.

Rolf waved and steered Jorn over to be introduced.

"Jorn this is Mordant, a good friend of mine." The raash looked at Jorn with a complete lack of expression. His eyes were violet. The effect was unnerving.

"I'm pleased to meet you. Rolf has often spoken about you," he said in a light voice. His tightly-chiselled mouth almost achieved a smile. "Sometimes first impressions are misleading; perhaps we should both hold back from passing judgement until we know each other better?"

"Um, er, yes," Jorn stammered, trying to hide his dismay, and Rolf shepherded him off towards the servery to get their meals.

"How can you possibly have one of those cold-blooded, murdering raash as a friend?" Jorn demanded as he slammed down his plate, still unsettled by the meeting. *"I don't want to have anything to do with him."*

"I understand your reaction, but it is misplaced. Mordant is a close friend and she — yes she; raash sexes are very similar in appearance — is a human-raash halfer who has no cause to love her father's people. She is an expert in glamours, which is an area of magic that I sadly lack, for I do not master ether. I think you will get on well with her, once you get to know her. She is a very experienced mage, and also a Sword Master."

Jorn devoted the next half-hour to steady eating, and felt far better by the end of his meal. Finally, he turned to his guardian.

"Rolf, I don't think I can really take all this in. My life has been turned upside down. Hardly anything is what I thought it to be, and that includes myself! I don't think I can cope with any more information or new faces right now. I need a bit of time alone again. I don't suppose that are any woods nearby?"

"Not woods, exactly. But there is a large grove. A few of the shian mages have their home-trees there. It's through the garden." Rolf led the way, out through the big dining room, along a back passage, where Jorn caught savoury smells wafting from the kitchen, and out of a door onto a flagged terrace. At the top of a wide sweep of stone steps leading down to a stretch of improbably short, neat grass, Rolf stopped and pointed things out.

"The Yew Close is over there. Then there's the rose garden, behind that hedge, with gravel paths and a pond. The herbaceous borders are that way. You walk past them, and past the grotto waterfall, and the grove is over

Jorn

there. You can see the tall trees on the left. Take a break and I'll come and find you in, what? Say an hour?"

"Thanks Rolf."

Jorn went quickly through the garden, without much appreciation for the beauty of its neat borders, clipped topiary and mown lawns, feeling deeply in need of shade and solitude. The trees were fine specimens, arranged in concentric rings of oak, beech, chestnut and maple. He touched the rough bark of one fine oak and lent against it for a while, beginning to feel better.

Following a narrow path through the trees, he reached a central clearing, in the middle of which stood a large stone statue. Jorn looked curiously at the carved figure; an older, bearded man, with a somewhat stern expression, tall and well-built, dressed in a simple tunic. On the base, the weathered inscription read simply; Myron, Founder. Jorn stared at the statue and the statue appeared to stare back.

He sat there for a while, running through the extraordinary events of the past days. It still felt more dream than reality. He had lost his foster family, gained strange new parents, and found a race of ruthless enemies. He had experienced his Gift and set his colours in order. The conflicting emotions tangled and left him feeling drained. He tried to push them to one side and focus on the future. He had to master his Power. He went back into his mental workroom and sat quietly, letting the familiar surroundings sooth and calm him. *I'm glad I have this special place to retreat to. It's so odd to think that the real weaving loft is just a heap of charred ruins. At least it lives in my mind. The raash can't take that, or my other good memories. I'm not going to let them do that.* By the time Rolf come to the grove to find him, the young mage was feeling much more settled.

"Time to show you to your room," his guardian said cheerfully, "and then I need to give you some basic information about the use of Power. You have enormous natural talent, but that alone will not make you a Master of Nine."

Jorn pulled a wry face. "There's me just having become a journeyman weaver, and now I'm back to apprentice again! I have my mental workroom all set up and ready to go, all my colours are neatly boxed and waiting, but now what?"

Rolf led the way back into Mage Hall and up several staircases until they reached a suite of rooms off a long corridor on the third floor. There was a comfortable sitting room with a fireplace.

"Space for you to study," said Rolf, indicating part of the room that had no furniture. "You can set it up as you please, just ask me for what you need; I'm only a few doors away down the corridor."

A door led through to a bedroom and a door from that into a bathroom. It appeared that Mage Hall was fully-equipped with the latest dwarran inventions, including lighting, plumbing and hot water. Rolf gave him a quick lesson in dwarran technology. Jorn looked round with amazed delight.

"Oh my, I have never had so much room to myself! And it will take me a week to get used to finding where it is! He flicked the light switch on and off, regarding the result with amazement. "Why don't humans know about this stuff?"

"Because the dwar techs take a great deal of trouble to see that they do not. I think they probably have a point. The dwarrans are very advanced in some aspects of science and engineering, even ahead of the raash in some areas, such as the uses of current. Humans lost all knowledge of such things in the long millennia that followed the Catastrophe. They haven't reached that stage of knowledge again yet, and they are not ready for it. No doubt they will get round to these inventions in their own time." He saw another batch of questions brewing and grinned. "You can read all about the history of Earth in the library. Now we must focus on the study of Power."

They sat in comfortable chairs, which Rolf pulled side-by-side in front of the unlit fire. The late afternoon sun painted long, bright ribbons across the polished oak boards.

Rolf smiled and said, "Now you must forgive me if I sound like a schoolmaster, but we have to start at the beginning. I'm afraid you are in for an intensive period of instruction. I will be your mentor, and what I can't teach you, one of our friends will. And once you understand the basic skills you will need a long time to perfect your techniques and achieve the full potential of your Power." He gave his guard-child a wry look. "It only took me ten years. We need you to do it rather faster, if you possibly can."

"But back there in Kayman's study, you implied I might not master my colours. What did you mean?"

"Getting your colours under control is not the same as mastering them so that they are available for use. Having them gives you the potential to control and master them; it does not guarantee it. Frankly, as we've never worked with a Nine before, we don't really know what to expect. Colours can be stubborn. Sometimes you have one there in store, but it refuses to obey. Until you have all Nine ready for use, you are not a true Master."

"Somehow, I didn't think it could all be as easy as just getting them into their boxes."

"Most mages do not find that remotely easy!" Rolf told him dryly. "Mordant managed to store her colours in a box, rather as you did, but she still had to fight to control them later."

The mage fished in a deep pocket and brought out a smallish book. "This is for you; it's the beginner's guide to constructs and the underlying theories of magic. Everything I'm about to tell you is written here so you don't need to take notes, but that does not mean that you don't have to listen right now. I'm going to start with the standard definition of magic: 'Magic aims to manipulate mind and matter, time and space, for a defined purpose, through the applied use of will and innate Power'. That is neat, but deceptively simple; however, it reminds us of the basic rules. Magic has an aim. To achieve it, the mage requires both a strong will and a natural ability to use Power, which we call the Gift. The mage makes magic by creating spell constructs from the colours in his personal spectrum. This is a mental operation that demands skill and intense concentration."

"What exactly is a spell construct?"

"It's a particular blending of colours that enables the mage to work magic. I'll explain more about that in a moment. Are you with me so far?"

"I think so. Whether I remember it is another matter."

"It all seems a lot to take in when you start. It will soon feel easier. Now, this next thing is important and I will no doubt say it again. The fact that something magical *can* be done does not in any way imply that it *should* be done. The study of the ethics of magic is an essential part of learning to be a mage. Power misused may not only damage the mage, or other people, but on a large scale, it has the potential to cause global disaster. The raash home-world is a prime example of that. From what Mordant has told me, they've destroyed it. Their climate is a mess, the raash are struggling to survive, and a large part of the planet is arid wilderness; that's entirely due to War-Mages such as Darric letting rip with destructive magic without considering the consequences. It is essential to have a full understanding of the appropriate and limited use of Power, and to be able to evaluate and predict all the effects of a working. I hope you understand that?"

Jorn nodded, looking serious.

Rolf set the book aside and fished into his pocket again. He produced a metal object on a chain, like a large pendant in the shape of a hollow square, with the corners joined in a cross. Each straight line was enamelled a different colour and there were coloured dots at each corner and in the centre. He handed the square to Jorn.

"So, what do you make of that?"

Jorn turned it carefully, feeling his inner sense tweak with interest. It was an important object.

"It has five dots and eight lines. They are in the Nine colours of magic, which you called the Spectrum."

"Good; it's a matrix called the Quincunx. It helps a mage to remember the relationships between the colours and serves as a guide to working." He noticed Jorn's eyebrows rise in enquiry and added, "Working means using the colours to create a structure to hold magic, which is called a construct. Your first task will be to establish an image of the Quincunx inside your mental workroom, and then activate the colours and transfer them into the Quincunx. This is not easy, as I told you before; having a colour in store does not always mean that you can master it. Sometimes it can take years to do so. Occasionally, it simply does not happen. Anyhow, you can see that there are four corner dots and a central one. Each dot is called a Nexus. Each of these is a major colour: red, ether, blue, yellow, and violet. The linking lines show the minor ones: orange, pink, azure, and green. The four outer dots represent the traditional elements of matter. Do you know what these are?"

"Earth, air, fire and water. So…" Jorn looked at the Quincunx trying to make connections, and thinking aloud as he did so. "The colours that go across the diagram must relate to the elements at the corners, in which case, let me see; fire must be red, and its opposite is water, which is blue. And that means earth must be golden yellow and air is… ether, I think you called it?"

"Excellent! So now, you have the elements. The central nexus, violet, represents control. Mostly the mage needs to work with the colours to form a spell construct, but major colours can be used without the Quincunx for simple operations as a shaft of pure colour. So now, what about the outer lines that link them?"

Jorn shook his head. "Apart from the obvious fact that these colours are a blend of the ones on each side of them, I have no idea."

"And you won't remember if I tell you! It's all in the book so you can study it in your own time." He turned the pages. "It's a very useful explanation when you start out and feel that there is far too much to remember! Look, here's the list of colours and their main attributes." Rolf passed the book over again and Jorn looked at the list with interest.

The Nine Colours also known as 'The Spectrum of Magic'.

Red Fire (end)
Orange Desire
Yellow Earth (seal)
Green Growth
Indigo Water (heal)
Azure Mind
Ether Air (send)
Pink Glamour
Violet Control

"Yes, I see," he said, scanning down the page. "But what's glamour?"

"A glamour changes the way other people see you, or an object. There are many kinds, all designed to make things seem other than they are. As I told you, Mordant is the expert in these very useful constructs. I am not in full control of pink, so I can only work with it enough to make a simple pass-me-by. Well now," Rolf continued, "from the Juncture Point, the Nexus at the centre of the Quincunx, the mage is in control of all his colours. When a mage is described as a 'Master of Eight', which is quite rare, or a 'Master of Four', which is the lowest level at which useful magic can be performed, the number signifies both the colours he can master and the level and limit of his Gift. As I told you, I only partly master pink, so I'm a kind of 'Seven and a bit', but I can only claim to be a Seven. Kayman is an Eight, which is as good as it gets, apart from you, of course. Some people are born with one, two or three random colours. These are not able to work with the Quincunx, so their powers are very limited. They become witches and warlocks."

"Oh my! That all sounds very complicated!"

"Well, if magic was easy, mages would be as common as daisies in a lawn. It's probably just as well that it requires a great deal of hard work and dedication, even when you have the Gift."

Jorn was silent for a while as he studied the Quincunx. "So all the colours work together?"

"Yes. You work with them in your mind, visualising the construct you need to make — the shape and pattern. It might be a plait of three or more strands, or you might form a twisted rope or a knotted cord. More complex constructs can take the shape of a woven ribbon or braid. Some of the really complicated ones look like a net or fine mesh."

Jorn was finally on familiar ground and nodded.

Rolf continued, "The Quincunx can also be seen as four triangles, meeting at the central nexus. These are the four Triads. Each has three majors, two minor colours and violet. The colours within a Triad are always compatible, each strengthens the other: Earth supports Water; Water combines well with Air; Air mixes with Fire to intensify its action; Fire complements Earth." He paused to allow Jorn a few moments to study the matrix.

"The Quincunx looked quite simple when I first saw it, but I can see that it has great subtlety. There's a lot to learn."

"Yes, there is, and we have only just begun to explore all the ways it can be used. However, I'll just deal with the essentials now. If you split the Quincunx down the vertical axis you get two larger triangles that comprise of two triads each. Or you could split it across the horizontal access and also get two large triangles." He paused to outline them each with a finger on one of the diagrams in the textbook, and pointed as he continued his tutorial. "Each of these larger triangles is a Sector of Command, known as Conjunct, Injunct, Adjunct and Disjunct, each of which has six colours. I'll run through them now, but you can go back to the book to study them later; it takes a while to remember all these relationships. He pointed at the lower Sector. "Now see, the line across the centre is the base of the triangle. Here on the left we have the red Nexus. What element does that master?"

"Fire."

"Correct. Now here's its connecting red line, leading across to the central Nexus of violet. Continuing straight past the violet Nexus, the blue line leads to the blue Nexus."

The mage paused and looked enquiringly at Jorn, who said "Water."

"Good. So from water, we follow the green line down to the yellow Nexus of Earth, at the point of the triangle. That yellow line connects back up to violet in the centre, and finally there is the orange line connecting back to the red and yellow Nexuses. Can you remember the rhyme about functions? What does Earth do?"

"Earth seals," said Jorn, pleased that he'd remembered. His brain felt as if it was swelling with all this new information. "So I guess that Conjunct must have something to do with that? But…" he paused, aware of an unfamiliar stirring in his mind, as if there was something he knew that was on the tip of his tongue. After a moment, he said, feeling for the words, "I get a sense of joining, and connection. But also something about being secure and safe."

"Excellent! Your intuition is right; you must learn to recognise and rely on that feeling. We call it Mage-Sense, just sense for short. Conjunct commands the tangible; it is used to create bindings of various kinds. It forms wards that protect the mage's mind or body from attack. It also combines and builds."

Jorn was relieved that he was starting to get a grip on the basics.

"Now, I'm not going to go through all the Sectors, you can do that using the book, but I'll just highlight their main areas of operation. Disjunct is very dynamic," Rolf continued. "As the name suggests, it is used to cut things. It is the attacking Sector where killing or stunning constructs are formed. And yet it has positive aspects also. Fire can destroy, but it can also help to create. It has warmth. Orange governs passionate emotions such as love and hate."

"A Sector with such innate opposites sounds hard to control."

"You are right; it requires a strong will to work with Disjunct. Injunct, being based on Air, is the opposite of Earth; it commands the intangible and subtractive. This is the Sector where you work apports, glamours, and manipulate the mental world of thought and imagination."

"Apports?"

"An apport lifts and moves things over short distances. Sadly, because I lack ether, I cannot do that at all. A pity because it is very useful. Finally, we have Adjunct. This governs living things. It controls all aspects of healing. It also multiplies. Just as orange stimulates passions, azure calms them."

Jorn was fascinated. "I'm looking forward to trying all this! But my head feels as if it is going to burst! I don't think I can take in much more right now." He took another long look at Quincunx. It was going to take time to understand how the matrix operated, but it did make sense. "Having trained as a weaver, I think I can understand the principles. But I am not sure how one turns a mental working of the colours into actual magic? How does it become real and have the effect you seek?"

"Well that is the part that takes the skill and practice. First, you make the construct to the particular design in your mental workshop, drawing the colours from the Quincunx. You can actually have many spell constructs hung, ready to use, and it is important to do that because, as you can imagine, a complicated working takes time to weave, and you may need to use a construct quickly in an emergency. So then, when you want to use it, you take the construct and, by an effort of concentrated will, you apply it. There is no point in trying to understand that by a description, you just have to do it. Now, that is more than enough for one session. You can go back to the textbook later. When you have rested and your mind is fresh, I want you to go back into your workshop and install an image of the Quincunx there. It needs to be quite large. You can place it anywhere you like, on the floor, or hanging on a wall. Anywhere that feels comfortable, so that you can use it as a focus. Once you have done that, I will explain what happens next."

*

Rolf, Kayman and Mordant sat in the High Master's study in anxious conference.

"This raid on Jorn's family is very disturbing," said Kayman flatly. "The raash have avoided Dart for years. And why target the weavers? Was this some random chance, Mordant, or did the raiders have a motive?"

"I have a very unpleasant suspicion that it was not an accident. I've been investigating the new raids, Kayman, as you asked, and I've had agents touring local villages and farms in some of the areas, to ask what people know about their lost neighbours. They also enquired about any strangers who may have come past in the days before the raid. I've been analysing their reports to see if I can find any pattern. Most of these new strikes are simply to create terror; it can be nothing else. Sometimes they take young children, as they did at the weavers, but more often, everyone is killed, buildings are destroyed and animals slaughtered."

Kayman nodded grimly. "It is appalling and senseless violence. And people are, rightly, very frightened. But Darric is careful. He does not target one area often enough to get the local ruler worried enough to start calling up his own forces. It could still, almost, be the work of brigands. But in the raid on the weavers, they did take the two boys. Was that unusual?"

"No, recently raash have started to take a few boys and young men. That may perhaps be due to their current need for fresh child slaves to work the mines."

Rolf winced. "I can't bear to think of young Rob and Red being sent down some dark crack in the ground to win coal or ore. It's vile. But you said 'mostly', is there a second type of raid?"

"Yes, I think so, but I need more evidence to be sure. It's very hard to get information about what happened in the settlement or village before an attack, because the raash leave no one behind to tell us, but I've discovered two significant things. There have often been one or two strangers in the area, sometimes apparently on business, at other times, just riding through. And, in several cases, there are rumours that a young person in the settlement that was attacked had started to show signs of emerging mage-power, not that it was usually recognised as such, of course.

"We know that raash agents are continuing their systematic search of Earth. They are still hunting for the Wand, and they are gathering strategic information. We've had very little success in capturing any of these spies, but we have found their traces, small, painted tags marking bridges, roads, army quarters, grain stores, you name it. I think that on their travels, these raash agents are also looking out for untrained mages, especially potential adepts. Any mage will know when someone in his vicinity has potentially strong Power that is not controlled. And when they sense someone who has, they take steps to see that he or she is killed or taken, to rob us of our seed-corn."

"By the Powers, Mordant!" exclaimed Rolf. "Then, if you are right, it was Jorn they were after, not his family!"

"Should we tell him?" asked Kayman.

"Tell him that he has caused the abduction of his foster brothers and the deaths of his foster-father and mother, and all the rest?" Mordant shook her head. "No. Why burden him with guilt and anger over something that was not his fault and could not have been avoided or predicted? I do not advise it, at least, not now, when he needs to channel all his mind and will into mastering his colours."

"I agree," said Rolf. "He has more than enough to deal with. There may come a time when he should know, but it is not now. I may ask him what he remembers about any visitors to the weavers in the days before the raid. Meanwhile, we must increase our efforts to find young mages and protect them."

Mordant looked at her two friends and spoke with quiet intensity. "Darric has already two of the Tools: the Knife and the Chain. He is intensifying his efforts to gain the Cup and the Wand. If he can obtain even one of these, he will reach the tipping point of power and launch his attack. If he gains all four, he will be all but unstoppable. We need our own Master of Nine more urgently than at any time in the past thousand years."

"One young halfer against a Mage-Lord with Tools and a large, merciless army? However good Jorn is, it sounds like a tall order."

"Well, let's wait until he has Mastery. Once we get past that, there may be something we can try that will shorten the odds," said Kayman.

Rolf and Mordant exchanged glances. They could see that their secretive friend was not going to reveal more at this stage.

Chapter 5

Jorn sat under an oak tree in the grove, closed his eyes and entered his mental workplace. The monochrome outline of his Quincunx hung on the wall of his weaving-loft much as a cartoon for a tapestry would have done. It had not been difficult to place it there, but this was just the start. Now he had to fill the matrix, with each colour in the right place.

He went into his storeroom and picked up a couple of boxes: red and yellow. Rolf had told him to start by installing the major colours into the Nexuses and along the connecting diagonal lines, which would later be filled in with the minor colours. What he had not done was to tell him how. He opened the red box. The symbolic hank of bright red wool lay there, ready for use. Working the colours was a matter of intention focussed by will. He went over to the Quincunx and lightly touched the Nexus of fire, filling his mind with red. *Here. I need you here,* he told the colour firmly. Nothing happened. *All right, then. Not like that.*

Any tapestry had to start with threading a warp through the heddle strings. He thought about that, wondering how he could relate the idea of creating a warp to getting the colour into the Quincunx. He picked up the soft hank and held it for a moment. Then he gently tweaked at the hank until he found the free end of the wool. He focussed his concentration, mentally grasped hold of the thread, and projected it towards the dot. A bright scarlet line shot across, landed neatly, and pushed itself down and into the Nexus hole. Jorn pulled the thread through and then visualised it moving along the connecting line to the central Nexus. He mentally snipped the required length, and tied it off. The Nexus of Fire now shone with ruby light that pulsed up the diagonal. He could feel the latent energy waiting to be tapped.

He had not been aware of making a huge effort, but he was suddenly far too weary manage another colour right now. He had made a good start. He returned the boxes to his store, left his workroom, and came back to awareness in the grove.

*

It took Jorn another 12 days to bring blue, yellow and ether into his control. Some needed several attempts, and it was incredibly tiring, so he had to take a day or so to rest between the workings. After each success, he took longer to recover. In the between times, he did little but eat and rest. A few of the other students had introduced themselves and made some attempts to be pleasant to the new boy, but his weary excuses and rapid retreats soon made them give up. He knew they thought he was odd. Well, they were right, he was, and he didn't want them to find out about it. He had no energy to play games of deception. It was easier just to stay in his room, or the grove, out of everyone's way.

Darric's shadow seemed to loom over his shoulder, making each tick of the clock sound louder and more final, but he knew that he couldn't push himself any harder. An exhausted mage was no use to anyone.

He'd managed to deal with the four outer Nexuses, but when he got to violet, he encountered some kind of barrier. It was like trying to grasp a piece of a rainbow. However hard he tried, the colour defied him, and the mental battle drained his strength. It irked him like an itch in a place too awkward to scratch, and his continued failure made him feel tense, irritable and depressed all at the same time. Hoping that his guardian would know what to do, he went to find Rolf.

"That's not at all unusual," the mage reassured him. "In fact, you have done remarkably well. Many mages take a year or more to achieve what you have done in barely half a moon. Take a break for a few days and then try some of the minor colours." He regarded Jorn with sudden attention. "You look tired. And you have lost weight. Are you getting enough rest, and remembering to eat well when you've been working?"

Jorn nodded. "I've been eating for six! And trying to rest. But you're right, I do feel very tired, and yet I'm not sleeping all that well."

Rolf patted his arm. "You take care. And slow down. I know we all have the invasion at the back of our minds, but mastery of Power comes at its own pace." As he watched his pupil leave, he felt a prick of unease tweak his Sense. Something was not right. Jorn was looking much thinner than he should, and there were lines of weary strain around his eyes.

Jorn took his mentor's advice and did very little for a while. He pottered about, read in the library, or made notes in his study area, and spent a lot of time sitting in the grove. He went for walks, exploring the farmland around the Hall. He longed for wild forest, but there was none nearby, and the manicured fields gave him escape, but little pleasure. He ate, and ate again, but he remained hungry. The rest did not make him feel much better, and only served to increase his frustration and sense of time being wasted.

And that was not his only problem. Something deep inside him was twisting and turning in acute discomfort. He had not told Rolf about the new nightmare that plagued his nights and ruined his sleep. In the dreams, he was in an enclosed space from which he was desperate to escape. He screamed and shouted, but no one heard him. He knew that the forest waited outside, but he couldn't reach it. He felt so weak. He hammered against the unyielding walls, knowing that if he did not break out soon, he was going to die. It was truly horrible and the dream did not fade away when he woke, but lingered at the edge of his consciousness, a threatening shadow, disturbing his peace.

*

After a few days, feeling no better, Jorn made a big effort to put it all out of his mind. He returned to his mental workroom, determined to complete the Quincunx. He managed to command orange and pink over the next few days, but the effort left him utterly exhausted. He was frightened that he was getting seriously ill, and even more frightened to talk to Rolf about it, in case he really was. More than anything right now, he wanted a big cuddle from Anna, or some of Aldrick's pragmatic common sense.

*

J'Louth were comfortably relaxing inside their home beech, when Louth's mage sense gave them an urgent warning. They shifted awareness to the periphery of the tree and felt their entire essence go cold with shock. A raash Envoy stood impassively in the centre of the grove, an ostentatiously large black flag of truce being held by the Herald at his side, and six heavily-armed guards as back up. It should have been impossible, but plainly, it wasn't.

"I call on J'Louth the mage," the Herald proclaimed loudly.

Powers! He even knows our name! J'Louth sent out an urgent mind-call.

"Idris, we need you, now! There is a raash Envoy standing in front of our home-tree!"

"I am on my way. What in the name of Nine is he doing here? And more to the point, how did he have a hook for this location?"

"We have no idea. Summon as many of our people as you can."

They had no time to do more. The shian mage shifted out of the tree and watched the Envoy silently for a few more moments, until Idris and another dozen or so shians gathered nearby. J'Louth took form and Idris materialised beside him. Other shians came into view, ringing the glade in grim silence. The Envoy ignored them. Idris could see that he was strongly warded. His aura was masked, which was itself significant. The Envoy plainly had much to hide.

"You will pardon the wait, Envoy." J'Louth bowed in minimal greeting. "We had not expected one of your race to grace our woods with his presence. My people assemble to welcome you. I regret that we cannot offer you either seating or refreshment, but we are unprepared."

The Envoy simply nodded stiffly in return and responded in fluent Basic. "I regret the lack of formal notification of my visit, but the matter is urgent. Do I speak to J'Louth, the Mage, of the Clan of the Glade?"

"You do," responded J'Louth, wondering again how the raash could possibly be so well-informed.

"I am named Oriel. I come on an errand of mercy. We know that you are a peaceful people, who have compassion for all living things, and you are skilled at healing. The Lord Darric himself, who begs your help, has sent me. My Lord's sister, Ajina, is gravely ill. Our healers have tried all they know to cure her, but in vain; she fails day by day. My Lord asks a great favour of you, that you will send one of your best healers, with the Cup of Water, so that she may be healed. We understand that you may be reluctant to do this, but you are assured of our protection. You may bring as many mages or soldiers as will make you feel secure."

"I am sorry to learn of her illness, but I can do nothing to help you. I know nothing of the whereabouts of this Cup of which you speak, and if your mages cannot heal her, then I doubt that ours will do better."

J'Louth spoke with honesty, knowing that the Envoy, who was certainly a Mage-Adept, would sense a lie. They had not told one. They did not know the hiding place of the Cup, although Idris did, being its Warden. J'Louth was certain that the Lady Ajina was as healthy as they were. It was a transparent ploy and Oriel must know it would be refused.

"Will you not consider further? Our Realms are not at war. We beg your help."

"And we refuse. There is nothing further to be said."

Oriel drew himself up and swept his gaze around the glade.

"I am sorry to hear that. And you will be sorry that you refused. It will not have escaped your notice that we know where to find you. My Lord has need of the Cup, and he will have it. The next request will not be phrased so gently."

The raash turned his back on J'Louth and produced a portal. Oriel and his guards marched through it without another word, and the cloudy gateway closed behind them. There was a babble of anxious debate as the shians discussed this extraordinary event. J'Louth looked at Idris in frank dismay.

"I cannot think how he came here so easily, or how he knows our name."

Idris shook his head. "They cannot have tagged one of our mages; any tag would be shed when the shian shifted out of form, and it is impossible to tag a *shi*. We have few visitors, and those are all trusted mages. I can only think that they have made transition at random, under cover of a strong glamour, to remain undetected, and have simply done so again and again until they have discovered our Clan. And your name is known at Mage Hall, as is mine; Kayman is always reminding us that there may be spies, even there."

"Darric could not possibly have expected that we would bring the Cup to them. By the Nine, we would not do so if the whole of Vard was riven by plague! This whole performance was no more than a way to deliver a subtle threat."

"Not that subtle," said Idris grimly. "It amounted to 'We know where you live'. I must leave at once and report to Kayman."

"Give Jorn our love."

"I will," Idris assured them.

The shian mage wove his portal to the Dolphin Transit Point where the resident mage created an onward portal to Mage Hall. Idris wished for the hundredth time that his own Spectrum was wide enough to manage the double translocation to the Dwarran Realm, but it was not and there was nothing he could do about it. He came through into the courtyard, hoping that Kayman would be available. Fortunately, he was, and Rolf was with him. Their faces grew grim as Idris told his news.

"None of that is good," said Kayman, a worried frown carving deep furrows. "Like you, I am deeply troubled that the Envoy could translocate so easily to the exact location of J'Louth's home-tree. How could he possibly have a hook right there?"

"Well, they have," responded Idris, "and there is nothing we can do to change that. J'Louth and I will set stronger wards, but we cannot guard an entire forest. The raash will undoubtedly be back. But they may as well look for one drop of water in an ocean; they will never find the Cup."

"Indeed." Rolf was winding his fingers through his full beard, a sure sign that he was anxious. "But what will they do next?"

"Oriel's parting threat suggested that they will use force next time. They may hope to frighten us into moving the Cup to a safer place, thus revealing where it is and giving them a chance to take it, or perhaps they think they can terrorise us into giving it to them. Whatever they plan, it will be violent and damaging. However, my people are not as defenceless as the raash assume."

"Perhaps J'Louth and his Clan should move to a new home?"

"No shian leaves his chosen forest and home-tree unless he is forced to. Those with young children cannot go. Even if J'Louth suggested it, I doubt if the others would agree."

Kayman sighed wearily. "I know they won't, but give them the advice anyway. My Mage-Sense is tweaking with forebodings. This is just one more signal that Darric is in the final stages of his preparation. And yet again, right now, we can do nothing to stop whatever it is that he plans. We have our Mage of Nine, but he has a long way to go before he can help us."

"I must see Jorn before I go back. J'Louth will demand a progress report. But I will not tell Jorn about the purpose of this visit. It will alarm him, and there is nothing he can do except worry. Is he making progress?"

"He learns amazingly fast," Rolf replied. "But he's still not gained control of violet. And he pushes himself too hard. I'm getting concerned about him, Idris, he's not looking at all well."

"Do you want me to examine his aura? If there is a blockage, I may be able to help him to remove it, although it would, of course, be better if he could do so in his own time."

"Yes, see what you can do, old friend. I don't want to put pressure on him, but time is so short."

Idris found Jorn sitting listlessly beside the waterfall and the healer was at once seriously concerned. Jorn's aura was dulled to a weak flickering, and his energy flows sluggish. The young mage was sick in both body and spirit. The shian took form and came to sit beside him.

Jorn looked up and gave a wan smile. "Hello, Idris. Good to see you."

Idris came and sat beside him. "What is the matter, Jorn? I can sense that you are troubled. It is no wonder if you are, considering what has happened to you of late. Maybe I can help you? You know am a healer."

Jorn shrugged irritably. "I don't know what's wrong, Idris. I wish I did. It's really starting to worry me, and it's getting in the way of my working."

"You carry a considerable burden of expectations for one so young. It is hard enough to master your powers and, at the same time, you are growing into an adult, which is not easy either, especially being any kind of halfer, never mind a shian halfer as well, which is beyond rare. Maybe you are just pushing yourself too hard."

"Perhaps, but I don't think it's that. Something deep inside me feels so tired and… hungry. Yes, that is the best way of putting it; hungry all the time, as if however much I eat it is never quite enough. Maybe it's just 'growing pains' as Anna used to call them. I feel so strange recently, as if there is something trapped inside me that wants to get out; and sometimes I feel… oh, it is so hard to explain… as if my body is just a coat I have put on, and I want to take it off…" He tailed into silence for a moment, unable to find the right words, and also afraid of admitting how bad he felt, but something about the quiet shian encouraged his trust. "I can't talk about it to Rolf, he really wouldn't understand."

Idris nodded. "Do you have a good appetite?"

Jorn pulled a wry face. "And then some! I can't stop eating. But I'm still losing weight."

"What do you eat? Is there anything you especially like or dislike."

"I eat pretty much anything, but I always want the sweet things, I love bread and honey and fruit with lots and lots of sugar. But nothing satisfies my hunger. And I've been having these horrible nightmares."

Idris listened to his description of the dreams, studying Jorn closely as he spoke. He was much thinner than he should be, with gaunt hollows showing under his cheekbones. He looked again at the young mage's aura and made a deeply disturbing discovery. The weakened human aura was no longer flaming with Power, and beneath it, there was a glimmer of something else. *By the Powers! A second aura? That's impossible in a human!* But as Idris scanned with urgent attention, he could see that there was indeed a second one, undoubtedly shian, flickering like a guttering candle, weak and shockingly close to death.

He kept his voice calm and reassuring. "That is interesting. Jorn, if I am to help you, I need to see your essence. May I enter your mind for a moment or two?"

Jorn nodded, "Please do, Idris. I really want to know why I feel like this." He closed his eyes and tried to open his mind to let the shian in. The entity that made contact was nothing at all like J'Louth. Idris was much less structured; he was large, immensely strong, an ever-changing stream of ebbs and flows and complex currents. Jorn felt the exhilaration of fast-moving water, full of tingling bubbles, a joyful laughter like a shallow brooklet running over pebbles, and beyond that, surging depths so alien that he drew back, afraid. Idris left him at once.

"I am sorry, I got a little too close for your comfort. But I have diagnosed your problem, although what to do about it is another matter. Jorn, do you remember that when J'Louth entered your mind, your *shi* rose to meet them?"

Jorn nodded. "It felt as if part of me wanted to leave my body. But J'Louth warned me not to try to release my *shi*."

"The warning was well-meant, but J'Louth was wrong. Releasing your *shi* is exactly what you must do, and urgently." Idris reached out and placed a cool hand on Jorn's shoulder. "Jorn, it is no wonder you feel so strange. There is no way to put this other than bluntly. Your *shi* is slowly starving to death."

Jorn felt the shock of that kick through him. "Oh, Idris, by the Powers! What can I do?" he asked, fighting against his surging dread. "Am I going to die?"

"If we do not do something fast, yes, you may. But it will not come to that. First, let me explain the problem. A shian of the wood takes nourishment from his host tree, feeding off the sugars that the tree makes, and the water and minerals that are drawn through the roots. This does no harm to the tree, for the shian does not take more than the tree can easily provide, and in return, he protects the tree and keeps it strong and healthy. A shian infant spends his or her first years inside the tree in which he or she was born. For about five years, the shian baby is simply a ball of *sut*; you might say, soul or essence, a developing consciousness, living in a small area deep within the trunk of the tree, absorbing nourishment and waiting until his energy form, the *shi*, grows large enough to contain him. When the *shi* is formed, he is able to explore his tree, but cannot leave it yet. When the child is about 10, his parents teach him to leave the tree and let his *shi* take its external energy form. Later on, his *shi* will learn to shift into his *tuka*, his solid form. J'Louth was sure that you have a shian essence deep inside you, bonded with your human body and living within it as if it is a home-tree. As you age, it is becoming stronger and more independent, developing its *shi*, though more slowly than a full shian would. Your shian essence has been drawing nourishment from the food you eat, but that is no longer providing what it needs. It is draining your body in the attempt to find it. Your problem is rather like that of the shian child, but in reverse. He has to learn how to leave the tree to take form.

Jorn

You need to be able to send your shi *into* a tree where it can absorb the food it craves."

Jorn's whole understanding of himself expanded as Idris spoke, and despite his fear, he felt a huge sense of relief.

"Oh, Idris, thank you! I'm sure that's right! That explains what I am feeling perfectly. So, can you help me to let my *shi* out, and show me how to merge with a tree?"

"I cannot, for I am of the water. You need help from a shian of the wood. But there is a shian Mage-Healer named Mara, whose home-tree is within the glade. Wait here and I will go and find her."

Jorn sat by the pond, his thoughts in turmoil. How could he help this dying inner self? What would happen to him if he couldn't find a way to release it? Was it going to be dangerous? So many people were depending on him.

Idris returned with two shians — a tall female, and a brown-skinned male.

"This is Mara and Kern. They will do everything they can to help you."

Mara looked serious. "We will certainly try. But you must understand the dangers. You are not wholly shian. That might mean that your *shi* cannot completely leave your body. But if it does, there is a risk that it will not be able to return. Certainly, to begin with, we must be very cautious. However, being a mage is a great help. I think you should be able to form a tether between your *shi* and your body, which will ensure that your *shi* can return to it."

"I really want to try. I can't go on like this."

Kern nodded. "You are right. If your shian self were to die, I think your human self will not long survive without it. We cannot afford to ignore that and hope that the problem goes away; it is certain to get worse. Mara and I have often helped shian children to take form, I am sure we can help you to leave yours."

"Thanks, Kern. I need all the help I can get. To be honest, I'm really frightened."

"I'd be amazed if you were not," responded the shian, "but you have three experienced Mage-Healers here to watch over you."

Mara gave his arm an encouraging pat. "I am sure we can solve your problem. Let me explain what we need to do. We will go to my home-tree. I will enter it. You must then try to let your *shi* emerge from your body and come to find me. Kern will merge with you, just enough to guide your *shi* across."

"You can think of it in human terms, as if I am giving you a hand to hold. We will take everything slowly, and if anything hurts or does not feel right, just tell us and we will stop. Do you understand?"

Jorn nodded, fighting his fear, not trusting himself to speak. He followed them to the grove, with Idris at his side. The big shian put his arm round his shoulders and sent a calming wash of azure to settle him.

"You can do this, Jorn. I know that J'Louth would have taught you if they had understood the need, but there is no time to fetch them now. This must be tackled at once. You have the courage. Now you must use your will."

They reached the big beech and halted.

"So, first the tether," said Mara. "Do you have yellow in your Spectrum?"

Jorn nodded. "I've mastered that."

"Good; you need a weave a strong, braided cord. Work within the Sector of Conjunct. Add whatever other colours within that sector that you feel are appropriate. Make it a long cord so that it will give you enough slack to reach into the crown of the tree. Don't rush it, we have plenty of time."

Jorn retreated to his weaving loft, engaged with the Quincunx. He focused on the Sector of Adjunct and worked swiftly and methodically until he had a full eight ems of neatly knotted and very strong yellow cord. He then added a few threads of green, which seemed an appropriately shian colour.

"I have it," he said, as he opened his eyes and returned to full awareness of the grove.

"Now for the harder part," said Kern. "You need to attach one end of the cord to your own body and the other to your *shi*. That is something we cannot help you with, because, of course, no shian needs to do this."

Jorn thought about that for a while. He visualised his body and considered where he could most easily attach a cord to it; *around my wrist would work. Now I need to think of myself in two parts and join them. But how?*

He remembered sitting in front of his tapestry and glimpsing himself reflected in the mirror that stood behind the work to show the good side of his weaving. *I need a big, long mirror; then I can imagine my shi reflected* in it and bind the tether between the mirror image and myself. I can imagine the mirror waiting for me inside my storeroom.

Visualising the image as strongly as he could, Jorn unlocked the door and entered. All his extra colours were neatly boxed, out of sight, though he could sense their latent power rising as they felt his presence.

The full-length mirror, supported on a wooden stand, was turned away so that he could not immediately see what it reflected. The young mage took a deep breath and waited, his pulse racing, fighting against his fear of what he would see. *Whatever it shows, it's part of me; it can't be so very dreadful, and anyway I have to do this.* Summoning his courage, he took two quick strides to the mirror and halted with a gasp of dismay, staring in distress at the tall, painfully emaciated and exhausted version of himself who stared back at him. *"Hello,"* he greeted his inner self, *"my, but you look famished! Just hold on; in a very few minutes, you are going to be able to leave me and find a tree and we'll both soon feel better."*

He tied the tether firmly around his own wrist, and his reflection did the same. Now the cord appeared to run between them, somehow into and through the mirror. *That should do it. My essence can't break that. The only way it will come loose is if I unbind it, or sever it, and I am not going to do either of those things unless I have a very good reason.*

He opened his eyes and found Mara and Kern watching him carefully. "I think I'm ready," he told them.

"Good; then I will wait for you within my tree." Mara disappeared.

"I need to link with you," Kern told him, "but first sit down beside the trunk of the tree and reach out a hand to touch it."

Jorn nodded. Despite the help Idris had given him, his heart was beating very fast and his mouth felt dry, but he could feel his inner essence straining to be free, and nothing was going to stop him from trying now. He caressed the smooth bark beneath his fingers and then rested his hand against the trunk.

Kern's mind touch was strong and confident. *"Come, Jorn, reach out, come towards the surface. Feel the tree. Let your shi run out through your fingers, through the bark, into the tree, Mara will guide you. Stop holding yourself back. All you need to do is to let go. Relax, let your body sleep but send your shi out."*

"Come on," Jorn told his inner self, *"come on, you can do this There is nothing to be frightened of. Shians do this all the time."* He felt his inner self respond with a fierce, urgent need. He let the hunger build and began

to reach out, desperately wanting, seeking, extending. A barrier burst open. His awareness of his human body faded and was lost. Kern's *shi* was somewhere beside him, steadying and reassuring.

A moment later, Jorn felt as if he had exploded into a million minute particles, which were somehow still part of one whole being. He felt himself enter the trunk in a great rush of joyous liberation, surging up towards the canopy of the tree, spreading out along branches, into twigs, into the tiny channels within each leaf, finally feeling the faint warmth of the sun. Sweetness flowed into him. He was suffused by it, expanding like a bud becoming a blossom all in a moment. He wanted it to go on forever. He poured more and more of himself into the tree, absorbing the lifesaving nourishment, until he was brought up short by an acutely painful jerk. He pulled against the restraint, striving to break the tether and be free, but he was blocked by Mara, whose strong *shi* surrounded him and began to push him down.

"Stop, Jorn. Stop! That's enough." The shian's mind-voice was tense with warning. *"You have done wonderfully well, but you must go back now."*

"Come, Jorn; this way, I will guide you back," said Kern.

Hearing his name called brought Jorn back to full awareness of himself. He instantly released his grasp on the tree. After a few moments, he opened his eyes. The mages were each kneeling beside him. Idris stood nearby watching attentively.

"How do you feel now?" asked Mara in a professionally neutral tone of enquiry.

"Wonderful!" said Jorn, sitting up, still brimming over with the rapture of his experience. "In fact, I feel stronger and more alive than I can ever remember." He looked across at Idris. "I actually went into the tree, all of me went right up into the leaves. It was so amazing and it felt so natural, as if I'd found the place I was always meant to be. I wasn't expecting that. I thought I'd just go to sleep or something and not remember."

Mara smiled. "Well, I will admit that that is a huge relief! Considering that none of us have ever done anything remotely like that before, it all went pretty well. There is no longer any doubt that you can release your *shi*."

Kern also looked relieved. "I can be honest now that it is over, I had no idea what to expect, but in fact, you managed it instinctively with very little help from me."

"I really didn't want to come back into my body; it felt so good to be inside the tree. It's just as well I had the tether in place."

"I think your *shi* will return to your body more easily once it is no longer starving. It is part of you. But it needs to feed regularly, or you will become ill again," said Mara.

"I understand. Do you think I'll be able to do it on my own soon?"

"I think we had better keep an eye on you for the next few attempts; you will need to practise. Once you can do it easily, you can shift it out as often as you need."

"But I would not do it too often," cautioned Kern. "You need to allow your *shi* to feed at intervals, but it would not do to become too reliant on that. There will be times when you are far from any tree."

"And you must be careful not to let anyone try to move your body away from the tree when your *shi* has shifted. I'm not sure, but I think if there was too great a distance between the tree and your body, the tether could break and you might not be able to get back. I believe that could be fatal," warned Mara. "Enough for now. Come and meet us here tomorrow and we will practise again."

"I can't thank you enough. There was always something missing, and now I know what it was, and how to feel complete," Jorn told them. "I think you've just helped me to change my life forever!"

The three mages watched him stride away, whistling cheerfully, with a lightness in his step that had been missing before.

"Have you ever seen anything like that?" Mara asked incredulously.

"Of course not; who could imagine such a thing?" replied Idris. *"I think that, for the present, there is little we can do but watch and wait. He may need our help again as his shi grows stronger."*

Idris returned to his pool, his mind full of anxious speculation. *We have solved one problem, but not the underlying cause, which, I suspect, not even Mara and Kern fully recognised. Jorn is certainly unaware, which is, of course, the key to the whole thing, but now is not the time to give him another shock. Perhaps he will come to understand his true nature, but if not, I may have to intervene again. I will keep this to myself for now, and watch him closely. I must speak to J'Louth, though, and tell them that Jorn can shift his shi, and about the second aura. The boy needs his shian parents more than ever right now, and I am a poor substitute. I had thought J'Louth would be pleased that their son is old enough to know the truth, and so they are, and yet they do not seem to know what to do with their human son or wish to be close to him. J'Louth knows that Jorn is afraid of them, which doesn't help, and shians of the wood do not have a human sense of passing time; they are content to let things be, for now.*

*

Jorn went back to his own sitting room, sat in his favourite chair, and basked in the memory of what he had just experienced. It was totally wonderful. Being bonded with a tree was such joyous freedom. He couldn't wait to try again.

After a while, he braced himself and entered his mental storeroom. The mirror showed a happier and healthier reflection of his inner self, although he could tell that he needed more of the sustenance that only a tree could provide. The braided tether still linked his *shi* to his body. Jorn found it uncomfortably odd and deeply troubling to see this image that was not quite himself, so he turned the mirror to the wall, shut the doors and returned to outer reality.

He was suddenly overwhelmingly happy and bursting to share his news with Rolf.

"You will never guess what I did this morning!" he exclaimed jubilantly, as he bounced into his guardian's study, and proceeded to explain in detail what had happened.

"Well, that's astonishing, and a great relief!" beamed the little mage. "I was worrying about you. Now you can really concentrate on mastering the Nine without feeling so tired all the time. Let's go and have lunch, and then you should rest and forget about mage-craft for a while. It may take you some time to build your strength again."

Jorn's stomach rumbled, reminding him that, whilst his shi had eaten, he had not.

"Great!"

*

Over the next three days, Jorn returned each morning to the grove and practised sending his *shi* into the tree, under the watchful tuition of Mara and Kern. Now that his need for nourishment was not so urgent, he was better able to control the whole process. The shian mages were soon confident that he could manage on his own without any difficulty or danger.

They encouraged him to select a tree to use regularly, explaining that this worked best. Jorn chose a large oak, which seemed appropriate, and settled comfortably by the stout trunk. He checked his tether, let his awareness of his body fall away, and allowed his *shi* to explore the tree on its first solo journey, starting to understand its wonderfully complex structure from roots to leaves. He found he liked the strong taste of oak. He was still cautious, however, and knew he must not stay too long.

When he returned to his body, he stood and stretched, feeling a wonderful sense of well-being. *I could spend days just getting to know this tree. I wish I had more time, but I must get back to completing my Quincunx. Maybe it's just as well that I have other things to do. It feels so good, it would be very easy to get too used to doing it, and forget that I have a human body as well. I must be careful not to let my shian side take over.*

Chapter 6

Mordant had been away, checking out her network of agents. Now she was back and slotting into her usual routine. She had completed her morning sword practice and was returning past the waterfall grotto when she was brought to a halt by an extraordinary sense of being transported into the past. Standing under the cascade was the scaled form of a shian, and she knew instantly that it was Idris. She had not seen him for 18 years. She had forgotten how impossibly attractive he was.

She went straight to the pool and said, "It's been a long time, Idris. You don't look a day older."

Idris came forward, his perfect features expressionless. Then his smile lit his face and the silver circle around his indigo irises shimmered.

"Neither do you, Mordant. Though your aura has changed greatly, and for the better. The blocks to your energy flows have gone."

She gave him her tight smile in return. "I've learnt a great deal. I was young, damaged, confused and angry. Now I am at peace with who I am, or at least as much as any mortal may be." She sat on the parapet with easy grace, and the shian mage came and sat beside her. "What have you been doing Idris?"

"Travelling. Exploring the waters of the worlds. Healing minds and spirits. And you?"

"Killing raash raiders. Although much less often than I once did. Spying — on Vard and on Earth. Studying. Tracking down chimeras. Practising the disciplines of the Warriors' Way."

"And growing vegetables?"

She laughed. "Sadly, not. Perhaps one day, when the raash no longer menace Earth. Who knows what the future will bring? I prefer to live in the here and now. What has brought you back to Mage Hall after so many years?"

"Several things. The worst is that we have had a raash Envoy portal into Arden. He stood right in front of J'Louth's home-tree and demanded the Cup, giving an obviously spurious reason. He left with a threat to return."

"By the Powers, but that is terrible news, Idris. The implications are appalling."

Jorn

"We cannot understand how it was possible. We have been considering little else. Kayman has summoned a meeting of the High Council."

"There must be a spy very close to us here, close enough to know names and somehow learn the Arden hook."

"Rolf wants me to read the auras of everyone in the Hall to weed out any spies. That will take me some time."

"The raash can't find the Cup can they?"

"No. I can assure you that it is far beyond their reach. But I fear what they will do next. Kayman urged J'Louth to move, but of course they will not."

"No, and there is no one in all the Realms more stubborn than a shian of the wood who has made up his mind. But you said there was another reason for you to be back here?"

"Yes. Rolf wants me to keep an eye on Jorn for a while, and teach him, once he has gained control of his colours."

"If he can master the Nine, he will become a powerful weapon against the raash, and that is game-changing. But there is still an 'if'. He may remain an Eight. Rolf has been quite worried about him. Last time I saw him, he looked dreadfully thin and tired."

"There was a problem, but we have solved it." He explained about Jorn's new ability to send his *shi* into a tree. "Now that his *shi* is properly nourished, his aura again flames with potential. But we have no idea how his shian side will influence his development as a mage, or as a man. No such blending has ever taken place before. It may help him, for the shian essence is very strong."

"That's extraordinary! Our young mage is unique in every way. I suppose we'll have to get used to being surprised by what he is and what he does."

"As you say. The future is unknown. Even Kayman, who has the Gift of foresight, is unable to predict what will happen to Jorn. But he should make rapid progress now that he has recovered his strength."

She stood. "I must go, I need to talk to Kayman. No doubt we'll meet again soon, Idris. And perhaps we may leave the past in the box where it belongs, and become friends?"

Idris nodded, made a graceful gesture of farewell and faded into mist.

*

Jorn went back to work with renewed optimism. Now that he was so much stronger, it would surely be easier to complete the Quincunx. He managed to get azure and green swiftly brought into place, but the remaining colour, violet, continued to elude him. He was puzzled and deeply frustrated at his inability to grasp this final major colour.

Rolf was not able to help him. All he could suggest was that Jorn should leave it alone and start to learn how to work the colours he had.

"After all, you do have eight colours, and that gives you enormous Power to call on. The sooner you begin to learn how to use it, the better."

Jorn huffed, his brows knitted in a frown. "That's all very well, Rolf, and of course I want to learn, but you exaggerate my potential. Without violet, I'm not even a competent Master of Eight; I can't construct a portal without it. A fine Adept I'll be, having to go and ask someone every time I need to travel. And an Eight is not a Nine. Suppose I never manage to control it?"

Rolf wanted to reassure him, but he didn't want to lie to the lad. It was possible that violet would continue to elude him, dashing all their hopes.

"Just try to put it out of your mind for now. Mordant has agreed to teach you the Sectors of Injunct and Disjunct. Idris will deal with Adjunct, especially healing. I will concentrate on Conjunct, particularly bindings. Of course, we won't all teach you at once; it would be far too confusing. I'm going to have to be out and about for a while. I think you should start with Mordant. You and she have more in common than you might imagine. Getting to grips with two Sectors is more than enough to keep you busy, and there is plenty to learn that doesn't require violet."

Mordant came to find Jorn that afternoon; he was sitting by his unlit fire, trying to work his way through a textbook chapter on the Sectors. She gave him her thin-lipped smile and sat in the other armchair.

"Swotting up I see. That's good, though frankly it may not help. If spellcraft was just a matter of reading a formula and following it, life would be a great deal easier. In the end, we all have to work out our own ways of doing things."

Jorn looked at the halfer mage. He was getting used to her, but her chiselled mask of a face still made him uncomfortable. It was a painful reminder of fear, loss, and fire in the night.

"I suppose so," he said irritably. "Though I'm not having much success with that right now. I'd be happier if you could show me how to master violet first."

"But I can't. Only you can do that."

"But it feels as if there is a block of some kind. The damned colour just melts away when I try to hold it."

"There could be a block, but if there is, you placed it there yourself for some deep-seated reason that you do not yet understand. That happens sometimes. I once blocked red because I feared to use it."

"So can someone help me to remove the block? You, perhaps, or Idris?"

"No. It is dangerous to have a block removed by another mage, even one as skilled in healing minds as Idris. The colour could break out of your control. It might go wild and wreck your reason. It must happen naturally, or not at all. Violet, especially, contains enormous energy, located as it is in the central Nexus. The more control you gain of the eight colours you have mastered, the better your chance of dealing with the last one."

He knew she was right, but it was hard to concentrate with the problem niggling away at the back of his mind.

"Rolf said much the same. So, where do we begin?"

"I said there are no easy formulas, which is certainly true for all workings that involve the Quincunx matrix. But there are a few standard constructs. Let's try a couple of very simple operations that don't even require you to use the Quincunx. These are things that even witches and warlocks can manage if they have the right colours." She picked up a small log and placed it on the hearth. "We'll start with a basic apport." Rolf had told her that Jorn had managed a spontaneous apport, so it seemed a good place to start.

"I want you to see ether in your mind, then fix it to the log, and lift it from the hearth and then set it back on the pile with the others. It helps if you point to indicate the lift when you are a beginner."

Jorn brought the colour into his mind, aimed for the log, and made a motion with his hand to direct the colour towards the log and then raise it. The log wobbled a bit and one end lifted a fraction, but then he lost control and it settled again. He snorted crossly and tried again. This time he was able to lift the log, hold it for a moment and set it down neatly.

"Not bad for a first attempt," Mordant told him. "But it takes a great deal of practise to gain fine control of your target. Look." She fixed her eyes on the book he had placed on the table beside him, lifted it, placed it neatly on her lap and then opened the cover and turned the pages without lifting a finger.

"Oh my! I can't believe I'm ever going to be able to do that!"

"You will, but it certainly won't happen quickly. You just have to persevere. Remember, you can only move something you can see, and it must be reasonably close. Now we'll try a similar exercise. Fill your mind with red and imagine it as a sharp blade. Slash that blade down hard on the log and slice it into two. Again, you can point if you like, or mime the stroke."

Jorn summoned memories of chopping firewood, felt for the scarlet blade, and brought his hand down in a sharp, slicing movement. He saw a momentary flash of red light and the log fell into two halves.

"Wow!" he said softly.

"Wow, indeed! Oddly, although red is one of the more active colours, it is not in fact as strong as some of the others. For most workings, you combine it. So, now let's try something where you need to engage with the Quincunx." She indicated the logs piled ready in the grate. "It's quite chilly today. Lighting a fire is one of the first exercises for the apprentice mage. Go to your workplace. Draw on the energies of red and yellow. Make a simple plait using three strands of those colours. When you have that ready, imagine you have wrapped it around a piece of kindling; then will the fire to light. And be careful — we don't want you to overdo it and burn the Hall down!"

Jorn went into his mental workplace and stood in front of the Quincunx. He focussed his will on red, and saw the colour flare into life; he held that and engaged with yellow. Then he pulled the colours out into use as if he was drawing thread from a spool, and rapidly constructed the simple plait. He opened his eyes, keeping the image in his mind, projected it, and wrapped it round a suitable piece of kindling on the grate.

Ignite.

The wood burst into flame at once. Jorn gave a small start of surprise.

"I know that is what I wanted to happen, but it is still a bit of a shock that it did!"

"It does take some getting used to. But that was an excellent first attempt," approved Mordant. "And the rest is just experience and a very great deal of practice. I know you need to gain Mastery as fast as you can. We will focus on the things you are most likely to need to use, rather than sticking to the usual curriculum. I'll come every afternoon for the next two weeks. Tomorrow we'll start on simple glamours. A never-mind is probably the most useful thing I ever learnt."

"Thank you Mordant. I really appreciate you giving me so much time."

"If you work hard, I won't begrudge it."

*

A battering ram of focussed power punches a tight swathe through the forest, felling everything in its path. Branches thresh, crack, trunks groan, stressed beyond bearing. Urgent warning penetrates their sleeping essence, but it comes too late. There is a mounting cacophony of destruction, a final hammer-blow. The great beech splits asunder, crashes in ruin, its roots ripping from the ground. A terrible agony sears though their being, exploding the bonds that bind it. Then everything stops.

*

Jorn awoke with a shuddering cry, his head pounding, feeling sick and disorientated. It was still dark. A few moments later, Rolf burst into the room, incongruously normal in his nightgown. Jorn sat on the edge of his bed, his head in his hands, shaking with horror.

"Easy lad. What happened?"

It took him a moment before he could answer. "A dream. Only I don't think it *was* a dream; it was much too real." He stood up and Rolf had to steady him as he swayed. "I must go to J'Louth… now Rolf, now, please help me. Their tree fell down and there was such pain… I feel sick."

Rolf wasted no time in pointless reassurances.

"That sounds like a far-seeing in the form of a dream. Get dressed at once, then meet me in the courtyard."

It seemed an eternity before Rolf joined him outside and Jorn paced restlessly, riven by fear, feeling that last dreadful annihilation in the very roots of his own essence. The Mage wove the transition to Earth. Jorn was so intent on reaching J'Louth that he scarcely noticed the discomfort, or bothered about where he had come out. Rolf took a deep breath and at once wove the translocation to the Shian Realm without waiting for the resident Transit-Master. The hook for J'Louth's home-tree failed to catch. That was ominous. Rolf had a hook for the nearby lake where Idris made his home, so he switched to that. It held.

He paused, his hand arresting Jorn as he was about to dash through the misty opening.

"Be careful lad. Everything may very well be fine, but we may find danger. In that case, I will take us straight back." He held up a hand to ward off the predictable protest. "Jorn, what can the two of us do? We'll need to get help."

They completed the translocation and both stood stock still, staring in horror. On the far side of the lake, there was a corridor of total devastation; not a single tree was left standing. Massive trunks lay crashed in ruin, all pointing in the same direction. With frantic haste, Jorn ran round the edge of the lake, and then began to scramble over the mass of fallen boles. Vast plates of earth and stone had been dragged up with each root system. Smashed branches heaped into impassable labyrinths. It was horribly quiet.

The glade had been obliterated. Jorn recognised one thing with sick certainty. The huge beech, his parents' home-tree, lay felled and splintered as if a lightning bolt had struck it. He was totally certain that they had not survived that appalling ruin. He clenched his fists and roared his grief, rage and denial at the sky in a bellow of wordless anguish that sent birds flapping out of the distant standing trees.

"No!" he yelled. "No, no, no!" Red erupted in his mind. He sent a bolt of unrestrained Power cracking across the shattered glade, pulverising a fallen oak-tree into an explosion of splinters that shot away into the distance. "No!" he screamed again. He was vibrating with fury, looking for something else to smash, because he wanted so very much to kill, and the enemy had long gone. He knew beyond all doubt that the raash had done this.

"Be still, Jorn. It is over." Idris materialised, standing a short distance away. *"My essence grieves with you, and I too am angry, but we can achieve nothing now. Come away from this terrible place and I will tell you what happened."*

Jorn took a few breaths, fighting for control, and finally managed a curt nod. Idris floated over the ruins in his mist form and Rolf and Jorn clambered awkwardly to a patch of slightly clearer ground beside the lake. Jorn sat on a fallen trunk, shaken to his core, overwhelmed by his grief and fury, feeling as if his legs could no longer hold him up. Rolf put an arm round his shoulders, but Jorn shrugged him off, still too angry to want comfort.

"*Why* Rolf? *Why?* I had only just found them, and now I've lost them again. It's so bloody unfair." He put his head down, stressed beyond bearing, his colours surging wildly out of the matrix, making him feel dizzy. He was on the edge of losing Mastery.

He felt cool, strong hands gather his own. Strength flowed into him and the dizziness faded a bit.

"Breathe deeply, Jorn, calm your mind, exert your will. Let your colours settle. Revenge will come, but it must wait."

Idris' calm voice and firm grip steadied him and doused the heat of his emotions like a cool shower. *It's over now,* he told his colours quietly. *I know you want to help me, but right now you can't. Ease up and go back to sleep.* Gradually, he felt them settle back into the Quincunx, like frightened birds coming back to their roosts when a hawk has passed.

Finally, he looked up. "I'm sorry I exploded. It was just too much."

Rolf patted him on the shoulder, and this time he did not move away. "You don't need to apologise, Jorn, we understand." The mage looked at Idris, his expression grim. "Only one thing could cause devastation on this scale; a massive war-hammer, made from Disjunct and Conjunct, powered by the Knife and the Chain."

"Yes; almost certainly wielded by Darric himself. The war-hammer came out of nowhere and took us all by surprise. We had no time to defend ourselves. It all lasted barely three minutes, but that was enough. J'Louth were sleeping in their tree. The first thing they would have known as they roused was that it was being uprooted. If a tree is suddenly felled and shattered when a shian is fully bonded with it, the shock is usually fatal."

Jorn looked at the mages in silence, hurting too deeply to find words.

Rolf said, grimly, "What about the others in J'Louth's Clan?"

Idris stood, shook his head. "Many are also dead. The attack was carefully timed. It has turned autumn. Trees slow down, and so do shians of the wood. They spend much more time asleep in their home-trees. And, you have to understand, some had children, not yet mature enough to leave their birth-trees. Their parents would not abandon them, even if they had time to do so. Those who survived the destruction, by luck or swift withdrawal, are deeply shocked. They have fled to find a new refuge. My own folk fared better; the effects did not penetrate our lakes and streams."

Rolf also stood and looked around him. "It's a deliberate demonstration of appalling Power."

Idris spoke with quiet determination. "Well, they can fell every tree in Arden and drain every pool; they still will not find the Cup and I will not give it to them."

Jorn got up. He was feeling steadier and he had put a lid on his deep anger. His colours throbbed, but he had them mastered.

"They will pay for this." His voice was quiet but full of authority. "The raash will pay to the last limit of my Power, I swear it."

Rolf looked at the tall youth, his young face set with a terrible, quiet control; the last remnant of his childhood suddenly and brutally stripped from him.

"We must go back to the Hall. Kayman must be told of this outrage."

"Yes, I will come with you," said Idris. "But there are things that must be done before we go. The unicorn is dead. My sense tells me that Jorn should take the horn, I believe that he will have great need of it."

Rolf looked hard at the shian mage. "Are you certain of this?"

Idris nodded. He led them to the place, slowly skirting the tangles of branches that could not be crossed. In the pale dawn light, they could see that something white had been trapped under a mass of fallen branches. Jorn clambered nearer, dreading the moment of discovery. It was a unicorn stallion. Flies crawled round an indigo eye, which stared sightlessly at the sky. Jorn sank down and gently touched the torn white feathers of the mane. He wanted to cry but the tears would not come.

"Take hold of the horn and give one sharp twist to the right. If the gift is meant, the horn will come easily to your hand," instructed Idris.

Jorn grasped the smooth spiral. *"Forgive me, lovely one."* He twisted sharply and the horn came away cleanly, leaving a round, bony plate on the head of the beast. He cradled the glimmering thing carefully and stood, the softly iridescent colours catching the light and changing as he did so.

"What kind of power does this hold?"

"That is so lost in myth that it's hard to be certain," Rolf replied, "but it may heal, or hurt, as the will of the user chooses. Be cautious. It is said to be a fickle tool."

"We must go," said Idris, "but first my people and I will sing. This rent in the fabric of our Realm needs mending."

The shians of the water were gathering, some thirty folk, all so much alike that Jorn found it hard to tell them apart. *So much loss. How does one bear so much loss?* His Quincunx pulsed in his mind, charged with his grief and anger, but his iron will held his colours in check.

The song Idris sang seemed almost wordless; a flowing river of melody holding the mourning of a people, the grief of a whole world, perhaps of all the worlds. The music entered Jorn, flooded through him, and finally opened the gates of his unshed tears so that his own grief had voice.

Then the other shians joined in. Their music spoke of dead beauty, lost youth, severed love, and betrayed peace. The voices turned to anger, climaxing in the wrath of water in full spate. The drums beat out a rhythm of determination and defiance then stopped abruptly. For a moment, there was silence. Then Idris sang again. His voice had calmed, and his simple, perfect melody sounded like a final note of hope.

The water shians faded into mist and drifted away. Jorn pressed his knuckles into his eyes. Tears were no help now. He looked around the shattered forest, gathering himself. Rolf and Idris were silent, respecting his need for a moment of silence and farewell.

He whispered, *"Ovrassedea, bibba, and goodbye.* I wish we could have had the time to get to know each other better." He paused. His fists clenched in bitter anger, and his final words were a firm assertion. "You will be avenged."

Idris nodded and spoke with a quiet vehemence. "Yes, Jorn, they will. We shians do not make war, but nor do we ever forget a wrong such as this. J'Louth was a close friend. You heard the anger in our song. If the raash come again, I can assure you that none will return to Vard." In the distance, deep drums began to speak. "Even now the news is being spread."

"Good. I'm ready, Rolf; let's get back."

Rolf turned to Idris. *"Tantar-alta,* I am tired from the two workings that brought us here; be so good as to take us back to the Dolphin Transit Point where a fresh mage can manage the return to Mage Hall."

Chapter 7

As soon as they got back, Jorn went to his room. He sat, cradling the horn, his feelings once more in turmoil. Shocked disbelief battled with anger and grief. The anger was dominant. The raash would pay. Jorn's colours surged again, but he held them in check within the matrix. The raash had killed. So would he. The moment he could master violet, he would learn how to work the constructs of war.

But beneath his anger was a prickle of guilt. He was uncomfortably aware that he had felt the grief of Aldrick and Anna's deaths more deeply than the loss of his own parents, and that made him feel bad. *I know did not really love J'Louth yet. I hardly knew them, and what I did know was so strange and unsettling. I should have visited before now, but I've been so busy these past weeks, and then I didn't feel well. I kept putting it off because meeting them was just so difficult.* He stared at the horn and ran his hands up and down the smooth spiral. It was oddly soothing. He sat staring into space, unwilling to move until Rolf came to find him and encouraged him to come down to the dining room.

Jorn found a safe place to hide the horn and reluctantly followed his guardian downstairs where he managed a small breakfast. They said very little. Jorn still could not find any words, and Rolf himself was silent and sad, stunned by the attack and the loss of his old friend. Then, very much in need of time to sort out his thoughts and emotions, Jorn went out into the chilly garden and sat by the grotto pool, trying to let the changing sounds of falling water sooth him.

His anger had died for the moment; he was sad and uncertain. A gentle voice came into his mind. *"Sometimes hard feelings are better shared. May I join you?"* Jorn had been unaware that Idris had taken up residence in the pool again.

"Yes, I'd like your company. I feel... Oh, Idris, I don't know how I feel! It's all such a muddle."

"The colours tangle at times such as these; sometimes talking helps to straighten them." The tall shian materialised and sat beside him. "You grieve for J'Louth, not because you loved them, but because you hardly knew them. You are angry because now you never will, because the raash

have stolen your chance of doing so. You want revenge, but you fear that you will fail to master your Nine. Is it not so?"

"Yes, that is exactly right. Was I thinking loudly again?"

Idris smiled. "No, you have excellent control, but your emotions flame in your aura, and any son would want the same."

"When Rolf told me that my father was still alive, I built up all kinds of thoughts about him in my mind. And then the raash destroyed my foster family and J'Louth saved my life. I knew who he was the moment I saw him, but I was in such a state that I could hardly take any of it in. And then J'Louth explained about their union and touched my mind with their essence. That was so unexpected, so extraordinary. It was good to know who I really was, but it was frightening, and so was J'Louth, if I'm honest. So I put off going back to Arden. I kept telling myself I'd go once I had Mastery. I wanted them to be proud of me. I was looking forward to explaining about being able to shift my *shi*, finding out more about my shian heritage. And now they too are gone. I will never see them again."

"Is that what you believe?"

Jorn sighed. "Dead is dead," he said flatly.

"Many humans believe that. It is not what shians think. We believe that the essence passes onward into another realm of being. I will try to explain, but these ideas are difficult for the human mind. We shians understand that the world is made of two kinds of substance; things you see and touch and another kind of thing that you cannot. We call these things matter and essence. Some things are only matter and these are not alive; rocks for example. But living things have essence as well. Shians are almost entirely essence, wrapped in the energy form of the *shi*. For us, taking form is like putting on a garment. Our shape is not who we are. But in humans, matter and essence are bonded in a way that makes it impossible for your spirit to leave your body until that body finally dies and releases it. Humans cannot feel their essence as something separate from their bodies, and so they have come to believe that it does not exist."

"I'd like to believe that my essence could survive my death, but I'm not sure that I do. I mean, if my spirit eventually has no body, where will I be? What will I do? How could I know anything without a body and a mind to know it with?"

"But, Jorn, when you shift your *shi* into a tree, do you lose awareness? Are you unable to think or feel?"

"No, I guess not."

"Then why is it so hard to believe that your human spirit can continue to exist without a form?"

Jorn rose; there was still a dull ache of anger and loss, but somehow he felt steadier.

"Thank you Idris. I really am grateful. I don't mean to be rude, but I need to go somewhere quiet and let it all settle. And you must need time to grieve also; J'Louth were your close friends."

Jorn sat for a long while under his oak, his back against the steady strength of its rough trunk, trying not to think too much, letting the spreading colours of autumn calm him until he felt ready to face people again.

*

Kayman was appalled by the shocking attack on Arden. The High Council had already been summoned to meet at Mage Hall to discuss Mordant's news from Vard. If this latest atrocity did not convince them that the raash were dangerous, then nothing would.

The senior adepts representing Earth and the Dwarran and Shian Realms portalled in later that day and assembled in the conference room. They donned their ceremonial robes and the atmosphere was tense with unvoiced agendas.

Rolf sat and watched them enter, his fingers absentmindedly combing through his thick, slightly grizzled, beard. Idris was beside him, as the chief of the Arden mages, robed in a thin silver tissue. He was already too hot and dry. He sipped from his glass and Read auras; it was hard to know who was on Kayman's side.

"I'm out of touch with the Council, Rolf; you'll need to remind me of names. But I do remember Professor Turner," Idris bespoke.

The head of the secret Mage School at the University of Errington was the first to arrive, accompanied by his deputy, Professor Sturminster. Turner's brusque response to Kayman's welcome radiated antipathy. The thin, elderly man swept to his chair, his dark blue robe billowing, and sat looking grimly impatient. Angela Sturminster wore a grey academic gown, trimmed with sable and edged with scarlet. She greeted the High Master with slightly more warmth and pointedly avoided sitting next to Turner.

"It doesn't take a Reader to see that he is already in a foul mood," commented Rolf dryly. *"We can count on him to oppose anything Kayman says as a matter of principle, and unfortunately, as the senior mage here, he takes the Chair."*

Jorn

"Right; his aura is already seething with resentment and suspicion. Professor Sturminster flares with dislike every time he speaks to her. They clearly detest each other, but that does not mean she is on our side. Who is this?"

The short olive-skinned, middle-aged man was robed extravagantly in violet satin, embellished with gold, and wore a heavily-jewelled cap.

"That's Justin, the new mage from Andrea. He's recently taken over from old Marcus."

"Not short of self-importance, is he? But I thought that mages were not allowed to practice in Andrea? Has that changed while I have been away?"

"No, the Andrean mages still have to work in secret, which makes them overcompensate with gaudy robes and a lot of added secret signs and rituals. But Justin is clever, and he has worked his way into a place at Court, so he's a useful contact. Whether we can count him as an ally is another matter."

Justin had bowed low to Kayman, smiled at everyone, and now made his way around the room with confident charm. Meanwhile a cluster of others arrived, and Rolf named them.

"The tall, dark-skinned man in red is Azabar from Sard. The thin one is Emile of Daunce and the blonde woman in green and blue is Erica from Norlond. We can usually count on her support, but the others will take sides as it suits their own agendas."

"Their auras are unremarkable. All Masters of Eight, of course. Ah, at least we have one firm ally."

Rolf smiled as he saw the slim dwar enter the room, wearing a robe of vivid orange, which suited her dark skin.

"Yes, Sarra is a good friend. You can always rely on her. She may be the youngest mage here but she is a strong Adept and full of common sense."

Professor Turner saw that all the members of Council were seated and tapped his glass to signal silence.

He began briskly. "Very well, Masters and Mistresses. Council is in session. We have been summoned urgently by Master Kayman, who has, however, refrained from telling us why. Perhaps you would be so good as to enlighten us High Master?"

Kayman bowed his head respectfully and said evenly, "Thank you, Master Chairman. Originally, I wished to report that a raash Envoy had portalled into Arden to confront J'Louth and demand the Cup. But now something even more serious has occurred. This is not my story to tell. Idris is the Warden of the Cup and he will report what happened."

"Yesterday the raash attacked the Clan of the Glade on Arden and used a powerful war-hammer to wreck a swathe of the forest. Not a single tree was left standing. My good friends, J'Louth, were killed, with many others of their people. It is obvious that this attack was both retribution for having refused to hand over the Cup, and a warning of what will happen if I do not."

"Well, I am sure we are all sorry for your loss," responded Turner, whose coldly-precise voice conveyed no sorrow at all. "But I do not see why that unfortunate event should prompt a full meeting of the High Council."

Kayman raised his eyebrows in dramatic disbelief and then looked round the table and spoke with careful control. "That was not why I originally called for this meeting, as you well know. However, I am surprised that a mage of your experience should fail to see the significance. The raash have a hook for Arden, which is worrying enough, and they are plainly trying hard to obtain the Cup. We suspect that they have also intensified their search for the Wand, but Kayman has it well-hidden. Darric already has the Knife and the Chain, and this attack demonstrates exactly how dangerous these Tools can be. A war-hammer of that magnitude would flatten a city wall and pulverise buildings."

"So, you have proof that it was the raash? Did anyone see them?"

"No," admitted Idris, "but who else would cause such devastation? And the threat was clear enough."

"It could have been a freak wind, a hurricane or tornado of some kind. These things are not unknown."

"I know the use of Power when I see it. How can you possibly persist in claiming that the Tools that the raash have been at such pains to obtain are unimportant?" asked Rolf angrily.

"They are simple focuses with no innate Power," retorted Turner. "I have proved it beyond doubt. I can assure you that my own experiments with the Wand revealed nothing of significance. It augments a working, but only by a small increment."

"Yet the raash are making every effort to find them. Perhaps we should ask why?" interposed Sarra quietly.

Turner shrugged. "I'm not pretending to understand the alien mind. Possibly the Tools have some religious or symbolic significance for them.

We must hope that the esteemed Wardens of the Wand and the Cup are doing their jobs more effectively than Rolf did in the past."

Kayman was visibly seething. He took a deep breath, and fought to keep his voice even.

"Dismiss this attack if you will. It is not the only evidence of what the raash intend. I summoned the High Council to tell you even more serious news. My best agent has recently been to Vard. We are no longer speculating. Darric has an army of almost 200,000, and he is undoubtedly in the last stages of preparing his invasion of Earth. His spies have tagged strategic targets across the length and breadth of the known world. The disaster, of which I have continually warned, is almost upon us, and yet you cannot see it. What more proof do you need?"

"Still singing the same song, Kayman? Your credibility wears thin; you have been telling us of this predicted invasion of Earth for nearly 20 years. So far it has failed to materialise, and frankly, despite what Mordant may have seen, I doubt it ever will. Darric may have rebuilt his army — the raash are a war-like race — and I have no doubt he has territorial ambitions, but turning them into reality by an invasion of Earth is quite another matter. How will he translocate this huge army? It is impossible. Darric may be a war-mage, but taking over Earth is surely way beyond his Power."

"So why is he bothering with these elaborate, long-term preparations for something he can never achieve?" snapped Kayman. "Yes, I have spent 20 years giving warnings to deaf ears; we always knew it would take this long for Darric to rebuild his army. Now he has done so. Are you going to wait for him to arrive before you believe me?"

Turner made a dismissive gesture and gave no reply.

"There have been new raash attacks in Norlond," contributed Erica. "That worries us. They destroy farms and villages."

"As they do in Daunce," said Emile.

"And in Sard," confirmed Azabar.

"We all know the raash take slaves. They have been doing so for years. This is just more of the same," said Turner dismissively.

"Perhaps, Professor, you would care to explain exactly why you consider slavery is so routinely acceptable that we can simply ignore it?" enquired Sarra acidly. "Each time the raash strike, they cause death and suffering, and leave families bereaved and destitute. It was my understanding that the Council of Mages exists to prevent that kind of outrage."

"When it is preventable," he retorted. "Would anyone here like to tell me how we can stop them?"

"Well, for a start, we could train our own war-mages," responded Kayman. "We are totally unprepared to counter this kind of Power." He sent a challenging stare round the table. "Which of you could form a war-hammer with enough impact to flatten a brigade of raash?"

Turner frowned. "The High Council has maintained the ban on mages being involved in warfare for over 500 years. It is simply too dangerous to have magic used for political ends. Once we lift that prohibition, there is no telling where it could lead. I see no reason to rescind the ban on the basis of rumour and speculation, and there will be no further discussion."

The frosty silence was broken by Justin. "Be that as it may Masters, your difference of opinion over these matters is well-known, and not likely to be resolved at this meeting. I am based at the Andrean Court on Earth, and I can tell you that Emperor Malchious has a most effective network of spies, and he has found no cause to place his army on a war footing. I may add that he can call on at least twice the number that this Darric is claimed to have, so if there should be any attempt to portal a force into Earth in our area, he would have little trouble in crushing it. Powerful though Darric may be, and well-warded, he is neither immortal, nor invulnerable. If he should attack, we can combine our Powers and work together to defeat him."

Professor Sturminster nodded. "We have many powerful adepts. And if we were to consider some planned response at this stage, what could it be? We have no idea where or when the raash will attack, if they ever do. One cannot prepare a defence that spans the known world. We cannot act on such scant information. However, we must be vigilant."

Turner nodded. "With that I agree. I propose that we note this report and take no further action. Agreed?"

Everyone except Kayman, Rolf, Idris and Sarra raised their hands.

"That motion is carried. Now, as that matter has been dealt with and we are assembled in Council, I have a number of other items to discuss, and it would be useful to receive reports from other Members."

Idris begged leave to go in search of water and left the room. Kayman sat silently, seething with fury and frustration. Turner spent the next hour dealing with routine issues at unnecessary length, and finally allowed the Council to end. Kayman called the servants in to serve wine and small refreshments, and left rapidly without saying goodbye, not trusting himself to speak further. Rolf circulated and did his best to mend bridges. As they had expected, The High Council could not see the truth under their noses. Kayman was on his own, as always.

Chapter 8

Jorn had been doing very little since the loss of his parents. He felt unable to master the calm concentration needed to work with his colours. He knew that he had to make progress, but it was hard to make the effort when he couldn't even think straight. He was still deeply angry, and that disturbed his mind and made his colours hard to manage. He spent some time in his oak tree, which helped to relieve his inner tension, but he still felt unsettled.

He sat in his room, once again running his hands up and down the smooth, cool spiral of the horn, trying to sense what power it might contain. Could it help him? If so, how? He knew that he must master violet, and sitting and brooding wasn't going to get him anywhere.

Then there was a light tap on his door and Mordant entered. "Don't worry Jorn. I'm not here for a lesson. I know you need some time off. I've been away for a few days and I've only just heard the terrible news. I just wanted to tell you I am so very sorry. J'Louth were very special."

"Thank you, Mordant. I just wish I'd had time to know them better. I hated the raash when they destroyed my foster family and ruined my home. Now I have another reason to hate them. But I have no way of getting my revenge."

"You will have. Professor Turner was totally obstructive at the High Council meeting, but despite what that blinkered idiot says, we mages have to learn how to fight back. When you become a Master of Nine, you'll have the Power to become a War-Mage such as the world has not seen since Myron's time. If, that is, you are prepared to kill with total commitment and no mercy. Are you?"

Jorn looked down at the horn. "I don't know, Mordant. I truly do not know. When I saw J'Louth's home-tree smashed to splinters, and the ruined forest, I was so angry, I could cheerfully have slaughtered every raash on Vard. But, back at home, I couldn't even kill a hen for dinner; I tried once and I was sick and couldn't eat chicken for three moons. I don't want to become like the raash; I just want to defeat them. But I guess I can't do that by just sitting twiddling my thumbs and wishing they'd go back to Vard and stay there."

"No, Jorn, you can't."

"Anyway, I have to master violet first. Until I do that, everything else is pie in the sky."

"Well, when you do, I have some interesting attacking constructs to show you." Mordant could see that Jorn needed to have something else to think about right now, and she was fascinated by the horn he was holding. "Idris told me about that. It's so beautiful. It shines like mother of pearl. Do you know, in all the years that I have studied chimeras, I have never see a complete unicorn horn close up. I glimpsed one, only once, in the far distance, on a fine stallion."

"Chimeras?"

"Strange beasts that have features of more than one animal. Researching them is my hobby, when I have time."

"And a unicorn is one of those?"

She nodded.

"Then you are just the person I need! Idris told me this horn is a Mage-Focus and I've been trying to find out about that, and about unicorns, but all I can come up with are some old folktales, which don't help much. Did you actually see one once? Was that on Arden?"

She sat in her usual chair. "Yes, it was. But they also exist on Earth, which is a mystery in itself. It's very hard to untangle truth from fiction. The legends of the Old Ones say that the unicorn is a shy and secret beast. It can only be entrapped by a young, female virgin when, being entranced by her purity, he will come and lay his horn in her lap, and that's when the hunters can ensnare him. It is also reported that if the beast is induced to charge at a tree, the horn will stick fast and he can be captured."

"Well, that sounds like a load of moonshine! I can't imagine that a unicorn would be stupid enough to do either of those things."

"Of course not. But the horn is commonly held to be magical. It's said to cure illness. Its touch will seal a wound. It can neutralise the effects of poison. Some people even believed that, in powdered form, it would produce a philtre to induce love or heighten passion."

"Is any of that remotely possible?"

"There may be some healing properties. Certainly the love-philtre is sheer myth; the horn is as strong as steel, so there is no way it could be reduced to any kind of powder. There is another odd legend that says that the horn can be used as a lethal weapon, but it must be used with caution. If the horn decides that the killing is without strong justification, the injury may rebound and kill the user."

"My word! So many stories."

"There is one more that may amuse you: to wield the horn with full power, the user must remain a virgin, having no intercourse with man or woman."

Jorn snorted with laughter. "Powers! I wonder if that is true? If so, it won't trouble me for a while. I guess I am going to be rather too busy to fall in love! But Mordant, all that's just tales for a winter fireside. What about the idea that it's a focus? I can feel some kind of connection with it when I run may hands over it, but I don't know what to do next."

"Well, I suspect that, like most things to do with mage-craft, you will have to discover the method for yourself. A Mage-Focus is a very personal thing. Many only work for a particular user. The object, whatever it is, acts to augment or channel power. The Tools are the prime example. No one is exactly sure how this works. We don't know whether it is some innate quality of the object, or whether it is a matter of the trust and belief of the mage who uses it. Perhaps both are needed. But if you engage your colours with it, in theory, it will help you work more effectively, with minimal fatigue. May I hold it for a moment?"

Jorn passed it to her. She weighed it in her hand. "Not as heavy as I had expected, but very strong. I can sense no Power. But then, I am not its Master. You will have to experiment. Why not just ask it to help? Worth a try. Anyway, I will leave you in peace for now. We must resume your studies tomorrow." She handed the horn back to him and left.

When she had gone, Jorn held it again, running his hand gently up and down the shaft.

"Can you help me? I wish you'd tell me how?" he murmured. To his amazement, he felt a responding warmth. "What is it?" he asked it softly, stroking it again. "Are you trying to tell me something?" There was an answering surge of heat. The colours seemed to ripple. Jorn was astounded, and slightly scared. *How could this dead thing be alive?*

"Can you help me to master violet?" he whispered. "The raash are so very strong now. I must be ready to fight them, but I can't unless I am Master of Nine. Can you help me to bring my last colour under control?"

The encouraging warmth came again. His fingertips began to tingle with latent energy. He took a deep breath, steadied himself, and went into his mental workroom, making sure that he was carrying the image of the horn with him. He stood in front of the Quincunx with the shining horn in his right hand. It felt solid and reassuring. He fetched his box of violet wool

Jorn

from the cupboard, opened it, and stood looking at it as he had so many times before. The horn throbbed with rainbow light. Jorn held his breath and, with delicate care, inserted the tip of the horn into the hank of wool and used it to fish a small bundle of violet yarn out of the box. He breathed out slowly, then his whole mind and will focussed on the bundle.

He very gently teased out a strand of violet thread with the tip of the horn. He then twisted the horn, using it as a bobbin for the thread. Next, he pointed the horn at the central nexus and willed the transfer. The hank unravelled speedily and disappeared into the dark dot. For a moment, nothing happened, and then the entire Quincunx flamed so brightly that he had to look away.

An explosion of transforming energy blasted through the core of his being. He was being re-made, charged and forged with Power. The surge was so strong that he thought it would tear him apart, but the horn in his hand fed him steady strength. With the totality of his will, mind and essence, Jorn accepted his Gift.

He opened his eyes. His Quincunx was complete. It no longer flamed with unbearable light, but all Nine colours glowed with a steady flame. It was perfect.

The horn was now cool in his hand. He looked at the box of violet, and found it filled again. Still shaken to the roots of his essence, he went to return the box of violet to its place in the cupboard. Having placed it back, he turned towards the storeroom, where he had neatly stacked all the other colours in their boxes. The door was open. He paused on the threshold in stunned amazement. The boxes had gone. The open pigeonholes were crammed with skein after skein of every possible shade, and a few that looked almost beyond the spectrum of normal sight, and every one of them throbbed and shone with Power. He stared in wonder, his sense pulsing with awareness of this enormous potential. It was going to take a lot of getting used to.

The Master of Nine left his workroom. He came back to awareness of the outer world. He was still sitting in his armchair, with the horn on his lap. Everything around him looked just the same. His body felt as it usually did, perhaps a little stronger, more tuned to his sense, but, in his inner space, everything had changed. His Quincunx pulsed with promise. It was not going to happen overnight, but once he had learnt how to use this incredible reservoir of Power, Darric and his sister had better beware.

Suddenly, his whole body trembled with the pent need for action. He wanted to shout, jump, dance. He surged to his feet, set the horn down on his chair and rushed to find Rolf. His guardian had returned to his study and looked up in some surprise as Jorn exploded into the room.

"I've done it!" he shouted. "I've actually done it!" The small mage took one look at the excited young halfer, instantly understood, beamed a huge smile, and went to pump his hand in congratulation, and then came to a sudden halt, an expression of stunned amazement in his eyes.

"What's wrong?" asked Jorn, anxiously.

"Nothing. You just look totally awesome! Your aura is so strong that even I can glimpse it. How do you feel?"

Jorn laughed. "As if I could point my finger at a mountain and turn it into dust! It's a bit hard to handle right now, but I think it will all calm down shortly. Oh, Rolf, I've finally managed it! I have all Nine colours, and all the other shades are ready as well, thousands of them, all glowing my storeroom. The horn helped me to do it."

Rolf completed his hug and gave a huge, relieved smile. "Let's go and find Kayman and tell him the good news. After today's Council meeting, he could certainly use some."

Like Rolf, Kayman did not need to be told the obvious. The High Master was so overcome with relief that he actually had to brush tears from his eyes.

"Jorn, my most hearty congratulations! I can't tell you how glad I am. For you, and for all of us. J'Louth would have been so very proud. Having a Master of Nine really changes so much. It gives me real hope that we can defeat Darric, though it's clear we will have to do that on our own." He saw that Jorn had not understood that last remark, and smiled. "I was speaking my thoughts aloud; I've had a difficult meeting and I have much to think about. It need not concern you right now. Look, you need to go somewhere quiet and let your colours calm down a bit. We must tell our friends about your triumph, and plan what to do next. Come here after supper, Jorn, and we'll talk it through."

Jorn nodded and followed Rolf out of the room. He looked up and down the corridor to make sure no one was near.

"I must get to my oak, Rolf. My shian side is very hungry, and I need a real rest, out of my body for a while, so I can lose some of this tension. I'm as wound up as a crossbow ready to fire."

"Fine, but before you go any further, cover yourself with a strong never-mind, young Master," said Rolf with a chuckle. "Your aura flames about you like a summer sunset! Even a first-year student with four colours will notice it right now. We don't want the entire Hall to know we have a Nine! This has to be kept secret at all costs, you understand?"

"Oh, erm, right." Luckily, Jorn had the required construct hung ready and he set it in place. "Better?"

"Yes, much. And don't worry, it will all calm down in a few days," Rolf told his now invisible guard-child reassuringly, privately hoping that was true. With a Nine, who knew?

Chapter 9

Within his home-oak, Jorn extended his *shi* from root tip to twig and drank deeply. His colours permeated his energy-form with rainbow splendour and an awesome sense of latent Power. It was one thing to have all Nine within his control, but learning to harness them to his workings would be something else entirely. As for the myriad shades that now stocked his storeroom, he had not the least idea what to do with them. Nine was more than enough to deal with for now.

He was conscious of a strange circle of events; the raash war-hammer had killed his parents and also killed the unicorn. Without the horn, he would probably not yet have mastered the Nine. It was a cruel irony. In so many ways, nothing could ever be the same again.

Eventually, the young mage left his tree and slipped back into his sleeping body. He awoke, got up, stretched, and realised that the solid part of him also needed feeding again. He covered himself with a light pass-me-by, just enough to make people not bother about him, and hurried off across the garden, towards the dining room.

He cast a quick glance at the clock as he went through the hallway, and gave a tut of dismay; he'd lost track of time resting inside the oak. Kayman's meeting was scheduled for six o'clock and it was already ten minutes past the hour. *No time for supper. Kayman mustn't be kept waiting.* He took the stairs two at a time.

Mordant, Idris, Rolf and Kayman were already there, standing in a huddle. Jorn's sense twitched, but he had no need of that to know they had been talking about him. He shed his glamour and went in. Everyone except Idris had a glass of wine, and they all looked delighted and excited. Mordant came and gave him an unexpected hug.

"Well done!" She stepped back and looked at the tall youth with a challenge in her eyes. "So, Wonder-Boy, now the hard work really starts."

He grinned at the black-clad mage. "And don't I know it! I can't wait to get going, but right now, my colours are still too volatile to handle."

Idris had been studying the young mage with close attention. His aura was almost too bright to look at, with the entire Spectrum of magic flaming out in a clear halo of extraordinary power. Was there only one aura now? It was extremely hard to be sure, because if there was a second, it was totally obscured under the other. Time would tell. He smiled warmly.

"And my congratulations also. The emanations will die down, and you are wise to wait until they do."

Kayman waved him to a chair. "I'd offer you wine, but I know you don't drink it. And now, at long last, we can make some plans. Sit down everyone, this may take some time." When they were all settled, he continued. "Jorn, I've been discussing the outcome of the High Council meeting that I called to report the attack on Arden, and the preparations for war that Mordant observed on Vard. I have to say, my esteemed colleagues refused to accept that there is any serious threat from the raash."

"But we know that's not true. Why won't they believe you?"

"Two words: politics and power. Plus, sheer blinkered, obstinate stupidity, and the fact that Professor Turner hates my guts and will do everything he can to thwart me and diminish my influence. I have to admit I was angrier than I have been for years. I am not going to let the Council off the hook so lightly. Over the next moon, I will visit each member to explain my evidence for the invasion in full. They may be persuaded without Turner breathing down their necks. If I can convince at least one or two more Councillors to take this seriously, it will help if it comes to another vote. And maybe one or two might decide to practice some attacking constructs. But, meanwhile, there is work to do. Jorn, your Mastery of Nine is the turning point I've been waiting for. It opens up many possibilities, and one in particular, which is what I want to discuss with all of you this evening. To understand about that, I have to go over some ancient history involving Myron, the original Master of Nine."

"I've been trying to find out more about him," said Jorn, "but there is remarkably little in any of the books, which surprised me. I mean, he was such a key figure. There's a bit about how he developed the theory and practice of magic, and founded the first school for mages."

"That's right," agreed Mordant. "And as far as we know, he somehow stole the Tools from the raash, brought them to Earth, and used them to get back to Vard, but he sealed up the portal so that no one could ever come that way again. He died at the end of that working, but again, we don't know how or why."

"But we can reach Vard now," said Jorn, feeling more confused than ever. "How come we can do that if Myron sealed the way in?"

"Look, we really know so little about all this, it's all just guesswork based on a legend. No construct will last indefinitely if untended, however powerful its maker. You have to remember it was all a thousand years ago." Rolf shrugged. "We assume the binding simply frayed out and wore away. As for Myron himself, a lot of records haven't survived. But there is probably more to it than that. His friends appear to have kept much of his work a closely-guarded secret, both during his life and after his death."

"I wonder why? You'd think they'd have been proud of someone who did so much."

"Just one of numerous questions with no answers," responded Kayman. "And there is one secret in particular that concerns us now. In order to work with, and control the Tools, Myron created something that he called a 'Juncture'. We do not know what it was, or how he used it, but it acted rather like your unicorn horn, as a personal focus that augmented his already staggering Power, and gave him the strength for long, immensely complex workings. After his death, this object was cut into five pieces and hidden in five remote locations."

Mordant leant forward with tense concentration. "I didn't know that."

"Very few people do", responded Kayman.

Jorn looked puzzled; his sense was tweaking, telling him this was something of enormous importance. "Another big 'why'?"

Kayman sipped his wine and made a small gesture of frustration. "You are going to get bored with hearing this; again, we don't know. The only clue to where the five pieces had been hidden was a Riddle Rhyme. Over the course of time, this Rhyme has been lost, or perhaps it was hidden as well. From time to time, mages have discussed the possibility of searching for it, but since only a Master of Nine could make use of the Juncture, there was really no point."

"Until now," said Rolf.

"Exactly. Now we do have a Master of Nine. And the Juncture, whatever it is, could be a powerful weapon in our coming war against the raash. Plainly, Darric can use the Tools he has; we have ample proof of that. But if the Juncture can be used to enhance Jorn's Power, then maybe it can enable him to wrest control of them, or at least block Darric from using them. We simply can't afford to ignore that possibility. It may tip the balance of the war in our favour at a critical moment. I believe it is time for us to start the search for the Rhyme again."

Mordant shook her head. "But where to begin? It could be anywhere. As you know, my hobby is hunting for chimeras, and in my search for archive material, I've trawled most of the major libraries, and many small obscure collections. It's incredibly time-consuming and frustrating. There's just so much stuff to sort through, and that's just what is on the shelves, or in the listings. In many places, there are records that have never been catalogued, just boxes and trunks full of old parchments, mouldering in attics and cellars."

"I certainly agree that it will be difficult. But I believe that we should try. In strictest secrecy, of course."

"Which will only add to the problems."

"This is not something I can help you with, I fear," said Idris. "I am of little use in dry and dusty archives. But if this mysterious Juncture has power, it must be worth trying to find it." He sipped his water and tipped a little into his hands to rinse across his face and body.

"Perhaps the Rhyme was not the only reference to its whereabouts?" suggested Rolf.

"Maybe." Mordant was still looking doubtful.

"So, what do we do next, Kayman?" asked Jorn.

"We can start with our own archives. We can assume that the Rhyme is not anywhere in the main collection, or it would surely have been found by now, but as you say, Mordant, there may well be uncatalogued material. You could look at that, Jorn. You have to stay here for the present while you continue your training."

"Powers! I'm not much of a scholar, but of course I'll try."

"Good. What about you, Mordant?"

"I suppose I could try the Library at the University of Errington. They are used to me going there to poke about in the Reserve Archive. Professor Sturminster can be quite helpful."

"I should not have thought she would be, bearing in mind that you were responsible for finding the Wand of the Wind and helping us to steal it!" said Kayman.

"Ah, she realised I was your spy, but she never saw my real face. I have developed a different identity for my visits. I use a whole body shape-change, which is very tiring, but effective. I do an excellent impression of an elderly male academic who is so absorbed by his studies that he hardly knows what day it is."

Rolf gave a quiet chuckle at the image. "I could try the libraries in Garamond. I am well-known in the City, and I can send agents to other places, if you can give me a list, Mordant?"

She nodded.

"Well, that's a good start." Kayman leant back in his chair and beamed with satisfaction. "I know it is a long shot. Even if it fails, we still have our Master of Nine."

"I do wish you would all stop calling me that. I may have the Nine activated and ready for use, but that is a million kays away from being a Master. And if Mordant and Rolf are away, who is going to teach me? I must learn more constructs."

"I will," Idris told him. "We can start with the basic principles of forming a portal."

Jorn smiled. "Great! I really want to tackle my first translocation!"

Kayman nodded his approval. "Right then, if that's all fixed, I suggest we all meet back here in thirty days to report on progress.

Jorn heard Mordant mutter, "Or lack of it," under her breath as she left.

*

Idris left Jorn alone for three days until he could see that his aura had returned to something like normal intensity, or, at least, what probably passed for normal in a Master of Nine. The autumn weather had turned chilly and windy so they had decided to meet in the sheltered, if slightly damp, environment of the grotto, where there were enough trickles running down the walls to keep Idris comfortable. Jorn was well wrapped in his thick cloak.

The shian had brought a fresh textbook and opened it at the page that showed a coloured diagram. "Here is what we call the Pattern. What do you make of that, Jorn?"

The young mage took the book, and studied the diagram. There were four overlapping circles, coloured pink, azure, green and orange, arranged as if confined within a square. The design formed a shape like a petal, where two circles intersected, four in all, each of which was a blend of the overlapping colours. The central area was violet, and next to that were four small black areas, formed where three circles overlapped. It had an elegant beauty. Obviously, since this was the topic he was to learn, it must have something to do with portals. His sense tweaked and suddenly he understood.

"It's a kind of map! It shows one how to get from Earth to another Realm. I know that violet is the key, and that stands in the centre. Let me think, the colours are the same as the Quincunx." He studied the page again and then nodded. "How very clever; now I see how it must work. You need to overlay the Quincunx like this." He traced the outline of the matrix diagonally on the Pattern. "The Nexuses must go on the outer edge, where the circles intersect, and that shows you the colours to use."

Idris was astonished by his intuitive leap. "Well done! The Pattern was invented by Myron to show how to weave transitions and translocations."

Jorn gave a wry grin. "Well, that's the limit of my brilliance. I don't have a clue how it works!"

Idris turned the page and showed Jorn that his assumption had been correct. "There is the overlay, just as you said. Each coloured circle represents a dimension. Pink is Above and green, Below. Azure is Behind and orange, Ahead. Above and Below are spatial. Ahead and Behind are aspects of time. Violet represents the Here and Now, the points in space and time where the Earth within the human universe is located. The Realms are in other universes, which are separated from the Here and Now by minute differences in time and space. When a mage forms a portal, he has to bridge those gaps. The entry point or wormhole lies between the dark petal-shapes in the centre. One has to find a passage between these."

"That sounds difficult."

"It is, and potentially dangerous. These dark areas around the centre are where conflicting dimensions clash; we call them Chaos Zones. You have to pass between them, but if you get dragged into one, you die. The constructs are complex. Only mages of six or more can weave a portal, and then, as you know, only if they have violet in their Spectrums. Now, when you translocated, you saw that a portal is like a doorway, and the first stage of making the portal is to form the frame for the door. Each Realm has its own set of framing colours, so of course, to reach them, you also need to have the right ones. Look, here is the list:

The Shian Realm — Ahead and Below, blue, green, azure, plus violet.

The Dwarran Realm — Behind and Below yellow, orange, green, plus violet.

The Raash Realm — Above and Behind red, orange, pink, plus violet.

"In theory there ought to be a fourth Realm, Above and Ahead, with ether, pink, red and violet, but this appears to be inaccessible. No one knows why."

"Rolf has taken me to an Earth Transit-Point. He said one cannot go straight from one Realm to another, only via Earth?"

"Yes, because Earth, in the 'Here and Now' dimension, is the point to which all the wormholes from the universes in the other dimensions are linked. See, it stands on the violet Nexus at the centre of the Pattern, so all journeys have to start and end there. It's the centre of everything."

Jorn considered the Pattern. Like the Quincunx, it was far more complex than it seemed at first sight.

"I think I can see the principles, but no wonder it takes so long to learn how to make them work!"

"Now, think what this use of the colours means for those of us who are not so fortunate as to have the Nine. For example, like most shian mages, my colours are in the Sector of Adjunct. That means I can form a portal between the Shian Realm and Earth. But I cannot form a portal from Earth to the Dwarran Realm because I lack orange, so I have to use an Earth Transit-Point, where another mage can help me to travel through. And I also have to use a mage at the Hall to send me back to Earth again so I can return home."

"My, that does sound complicated! And pretty frustrating if you are in a hurry."

"It is that. I have to rely on the magic of others. Mordant's colours are in the Sector of Disjunct, so she can travel between Earth and Vard, but she cannot portal from Earth to the Dwarran Realm or to the Shian Realm. It is indeed hugely frustrating, but of course, not something you will ever have to worry about."

"I see. I think I'm following. Idris, you can sort out another confusion for me. I've heard Rolf mention a transition, although mostly he says translocation. I don't really understand the difference."

"That is relatively straightforward. It is possible to travel across time and space using three related techniques: the translocation, the transition, and the cross-step."

"A translocation is a transfer from Earth to a different location in another Realm, or the reverse. This requires a hook, a familiar and easily recognisable destination, to act as a focus. You form a seeking cord called a 'fishing line', visualise the hook, cast the line through the portal, catch the hook, and pull yourself through."

"So, you cannot translocate to a place you have never seen?" Jorn asked.

"No, you need a hook."

"Right, and what about the other methods?"

"Well, except for Vard, the planet in each parallel universe is geographically very similar to Earth. A transition is used to cross from Earth to another Realm and come out exactly where you started, but of course, in the other world. That is seldom useful, although it was probably how the first portal to a new universe was first opened, when no one had a hook, or even knew for certain that it was possible."

"Heavens, the first mages who tried that must have been either very brave or totally lacking in imagination! Fine, so for translocation you need a hook for another destination, transition just takes you to the exact same point on another planet, but what about the cross-step?"

"A cross-step is used on Earth in order to move relatively short distances between known places without forming a portal. It does not involve any change in time, only a transit across space from here to there on the same planet, but it is only practical for very short hops because long journeys place too much strain on the body; humans get very sick and can even die. It can be a good way out in an emergency, but on the whole, one is better off using a portal."

"Dear me, this gets worse! This is clearly going to take a lot of time and practice."

"Yes, it will. But we will take it one stage at a time. First, study the theory. Then you can construct a portal, and finally, you will attempt an Earth translocation. You will have to ask Rolf to take you to a Transit Point first so that you can learn the hook. I favour the Dolphin because it has a fountain; I suggest we use that one."

Jorn picked up the textbook. "Thanks Idris. If I can learn to do this, I'll start to feel a bit more like a real mage!"

But however much he would have preferred to continue his own translocation studies, his next job was to start work in the Library, looking for the mysterious Riddle Rhyme. He had already spoken to Marilyn, the mage-librarian, explaining that he wanted to do some research in the ancient, uncatalogued archives.

"It would help me to find the right documents if I knew what exactly you are researching?" she had asked, predictably. He had fobbed her off with something vague about looking for new information about the life of Myron. "Well good luck, although I can tell you now, you are almost certainly wasting your time. But I'll pull some boxes out for you. I'd appreciate it if you could list the items you find, as I never get time to rummage."

Jorn settled in a quiet corner, with a pile of fragile scrolls, fragments of discoloured and illegible parchment, and battered, crumbling books with half their pages missing. His task already looked quite impossible. He reminded himself that the Juncture could be the deciding factor in the war with the raash, but that did not make a mountain of ancient documents look any more appealing. With a sigh, he picked up the first item and began to examine it.

*

The thirty days soon elapsed and Jorn joined his friends in Kayman's study to hear how they had got on with their search for the Riddle Rhyme. He suspected that they would have had as much success as he had; namely, none at all, and he was almost right. Rolf had found nothing and was as fed up as he was with shuffling through musty archives. Mordant had also found no trace of the Rhyme, but she had got one thing to report.

"It may mean nothing at all, but I did find one new account of Myron's final working. It was written many years after the event in the form of an epic verse, and this phrase may simply be a fanciful, poetic flourish, but the author describes Myron as being 'crowned with mighty power'. It did make me wonder whether the Juncture might possibly be a crown of some kind."

Kayman shook his head. "It's an interesting thought, but it doesn't get us any further."

Rolf had been absent-mindedly twiddling his beard with his fingers, a sure sign he was frustrated and worried.

"Is it worth going on? It is taking up a great deal of time. I ought to be back on the road, checking my networks."

"As should I," said Mordant. "But I hate to give up on a project, and there's still a mass of material to go through at Errington, so I'm willing to give it another moon. After that, if there is still nothing, I'm afraid I'll have to call it a day."

The High Master sighed. "Well, it was never going to just walk off a shelf and say 'I'm here!' was it? But we have to keep trying while there is still time. Finding the Juncture is more important than anything else right now."

"Did you have any success in your visits to the Council Members?" asked Rolf.

"Some, but not enough to make any great difference. Humans are so very good at denying unpleasant facts that don't fit with their comfortable view of reality. I can do no more for now. I fear it will take some further massive demonstration of Darric's Power to break through the inertia."

"Seeing is believing," said Mordant. "If I could take a few Council Members to Vard and show them Darric's army, they'd have to take it seriously then, surely?"

Kayman shook his head. "You'd hope so, but first I'd have to persuade them to go. Still, it's a thought."

Chapter 10

Jorn sat in his room and braced himself for yet another tedious session in the Library. Mordant might enjoy the thrill of exploring the deep past, for she clearly had a genuine passion for research, but he certainly did not. Only the thought of how important the Juncture might be kept him going, but he was finding it increasingly hard to concentrate as he ploughed through box after box of dusty parchment. The librarian was enjoying the challenge of keeping him supplied. He sighed at the thought of the next batch that would be waiting for him. His brain simply did not want to play this boring game for hour after hour, especially when there was so much else to learn. On the other hand, his sense told him that there *was* something to find, but the feeling was far too dim and uncertain to be of any use in directing his search. Perhaps he was just not looking in the right place.

He sat down to consider the problem. *If only I had a means of focussing this faint feeling I have.* He had propped the unicorn horn up against the edge of the fireplace, and his eyes were now drawn to it. He picked it up and began idly running his hand up and down it, as he now did when he needed some comfort or an answer to a problem. *I need a focus,* he repeated, and then sat up straight with a jerk as the answer hit him. *Idiot mage! You have one in your hand! Why do things the hard way when you might be able to use your Power instead? Maybe the horn can help me to find the Rhyme.*

The shaft warmed under his hand. "Are you trying to tell me you can?" he whispered. The horn warmed again, decisively. *That's great, but how?* He thought about that for a bit. He closed his eyes and saw himself back to his old home, sitting by the fire on a wet winter evening, playing 'hot or cold' guessing games with Rob and Red. "If you could go warm if I get close to something interesting, or cold if I am not, it would speed things up a lot. Can you do that horn?" he asked hopefully. The horn grew quite hot.

Jorn was excited by the idea and would have liked to try it out at once, but he realised he would have to wait. *If I'm going to search the shelves, I needed privacy; I'll have to wait until the evening to try to sneak in when it's quiet, perhaps while everyone else is having supper. And it's no use carrying the horn in plain sight. I've taken great care to keep it hidden so far. Pity Mordant hasn't shown me how to work a full shape-changing glamour yet, but I could wrap it in something. My next instalment of boxes and bundles will be waiting on my table. I can use the horn to dowse to indicate if any are worth looking at. That should really speed things up.*

To distract himself, he spent most of the afternoon inside his mental workroom. He fabricated some of the simple constructs that Mordant and Idris had taught him, aiming to get his working faster, smoother and generally more elegant. He had already noticed that a well-made braid or mesh acted more effectively than a messy one. *And quite right too! After all, I'm a weaver; absolute precision is the key to good work.* Since gaining control of the Nine, he could work for many hours before the fatigue that limited an ordinary adept caught up with him, but Idris had advised him not to push himself too hard.

Eventually, his rumbling stomach reminded him that it was almost suppertime. Jorn concealed the horn inside a cloak, with the added distraction of a light never-mind. He went downstairs, along the panelled corridors and into the refectory, and settled for bread and cheese, and a slice of apple pie. He nodded at a few people he knew, but picked an empty table, and no one joined him; thankfully, the students had decided that he was a loner and had given up on getting him to chat, and right now, he liked it that way.

He ate fast and then headed for the Library.

Bother! Have to wait a bit.

There were still a dozen or so people there, but most were too engaged in their studies to look up as he walked casually to his table, where two new boxes and a tied bundle of scrolls awaited him. Feeling keyed-up with the need to get on with his experiment, the young Master sat down and went through the motions of looking at the documents.

One by one, the other users packed up and left. After half an hour, the big room was finally empty. Jorn allowed a few more moments, went to the door to check that no one was heading his way, then took out the horn. He pointed it at the heap on his desk and focussed his full attention on it.

"Horn, please tell me, is the Rhyme there?" he asked.

The horn remained cool and inert, which was no surprise, but did not necessarily represent an answer. He needed to test its ability to respond accurately.

"Where are the books on herbs?" he asked, and scanned the tip of the horn across the nearest bookshelves. It warmed at the middle shelf of the third one, which, as Jorn quickly saw, contained a row of illustrated herbals and related books. To confirm that it had not been a lucky accident, he repeated the question and scanned the rest of the room. He had expected a negative, for the books were strictly arranged in topic order, so he was surprised to feel a faint warmth when he pointed the horn at the far end of the room.

Jorn walked to the area indicated and ran his eyes across the shelves, careful not to miss anything. There were no herbals, or anything else that might have triggered a response. He stood, looking round, his face perplexed by indecision.

This is not good; maybe the horn isn't giving me reliable signals. Now what?

In response to his thought, the horn grew quite hot. He felt a distinctly angry pulse of Power throbbing up from it.

"Sorry, I guess I'm just not looking in the right place. Please show me again."

He pointed the shining spiral and scanned methodically round the area until it grew warm again, and then moved in that direction. The horn pulled him insistently towards a dark alcove in a remote corner, where a floor to ceiling stack of oak shelves was laden with huge, battered tomes. The light was fading now as the autumn evening advanced. Jorn found a switch and turned on the lights. He peered at the faded label on the section: 'Mage Hall Administration Archive'. The bound ledgers appeared to continue in series for several hundred years.

These have to be the most boring books in the entire library. So why has the horn led me to this section?

"Is there something of interest here?" he whispered softly. The horn grew so hot, he almost dropped it. His sense tweaked sharply.

Surely it can't be indicating the Riddle Rhyme? How could that possibly be here?

"Is the Rhyme here?" he asked aloud. He hefted the horn again and methodically scanned the shelves from bottom to top. The horn got warm again when it brushed along the top shelf, and then intensely hot as it touched one volume. The faded gilt lettering on the old spine was hard to read, but Jorn eventually deciphered *'Mage Hall Accounts. MH years 400-450'*. He reached up and gingerly removed the ancient volume, releasing a shower of dust, which made him sneeze.

Jorn

Jorn took the heavy ledger to a table, folded himself into a chair, and began to turn the pages methodically, finding nothing but list after list of purchases, expenditure, and calculations in a neat, archaic script.

Only a dedicated accountant could find this remotely interesting. If there is a code, or a hidden message, I'm not seeing it. This is pointless; the horn must be mistaken. He sat back and let his sense explore the book, fighting an urge to give up and put it back where he found it.

Interesting; I think there is a small glamour at work here. A little pass-me-by to put people off, if the title has not done that already. So, what are you hiding?

He produced a small blade of Disjunct and applied it. The pass-me-by snapped, but the book was no less boring. He turned it over, examining the covers, which felt looser than usual, and the spine, which felt fatter than it should be. He rummaged in a nearby drawer, found a slim, wooden ruler and, with patient care, slipped it into the gap between the spine and the book. A single sheet of folded parchment slid out.

As soon as Jorn touched it, he felt his colours flare out with the recognition of its importance. Trying to contain his impatience, he carefully unfolded the dry parchment and saw lines of beautiful calligraphy.

Searing is my power and sharp,
Fit to test the bravest heart.
I am not within death's keeping,
Seek me where dry kings lie sleeping.

I command a force unseen,
Edgeless and yet always keen.
Hunt me in a place on high,
Where mighty eagles dare not fly.

Drear the world that knows my loss,
Reduced to barren drought and dross.
Seek me far from light of day,
Where mapless mazes bar the way.

Without beginning I or end,
All things I firmly hold or mend.

Earth's opposites me safely hide,
Where burning ice and freezing fire collide.

Seek me somewhere that you know,
I am neither high nor low.
I do not lose or win the race,
The still centre is my place.

Master of Nine, be strong and wise,
Complete the quest and win the prize.
Resolve the verse, perform the task,
Unlock the truth; reveal the mask.

Jorn re-read the enigma several times, but was none the wiser. He put the old ledger back on the top shelf, where it would no doubt remain unread for another hundred years. He wrapped the horn in the cloak, covered himself with a never-mind, and sent a terse mental message to Kayman.

"I have found it. Meet you in my bedroom."

"I'll be with you in five minutes," Kayman replied, his excitement evident.

Jorn had only just returned to his room and discarded his glamour when the High Master almost ran through the door, puffing for breath.

"Where?" he demanded.

Jorn silently handed him the small piece of parchment. "It was hidden within the spine of an ancient accounts book in the archive section of the Library."

"Are you sure it's genuine?"

"My sense tells me so. My colours flamed when I found it."

Kayman rapidly read the Rhyme and looked at Jorn with sharp attention. "This is astonishing. How did you come to discover it?"

"The horn led me to it. It was concealed by some kind of pass-me-by that would prevent any casual discovery; but perhaps there was something more. I think I was being drawn to find it."

"Remarkable." Kayman read the Rhyme again. "It is certainly a riddle, deliberately enigmatic. It will not be easy to solve these verses."

"But we have to try."

"I think we must. And it may not be a coincidence that it has turned up at the very moment that a new Mage of Nine appears, or that he himself has discovered it." He handed the precious text back to Jorn. "Please make five copies. Let me have one as soon as you can. Hide the original. I'll send messages to Rolf, Mordant and Idris. Meanwhile, I'll start to think about what it means."

He clapped Jorn on the shoulder. "Well done Master, very well done. I feel more cheerful than I have for many months."

*

Kayman dispatched urgent messages for Mordant, Idris and Rolf. The summons was short and deliberately obscure, except, of course to the recipients.

"Found it. Return at once."

A day later, Mordant and Rolf had portalled in and the whole team met up again in the small meeting room next to Kayman's office. The sense of anticipation was tangible.

Jorn briefly repeated the story of his discovery, and then Kayman handed out copies of the Rhyme. There was a tense silence as everyone read it several times.

Mordant leant back in her chair and shook her head. "Riddle Rhyme is right! This won't be easy to crack."

"No it won't," agreed the High Master. "At least, not the parts that give the clues to the locations of the hiding places. But Jorn and I spent several hours yesterday looking at the text line by line to see what we could pull out of it." He nodded at Jorn to continue.

"Well, the first thing is fairly obvious; the first five verses must correspond to the five hidden parts of the Juncture. The sixth is more of a mystery. It seems to be about something else that can only happen when the quest is completed. In the first four verses, the opening two lines relate to one of the elements. For example, 'Searing is my power and sharp, fit to test the bravest heart,' must be Fire."

"Of course!" Rolf studied his copy intently. "So, 'I command a force unseen, edgeless and yet always keen,' has to be Air."

"And, 'Drear the world that knows my loss, reduced to barren drought and dross,' is obviously Water," said Idris.

"Right, which leaves the one about, 'All things I firmly hold or mend,' as Earth," continued Jorn. "You will notice that the first line of that verse is, 'Without beginning I, or end,' which made us think of a chain."

"And, 'Searing is my power and sharp,' could be a knife," Kayman added, and then looked round at the others. "So what do you think that indicates?"

"The lines might also relate to one of the Tools?" suggested Mordant.

"That's what we thought. Which might also indicate which Sector and/or Tool that part of the Juncture controls."

Idris smiled. "Well done for getting so far so quickly, my friends. But what about the last two verses?"

Kayman shook his head. "The final verse must refer to the last part of the Juncture. But the other is very obscure. Anyway, that was as far as we could get. We have to start with the ones that make some sense at least. The second part of each verse is the enigma that conceals the location, and that is where we run slap into a stone wall." He handed them each another piece of paper. "We've separated these lines out to make it easier to study them."

The mages reviewed the text with silent concentration.

I am not within death's keeping,
Seek me where dry kings lie sleeping.

Hunt me in a place on high,
Where mighty eagles dare not fly.

Seek me far from light of day,
Where mapless mazes bar the way.

Earth's opposites me safely hide,
Where burning ice and freezing fire collide.

"Any ideas?" Kayman asked hopefully after a few minutes.

Everybody shook their heads.

"We need to take this away and think about it." Rolf looked intently at Kayman. "What happens if we think we have found a location?"

"I think we should set up a team and go there. A small taskforce, operating in secret. All of you, if you are willing, and perhaps one or two others who have our absolute trust."

"I'd like to include Commander Clarriss," said Rolf. "She is a logistics expert, and a soldier, and, of course, a Spy-Master. She also happens to be an excellent trail-cook. It's a useful skill set." Kayman nodded.

Mordant said nothing, but she knew very well who she would like to include. Unfortunately, Sar Brett Darnell was now a much-married man in his mid-40s, busily engaged in the traditional Darnell occupations of running a large estate and breeding a brood of boys. Since his marriage, she had, as she had promised, kept a tactful distance. But she still missed her 'Beaky Boy', both as friend and lover. Their raash-hunting partnership was long over, but he was still an expert Sword-Master, and the person she would most like to have at her side in a tight corner. She decided to send a coded message to ask him, although she would place her bet on a refusal. And then there was Sarra; her dwarran best friend was now a powerful Mage-Adept, but she had many commitments, and maybe a dangerous quest into the wilds was not playing to her strengths.

"Let's meet again tomorrow," Idris proposed. "We might have got some inklings by then."

"I surely hope so," said Jorn. "It would be maddening to have found the Rhyme after all these years and then not be able to solve the clues."

"And that timespan may be an important factor," suggested Mordant. "We don't know *where* the mages hid these things, but we do know *when*. We are looking for places that existed a thousand years ago."

"There speaks our historian," said Idris with a smile. "We rest our hopes on you!"

*

When Jorn went to meet the others the next afternoon, he was very much hoping that someone had an idea, because he certainly did not. There was so little to go on that the horn could not help, and his knowledge of Earth's history and geography was minimal. But he saw that Mordant had a gleam in her eyes. She was the first to speak when Kayman asked for progress reports.

"Well, I do have a clue, but it's a long shot. The lines about 'mapless mazes' rang a faint bell. There is an ancient legend about a cave system in Daunce that contains an endless labyrinth. People who enter are never seen again. It is also cursed. It rejoices in the name of 'The Cave of the Damned'."

Rolf winced. "Delightful! If there is one thing I detest more than a cave, it's a haunted one! But is it any more than a legend?"

"Possibly. It's somewhere in this region." Mordant bent down and picked up a rolled map from the floor beside her chair. She unrolled it and pinned it down under the water jug and a couple of glasses. Everyone got up and crowded round to look. Jorn had little experience of maps, so the squiggles and lines meant nothing to him, but Mordant stabbed a finger down on a particular spot.

"This high area of southern Daunce is limestone — all mountains, valleys and gorges. It's famous for its caves."

"Which is not much help," said Rolf. "It could take several lifetimes to explore terrain like that."

Jorn's sense was tweaking. "Hang on a minute," he told the others. "Just going to get something." A few moments later, he was back, carrying the horn. "I think the horn may help us again here. I need to ask it a precise question. If the answer is positive, the horn will go warm in my hand. If it is negative, it gets colder. Shall I try?"

"Indeed you must!" Kayman told him.

Jorn pointed the tip of the horn at the map in the area Rolf had indicated. "Is part of the Juncture hidden here?" he asked. There was no response. He moved it a little to the left, repeated the question, and was instantly rewarded by a warm glow. He gave a triumphant "Yes!" and there was a chorus of amazed and excited exclamations.

"Well done, Wonder-Boy!" sent Mordant.

Kayman was beaming with satisfaction. "Well, my friends, it looks as though we are in business! We absolutely have to go to the area and find that Cave."

"By 'we' you mean 'us', of course," said Mordant dryly. "Unless you intend to come with us?"

"I'd like nothing better, but I can't be away from the Hall."

"Well, in any case, this mission can't be put together in five minutes. It will take a great deal of practical preparation."

"Mordant's right," confirmed Rolf. "May I involve Commander Clarriss? This is just the kind of task she excels at."

"Certainly. Should we include anyone else?"

Mordant was still waiting for a reply from Brett. "I might have a suggestion. I'll let you know shortly."

"Excellent. And, needless to say, this has to stay absolutely secret."

Mordant gave a quiet snort and Rolf shook his head.

Jorn

"As Mordant knows full well, absolute secrecy is a myth. However careful we are, someone will notice our preparations and mark our departure. The best we can do is to hide our destination and lay some false trails. Anyway, we are well used to doing that."

Kayman looked enquiringly round the table. "Anyone else got any suggestions about the other verses?" Idris, Rolf and Jorn all shook their heads.

*

Mordant received her reply from Brett later the following day.

I regret that I cannot help, I'm sure you understand why. But there is someone else who can; my younger brother, Sar Braidart. He has the skills you seek and he is currently unemployed, bored, and in need of adventure. Meet him at the Transit Point of the Horse at noon in three days. My best wishes to my FF.

BB (By the way, he does not know of our past association, professional or otherwise!)

Mordant felt a small twinge of bittersweet regret. It had, of course, been a foolishly nostalgic hope. But Braidart? She cast her mind back and found only images of a small boy playing with his brothers, chasing round Darnell Hold with a toy sword 'repelling invaders', getting into endless mischief, and generally doing what all boys do. But time had passed for him too; he must be in his mid-20s now.

Well, if Brett recommends him, he must be useful. Two swords are better than one, and an expert woodsman is a bonus. And it would be good for Jorn to have another young man on the team. I'd better just check it out with Kayman first, though.

*

Well ahead of the appointed hour, Mordant formed her portal to the Transit Point. It was a grey autumn day on Earth. The Transit-Master, Philip, came out to greet her as usual.

"Where are you going today Mistress?"

"Straight back to Mage Hall," she told him, "as soon as my visitor arrives. How are you, my friend?"

"Keeping busy as always," the man laughed. "What with all the comings and goings to Mage Hall and the postal and pigeon services to manage. But you know I like it that way. When I have time off between shifts I get bored."

They chatted amiably for a while. Philip had been running the Transit Point with exemplary efficiency for 10 years, so Mordant knew him well, and he was a useful source of gossip. He was heading for middle-age, a tall, thin man with a slightly grizzled beard and a rapidly balding head; the kind of person who seemed to actually enjoy running routine systems, and stayed remarkably calm, pleasant, patient and helpful while he did so. That kind of life would drive her to distraction inside of a single moon, but it suited others.

Just before noon, there was a sharp knock on the outer gate of the courtyard. Philip went to open it. She watched through the gateway as a tall man dismounted and handed the reins of his horse to the servant who had accompanied him. As Braidart hitched a light pack over his shoulder and strode forward, Mordant felt a visceral pang, which made her catch her breath. He was a true Darnell, with the trademark dark hair, blue eyes, and that proudly jutting nose that just stopped them from being conventionally handsome. In fact, he was so exactly like her young 'Beaky Boy', down to the well-worn set of brown leathers, and the sword slung at his hip, that it was all she could do to stop herself from running across the cobbles to give him an inappropriately passionate welcome.

Instead, she stood still and watched his reaction, wondering if Brett had warned him to expect a raash mage to welcome him. Plainly he had, because Braidart came straight to her without as much as a blink of surprise, wearing a charming smile.

He gave a court bow and said, "Mistress Mordant? I am delighted to meet you. I can't wait to find out what all this is about."

She gave him her own approximation of a smile in return. "And I look forward to telling you. But first, we must travel to Mage Hall in the Dwarran Realm. Have you used a portal before?"

"No, Mistress."

"Ah, well, there's a first time for everything. I must warn you that most humans find the experience unpleasant. You will feel as if you have been pulled to pieces and put back together again in a great hurry. You will certainly feel dizzy and you may well be sick. But it will pass rapidly."

He pulled a wry face. "How could I refuse such an attractive invitation?"

Mordant nodded at Philip. "Be so kind as to make the portal for us." Braidart stared with unconcealed amazement as the mist-filled gateway formed.

"After you, M'sar."

To his credit, he did not hesitate, but walked swiftly through, and she followed. The young nobleman was, as she expected, on his knees, looking decidedly green. He took a while to recover.

"I see you are going to be one of *those* humans," she told him unsympathetically. "Never mind. Come in and meet the rest of the team. I believe that Kayman has some wine waiting. Oh, and I should warn you, the others are not all human."

By the time Mordant had escorted their newest team member up to the meeting room, everyone else was already there, having a light lunch of bread, cheese and fruit. Braidart halted just over the threshold and looked at the company with frank astonishment.

"I, um, see what you mean," he murmured.

Mordant took him on a tour of introductions, pressed a glass of wine into his hand, and sat him down in a corner for a rapid briefing.

"You are being thrown in at the deep end," she told him briskly, "and I haven't got time right now to do much more than toss you a few straws to clutch at! Everything you see or hear from this moment on is completely secret. This team has been set up to find a magical object called the Juncture, which may make a significant difference to our success in the coming war with the raash." She looked at him sharply. "You do know about *that*, don't you?"

He nodded. His sapphire eyes were alert and intelligent. "You can't be a Darnell and not know about that. But my father is not generous with his information, so I expect there are a lot of gaps."

"Right. We'll fill those in as we go along. To get back to our mission, the Juncture was hidden a thousand years ago in five secret locations. Clues to these were given in a cryptic Riddle Rhyme. We have just found this. We think we may have solved one clue, and we are about to plan a mission to go and conduct a search. It will undoubtedly be a difficult journey through wild country, and it may well be dangerous, hence your presence here. There are times when a Sword-Master is more use than a mage." She was interrupted by Kayman, tapping his gavel on the table to signal the start of their meeting. "And that will have to do for now. I can answer any questions you have left after the meeting."

Kayman looked round with a smile. "Now the real work begins. Firstly, as High Master, let me formally welcome Commander Clarriss and Sar Braidart Darnell who have agreed to join us. Now, we do not all know you, and you do not know all of us. You all have skills to bring to the mission, and modesty is not going to assist us, so I think it would be a good idea to share what you know, and admit to what you do not. Sar Braidart, you begin."

"I'm the hired muscle. I have served as a mercenary captain. I have some skill with my sword and other weapons. I can hunt and track and live off the land. Needless to say, I have scant knowledge of anything to do with magic."

Kayman chuckled. "I suspect there is more, but that will do for now. Commander Clarriss?"

The uniformed dwar spoke briskly. "I have 45 years of service in the Dwarran army. I have attained the rank of Commander. However, you will be aware that we do not go to war among ourselves. Whilst the army is battle-ready in theory, its main function is ceremonial. I doubt if my active service record equals yours M'sar." She gave Braidart a small nod of acknowledgement. "But my army role is, to be frank, simply a front for my real job, which is running the Dwarran Intelligence Service. Apart from that, my strengths, to use the old adage, are three: organisation, organisation, organisation. I am a logistics specialist. I can set up camps and bivouacs. And I'm a good cook."

Kayman nodded and turned to Mordant. She looked at Clarriss and Braidart with a deliberate challenge in her violet eyes.

"I look like a raash. If a thing looks like a duck and quacks like a duck, it is generally assumed that it is a duck. Please do not make that mistake with me. My mother was human. I was born on Vard, the result of a raash breeding programme that aimed to create mages who appear human on the outside, but are pure raash on the inside; such people are used as spies in the human world, as I am sure you know, ma'am," she nodded towards Clarriss. "With me, they produced the opposite; I look raash, but inside I am entirely human. I have more reason than most of you to hate my father's people. I managed to escape slavery in the Raash Realm. Since then, I've worked closely with Rolf and Kayman. I am a Mage of Six. I master the Sector of Disjunct, plus violet. My speciality, like that of many raash mages, is the casting of glamours; weaves of deception that make things seem other than they are. I am also an expert Sword-Master. Oh, and, just to avoid any later confusion, I'm female." She noticed a flicker of surprise in the dwar's eyes, and interest in Braidart's. "Yes, the raash sexes look alike, and I prefer, as you observe, to dress as a male." She smoothed the sleeve of her well-cut black jacket and touched the silver lace on her cuff. "In recent years, my main role has been that of spy. And unfortunately, I can manage to burn water, so I can't volunteer for the cooking rota. That will do for now."

"Well, my turn," said Rolf. "I'm a dwarran halfer and a Mage of Seven. I lack ether, and my control of pink is very limited. I am also a spy. Using my disguise as a trader, I travel widely in the human world, which is useful because I have been able to memorise many hooks, and that may be helpful for our mission. I speak a number of human languages."

"What is a hook?" asked Braidart.

"Well, let's see if Jorn can answer that?" said Rolf. "He's been studying the theory of translocation."

"A hook is a marker point by which a mage can remember a specific location in order to construct a portal to go there again. It's not possible to translocate to a place to which one has never been, unless one can find a very accurate picture of it, so Rolf's travels will come in very useful."

"Indeed," agreed Kayman. "So, that brings us to Idris." The mage had been sitting quietly near the open window, sipping water, soaking his feet in a tin bath.

He responded quietly. "I am a shian of the water. I am also a Mage of Six, in the Sector of Adjunct. I have some skill as a healer."

Kayman shook his head very slightly, as if to indicate that Idris had left out more than he had said, but he looked at Jorn, who had decided that brevity was the safest strategy. "Now for you."

"I'm a shian-human halfer. I am a Master of Nine. I am still trying to discover exactly what that means."

"As are we, Wonder-Boy!" said Mordant dryly. "But for the benefit of our new team members, Jorn is the first mage for a thousand years, since Myron, to have gained control of the entire Spectrum of magic, and that means that his Power is many, many times greater than any ordinary Adept. We have to keep that fact a secret for as long as possible, and it is our duty to protect Jorn at all times. He is our most potent weapon against Darric."

"But I still have a huge amount to learn before I can be any real use."

"So, we have a strong team. Your first task is to plan the mission to Daunce. I am going to leave you to it. However, as Idris reminded us the other day, winter is coming, so you need to depart as soon as you can." Kayman left the room.

Rolf unrolled a large map and spread it on the table. "Unfortunately, it appears that this area has not been mapped in any detail; but this is the best I can find. The Hackfells are here in the mountains of southern Daunce. Using this map, Jorn has dowsed with the horn and he has been able to narrow our search area. It looks as if The Cave of the Damned is somewhere here, off this valley."

"Attractive name. Any reason for it?" asked Braidart casually.

"A lot of legend, but no fact. But we think it is where the object is located."

Braidart looked round the table with a disarmingly apologetic grin. "Forgive me if this seems rude, but we are not exactly going to blend in with the crowd are we? I mean we have a raash, a water-spirit, two black dwarves, and a tall boy with unusual hair and eyes. And me, armed to the teeth, of course."

Rolf chuckled. "Well, yes, we'll need disguises, and good cover stories for the first leg, when we're in the public eye. Using a glamour is tiring, and besides, there are always spies; this time, we *want* them to see us, and remember us heading off in the wrong direction."

Clarriss and Rolf took the lead in the next discussions, planning routes, accommodation and supplies with the competence of old campaigners. Braidart held back, mostly simply watching proceedings, but adding useful comment and suggestions.

Mordant was finding the long meeting trying for several reasons. Clarriss' automatic assumption of the role of leader was just plain irritating. The dwar was certainly an extremely able organiser, and she had a long experience as an army commander, but by the Powers, did she have to say the same thing three times and treat everyone else as raw recruits? Mordant was well aware that dwars were used to having their males firmly under their thumbs, but she was female, for heaven's sake, and she had been running her own operations for years. It was hard work keeping her mouth shut and not saying something she would later regret.

She was also still acutely aware of Braidart's unsettling resemblance to Brett. She kept telling herself that this was a different Darnell, but then he grinned, or laughed, or said something in a particular way, and his brother was there in the room. It was going to take a lot of getting used to.

And then there was Idris. Despite his water bath, he was so obviously uncomfortable in this hot, dry room, but he stayed on, determined to play his part, although he was being totally ignored for his pains. The others seemed to forget that he was there. Just because he couldn't rattle on about tents and camping gear, dried food supplies and the right kit for caving, it didn't mean he lacked brains. His calm alien beauty troubled her in a way that she really did not understand. What was he thinking? After an hour, the shian begged leave to go and soak under the waterfall, and she felt relieved for him.

Jorn was no happier. He rapidly got lost in all the tedious detail. *"Do I have to stay?"* he asked Rolf, plaintively. *"This is all so boring and they really don't need me."*

"Of course they don't, but just sit it out. Watch and listen. You may learn something."

What he had mainly learnt, by the end of a long and tedious afternoon, was that organising a major expedition took a great deal more time and effort than he had ever imagined, even with experienced experts in charge. The messaging services would soon be humming with exchanges about supplies, caving gear, horses, tents, and other essentials.

Jorn listened with half an ear to the final discussion. He was bothered about the unicorn horn. He must take it with him, and have it ready for use, but he was stuck as to how to disguise it. A simple never-mind would ensure that it went unnoticed in public, but it was still a largish object that would not be at all easy to carry, especially if they had to climb, as seemed likely. Braidart had turned out to be an experienced mountaineer and his descriptions of all the gear you needed in order to hang by your toes and fingertips from some tiny ledge halfway up a cliff did not sound at all encouraging.

Finally, Commander Clarriss straightened up and said briskly, "Well, that is as far as we can get for now."

The team got up. Braidart stretched wearily. "My tongue feels like old jerky. I could murder a top of ale!" He looked at Mordant with sudden alarm as an unpleasant possibility hit him. "Blood's death, don't tell me this place is dry?"

She laughed. "No fear of that; Mage-Craft is thirsty work!"

He wiped imaginary sweat from his forehead with a flourish of relief. "Then lead the way! Coming, Jorn?"

He nodded. "Mordant, I need to find a way to carry the unicorn horn so that it doesn't get in my way, and also makes it easier to hide. Is it possible to change it in some way? Make it smaller and lighter, for example?"

"It is possible to make it smaller, but not lighter. You can't just lose substance from a solid object and then regain it at will, but you can condense it. The horn will weigh the same, but be smaller. It's like forming a whole-body mask that completely changes one's appearance. The closer you can keep to the original shape, the better."

"So, it would need to be something long and thin, like a wand, or perhaps a knife?"

"That's the idea. Look Jorn, it's been a very long day, and Braidart missed his lunch. We're heading for the dining room. Why don't you join us, and then I can show you the construct later on?"

"Great!"

The young mercenary had been listening to this exchange with some bewilderment. "Did I really hear you say 'unicorn horn'?" he enquired incredulously.

"You certainly did!" Jorn told him. "I'll explain about that over supper."

"Thanks. I think I need an intensive course on magic or wizardry, or whatever it is you all do. Half of what you're saying might as well be in Kardashian for all the sense it makes to me!"

"We'll do our best," Mordant told him. "But you'd better start by remembering that we are mages, definitely not witches, wizards, magicians, warlocks or conjurers, and we hardly ever talk about magic as such."

"What is that useful phrase? A steep learning curve? I think I just started to climb one, without a safety rope!"

Jorn gave an answering grin. "Then you can join me. I've been ascending one ever since I arrived at Mage Hall, and I don't see any sign of reaching the top!" He led the way downstairs, having decided that he was probably going to enjoy having Braidart on the team.

Chapter 11

The raash force portalled into Arden, with two mages, prepared to cause havoc. Darric had been infuriated by the obduracy of the shians, and he was determined to continue inflicting punitive damage until they changed their stubborn minds and gave him the Cup, or Arden was reduced to ashes.

The mages surveyed the area. The autumn woodland was bare. There was plenty of fallen leaf litter and dry branches. A fire would take hold rapidly, not perhaps as well as during a summer drought, but well enough.

The soldiers spread out, holding their ugly flamethrowers at the ready, forming a wide semicircle. It was very quiet. The lead mage, Oriel, was uneasy. Something pricked his sense, but he could see no threat. Then a distant drum began to beat. It was a slow, ominous thud. The soldiers looked up, hands falling to sword hilts. But there was still nothing to see.

"Get on with it," Oriel snapped. His colleague had the return portal hung ready; the sooner they left the better.

A thin mist began to swirl across the forest floor. It reached the first soldiers and twined around their legs. A half-seen shimmering swept across the Glade at head height. The raash hesitated, uncertain, not seeing any enemy to confront or sensing any magic. It was a fatal delay.

The soldiers fell, or tried to run. The screams began. Those targeted by the shians of the water never fully understood the nature of their excruciating, but brief agony, as the life-water was sucked remorselessly from their bodies.

The ones attacked by shians of the wood died a little faster. The shimmering, angry *shis* penetrated their skulls and exploded outwards, carrying bone and brains with the raw power that propelled the energy-forms into and through a living tree.

The mages had their mind and body shields in place. In the few seconds before death, they realised they were useless. They were not confronting magic, or any kind of force they had ever met before.

A *shi* did not recognise the barriers of matter or magic; it operated at a different level of being, where the distinctions between substance and pure energy were meaningless.

The big drum boomed its message and fell silent, and then a cacophony of timpani celebrated victory with rapid rhythm. The shians took form and danced.

The report finally reached Idris, who hurried to tell Kayman, Rolf and Mordant the news with more than a little satisfaction.

"A raash attack group and two mages have been wiped out by the shians. Darric will never know what happened. And if he tries again, his soldiers will get the same reception every time. There will come a point when he has to realise that the stakes for this particular game are far too high."

Mordant looked at the big shian with curiosity in her violet eyes. "May I ask exactly how the unarmed people of Arden managed this?"

"You may ask. But a secret defence is no longer useful when the secret is known. Just take my word for it that shians have their own ways of protecting themselves. If J'Louth and his clan had not been surprised by an attack they never believed possible, the result might have been very different. But my people have always been fast learners. No raash can now set foot on Arden and live." He grinned at Mordant. "So I advise you not to go there!"

"I suppose it is too much to hope that Darric himself might try again, and gift us the Knife and Chain in the process?" said Kayman rather dryly.

"We can always hope," responded Mordant, "but I fear he is too wily for that, and much though he desires the Cup, he desires his invasion more. However, I hope the Wand is equally well hidden and warded, for he is certain to make a final effort to locate it before his window of opportunity closes."

Kayman looked uncomfortable. "I have done what I can. I suggest we keep this news from Jorn. I want his mind uncluttered by extra emotions right now. I think it is time to perform his initiation. I have not the slightest doubt that he will pass the test, but it confirms his status as Master, and that will give him confidence before he goes on the quest."

*

There was an unavoidable wait while all the necessary arrangements were put in place for the mission. Commander Clarriss and Rolf portalled out to Fairhaven and got down to managing the logistics. Braid was sent home by portal from the Horse Transit Point, so that he could update Lord Barrass and get himself ready for the mission. Idris too returned home, anxious to see how the remnants of J'Louth's clan were coping, and if any were in need of healing.

Mordant got into her fighting leathers and exercised several times a day. Jorn watched her with awed respect. She found time to teach him a few attacking constructs — tangle-web, stunner, blinder — and basic wards and bindings. The next seven days passed swiftly.

*

On the evening before they were due to leave for Daunce, the team assembled for a brief, final meeting with Kayman. Clarriss took control as usual.

"I'm just going to run through the arrangements one more time. You know this already, but I just want to check that there have been no last-minute changes. We are going to start the journey in three stages. First, we will translocate to Earth at different times in three groups to three different Transit Points. Mordant and Braidart will go to the Horse Transit Point. Rolf and Jorn will go to the Oak Tree Transit Point. Idris and I will go to the Dolphin. Then we'll all rendezvous at the safe-house at Fairhaven where our people will have our heavy gear and supplies ready for collection. Then we'll make a transition to a marker tag a short way from the Cook's Kettle, where we'll be met with a cart and some packhorses. We'll pick up the riding horses at the inn. We stay the night there and start our journey up the Highway the following morning. It should take about five days to reach the mountains, and an unknown time to locate the caves where the Juncture is hidden."

Mordant and Braidart exchanged glances; Jorn could tell that they were both keen to stop talking and start moving. They gave the dwar the minimal polite attention. When she finally ended, Kayman looked round the group.

"Well, no more to be said. You all know that a great deal hangs on this quest; I know that if the Juncture can be found, you will do it. You will leave at first light tomorrow. In that kind of terrain, it may take time to find the right place, but if you have no success within 10 days of commencing your search then someone must portal back and report to me; we cannot waste time on chasing a mare's nest. Good luck attend you, and the Powers be with you."

"Jorn, stay behind for a moment," he added silently. Kayman waited until everyone had left the room except Jorn and Rolf. "Now Jorn," he continued out loud, "I have decided that you should be initiated as a full mage before you leave on the quest. You are a Master of Nine and we should acknowledge that with due formality. Rolf and I will meet you in

the garden in half an hour. You know the Yew Close where there is a replica of a Quincunx set out on the gravel?"

"Yes."

"Meet us there."

Jorn's imagination conjured up a number of alarming ideas associated with the word 'initiate'. "What do I have to do?" he asked rather tensely.

Rolf smiled. "It is a serious rite, but nothing to be alarmed about."

When Jorn reached the Yew Close, he found Rolf and the High Master waiting for him. Kayman had donned his ceremonial brown and gold robe and chain of office. He carried a white staff.

"Be welcome," he said, warmly. "Master Rolf, name your apprentice to me."

"He is Jorn."

"Is he fit to be named Mage?"

"He is fit."

"To what does he lay claim?"

"He claims the Power of Nine."

"Then let him show us his Mastery. Jorn, take your place." Kayman pointed to the centre of the Quincunx, which was laid out in paving stones, seeming no more than just an ornament in the gravelled square. "Name your colours. Show them to us, one by one, claim them by name and place them in the Quincunx here."

Jorn stood on the central spot. Somehow, he now felt totally calm. "I claim violet." he said quietly, and focussed his mind on the colour, sending a thick thread of it to swirl around and then fill the circle at his feet. He turned to face the point on his upper right. "I claim blue." A clear blue line sprang from his feet to run up the diagonal towards the corner nexus. The young mage named each of the diagonals, and then started to work round the square, until each colour was drawn in its place.

The watching mages felt goose-bumps prick their skin as the contained energy throbbed within the confines of the Matrix.

"How many colours do you Master?"

Jorn took a deep breath. "I have Nine."

"Braid them," Kayman commanded.

Jorn raised his arms and mentally summoned the colours. The rainbow threads swarmed round him, forming a spinning vortex, threatening to burst from his control. Slowly he calmed them, mastered the maelstrom of power, and brought the nine individual threads down into his hands. He held the shimmering tassel for a moment, mentally readying the construct, and then, with confident skill, he wove the nine threads into a single round, complex braid.

There was an instant of blindingly white light that made the watching mages flinch and avert their eyes. When they looked again, Jorn was standing quite still in the centre of the Quincunx. The colours had gone.

"I name you Master of Nine," declared Kayman. The High Master stepped forward and gave him a ceremonial kiss on each cheek. The elderly mage stepped back and lost his professional solemnity, surveying the silent, young man in some amazement.

"It was a privilege to be witness to such a demonstration of supreme control."

Jorn smiled with obvious relief. "That was the first time I have brought all my colours into use at once. It was quite a challenge. But as for the rite, somehow I expected a bit more drama; an oath or something."

Kayman regarded him with a quizzical expression. "Jorn, you have the Power to raze Mage Hall to the ground and uproot every tree in the grove. Will you do that?"

"No, of course not."

"Why not?"

"It wouldn't be right. At least, not unless there was some extraordinary over-riding reason why it had to be done. I can't imagine one."

"Exactly. Like all right-thinking mages, you will strive to use your Power wisely. If you make mistakes, as we all do from time to time, they will be for good reasons. An oath is redundant. And if you were the kind of mage who would use Power for all the wrong reasons, would an oath prevent you from doing so?"

"No, I guess not."

Kayman nodded. "You have the Power. Cultivate the wisdom to use it." He strode away. Rolf beamed and came over to give his guard-child a warm handshake and a reassuring pat on the back.

"That was quite simply wonderful!" he told him. "I can't wait to see what you manage next! *J'Louth would be so very proud of you,*" he added silently, *"and so am I."*

"Thanks Rolf. I wouldn't even be here if it were not for you." Jorn bent to give his guardian a big hug, which helped to hide his welling tears.

*

Rolf had insisted that his 'apprentice' should look smart for the mission. Jorn had risen before dawn, too excited to sleep, and dressed with care in his new clothes. He hardly recognised the reflection in his bedroom mirror. The well-fitting russet brown jacket with a flared cut and dark brown britches complemented both his rich auburn hair and his green eyes. His new riding boots gleamed with polish.

My word! Though I say it myself, I look pretty good. I've put on weight, and I think I've grown even taller. At this rate, I'll be hitting my head on the ceiling even in Mage Hall!

He put a few necessities into his pack and checked them through: two shirts, warm britches, walking boots, six pairs of socks, underwear, soap, toothbrush, and a comb. He had no need to shave; he had now realised that his shian ancestry meant that he would probably never grow a beard. He added a warm muffler, and a hoard of toffee in a tin. Finally, he hung his weatherproof leather hat on the outside. He patted his knife, checked his purse, hooked his hooded winter cloak over an arm, and wondered what he had forgotten. There was always something.

Jorn hefted his pack, took a deep breath, and paused to look round his room before he left.

I wonder what will have happened between now and the next time I'm here? With a mixture of anticipation and a touch of nerves, he went out and closed the door.

Rolf was waiting for him in the yard, back in his character of a prosperous travelling trader. Kayman bustled out of the Hall to wish them good speed and see them off.

"Where's the horn?" he enquired. "You are surely not leaving it behind?"

"It's here!" Jorn gently patted the small wooden wand, which hung heavily in a sheath at his belt. "But I've given it a disguise." It had been a complex working and he was proud of it, so he was pleased when the High Master looked impressed.

Rolf constructed the portal to the Oak Tree Transit Point. Jorn made a point of remembering the hook, even though he could not yet translocate. When Rolf had recovered from his first working, he made his second portal for the transition from the Oak Tree to Fairhaven, and Jorn followed him through, only feeling slightly dizzy this time.

He was standing in the courtyard of a large stone house, which stood on a hill overlooking the town with its wide estuary and harbour. Fairhaven was a major port. A gate in the yard wall stood open. A lane meandered down

Jorn

towards distant houses, and the horizon was defined by a wide band of grey-green, shot with a silver sparkle, which gave Jorn a thrill of surprise.

Oh my! That must be the sea! I have always wanted to get close to it, but I don't suppose there will be time for me to explore.

The two mages sat in the sun for a while, waiting for the others to arrive. Rolf said nothing, and Jorn was happy to relax for a moment and leave the anxieties of the quest for later.

Soon after that, Clarriss and Idris arrived. She was posing as Rolf's wife and had selected a becoming dark red dress, and attached some false braids to her short, military haircut; the change was striking and Rolf did a double-take. They went inside together.

Idris was in character too, as Braidart's manservant. He wore a drab livery, his face shadowed by a slouch-brimmed hat. The shian mage at once went to the gate to stare at the distant sea.

"It is a long time since I have had a chance to immerse my *shi* in salt water but alas, I must continue to wait; I have no time for such leisure. But these clothes chafe horribly and dry me out, and I need to get back to water before I take form again. I sense a river nearby. I will be back in an hour or so." The handsome shian checked that no one was observing from the house, walked into a corner and faded into mist, leaving a pile of discarded garments on the ground.

"Oops! Sorry, I forgot."

"Don't worry; I'll fold them for you. Go and have a good soak." Jorn told him. He picked up the clothes and made a neat pile on the bench. He sat for a while, looking at the distant sea and enjoying the sunshine, and trying not to think too much about whether they would find The Cave of the Damned, and what they would discover there if they did. He couldn't squash his restlessness, and thinking wasn't going to help, so after a while, he retreated to his mental workshop and began to check his constructs and hang a few new ones.

An hour later, another portal opened and Mordant and Braidart came through. The young mercenary sagged to his hands and knees, his bent face a picture of misery. He took a while to recover, and the others let him be, knowing that there wasn't much anyone could do for him. He had let his beard grow and looked exactly like a shabby, tough, hired guard.

"Urggh!" he said as he got unsteadily to his feet. "Death's blood! Twice in an hour is too much! It feels like the morning after a night spent doing the rounds of all the taverns in Jarlstown, only without the benefit of having enjoyed the drink." He sat on a bench, waiting until the world stopped spinning.

"Feeling better?" asked Jorn after a while.

"A bit. Fortunately, the nausea and dizziness doesn't last long. Though translocation does have its advantages; what I wouldn't have given for a portal to move supplies, or send a raiding party behind enemy lines when I was trying to break the siege at the Burg!"

"That, M'sar, is why we mages take such care to keep the whole thing a secret from human kind!" said Mordant dryly. "And that is precisely what the raash will do when they attack. Let your imagination run as it will, Braidart; you won't get near the half of it."

Mordant and Braidart disappeared into the house to check the supplies and camping gear. They didn't seem to need him, so Jorn sat on a bench outside the kitchen door, the smell of fresh rolls making him feel peckish again.

"Come and join us Jorn; we need some muscle," sent Rolf after a while. *"We are in the storeroom, just down the back corridor."*

Jorn helped the others to lug the heavy packs and bundles into the yard. "There seems to be an awful lot of stuff; do we really need all of this?"

"I can assure you we do," responded Clarriss. "We have to plan for at least three weeks camping out in the wilds, and we need caving equipment. We have to carry some trade goods for Rolf too."

"But do we have to take it all now?" Jorn asked.

"I know we could translocate back to get things if we have to, but we want to avoid that. The less other people see us coming and going the better."

"Anyway, at least for this leg, we can load it all on the horses once we get to Daunce," added Braidart. "When you have to march all day over rough territory, with a pack that weighs half as much as you do, you get a bit more selective in your view of what is essential."

"We'll have to carry it all through the next portal; that will be quite enough," Rolf told him. He looked round. "Is Idris away somewhere getting wet?"

"Yes, he'll be back soon."

"Very well. Let's grab some refreshments while we can." They followed the mage inside, and settled round the scrubbed deal table. The cook arrived with jugs of ale, cheese, apples, pickles and fresh rolls.

Jorn

"Go easy on the food Braid, remember you have another portal coming up in half an hour or so, and come up is just what your meal will do if you eat too much," Mordant warned him.

"I'll be sick whether I eat or not, so I might as well enjoy it now. I keep forgetting to ask; why do we always translocate from out of doors? Doesn't it work inside?"

Jorn smiled. That had been one of his early questions too. "You have a solid body, don't you?"

"Yes." The young nobleman flexed an impressively muscled arm. "Pretty solid."

"So, imagine what would happen if you tried to drag it through a thick stone wall at high speed?"

Braidart considered the deeply unpleasant image this presented. "Yurg! I'd rather not!"

"Exactly."

Clarriss stood up. "Right team, I'll just do a final check. Meet up in the courtyard in half an hour for the next transition."

Braidart muttered a sardonic "Yes *Ma'am!*" under his breath.

When the team assembled beside the heap of luggage, they looked at each other with some wry amusement, taking in their various disguises. Idris was waiting, once more in his livery. Braidart stared in surprise at the dowdy serving girl who had gone to stand beside him.

"I suppose that *is* you Mordant? If you're doing human, couldn't you at least be an attractive one?"

"Not on mission," she told him firmly.

He raised his eyebrows. "How about a demonstration when you're off duty?"

She cast eyes to heaven and moved off to pick up a large bundle.

Clarriss assumed command. "Right, Rolf will open the portal. Braidart, just take two bags and go through. You won't be able to do anything else; it will take you longer than usual to recover because it is not that long since your last jump. Mordant, Jorn, Idris, you grab as much as you can carry. Dump it fast, and to one side of the portal. I'll take a load. Wait until everyone else is through and then Mordant and Jorn go straight back for the rest. Please be as quick as you can because Rolf cannot hold the portal open for long; we don't want it snapping shut on you. When we've all gone through, we'll need some time to rest."

The portal formed and Jorn was first to go through. He didn't feel dizzy this time. He dumped his bundles on the grass and looked swiftly around. He was in a woodland clearing and no one was in sight.

Braidart came through. He shed his packs and collapsed on the grass, gasping for breath and, predictably, was very sick. Jorn had no time to worry about him because he and Mordant had to dash back through the misty portal, grab the remaining packs, and hurtle back through. This time, he did feel a bit dizzy, and had to sit down. A moment later, Rolf followed, and the portal snapped shut. Jorn took a while to get his breath back. As he recovered, he scanned round the featureless glade. "Where's the hook? Surely Rolf can't just be using a tree?"

"Well, in a way he is." Mordant took him over to a tree trunk and showed him a small marker disc that bore a distinctive pattern. "He is using a tag," she explained. "It's a trick we borrowed from the raash. Very useful for nondescript locations like this."

It took the group a good five minutes to recover and check that nothing had been forgotten. Mordant replaced her mask which the transitions had removed. Finally, Clarriss said briskly, "Jorn, if you take the path over there, you will come to a road. A short way down is a crossroads where you will find a cart waiting. The driver is named Tom. Tell him we are here. And take a pack with you."

"Yes ma'am," said Jorn.

"Better get used to it. She's very good at her job; bossiness comes with the territory."

Idris had read Jorn's irritation and was mildly amused.

At the crossroads, a large farm cart drawn by a pair of heavy horses awaited, the well-wrapped driver apparently dozing. The sleeper was quickly aware of Jorn's approach, however.

"Arr, there ye be," he said laconically.

Jorn dumped his baggage and went to tell the others that all was well. Tom touched his grey forelock as he saw Clarriss.

"All as ordered, ma'am, an' no changes. Load 'em up and I'll get ye down to The Cook's Kettle."

Clarriss, Rolf and Idris found places among the luggage whilst Jorn, Braid and Mordant walked beside the slow-moving vehicle.

"Is the Kettle an inn?" enquired Braidart, brightening up.

"Yes, a large one," Rolf explained. "The mail coaches stop to change horses. There will be other travellers, so keep in character at all times. I often stay there, and the owner is one of our agents, so very discreet, but we must still be careful."

The Cook's Kettle was in a well-chosen location near the junction of two main roads. The tall, half-timbered exterior rambled across several levels and turned corners at random as if the past owners had just added new wings as the need arose. A large, arched gateway led into an oversized stable yard. Everything seemed clean and well ordered.

A capable-looking, middle-aged woman hurried out to greet them. "Master Rolf, it's good to see you again. And I am delighted to meet your..." a slight hesitation, "...wife; ma'am, you are most welcome."

"Thank you Maggie. It's a pleasure to be back. This is my apprentice, James, and our maid, Mary. Brad is our escort; he has his servant, Ivor, with him."

Maggie called a servant to show them where to stow their gear, and then escorted them to a suite of comfortable rooms on the first floor.

"Our best rooms, Master, as always, and you have a private bathroom downstairs."

Rolf smiled and made appropriate polite remarks. Once Maggie had gone, he relaxed visibly and looked around with satisfaction. "Well, this is pleasant. No point in roughing it before we have to. Maggie will send our supper up so we can keep away from prying eyes, and I have asked for tea in half an hour, so do join us; I must eat and then rest. I'm very weary after working three translocations in one day."

Everyone went to get settled in their own rooms. Jorn found his small chamber at the end of the corridor, and was glad to lie on the bed and be quiet for a while. Braidart's room was next to his. The 'maid' and 'valet' went off to their more basic accommodation up in the attic.

Jorn went back to Rolf's private sitting room when he judged the half hour had passed and was well pleased with the spread of cakes, fruit, drinks and biscuits. Rolf had his lemon tea.

Mordant came in with Braidart, and at once, dropped her 'servant' mask.

"Idris has gone to find water. He says there is a river nearby. After tea, Braidart will go and check the horses. What time is supper?"

"At eight."

"Oh good, that means we can have a drink in the bar beforehand. And probably afterwards as well!" She gave Clarriss her most inscrutable stare. "And before you say anything, no, we are not going to get drunk, gamble, start a fight, inadvertently use inappropriate magic, or talk loudly about this amazing quest we are on. I'll weave a never-mind so no one gets a good look at us or even remembers that we were there. And we'll have a relatively early night. I have done this before, you know."

*

After an early breakfast, they loaded two packhorses and got ready to leave. Rolf had Tricky to ride.

"How did she get here? I thought horses won't go through a portal?" asked Jorn in surprise, bespeaking to keep his question away from the ears of a passing ostler.

"Tricky is an exception to the rule! She's an old pony now, past 20, and she has been going through portals since I first had her," explained the mage. *"Doesn't much like it, but she will go, especially as she knows she gets a treat on the other side. As soon as she is through and crunching on an apple, she seems to forget about it."*

Clarriss had a smaller pony and Jorn could tell she was not keen on riding, but determined not to show that it was a problem. Braidart chose a big roan gelding, which he managed instantly with practised skill. The young nobleman was now well-armed and dressed in a lightly-plated and studded cuirass with a tight, round helmet. Idris was given a large grey, equipped with a special saddle so that Mordant could ride pillion behind him, since she could not ride alone in her role as the maid.

"The shian form is simply not designed for riding," he grumbled to Braidart.

"Having trouble stowing your tackle are you?" asked Braidart mischievously.

He was somewhat surprised when Mordant snapped sharply, "Leave him alone, Braid. He really is very uncomfortable, and in danger of drying out."

Jorn regarded his large bay mare with considerable misgiving. He had occasionally ridden a pony when he was younger, but most of the errands he had run for Aldrick or Anna required the trap or a cart. Otherwise, he walked everywhere.

"What's her name?" he asked.

"Storm," was the discouraging reply.

Storm moved restlessly and sidled away as he picked up the reins and gripped the saddle, obviously sensing a beginner and taking advantage.

"Now you just settle down," he told her.

Storm turned to stare at him.

Maybe she hears me? Worth a try.

Jorn

He ran his hand soothingly down her long neck. *"I am going to ride you, and you are going to behave,"* he told her firmly. *"And if you do, I will see that you get a good grooming, and an apple."* He imagined a small, ripe fruit held out on his flat palm and projected the image. *"Apple, see? For you, later."* Storm snorted gently, flicked her ears, and let him mount.

They left The Cook's Kettle and set off along the wide, well-maintained trade road, which was broad enough for laden wagons to pass with room to spare. The thoroughfare was paved with stone and a wide drainage ditch ran along each side. Parallel bridleways surfaced with sawdust and shredded bark reduced the mud and provided a kinder footing for riders.

Braidart's roan was fresh and restive, pulling against the bit and giving trouble. He eased the eager horse alongside Tricky.

"Rolf, I'll have to give Pickle here a gallop or he'll be fighting me all day. There's not much traffic yet; I'll go up the bridleway for a few kays and let him have his head. I'll wait for you to catch up when he's ready for a rest. I doubt you'll run into anything you can't handle in the next hour or so."

"Fine, Braid, you do that."

The horse shot off down the bridleway, kicking up a spatter of divots. Jorn nudged Storm up to ride next to Rolf, thankful that his mare showed no inclination to do more than a steady amble, despite her name.

"I guess you've been up and down this road before, Rolf?"

"A fair few times." The mage laughed. "Though I confess that I do cheat and take a short-cut through a portal at times."

"I've never travelled on such a wide road. It must have taken a huge amount of work to drive it straight across country like this. When was it built?"

"Some four centuries ago, in the reign of King Justinian the Wise. But he didn't begin from scratch. He uncovered the track of one of the great highways that the Old Ones built, and simply cleared it and resurfaced it. It was a big job, even so. And once other rulers saw how well it worked, and what a fine income Justinian raised from the tolls, they all wanted to connect up, and more and more of the old roads were excavated. The original road beneath all this must be 20,000 years old at least."

"Heavens! I can't get my head round such a stretch of time."

"Indeed, a sobering thought. But it does make travel pleasant. The surface is well-maintained. No trees are permitted within 30 ems on each side of the road, so that cuts the risk of being ambushed by robbers. At regular intervals, there are watering points for horses and cleared areas for campsites with good latrines, and you get enterprising stallholders selling snacks and ale, and small necessities for travellers."

They rode in silence for a while. Jorn watched as the traffic began to build as people got up and moved off on their journeys. A few walkers with baskets and barrows, a medley of riders, lines of pack ponies, fast traps, slow carts, crawling ox wains, and the occasional smart carriage. A flock of sheep herded along the verge got away from the dogs and caused a flurry of commotion and swearing until the shepherd got them back under control.

Jorn was suddenly acutely aware of how little he knew about other places, other people, anything, really. He hadn't realised until now how very sheltered his life as a weaver had been.

Rolf bespoke, *"How are you doing lad?"*

"I'm all right. I guess I'm going to be aching by the evening though."

"Too right, you will! But that wasn't what I meant. In the past few months, you've had to cope with more shocks and losses than many people suffer in a lifetime. And on top of that, you've Mastered your Nine, and discovered things about your shian side that must be difficult to come to terms with. You are holding up amazingly well, but it can't be easy, and we haven't given you much chance to talk about it."

"I guess I'm managing, most of the time. Sometimes, I just long to be back at my loom, doing the work I love, walking in the woods when I need a break. But I know I can't go back, even if there was something to go back to. That's the hardest part, knowing that it's all gone: no home, no loom, no family. It makes it painful to remember the good times, because doing that just brings back the loss, but I do think about them, and try to hold onto the memories, because I'm not going to let the raash rob me of those as well."

"I understand. Your parents and foster parents were my friends. I miss them too. Aldrick and Anna and the children were like kin-folk."

"Rolf, I've been thinking, I've known you all my life, and yet I hardly know anything about you. And even the things I thought I knew might not be exactly right. You used to come and tell your stories, and bring us presents, and make us laugh, and disappear again. But I've realised you never really told us anything important. I don't know where you live, or what you really do, or whether you are really even a trader. You might

have a wife and nine children for all I know! You are very good at keeping secrets, and avoiding questions, aren't you?"

"My, it took you a while to see that, didn't it? The secrecy comes from being a spy, and all mages are expert at not giving straight answers. No, I don't have a wife, or children, or a dozen lovers spread around at convenient distances. Yes, I really am a trader, and a very successful one at that. I don't lack for coin, or comfort, and apart from my rooms at Mage Hall, I have several fine homes that I can open up and use when I need to, mostly at ports around the Middle Sea and the Inner Sea. There are few places within the Western World I haven't visited in the past 50 years, and most of my tall stories are true — allowing for a bit of embroidery, of course! But that gives me the freedom to go where I want and see what I need to see. I have a network of informers to run. And then, as a mage, I specialise in looking out for young humans who have the Gift, and need to be brought to Mage Hall and shown how to control it. But a rolling stone gathers no moss. It can be a lonely life."

"I'd really like to know more. Rolf. I feel I've got a lot of catching up to do."

"Well, we have time right now, so ask away."

Jorn smiled down at his guardian. "Now, there's an invitation! But with a million questions, where do I begin?"

*

As dusk gathered, the team made camp in one of the roadside resting places, and Mordant wove a pass-me-by to keep curious eyes away; people just glanced at their small group and instantly looked away or to one side as if seeing nothing of any interest.

Braid gave Jorn his first lesson in preparing and lighting a campfire, and the young mage was surprised to discover that it wasn't just a matter of piling sticks together. He watched Clarriss' expert preparations and sniffed the smell of stew with a rising appetite. He peered at the pot that she was busily stirring.

"What's in it?"

"Don't ask," replied the dwar crisply. Jorn was about to make a sharp reply when he noticed a twinkle in her eyes. He couldn't see what was funny.

Braid grinned. "Soldier's slang! This is mutton, but when you start living off the land the contents can get a tad more unpredictable; I've eaten mice, rats, slugs, lizards, snakes, snails, bugs and worms in my time, and one or two things I won't mention. You can get to the point when you're just grateful that it's been cooked. Curiosity is not an aid to appetite. So whatever's in the pot, just 'don't ask'," he explained.

The stew took a long time to cook, but it tasted fine. Then Clarriss landed Jorn with most of the washing up and tidying. Finally, they all settled round their small campfire, aware of the peripheral noise and bustle from other parties who laughed and drank and did deals all round them.

Jorn stretched stiffly. "My bottom's sore and my legs feel as if I can't hold them together after they've been stretched across a saddle all day."

Braidart grinned. "It'll go; you just have to work through it. How about a game of dice before we turn in?"

Idris was sitting in the shadows at a distance from the fire. Since their campsite was covered by a glamour, he had left off his clothes with considerable relief. The flickering light glinted off his scales. Mordant gazed across at him, intrigued anew by his strangeness. She had been in close contact with him all day as she rode pillion, and the intimacy of that was disturbingly pleasant.

His hybrid, scaled form reminded her of a chimera. Why did shians take human shape? She had seldom met another shian of the water. Were mages of his race rare? He was calm, kind, brave, polite, quiet, and totally enigmatic. She sensed an unseen barrier. She wondered if the lingering echoes of their disastrous parting 18 years ago were still blighting the development of their new friendship.

Is he lonely? It was very hard to tell. He did sometimes speak to Rolf, his old friend, and Jorn, who was, after all, half shian himself, and was still learning from the mage. Clarriss ignored him. She plainly did not know what to make of the big, ostentatiously handsome and naked male who had no need of her meals and made no response to her orders. Neither did Braidart, who mostly resorted to barrack-room humour in an effort to cover his unease. They seemed to have no idea how hard and potentially dangerous this journey was for him.

Mordant got up went over to sit beside him. She knew by now that shians preferred to be quite direct.

"How are you doing, Idris?" she asked. "I was concerned for you today."

"I am well enough. But I cannot ride any further, or wear clothes, it is painful to my form and it dries me out too fast." The shian's soft, precise Basic was as unemotional as always, but failed to hide his fatigue.

"I understand. I'll take the grey tomorrow. We have done what was needed to enable us to pick up the horses and leave the inn as a normal group of travellers. I doubt if anyone will bother that much tomorrow about a maid riding."

"It would be better. I can easily keep up in my *shi*. I'll slip away in a moment. I can sense water somewhere off to the left. I will quickly recover when I have fed and rested. The great advantage of being able to shed form is that the aches and pains are shed with it."

Mordant produced her best smile and said, "Forgive me if I am intrusive, Idris, but I know so little about shians of the water. Does your race avoid others?"

"We are a shy and somewhat secretive people, as indeed are shians of the wood. It is only the mage-born shians who travel, and even then, only to train so that they can master their colours. Mostly, they then return to Arden and seldom leave it. But I am cursed with restlessness and curiosity."

"Cursed? But that is the curse of every mage! Powers, didn't I just start my conversation with a question? You know it's said that a mage-child's first word is 'why' and his second is 'how'. And no Adept stays in one place for long."

Idris' rare smile lit his handsome face. "Even so, it is a curse nonetheless for it disturbs the still centre of my essence. Yet I have journeyed far across Earth and Arden, exploring rivers, lakes and seas, and that has given me much pleasure."

"Well, I'm determined to satisfy my own curiosity. Why do shians take human form?"

"Why do you breathe? Why does your heart beat at a steady rate? It just happens that way. But there is a legend among our people that, in the most distant past, eons beyond the reach of memory, shians were primitive shape-shifters who took whatever form they pleased, be it animal, bird or fish. And then, somehow, humans came to the Shian Realm. Inevitably, after a while, shians began to shift into human form. And they discovered that it had many advantages. Bit by bit, they ceased to take the forms of beasts, and finally could no longer do so. Who knows? We are as we are. And it may be significant that all the intelligent races that we know of have the same basic form; perhaps it is simply the most useful shape."

"But I remember that you told me once that form is not the same as essence."

His expression was serious again. "You remember that? Well, it is a deep truth. 'I' am not just what you now see. Nor am 'I' the mist form that I also take. My essence is not something you can see or feel, although you could experience it in part if I were to touch your mind with mine. Shian relationships happen at the deep level. Sadly, that is not something a fixed-form can share."

"J'Louth managed it."

"At the cost of Jelda's physical death. J'Louth knew I did not approve of that, even if Jelda did consent to it. Theirs was a unique bonding that broke all the rules." Idris glanced across to where Jorn and Braidart were playing dice. "Though we may yet have cause to be glad that they did so." The shian looked back at her. "You like our new Darnell recruit? He greatly resembles his brother."

"Yes he does. Rather too much so for my comfort. But he hasn't got the maturity that Brett had at his age. He's been around soldiers and it's rubbed off; he's got used to that rough style of male humour. He thinks quite a lot of himself. I've watched him at sword practice. He's good but he hasn't got Brett's style or focus. Lethal enough, but not a true warrior. But I can't help liking him, and he is amusing company."

"I fear I cannot amuse you, Mordant. We shians are rather solemn folk." He stood up rather abruptly and stretched. "I must find water. Goodnight."

Mordant watched Idris walk away and felt that she knew little more about him now than when she had started the conversation. It was so hard to tell what he was really thinking or feeling. *Still waters do indeed run deep. But then, I'm no better, with my stiff raash face.* She remembered his *shi* tickling her toes when she had dangled her hot feet in his pool so many years ago. He had not seemed so solemn then. She really would like to have him as a friend. Perhaps it would just take time.

Chapter 12

The following morning, the team packed up and left early, hoping to make good time along the next stretch of road.

Pickle had settled into the journey and was happy to walk alongside the other horses. Jorn found himself next to Braidart, who was looking relaxed and comfortable. *He's only eight or nine years older than I am, and he's already done so much. I feel like a school kid in comparison.*

Braid saw his companions eyes on him and gave his easy grin. "Can't tell you how good it feels to be out on a mission again," he observed. "I get bored very fast!"

"Well, I doubt if any of us are going to be bored on this trip," responded Jorn. "Did you say you're a mercenary? That's a hired sword, isn't it; someone who fights for whoever pays him?"

Braid snorted. "I don't fight for just anyone. I'm pretty choosey. But yes, I make my living out of warfare: big wars, small battles, sieges, petty feuds. As long as there's danger and a good fight, and a nice fat pay-out at the end of it, I'm happy."

"But why? Why put yourself through all that, and risk being killed or badly injured? The money can't be that good, and anyway, what's the use of a fat purse if you're dead?"

Braid raised his eyebrows. "You really don't get it, do you? Risking death is the only way I know to feel properly alive. When you are pushing yourself to the limit, testing the boundaries, working with your mates as a team, and looking out for each other, you actually have something worth living for. And then, when it's all over, the beer tastes better, and the air smells sweeter, the women all look beautiful, and you forget the pain and the mud, and the times you wished you were dead, because the other bastards *didn't* get you this time. And you can do it all again, when the coin runs out."

"But you have to kill people."

"There is that. But mostly they are trying to kill you, so you take them out any way that works."

"I can't imagine doing that. I'm going to have to, I guess. Not with a sword, face to face, but with magic, which means I have to prepare for it in cold blood. I don't know if I can do that."

"You will if you have to. And I can't imagine what it feels like to use Power. Is it good?"

"Sometimes, when it works well, it's wonderful. I'm still learning. But it's frightening too. I've got these colours inside my mind, seething like a pot that's been left too long on the range, and I have to keep the lid on them. All that wild potential just waiting for me to catch hold of it, and use it and make it obey my will, and take the shape I tell it to. It's very hard to explain."

"It seems a lonely thing, being a mage." Braid looked round at the others. "It's as though you all have to shut off some part of yourselves to make it work. I can understand that. My father is the same, being Lord Governor and Clan Lord, he always has to be one step away, never quite one of us."

"I keep forgetting you are high-born. Where's your home?"

"Darnell Hold. It's a huge, old fortress, with a moat and battlements, the works. Impossible to heat, always leaking, enough rooms that we could use a new one every day for a year and have a few left over. But I love it. Or rather, I love the memory of it. As I told you, I bore very easily. A few weeks of riding round the estates and hunting, and attending balls, and I've had enough."

"Have you got any brothers or sisters?"

"I've got six brothers and one sister. The eldest, Borodin, will be Clan Lord one day. Brett is second in line. By the time you get down to me, there isn't much real work left to do. I had to find my own way in life. The thing I do best is fight. I thought I might be a professional Sword-Master, like Brett used to be, but I haven't his skill, or his patience. Teaching spoilt brats how to fence isn't my idea of fun. What about you? You were trained as a weaver weren't you?"

"Yes I was. And up to six months ago, that's all I knew, and all I wanted to know. It was my whole life. You probably find it hard to believe, but I'd never been away from home for more than a few days, and then only to visit another weaving firm in Corscombe. Braid, when it comes to coping with the real world, I'm greener than the first leaves of spring. I feel such an idiot."

Braid laughed. "I'll tell you a secret. Most lads your age think adults have got it all together, and never put a foot wrong. Don't you believe it! Mostly we just get better at *looking* as if we know what we are doing. And you are no idiot; you just have some fast catching up to do. Now, how about giving that mare of yours some exercise?"

Jorn

He kicked Pickle into a fast canter, and Jorn gathered Storm and chased after him.

*

Around noon, the team quietly slipped off the thoroughfare under the cover of Mordant's never-mind to ride off into bare forest.

After a couple of kays, they stopped, dismounted and secured the horses. Mordant snapped the glamour, dropped her face-changing mask and heaved a sigh of relief.

"My, but all that continuous working is hard. I need a rest! And then I want to be back in my comfortable leathers, ready for action, with my longsword on my back. I feel undressed without it."

Idris had been following them in his nebulous *shi* and now reappeared, happily naked. "I can't get used to you doing that mist thing," Braidart told him.

"Mordant is not the only one who wants to change!" exclaimed Clarriss. "I loathe skirts, and these false braids are making my head sore. Give me a few minutes!" She took her own pack and disappeared into the woodland.

Jorn was also very glad to dismount for a while, but he was getting on well with Storm. He felt in his pocket for a small apple, which he had begged off Rolf, and gave her a reward. He watched as his guardian made a stash of the packs of supposed trade-goods, which had been included in case they were subjected to an official search, but were now nothing but an unnecessary burden. Jorn could see it hurt Rolf to the core of his merchant's soul to have to abandon items of value. He asked him if he could bag one of the small travelling sets of Gambit.

"Then you can teach me, if we have some spare time in the evenings."

Mordant returned, dressed in her black fighting leathers. She dumped her disguise and went to rummage in the baggage. A few moments later, she emerged with a scabbarded longsword. She patted it affectionately. "Now I feel dressed!"

Braid raised his eyebrows. "Where the hell did you hide that?"

"I used a glamour."

"Not a weapon I'd want to carry on a trek like this. It's no light weight."

"Each to their own, M'sar," she said tartly, and strapped the weapon to her saddle with practiced ease.

Rolf consulted a pocket compass and looked at the crude map. Braid came and looked over his shoulder.

"We need to go mainly east. It won't be easy, trekking across country. This woodland extends up to the foothills of the Greyhacks. As the name suggests, that is limestone upland, bisected by steep valleys. We need to find the Cut River and follow its valley up into the hills. Then there's that side valley, very narrow, almost a gorge, and somewhere in there are the Caves."

"Oh, I do so enjoy getting totally lost in a trackless wilderness with winter coming on," said Braidart in a resigned tone. "How long before we have to walk instead of riding?"

"No idea," Rolf told him briskly. "Certainly the last leg will be on foot, so at some point, we'll have to set up a base camp and picket the horses. One day at a time. But I'd appreciate your scouting skills to help find us the best route."

Clarriss returned, back in uniform. "So, have we got our bearings? Are we set to move off?"

Rolf nodded. "This is where the quest begins in earnest. Good luck everyone, and take care."

"And stay alert," added Clarriss. "This may be remote, but that does not mean that it's safe. There are very few people here, but we must avoid any contact with strangers from now on."

Jorn looked at the small group as they moved off, and wondered anxiously how their quest would end.

Well, warp before weft. First comes the finding. I just hope the Juncture is worth all this. But at least I'm back in real wild forest. I can easily find a tree to feed my shi here.

He gazed around with pleasure, feeling his shian essence relax happily, but he was also acutely aware that this journey was likely to change him, and his future, in ways he could not begin to imagine. The young mage clicked to Storm and followed the others into the forest.

As dusk came on, it got chilly and the weather worsened. They made camp and prepared for an early night. Jorn huddled down, pulled his hood up, and wrapped his cloak more tightly round his hunched shoulders. Although the trees were sheltering them from the worst, the bitter, gusting wind whipped the thin wood-smoke into his eyes, and the cold was winning the battle with the small fire.

Across the blaze, the other four members of the team were hurriedly finishing their meal. Jorn sucked his toffee and pondered his companions. It was the first time he had taken a journey with people who were not family, and he was finding it unexpectedly difficult to be with comparative strangers all the time. He felt oddly lonely, even though he had company. They were still getting to know each other, and not all the relationships were easy.

Rolf and Clarriss seemed to have a lot in common and often sat together after supper as they were doing tonight. Rolf was a comfort; the one familiar, caring person who understood him and was easy to talk to, and Idris was fast becoming a good friend. Braid was good company too, and seemed happy to pass on his skills.

Clarriss was another matter. Jorn found the dwar's patronising assumption that he was just the boy who did the chores totally infuriating. He didn't see why he always had to be the one who was sent off to dig a latrine pit, or fetch wood and water. He could see that her bossy manner also irritated Braidart and Mordant. Of course, they all respected her abilities, but she did have a habit of telling people how to do things that they were actually managing quite well already.

He was used to Mordant now, and he respected her expertise. She was a good teacher too. She had spent the first evenings of the journey with Idris. Jorn suspected that she was trying to get to know him, but he would never come within more than 10 paces of a campfire, and made a habit of going off alone at nightfall to find water to rest in, so she wasn't getting much opportunity.

Tonight, Mordant was sitting rather close to Braidart, playing dice in the firelight and giggling girlishly when she won. Her sculpted face had a certain kind of fierce beauty once you got used to it. The young nobleman was making teasing remarks and cracking jokes. From time to time, his hand brushed hers, or touched a shoulder. Jorn could sense a strange tension between them. Idris had watched the pair from a distance and then got up rather abruptly, shifted into his *shi*, and disappeared into the woods.

"What are they playing at?" Jorn asked Rolf.

"A game."

"I can see that; I didn't mean the dice."

"Neither did I," responded Rolf dryly.

Jorn sighed, decided that he really did not understand adults, whatever their races, rose to his feet, stretched wearily, and prepared to turn in. With any luck, they would be within reach of the Caves in the next two days, and then the mission would begin in earnest. Try as he might to imagine himself in possession of the Juncture, whatever that turned out to be, and working wonders with the Nine, he couldn't. His Quincunx thrummed with the need for action.

Once inside his tent, he retreated to his inner space to check that all was well and, on an impulse, wandered into his storeroom. The fabulous range of colours was a delight to his weaver's eyes, but they frightened him with the mystery of their purpose and potential. He'd asked all his mage tutors about them, but none of them had ever heard of a person having hundreds of shades of the Spectrum. He glanced at the covered mirror that held the image of his inner self and, for a moment, felt an urge to go and look to see if his shian essence was fully recovered. But his unease held him back; he wasn't ready to confront the reality of his dual nature right now. He closed the door, left his workspace and came back to awareness of the gusty wind tugging at the canvas, and the need for sleep.

*

Idris was resting in a small stream. It was enough to refresh him, but too shallow to give him much pleasure. He longed to immerse himself in a great rushing river full of rapids, where the icy, oxygenated water would make his *shi* tingle with life. His sense pricked. Someone was coming. A high moon, half-hidden by scudding clouds, gave a little light. A *shi* came hesitantly through the shadowed trees. He knew at once exactly who this was. He had been waiting for this moment.

"Idris?"

"*I'm over here. I've wanted so much to meet you, tantar-issa.*" He took form and waited, sensing the others fear, and his need for help.

"You knew? How?"

"*I could see two auras, one masked beneath the other. I am glad, and honoured, that you have come first to me.*"

"Who else? You are shian, and Jorn's good friend. No one else would understand, or know how to help me."

"*I knew you would find a way to leave him, eventually. How did you manage it?*"

"It was very hard. I was so afraid of hurting him. And until he let me out to shift into a tree, I was just too weak to even try. And then, when I was strong enough, I had to find my courage. It was a step out into the unknown, but I knew I had to do it. I finally managed to slide out of him a couple of days ago when he was asleep."

"*It must have felt very strange to be out on your own in the open for the first time.*"

Jorn

"It did. It was terrifying. I've so much to learn, so many new things to experience all at once. I feel so exposed without him, naked and vulnerable, scared of quite ordinary things. I'm so used to having him around me. His body has been my whole world. When I am bonded with him, I see what he sees, feel what he feels, I know his thoughts and emotions as if they are my own. Part of me just wants to go back inside and hide."

"But you are a separate person, with your own mind. You must become yourself."

"I know. It means I can go into a tree to feed when I need to; he never realises when I am hungry, unless I'm half-starved. Idris, I have to find out how take tuka. Can you help me? I'm frightened to try on my own."

"Taking form is not so very hard. You need to imagine the shape you want and have that clearly in your mind. Take time to get it right, because that will be the tuka you always take after the first time. You draw the solid elements you need from the air and earth around you. You are fully shian, your aura shows that. The process is instinctive. Just concentrate on becoming. It will feel strange the first time, but you will soon get used to it. It has advantages."

"The shape is easy to imagine. I've been living inside it all my life. We have met twice, in the inner space, and I've watched him, these past two nights. I know exactly what he looks like. Would it be all right if I look just like my brother?"

"Of course. You are his twin. Identical twins are not that uncommon in humans. Try that. Do it now. I am here, you will be quite safe."

Idris could see the fear in the young shian's aura, and the effort he had to make to master it. His *shi* shivered and strained with effort. After a few moments, his outline began to condense into a thickening, rather lumpy shadow, wavered, and then coalesced into a solid body. He was shian, naked, except for the usual small kiri, tall and strong, and as like Jorn, as one acorn is to its neighbour. The tall youth stepped forward uncertainly, wobbled as if dizzy, and then stopped.

"Oh, Idris this feels so very strange. Heavy and awkward."

"I know. Just stand still and get your balance. Breathe; feel the boundaries of your tuka, the solid weight of it. It takes a while to learn how to use your limbs and senses."

Jorn's double stood in silence for a few moments, full of uncertain wonder at this new experience. Then, shaping the spoken words slowly to begin with, he said, with quiet desperation, "Idris, I am so tired of being alone. Jorn still doesn't know I'm there. He can't hear me. He just has some dim sense of what he thinks of as his shian essence, and he believes that is part of himself. He was near tonight, and I tried so hard to make him come to me, but he wouldn't. I think he was afraid. I can only communicate indirectly, using the horn as a focus. He has no idea that it is me; he thinks he is focussing his own Power. I don't know what to do."

Idris held out his arms. "You are not alone any more, *tantar-issa, my young friend.*"

Jorn's shian twin came to him and let Idris enfold him in a gentle hug. "I've never felt anyone hold me. It's comforting."

Idris let him go and looked carefully at his aura. "You are also a Master of Nine."

"Yes. I've been using my Gift to help him, through the horn, but we could do so much more if we worked together. It's very, very frustrating."

"Do you have a name?"

"No, I don't. J'Louth didn't know they had given birth to twins, so of course, they didn't name me. I've been so entwined with Jorn, I think of myself as if I'm him."

"But you are not. Let me be your name-giver. Jorn means acorn. You shall be *Jan-Keb*, which is oak-cup. But we'll shorten it to Jan. How does that sound?"

Jan smiled. "I like that. Idris, I can't hold form any longer. I must go back, but I'll come again when I can. Perhaps you can help me to find a way to get Jorn to realise that he has a twin. I can't leave him properly, when he is awake and aware, unless he invites me to come out, and he'll never do that until he knows I'm there. But I can't tell him. It's such a tangle."

"It will unravel, given time. And I will help you both, in any way I can."

Jan gave Idris a quick hug, and then shed form and moved swiftly away between the trees. Idris watched him go with a feeling of deep sympathy for his impossible dilemma. He had long suspected the presence of a shian twin, but not one so very obviously independent and full of his own Power and personality. No wonder Jorn had blocked him from his consciousness. It was a matter of sheer necessity. The human mind was not equipped to deal with a second strong individual living in the same body. Jan was right; forced awareness could be enough to cause Jorn a major trauma. But on the other hand, this situation could not continue indefinitely. It was amazing that Jan himself had coped so well with the knowledge, and the terrible isolation.

*

The following day, as the land began to rise more steeply, the team were often obliged to dismount and lead the horses. Around midday, Idris disappeared in his *shi* to look for the River Cut. Everyone was glad of a few hours rest. Jorn was happy to be in wild, old woodland, but he was aware that his essence was getting hungry again.

After a while, he said silently, *"Rolf, I'd like to go and find a tree. I won't be long. But I need to tell Clarriss and Braidart about this. I mean about leaving my body beside a tree; they need to understand that I must not be moved, and I might need someone to keep watch."*

"Yes, you are right. Better that they know."

"Erm... I need to go off on my own for a while."

Braidart and Clarriss looked enquiringly at the young mage.

"You know that I'm part shian. You've become used to Idris going off to find water. Well, I'm kind of similar. Every so often, I need to find a tree to get some special nourishment that human food doesn't provide. I look as if I'm asleep, but actually I'm partly inside the tree. It's very important that you do not try to wake me up, or move me. However, as we can't be sure that there are no predators here, I'd be very grateful if someone would stand watch for me."

"*Inside* a tree?" Braidart shook his head. "I'm not going to pretend that I understand that, but I'll be happy to do guard duty."

"Thanks Braid." Jorn could see Clarriss hiding her surprise and incomprehension behind a carefully neutral expression. He and Braidart went off into the woodland.

"So, what do you need, tree-boy?"

"An oak for preference, though a beech would do. Those are my favourites."

"Let me try and get hold of this; you are going to go *into* a tree?"

"Yes, but not all of me. My body stays outside, but there is an inner part of me, my *shi*, that can come out, and enter the tree. That part of me needs the sugars in the tree to feed on."

After another hundred strides, a mature tree came into view, already almost leafless. Their feet crunched on yellow leaves and fallen acorns.

"Look, here's a fine oak. This will be perfect."

He ran his fingers across the rough bark, feeling the life welling up through the trunk. Despite it being late in autumn and past leaf-fall, this old tree still had plenty of stored sap.

"I may be away for half an hour."

"Well, you go and have your top, and I'll sit and dream about ale. Getting outside a decent tankard-full is one thing I really miss when I'm in the wilderness."

Jorn sat down, closed his eyes, and extended with joyful release into the trunk, letting the powerful sweetness flow into him. When he was satisfied, he allowed himself a little longer to explore the big tree, searching down into the roots, mapping the great limbs, and finally flowing out into the wide canopy of twigs. As always, the hardest part was keeping track of time and making himself leave, but he reluctantly pulled his *shi* together and flowed back into his body. He opened his eyes, stirred and stretched.

"Back with us, are you?" Braidart looked curiously at the tall youth as he uncurled and stood up.

"Back, and feeling better," Jorn agreed. "Thanks for body-sitting!"

"Do you need to do that often?"

"No, about once every 10 days or so is enough, unless I use a lot of Power. Then both parts of me need to eat extra."

Braidart gave him a wry grin. "I've just about got used to 'Dris the Mist' coming and going, and now you do it too. You know, most of the time I look at you and I just see a tall, redheaded lad who is trying to grow up in a hurry. And then once in a while, I catch something in your green eyes and I know there is a whole lot more."

"Oh, there is!" Jorn told him. "And you don't know the half of it — but then come to that, I'm not sure that I do either!"

They rejoined the others and rested, while the horses stamped and blew and nosed for thin grasses. Idris returned about an hour later and took form. Jorn could see that he was refreshed, so must have found the river; his taut, naked body shimmered as the scales on his back and legs caught the light and his silver hair was wet and slicked flat. His handsome face was alert and vibrant with life.

"The River Cut is about a day's ride from here," he told them, "and a fine, pure river she is too! Water straight from the deeps below the hills, filtered through rock, eons old. I feel better than I have for many days." The shian sat down and Jorn went to sit beside him.

"What does it feel like, when your *shi* is in running water?" he asked.

Jorn

"It is not a thing for words. Imagine being as thirsty as you have ever been, and you quench it with something cold and delicious. Or think of swimming naked on a hot day when the touch of the water is like silk. Remember the time you were happiest, when joy flowed through you like a great river. It is like all those things, Jorn, only sweeter and stronger. I cannot describe it any better."

"You don't need to. That is what I feel when I am bonded with a tree. It frightens me because it's so very hard to leave. Do you think I might forget one day and stay too long?"

"No, I do not fear that, *tantar-issa*, at least not at present. You have a strong sense of duty. As long as you have the quest or people need your Gifts, you will always return."

"Thanks Idris. What did you call me just then?"

"Tantar-issa; it means something like 'my dear young friend', a word to show that we are close. You may call me *tantar*, 'dear friend', if you wish."

"I am honoured Idris. I am in need of a friend. You know, I'm so very glad you are on the quest. You understand the shian in me, and that really helps."

Idris watched Jorn walk away and sighed. *If only he knew the truth of that.*

The team was getting ready to move out, so Jorn went to get Storm saddled. Everyone's spirits had lifted at the prospect of reaching the valley and nearing the Caves, but somehow, no one wanted to talk about what they would do when they got there.

Later that day, the land began to rise very steeply and the tree cover thinned to a scrub of stunted pine and bare dwarf birch. There was better grass in the glades between the lighter cover, so the horses grazed hungrily at every pause.

*

The next day, everyone had to walk, leading the horses and ponies up the increasingly rocky terrain. Mordant stayed close to Braidart. The two of them could be heard talking softly and laughing often. Rolf and Clarriss also kept company but spoke little. Jorn and Idris walked silently at the rear. They climbed steadily until they had left the trees behind and were out on the bleak upland, where a wickedly bitter east wind had them huddling into their cloaks. The sky loured and slate-grey thunderheads were building in the distance.

"Hope we get to shelter before that lot hits us," observed Braidart, pulling down his hood for the umpteenth time as the wind tried to whip it off.

"Not far now," responded Idris. "When we top the next shoulder, you will see the river below."

The Cut could be heard long before it was seen. They descended into a broad, steep-sided valley, where the lively river ran past rocks, which churned up white water. As they went further, the valley walls grew higher, closing in, and there was more vegetation and some low, twisted trees, including pine and juniper. It was a touch warmer out of the wind.

Progress was slow as they detoured around rocks and trees. They were keen to get as far as they could that day. When they finally started thinking about making camp, the sunset glared in an ominous red line from behind mountains of cloud. Then the first fat drops of cold rain began to fall. The only person to be happy about that was Idris.

Clarriss objected to the first three choices for campsite on the grounds of danger from flash floods, and the need for better shelter. Braidart looked increasingly fed up.

"If our esteemed commander doesn't make her mind up soon, we are all going to get drowned anyway," he huffed crossly to Mordant.

The dwar pretended not to hear. She finally selected a site on higher ground, where a rocky overhang and some stunted pines provided a little shelter. The rain was hammering down now. Rolf shook his head and then closed his eyes; Jorn could tell he was working. A short while later, the rain above the campsite stopped, and they were able to get the tents up in comparative comfort.

Once they had shelter, Rolf let his 'umbrella' unravel.

"Can't do it for too long," he told Jorn, "but it comes in handy. I'll show you the construct later." The rain drummed against the canvas and dripped in unexpected places. It was too wet to make a fire, so they made do with dry rations and decided on an early night.

Jorn's last thoughts as he went to sleep were to wonder, yet again, why The Cave of the Damned had acquired its cheerless name, and how long it would take them to find it.

When Jorn was deeply asleep, Jan carefully left his body and went to find a tree, aware that it might be the last time that he could do so for a while. He needed to be strong to help his brother. When he had fed and rested, he left the tree and took form. It still felt very odd. He stretched his limbs, walked about a bit, tried picking things up, and threw a few stones. He was still terribly clumsy, but improving. He could see that it was just a matter of time. It was also very tiring. He went into his tree again for a while, and then shifted out and drifted back to his sleeping twin.

He stood, looking down at Jorn with deep affection, and huge frustration, wondering when his brother was ever going to wake up to that fact that he was not alone, and that his indweller urgently needed to come out. He sighed, and slipped back into the comforting safety of his hosts body.

*

Mordant tossed restlessly in her tent, finding it hard to sleep. The idea of having to enter deep, dark, underground tunnels disturbed her more than she wanted to admit. It brought back all the vivid and horrible memories of being confined in the dreadful Punishment Box as a small child. She had experienced nightmares about closed spaces ever since.

But it was not just tomorrow's journey into the Cave that was disturbing her sleep. The enigma that was Idris troubled her on many levels. She had tried her best to get to know him better, though he gave her scant opportunity, and there always came a point when she felt his barriers shut down and he made some polite excuse and walked away. And yet, her sense told her that he did like her, and his beauty stirred her in a way she barely understood. She wanted to explore where that attraction might lead. Why wouldn't he allow her to get any closer? What could she do to get him interested?

And then there was her Blue-Eyed-Boy. Braid was undoubtedly great fun to be with, and he had flirted with her for days, totally assured of his power to charm any female in his vicinity. His boyish arrogance was amusing. He obviously assumed she was young and available, and if there was no human female nearby, a raash halfer would do. If he knew she was almost old enough to be his mother, it might cool him off a bit, but she was not about to tell him. He still reminded her so much of Brett that it was almost impossible not to respond to him. And that was likely to end in one of two ways, either of which would bring complications.

*

They rose at first light, all anxious to explore. It was a fine, dry day although the vegetation dripped and the river was running in full spate, swollen to a wide, churning torrent after the heavy rain. They secured the camp and hobbled the horses so that the animals could nibble the thin, patchy grass and reach water, but not stray. No one was left on guard this time, as even Clarriss agreed that there was little chance of any intruder in this wild place.

Their first challenge was to cross the Cut. The deep water foamed fiercely between the boulders; it was much too wide to jump, and they had to get heavy packs over as well.

"I'll cross first," said Braidart. "I can rig a line from that stump, and the rest of you can follow. We can swing the packs across once we have a rope rigged."

"It would be better if — " Idris attempted to speak.

"I said I'll cross." Braidart cut decisively across Idris' quiet protest. The shian mage shrugged and stepped back.

The young nobleman shucked off his pack, got out some rope, and tied it off round the stump. He went to the edge of the raging torrent and searched for a possible stepping-stone. He turned and grinned at Mordant.

"Haven't done this for a while. Keep the rope under control for me."

He selected his spot, took a long leap onto a half-submerged boulder, and then regained his balance. He moved to the next one, which was a bit higher, unreeled some slack, and made the next jump. He landed on the next stone with a large splash as it was completely under the water, but caught his balance.

Idris called urgently, "Watch out!" but he was too late. The shian had seen a long, fallen branch sweeping down the river. Braid had his back to it, but he could have done little to avoid it. The wood hit him hard, just below his knees, and toppled him into the white water. His head met a rock on the way down. The current picked the big man up and tumbled him away like a log.

Mordant yelled, "Braid!"

Clarriss used a word Jorn was surprised she knew.

Idris had already shed form. A few seconds later, they saw a column of mist curl around Braidart, pick him up, and carry him safely to the bank. Idris at once materialised and knelt by the prostrate body. The others ran over.

"Is it bad?" asked Mordant anxiously.

Idris shook his head. "Some bruises and a bump on the head. He has mild concussion. I will soon have him right."

After a few moments, Braidart stirred, groaned, and coughed up some water. Idris helped him to sit up. Clarriss and Mordant fussed around with a towel and a cloak. Braid finally brushed away the attention and looked up at Idris.

"Thank you, my friend. And please accept my apologies. Next time, I will listen to your advice, at least where water is involved."

Idris nodded, his face unreadable. He turned away and left the others to get Braidart back to base camp, where he got out of his wet clothes. Rolf produced a fire.

"*I had no idea your shi is so strong,*" Jorn told Idris. "*I thought it was just mist.*"

"*Not mist; the essence of water. Look at the river and see the strength of it.*"

"*At least Braidart is all right.*"

"*It could have been much worse. He has a sore lump on his head and his pride is somewhat damaged. Let us hope he has learned the lesson. We have no room for male mating displays on this quest.*"

It took them another hour to sort themselves out and get ready to start again. This time, they crossed the river in safety because Idris simply divided the flow around them and gave them an almost dry passage straight through the torrent. Braidart took that in with quiet astonishment, although he said nothing. Jorn could tell he was rapidly revising his opinion of the mage's powers. They transferred their essential gear and made a tidy dump.

Then Clarriss took charge again, organising their expedition with her usual efficiency. This time, Jorn did not resent her bossing him about, because she plainly did know what she was doing. Each person was given a close-fitting, hard leather helmet, a whistle, a coil of rope, and a belt that held a small pick and climbing pitons. The dwar brought out and demonstrated some strange, cylindrical objects, showing how a handle at one end should be vigorously wound to produce a soft light at the other end of the cylinder.

"You need to turn the handle again for a few minutes at intervals to keep the light going, but it's a lot easier than trying to keep smoky torches alight in awkward, draughty places. The light looks dim in daylight, but it will be quite sufficient in the underground darkness. This switch turns the light on and off; don't let it waste. I would appreciate you keeping the knowledge of this secret," she added sternly.

Clarriss handed out bulky packs that contained blankets, water flasks, dry rations, first aid items, and a host of other things she considered essential.

They had left the tents, because there were more than enough caves to shelter in. The weight was a bit less than Jorn had expected, but he had a feeling it would seem a lot heavier by the end of the day. Idris agreed to carry a bag of kit, but he refused the climbing gear and helmets, which would only be an uncomfortable burden. With just the kit bag, he could shed form if the going got difficult.

Mordant took her pack and strapped her longsword across her back. She had her silver-hilted kring and kor as well; she was taking no chances. Braid pulled a disapproving face at the added load but said nothing.

They set off up the gorge at last. It was soon clear that the search would not be easy. The rocky cliffs were as full of holes as a dry sponge. It was impossible to tell which of these were shallow and which might lead further into the labyrinth. They stopped by four dark openings.

"Which first?" asked Rolf.

Mordant shrugged.

"Bogel, bagel, beegel, by; lose a bee and catch a fly; this one choose I," she chanted in a bored voice, pointing at each in turn, playing a child's elimination game with the dark slits. She and Braidart ducked under the low arch of the chosen cave, but soon emerged, shaking their heads. "Another dead end."

"We could search for a year and still miss the entrance," said Braidart crossly. He was still suffering from a slight headache after his ducking.

"It doesn't look good," agreed Rolf. "But whoever hid the portion of the Juncture needed to be able to get into the cave without too much trouble. Perhaps there is some kind of clue that a mage would recognise?"

"Or a marker tag?" wondered Mordant.

Jorn was absentmindedly stroking the wooden 'wand' at his belt. His sense began to tweak. He felt the wood warm slightly.

"Are you trying to tell me something?"

The wand warmed again. He took the wand from his belt, laid it carefully on the ground and unwove the disguising glamour. The others watched with interest.

The wand blurred, lengthened rapidly and became the horn. Jorn picked it up and stroked the glittering, rainbow-hued spiral affectionately.

"Good to have you back. Now, about this cave, could you tell me when we get to the right one, like you did when I was searching the Library?"

The horn warmed decisively.

Jorn

"*So, hot for right, and cold for wrong, mmm? Well, that still leaves us a lot of searching and walking to do, but at least we won't waste time going in and out of every wretched hole we see!*"

"I can cut down the search a bit," he announced. "The horn can indicate when we get to the right cave. I know that still leaves a lot of holes and crevices to search, but now we only have to find the entrance. Once the horn tells us we have the correct one, we can explore properly. I'll need to stop quite often. Don't want to walk right past it. I'm afraid someone else will have to carry my pack for a bit so I have my hands free and I can climb if I need to."

Idris picked it up. "Leave it with me."

They hiked over and around massive boulders and cliff falls, and occasional slides of loose scree. A tiny trickle of water flowed down the ravine. It was bleak and bitterly cold, silent apart from the occasional call from the crows that populated the towering cliffs, or the mew from a hunting buzzard passing high up.

"No wildlife," commented Braid. "I'd expect plenty of rabbits, and possibly mountain goats, or even deer, we are not that high up; it's sheltered, and there's good browsing along the bottom here. That suggests predators; wolves maybe, or mountain lion, or even a bear. We must beware at night."

At intervals, Jorn gently stroked the horn and asked the question, but it remained stubbornly inert. Finally, when they were all tired and getting hungry and irritable, Jorn felt the horn warm a little under his hand.

"We are getting near!" he announced. "Start looking for suitable openings."

The horn grew steadily warmer as they walked. There were several dark holes spaced along the cliffs above them.

"*Is it near here?*"

The horn warmed decisively. Jorn stopped and very deliberately pointed the horn at each entrance in turn. When he pointed at a long, slanting fissure, half-hidden behind an outcrop of rock, the horn got hot so suddenly that he snatched his hand away and almost dropped it.

"Ow! I guess that is it!" he said, jubilantly, and added silently, "*Thank you horn, that was just what I needed. Now all we have to do is find the Juncture.*"

"Well, that's a relief," said Clarriss. "We should just about have time to explore before nightfall."

"Yes, but I'd like you to stay outside," said Rolf. "We need someone to set camp and mind the packs." There was a tense silence.

"I thought that would be Idris," the dwar snapped.

"I can sense water below," responded the shian. "I may be useful if there is a deep lake or rapid stream to cross."

"So, I'm just the camp cook and bag minder am I? But then, if four mages and two expert swordsmen cannot keep themselves safe, I am sure that one small dwar is not going to contribute much of a rescue. What exactly am I expected to do if you all fail to return?" inquired Clarriss with rather laboured sarcasm. "I suppose you simply expect me to trek back across a hundred kays of wilderness on my own and tell Kayman that you are probably all dead and the quest is a washout?"

"Something like that," responded Rolf.

Much to Jorn's surprise, Clarriss did not argue, but simply put on a disgusted expression and sniffed. "I'll have supper ready."

Chapter 13

The team checked their gear. Mordant strapped her short sword across her back and Braid did the same.

"Wish I could take my longsword," she told him ruefully, "but I guess it may get in the way."

"I'll be happy if we don't need to use our blades, but I'm not going in without one." He wound up his torch and led the way into the dark slot, followed by the others.

The narrow passage soon opened into a much larger space. Their small torches showed that three passages led off from this cavern. The first one reached a dead end after a few ems. The second led down, and the third was blocked by rock-fall after a short way.

"Huh! Let's hope it's not that one," grumped Mordant, already fighting down on her fear of enclosed places.

Jorn pointed the horn at each in turn. It warmed initially at the second opening, which led down, but then went icy cold. Jorn was puzzled.

"Is this where the Juncture is hidden?"

The horn warmed, but then went cold as before.

"You are trying to tell me something. Is it a warning?"

The horn warmed.

"So, the Juncture is down there, but there is something dangerous there as well?"

The horn grew hot in agreement. He realised that the team were looking at him with impatience, waiting for the verdict.

"The Juncture is down there," he confirmed, "but the horn warns that there's some kind of danger also."

"Why am I not surprised?" said Braidart.

The passage was too narrow to allow more than one person through at a time so they went in single file. Braidart again took the lead, a dagger in one hand and a torch in the other. Mordant went next, trying to ignore her rising discomfort. Jorn followed with his horn, and Idris and Rolf brought up the rear.

After some hundred paces of going downhill, squeezing between narrow gaps and ducking under places where the rocky ceiling lowered, Jorn sensed that they had emerged into a much larger space. Soon, his suspicions were confirmed. He lifted his surprisingly powerful torch; the narrow beams were enough to pick out the rocky walls and bumpy floor of a massive cavern. Great shawls and drapes and spikes of cream, rose and ochre stone hung from the roof of the cavern, and here and there, small crystals caught the light. On the far side, a dark pool glinted, and they could hear dull drips. Otherwise, it was silent.

"Wow!" said Jorn.

"What an amazing place!" exclaimed Braidart.

"Wowwww... aaaccce..." responded hollow echoes.

Mordant made a flourishing gesture. "Welcome to The Cave of the Damned!"

Beyond the dark pool, long, twisted, pale icicles of stone hung down from the roof in clusters and matching pinnacles rose from the floor to meet them, making stone pillars of many shapes and sizes.

Braidart made them all wait while he searched the cavern floor carefully. The team rewound their torches and watched.

"There is no sign of life," he told them, "except for some scratch marks near the pool. And there's some dry animal bones in a corner; they could be the remains of prey, or just something that crawled in here to die."

"Well, we are certainly 'far from light of day'," said Rolf, looking around at the surrounding darkness. They went across the cavern towards the pool, and got a better look at the stone formation that extended into the distance like a petrified forest. One group of humped pillars that rose from the floor looked uncannily like a huddled crowd of cloaked and hooded figures. There was no obvious route to follow through the extraordinary labyrinth. They looked at each other in glum realisation of the challenge ahead. 'Mapless mazes' suddenly made sense.

"At least the pool is shallow," said Idris, "but I sense much deeper pools further on, and there is fast-running water at lower levels I think."

"So, where is the Juncture? Do we really have to go into that?" asked Braidart, staring at the twisted pillars that blocked their way beyond the pool. "Because if we do, we must rope a back trail. One could get lost and disorientated in no time."

"Or it could be just a narrow belt that we can get through quickly," said Rolf, "but we won't know until we try."

"Maybe we don't have to," said Jorn, thoughtfully, as his sense tweaked again.

"Let's see what the horn says first," agreed Rolf.

"Horn, should we go into the maze?" The horn went icy cold. "The horn says not to enter. It's dangerous," Jorn reported. "And if you think about it, that makes sense. The Rhyme says, 'Seek me far from light of day, where mapless mazes bar the way'. We have assumed that the maze bars the way to the Juncture, but now that I'm here, I don't think it does. It simply bars the way forward. In which case, the Juncture could be down here in this cavern, or nearby."

"Horn, please show me where the Juncture is hidden." Jorn hefted the horn and did a survey of the Cave, slowly turning in a circle, with his left hand resting lightly on the twisted spiral. It remained cool under his hand until he was facing the tunnel entrance again, and examining the rocky wall on his right, when it started to warm. He walked in that direction, scanning all around the area until he located a narrow fissure. He shone his torch into it. The passage led downwards. He pointed the horn down the fissure, and it warmed decisively.

The others were watching tensely.

"It's down there," he confirmed. "But now what do we do? The entrance to the crack is very narrow, and it's not much better further on. I can't get into it, I'm far too big and tall, and I doubt if Braid or Rolf can either. Can you manage it Mordant? You're the slimmest one."

Mordant said nothing. Every part of her was begging not to have to go into that horrible, cramped place.

Idris saw the changes in her aura and understood the reason. He said quickly, "Let me go in first. I can at least see if I can find it. I may be able to bring it out."

The shian shed form and slipped easily into the cleft. It was pitch dark. The low passage widened a little, but then narrowed again, and finally dropped into a tight crawl-way. At the end of that, he sensed that it opened out. He had no way of telling whether the Juncture was there or not. He needed light, and hands, and it was far too dry down here. He went back to report.

"I will have to go and soak in that pool for a while before I try again."

Mordant sighed. Her sense had already told her that, fear or no fear, she had to do this. "Exactly how tight is it?"

"You can ease down the first part sideways. The worst bit is the crawl, you would have to do that on your stomach, but I think it is only about three ems. After that, it feels a bit wider."

"Then I'd better try. I can't say I like the idea, but it has to be done. We don't want to be down here longer than we must." She had made her voice deliberately casual, but her heart was hammering. This was not going to be pleasant.

"Let's rope you," suggested Braid.

"No, it might get in the way," Idris cautioned. "If anything goes wrong, I'll get you out, Mordant, trust me. I'll be back in a few moments, once I'm rehydrated."

She gave him a grateful smile. "Thanks."

He nodded and headed off towards the pool at the end of the cavern.

"Don't worry, Mordant," Jorn reassured, "the horn says there is no danger down there."

"I wish that made me feel better."

She got rid of her sword, dagger and any other bits of kit that might snag on something, and went to the crack. Turning sideways, she eased in awkwardly, past the tight place, and edged as fast as she could down the passage. It opened up a little, but her torch showed her the tight, low entrance ahead. She wondered if she could possibly fit into it, knew she couldn't and that she shouldn't even attempt it, but she got down on her stomach and went to try anyway.

It was a horribly tight fit. Her heart was running much too fast and she was breathing too shallowly. She couldn't use her torch down there, which made it worse. She took a few long, deep breaths and, in total darkness, wormed her way into the tunnel, inching painfully across the rough rock, avoiding bumps in the roof and trying to blank her mind to the thought that she was going to have to go out the same way, possibly, backwards.

After what felt like an hour, but could only have been a few minutes, she wriggled out into a small, open space. Relieved to have some room to manoeuvre at last, she whipped out her torch, switched it on and gasped. She was in a tiny grotto. White and pink crystals encrusted the surface of the walls, sparkling in the torchlight. More crystals and delicate, needle-thin spikes clustered the ceiling. It was still too low to stand so she stayed in a crouch and surveyed every nook and cranny. There was no sign of anything manmade that might be the Juncture.

She used her sense and picked up the faint traces of a pass-me-by. She produced a counter-construct and snapped it with practiced ease. On the floor at the back was an uninteresting piece of metal. Without bothering to examine it, Mordant picked the thing up and braced herself for the return journey.

When she squeezed from the fissure, she gave out a long, shuddering breath of sheer relief.

"Got it!" she told them triumphantly, and passed it hurriedly to Jorn before he could notice that she was shaking with reaction.

Idris was back, dripping from his immersion. He smiled and came to her; his indigo eyes were silvered with sparkling flecks. "Success, I see! Well done. But what have you found?" Switching to mind-speech, he sent softly, *"That was immensely brave. I salute you. Your aura shimmers; your essence is bright within you."* He reached out and touched her gently on her cheek, a butterfly touch, barely a brush with the back of his fingers. *"So very bright, so very beautiful."* Then he made a tiny, almost imperceptible, hissed intake of breath, a minute flinch, as if her skin had suddenly turned too hot to touch, and withdrew his hand. It was so fleeting, she wasn't even sure if she had imagined it. He withdrew abruptly, turned away, lost form, and slipped up the exit passage.

Mordant stared after the shian, still feeling the cool, slightly tingling contact. She wasn't sure what had just happened between them, or why he had left without a further word, but he had touched her, and that was astonishing. The others were too busy examining the piece of Juncture to have noticed anything. She regained her weapons and went to join them.

"Not much to look at though, for all the trouble," Jorn observed as the group clustered round. The object was made of a metal strip about four cems wide and some fifteen cems long that had been bent into an L-shape, and it looked as though it once formed the corner of something. Jorn placed the L-shaped object flat on his palm and held it out for the others to see. A metal spike, which housed the blue gem in a clawed clasp, came out of the apex of the corner, pointing straight up. Halfway up that spike, another thinner piece of metal stuck out at 45 degrees to his palm. This too had been cut short.

"Each end of the metal is bright. It must have been severed completely," observed Braid.

"Yes, that's what we'd expect. The story says five parts," agreed Rolf.

Jorn squatted and placed the thing on the ground. "Look, this must be one corner of a square. You can imagine three more just like it, all joined together. The fifth piece must have four parts, which join these cut straps and fit in the centre," he suggested.

There was no sense of Power; the fragment was as inert as a horseshoe. Jorn got up and stared down at it, trying to make sense of the strange object. Seen from above, the structure resolved into simple lines and he suddenly understood.

"It's a three-dimensional Quincunx!" he announced, excitedly. "See, there's the square for the outside, and the gems are the Nexuses, and these straps will form the central cross. I bet there is another spike in the centre, with a violet gem."

"Of course, so it is!" agreed Rolf. "That makes a lot of sense. A controlling matrix made from metal and gems."

Mordant had joined them. "So perhaps it *is* some sort of crown? Seems rather large to fit a head though." She picked it up and shone her torch on the metalwork, revealing twisted, engraved patterns that writhed across the outer surface. "It's strange, but these look a bit like raash motifs. I think this bottom part is copper. But the centre part is different, it might be steel." She paused thoughtfully then continued. "The Cup is trimmed with copper, isn't it? The other Tools are made from gold, silver and bronze. I wonder if the Juncture is also made from different metals."

"Well, we'll know when we find the next part. That's one down and four to go!" said Rolf cheerfully. "And well done all of us, especially you Mordant! Mission completed! We found The Cave of the Damned and located the Juncture. Now let's head back into the open air as fast as we can; I have no wish to linger down here longer than I must."

Mordant passed the Juncture back, and Jorn tucked it into the bag he had brought with him and slung it securely over his shoulder. He picked up the horn and caressed the tip in gratitude. His fingers chilled on its icy surface. Goosebumps ran up his arm.

Almost at the same time, a small sound came from across the cavern, and Mordant's mind-voice shouted, *"Beware behind!"*

Everyone span round. The team swept their torch beams frantically to locate the danger.

Three big creatures like giant maggots, about an em and a half long, had emerged from the stone forest beyond the pool at the far end of the Cave. Their large, segmented bodies were whitish. They had no real heads, and no eyes, but a huge, round maw, ringed with teeth, dominated the front end. They launched themselves into the pool and rapidly swam across.

"Freeze and don't make a sound!" Mordant urged Braidart. She grabbed his sword arm to prevent him from drawing his weapon, and urgently mimed rigid silence.

"What are they?" demanded Jorn.

"Blind-wyrms. They hunt by scent and vibration. They are very fast. They can strip a person to the bone in less than five minutes."

The wyrms wriggled forward and more emerged behind them. *"We cannot outrun them; we must prevent them from reaching us. Tangle-nets will help to slow them. Do you have any ready?"*

"I have one," replied Jorn, hoping that Rolf, Idris and Mordant were better supplied.

"We need to spread out. Rolf and Idris, move very slowly to your left. Jorn, go to your right. If a wyrm turns towards you, stop at once. They can sense us, but until we move, they do not know for certain where we are."

With immense caution, Jorn edged to his left. A wyrm turned towards him, its head raised, circling, trying to sense his location. He froze, waited until it turned away again, and then moved a little further.

Mordant inched towards the nearest wyrm, edging Braidart with her.

"Ready?" She checked that the others were in place. *"Then we attack now!"*

Her blade swept out of its sheath, echoed by the hiss of Braidart's, and they threw themselves into the attack, their torch beams swinging wildly in their left hands as they tried to keep track of the wyrms. Mordant hacked into the nearest one as it reared up, blindly seeking her, and almost sliced it in two. It fell back, both parts wriggling and oozing. Braid decapitated the nearest creature and headed for another. Rolf had killed two with lethal shafts, and span to find a third almost upon him, but Mordant killed it. She swept her torch round the cavern.

"Six down!" she shouted. "But there are more."

Jorn was only peripherally aware that his friends were fighting near him. His whole attention was fixed on the wyrm that was heading straight for him. He projected his tangle-web over it, and it rolled over, trapped, convulsing, twisting and writhing to escape. A second wyrm sensed the disturbance and lunged towards the other, as fast as a striking snake, thinking it was prey. Another wyrm was now coming straight for him. With no time to cast another construct, Jorn lowered the horn like a spear, and as the wyrm lunged at him, he stabbed it straight in the mouth with all his strength. Still propelled forwards by its original momentum, the wyrm's weight landed on him and Jorn fell backwards with the heavy creature on top of him, winded by the impact. Blood and foetid breath gushed as the monster writhed, still trying to reach him, but the horn had struck deep into its gut, and a moment later, it convulsed and died.

Braidart came over at the run and hauled the carcass aside. He knelt anxiously beside the young mage, seeing the blood on his chest.

"It's not mine!" Jorn gasped as he got his breath back. Braid pulled him to his feet.

"Good fight! I think we've finished them, but I don't fancy hanging around to find out if there are more."

Jorn put his foot on the dead creature and heaved hard until the horn came free. Its colours flamed briefly and the caked blood vanished.

Rolf was breathing hard, but he too was unharmed. Nine contorted wyrms sprawled in death on the rough floor. One more was crawling slowly back towards the pool, but Mordant followed it up and halved it with one swift stroke.

"Where's Idris?" asked Jorn anxiously, suddenly noticing his friend's absence.

"He went up the exit passage just before the wyrms' attack," replied Mordant.

Rolf suddenly froze as he received a mental summons. "Idris needs us! He says Clarriss is in danger!" He left at a run, and the others followed up the narrow passage and out through the smaller cave, heading towards the welcome daylight. They burst out of the cave entrance and were confronted by the remains of a blind wyrm. There was no sign of Clarriss.

Then Idris came towards them, looking his usual imperturbable self. "I dealt with the wyrm, but Clarriss has got herself stuck up on the cliff over there. I think it will be better if one of you fetches her down; she is too terrified to move. I must find water." He shed form and slipped away.

The small dwar was clinging in a frozen position, facing the cliff on a very narrow ledge an improbably long way up.

"What took you so long?" she enquired crossly. "And will someone please help me down? Frankly, I hate heights. I'd have refused a hundred in gold to do this climb, but it's amazing what one can do with mouthful of razor-sharp teeth at one's heels! However, I have no idea how I managed to get up here, and I don't much fancy climbing back down."

Braidart started towards the cliff but Mordant stopped him.

"Don't worry, Clarriss," she said gently. "Just close your eyes, and don't open them until I tell you. I will pick you up with an apport and bring you down. Trust me."

Mordant concentrated inwardly for a few moments and then looked up at the motionless dwar. "Can you feel the support?" she asked. Clarriss nodded, tensely. "Good; then close your eyes and let go! I can't move you if you're hanging on to the rock like a limpet!" Clarriss released her grip, finger by reluctant finger. The next moment, she was lifted smoothly from the ledge and brought gently to the ground where Rolf and Idris caught her and steadied her landing. Braidart simply gaped. Jorn put the apport on his 'to learn' list.

Clarriss dusted herself down and saluted Mordant crisply. "My thanks. So, have you got it?" she demanded. "And what happened down there? I want a full debriefing. But not until you have all eaten," she added. "I know how hungry you mages get when you have had to use Power. Emergency rations though, I'm afraid. I threw the boiling stew at that thing, not that it helped!"

"Yes, we got the Juncture; it's not exactly exciting. And we do all badly need food and a rest," agreed Rolf, "but not right here! It will soon be dark. I have no wish to find another blind-wyrm coming out of that hole in the middle of the night!"

"I spotted some high caves as we came up. If we can find one with a good ledge outside, we should be safe. I don't think those creatures climb too well," suggested Mordant.

"Well, now we know why there is so little wildlife round here. What the bloody hell were those monsters, Mordant?" demanded Braidart. "They were like something out of a bad nightmare."

"One of the less attractive chimeras, I'm afraid. That is the larval form, a kind of giant maggot. The adult is an insect like a giant roach that simply breeds and dies. These things eat anything, and when prey runs out, turn cannibal. And in really hard times, they simply pupate and go into suspended animation. Fortunately, they are rare. They usually favour old mine workings rather than natural caves. I've no idea how these got here."

"Maybe deliberately placed as guard?" suggested Braid.

"A thousand years ago? I doubt it, but who knows?" Mordant shrugged.

They grabbed their gear, packed in haste with one eye on the dark crevice, and set off to find a campsite, munching on some sugary trail-bars as they went. About half a kay down the gorge, Braidart found them a small, dry cave a short, steep scramble up the cliff, protected from the wind and with a long, wide ledge outside.

"This will be safe." For once, Clarriss agreed, and was happy to accept Rolf's help with the steep climb. No one liked the idea of being within reach of a hungry wyrm.

The team hauled their packs up to the ledge and set about getting comfortable. Jorn changed out of his smelly, blood-soaked jerkin and was at once dispatched to gather firewood, which took him a while, as there was little around. Braidart went off with his sling in search of pigeons, which were roosting in their hundreds along the inaccessible ledges.

Idris reappeared and took some water flasks to the tiny stream he had found, to top up supplies for the others. "There is an underground river nearby; I will spend the night there and join you in the morning at the main campsite," he told them when he returned, and moved away before anyone could answer. Mordant stared after him for a moment, her eyes puzzled.

Clarriss got busy with her pan, melting some fat to fry the pigeon breasts, and when Braidart returned with six plump birds, she, Rolf and Mordant began plucking and preparing them.

While the birds were cooking, Rolf provided a celebratory nip of strong spirit, and everyone but Jorn toasted their success and survival.

"Don't you ever drink?" Braidart asked curiously.

"No, alcohol just doesn't suit me. I've no idea why, but whatever it is, it always tastes vile and makes me ill, so there really isn't any point."

Braidart shrugged and held out his glass for a refill. "Don't know what you are missing."

"Oh yes I do!" laughed Jorn. "The headache you are going to have tomorrow if you have too much of that stuff! Rolf's special is lethal!"

The rest of the team chatted merrily, but Jorn turned the piece of Juncture in his hands, trying to sense its Power. He could still find nothing remotely magical about it.

Maybe the quest is just a wild goose chase? Maybe there was a good reason for taking such trouble to hide the thing. But the horn seems to want me to find the Juncture, and I trust it. I guess we have to hope that it will all make sense when we have all five pieces. But I still haven't the slightest idea how to use it, when and if we do.

After supper, Braidart unsheathed his sword, made sure it was clean, and began to go through a set of exercises with it, stretching his leg muscles and then shadow fencing. Jorn watched the young mercenary with interest;

he came alive with a blade in his hand, although he did not, he thought, have Mordant's skill. He noticed that she was watching too. Braidart felt their eyes and stopped.

"Needed to loosen up a bit." He held the sword out to Jorn. "Ever tried?"

Jorn shook his head. "But I've been wondering if I ought to learn, especially after those wyrms. You don't get much time to use constructs when you are about to be torn to pieces!"

He went over and took the blade, hefting it and feeling its fine balance. Braidart noted the ease with which he handled the unfamiliar weight. "Strong arms," he observed.

Jorn grinned. "You'd be surprised the strength it takes to work at the loom all day. It seems like a lifetime ago, but it's scarcely four or five moons."

"Would you like to learn how to use the blade? No doubt there will be some time on our journeys when we can practise."

"Yes, yes I would." replied Jorn, pleased at the offer.

Mordant got up and stretched. "I have missed my own exercises for many days. You are right; it would be a good idea to have a session. I'll need space. There is just enough at the far end there. Please be kind enough to respect my killing circle."

She picked up her big scabbard, moved to one end of the ledge, and drew her longsword. Rolf and Jorn were used to seeing her train, but Braidart and Clarriss were not. Jorn watched their faces with some amusement. Clarriss raised her eyebrows, pulled a face, which might possibly indicate that she was slightly impressed, and then ignored the effortless display of total mastery.

Braidart looked amazed, and then deeply respectful. The Sword-Master finally halted, kissed the hilt of her blade and sheathed it.

"I have only ever seen one other person use a blade like that and that is my brother, Brett. You put me to shame. Brett tried his best to teach me, but I never had the patience to work at the Warrior's Way. I am good, but I'll never be *that* good. My time as a Tullish mercenary ruined what little style I had. I can kill people, no problem, but it's not elegant."

"I too had a good teacher," she told him. "And I enjoy the discipline of body and mind."

Later that evening, they all huddled round the meagre fire to get as warm as possible before turning in.

"So what happens next?" asked Jorn.

"We are stuck again, it seems," said Braid, adding the last of the fuel and poking the dying fire with frustrated jabs. "We can't continue until we know where we are going. And that, of course, means that we must solve another verse of the Riddle Rhyme."

"We have no choice. We must return to Mage Hall and tell Kayman that we've found the first piece of the Juncture," affirmed Rolf.

"But that leaves the problem of the horses and ponies," objected Braid. "We can't just abandon the poor beasts with winter coming on."

"That was always going to happen. We could leave them hobbled for few days. Once we know what we are doing, you could send some students through to ride them back, or turn them free, whichever is easier," suggested Mordant.

Rolf yawned, setting them all to stretching their jaws. "I'm finished. Let's get some rest. We can go back to our base camp and make our final decision tomorrow."

*

After an unremembered dream, Jorn woke suddenly, wondering why he was icy-cold, only to find that he had tossed off both his blanket and cloak. He had kept the section of Juncture in a bag tucked under his arm and now he had pins and needles. The stone floor was chill and comfortless. A pale moonlight filtered into the cave mouth. The humped outline of his companions showed as dim shadows. Jorn sat up, huddling into the blanket, feeling tense and restless, and now far from sleepy. Then a small light attracted his attention. He got up and found Mordant sitting by the glowing ashes of the fire with a blanket round her shoulders. She was playing with an intricate weave of glimmering threads held between her fingers. She looked up, her violet eyes invisible in the shadows; her gaunt face as tautly expressionless as ever.

"You awake too?" he asked. *"I feel all fidgety inside. What are you doing?"*

"Playing with Irien's Knot; it's a puzzle game that raash mages use to amuse the children. A bit like cat's cradle."

"I can't quite imagine raash playing or having toys, even as children."

"Even raash are kind to their own children. Well at least on Free Vard they are." Mordant sighed. *"Not all raash are just ruthless killers, even now. In the deep past, they were a great people. But then some of them changed, especially the clan of the Hyakin. And of course, these were the*

high-raash who wanted to rule, lived to fight. Their gentle low-raash cousins were no match for them. They were all enslaved."

"And now Darric rules them?"

Mordant paused for a long moment before answering. "Yes. Many years ago, the Candrim, the last of the remaining clans to retain any real power, launched an attack on Darric's home and killed his father, and his wife and children. Darric declared an honour war. That meant that neither side would give up until the other had been totally annihilated. Even by raash standards, the war was savage. Finally, about 20 years ago, Darric won. He held a great triumph. I can still remember the screams when they impaled the children of Peridor, the last Clan-Lord of the Candrim. Darric flayed Peridor. Everyone was made to watch."

"Flayed? Do you really mean...?"

"Yes; skin taken from the living body, strip by strip. The art is to keep the victim alive for as long as possible. Darric is an expert. Peridor took four hours to die."

"Oh, Powers!" Jorn felt sick to his essence. *She has to carry the memory of that.* And then, the other thing she had said struck home. *She said she saw that, and it was 20 years ago!*

"But you hardly look more than 20!"

She laughed softly. "Flatterer! The raash easily live to 300. We age slowly. But I was still a child-slave at the time."

Despite her light tone, Jorn's sense tweaked sharply. Mordant was hiding something from her past that disturbed her deeply. He tried to find the right words to get the secretive mage to unload the emotional burden that so clearly troubled her.

"It's not easy, is it, being a halfer? I'll never forget the total shock when Rolf told me about my real parents. Suddenly, I wasn't who I'd always thought I was. And meeting J'Louth and finding them so fundamentally alien didn't make it easier. Sometimes I feel I don't belong to either race. Idris says being unique is good because I can truly be myself, but it doesn't always feel like that, does it?"

Mordant looked at him for a long moment, debating whether to tell him the ghastly truth, and knew she couldn't, at least not yet. "No, Jorn, it doesn't," she told him flatly. "Forgive me, but I cannot speak of my life on Vard."

Jorn reached out and gave her arm a quick squeeze. *"Forgive my intrusion. I do understand."* He left her hunched by the fire and went back to his lumpy resting place. Eventually he slept.

Chapter 14

In the morning, the team made a dawn hike back to their base camp. The Cut had subsided, and the ropes remained in place, so fording was thankfully not a problem, though it took time to manhandle the packs across. The ponies and horses were fine, and their tents looked like the height of comfort after the night in the cave.

They had an early breakfast, huddled round the fire, speculating about the location of the next part of the Juncture and debating what to do with the horses and ponies. Jorn kept out of the discussion, partly because he had nothing to say, and partly because he felt tense and irritable and slightly headachy, as if a thunderstorm was threatening. He went off to relieve himself in the bushes. He returned and sat down, and stretched out his hand to take some newly-baked flatbread.

"Have you washed your hands?" asked Clarriss.

In fact, he had not bothered, but the remark acted like a spark to dry tinder and Jorn's temper finally exploded. His colours flared. He snatched his hand away and stood, tense with fury.

"When are you going to treat me like an adult! 'Do this Jorn, do that Jorn, have you wiped your arse and washed your hands, Jorn?' Just quit bossing me about and nannying. I'm not a child!" he stormed, glaring at the dwar.

"I'll treat you like an adult when you stop having to tell me that you are one!" she snapped. "If you want to go down with trail-belly that is your affair. Don't blame me."

"Keep your bloody bread!" Jorn stalked off down the valley, feeling a mixture of seething rage and humiliation. He would have felt better if he could have slammed a door on his way out. "How dare she talk to me like that? How dare she?" he muttered furiously. He finally halted by a clump of stunted birch and alder near the river and slumped down, feeling totally miserable. There wasn't even a decent-sized tree for him to take refuge in. He sulked crossly for a while, his headache getting worse by the minute.

"Want to talk about it?" Jorn looked up. Idris was watching him, half submerged in the rushing water. He came out and sat down next Jorn, the water running off his scales in shining drips. "You have been looking restless for the past hour. What is eating you?"

"Nothing; everything. Oh, I don't know. Clarriss just got right under my skin. She keeps treating me like some idiot boy who is only good for doing the chores."

"She does that to everyone, or had you not noticed?"

"I know. Usually I can cope, but just now, I couldn't. Something inside me just exploded. I feel... I don't know... I've got a headache and I'm all wound up inside. As if something bad is going to happen, has happened... Oh Idris, I don't know."

Idris got up and laid a cool palm across his forehead. "Mmmm... Jorn, what you describe sounds a lot like the feeling one gets before an unsought far-seeing. Come with me."

He led the young mage down to the river where a puddle of rainwater had got caught among some rocks, making a dark, still pool.

"This should do. Settle down comfortably. Look into the water. Try to open your mind to whatever images come into it."

Jorn knelt by the small pool and stared at the water. He felt tense; the water seemed to pull him forward. It went black. All at once, he had the sensation of being wrenched elsewhere, as if a part of him had translocated.

"Tell me what you see."

"Fire! Fire everywhere! People running. Ahh..." Jorn gasped as the vision came in a series of disjointed images. *"A building is burning. Some kind of stronghold, I think. There are flames coming from the windows. Part of the wall has fallen, it looks kind of melted. People are running along the battlements, it's horrible, some of them are burning too. I can see raash watching, attacking!"*

His viewpoint changed as he homed in on one area of the inner courtyard. *"There is a portal. I can see a mage, and he's helping people go through, women and children; someone is being carried. There's a tall man, very like Braidart. There is fire everywhere. He can't hold the portal much longer... they are all through; it shuts."*

The seeing wavered and disappeared. Jorn came back to awareness of his surroundings with a shuddering sigh, his heart pumping overtime.

"Easy now, tantar-issa. Take some deep breaths."

After a few moments, Jorn looked up and said shakily, "I think that was the Darnell Hold. Under attack by raash. It looked really bad. We must tell the others at once, Braid will go crazy."

Jorn

Idris helped the young mage to his feet. They went back to the campsite. Idris told Rolf what had happened. "A far-seeing?" asked the little mage, anxiously.

Jorn nodded. Rolf got him to the fire, put a blanket round him, and thrust another trail-bar into his hand. "Eat something. A far-seeing drains Power. You need a moment to recover before you talk about the vision. However urgent it is, we can do nothing about it right now, so take your time. At least we now know why you acted so unlike yourself."

"I'm sorry," muttered Jorn, looking at Clarriss. He took a few bites of the sugary confection and started to feel better. He explained what he had seen. Braidart heard him out in silence, but his face was tight with anxiety and his hands clenched until the knuckles showed white. Rolf caught his breath sharply and looked stricken.

"You saw people leave through a portal?" Braid asked tensely.

"Yes, not sure who though. A man who looked a lot like you, but older. Someone was hurt."

"Where did the mage take them, I wonder?"

"A Transit Point, and then Mage Hall, I expect. Easiest in an emergency," answered Mordant.

"How many raash?" demanded Clarriss.

"I couldn't tell. Many; some had tubes with flames coming out of them."

"And you said the walls looked melted in places?"

"Yes. Running like candlewax."

Braid looked sick with worry.

Mordant shook her head with angry frustration. "I wish I could say I'm surprised, but I'm not. The Darnells have been giving Darric trouble for years. He knows that Barrass has worked closely with Kayman for decades, and he will want to eliminate him before the invasion. But the scale of the attack is troubling. Darric has gained sufficient Mastery to send a large force through a portal, and they are prepared to attack a fortress, not just defenceless settlements. He was obviously using the Knife."

Rolf had been silent. Now he spoke in a quiet, grim voice, which grabbed their attention. "It is far, far worse than you know. Darnell Hold is where the Wand was hidden. If Darric has taken it, we are in even deeper trouble. This could be what he's been waiting for."

"Oh by the Powers," breathed Idris. "Kayman will be devastated. But do not yet despair *tantar-alta*. We do not know that the raash have found it."

Jorn was gripping the horn for strength and comfort. It went icy-cold under his hand. *Have they found it?* he asked tensely.

The horn warmed in response. Jorn looked at Rolf. "I am truly sorry, but I fear that they probably have."

"We all need to get back to Mage Hall at once," decided Mordant. "If we have to leave the ponies and horses behind, so be it."

"I will stay with them," offered Idris. "I am very weary of holding form and I could do with a few days of solitude in the Cut. I doubt that I can help much with this emergency. But be sure to send someone back to let me know what is going on. I will return if you have need of me."

"Thank you my friend. Very well, pack up any necessities as fast as you can," said Rolf. "I can take Tricky through."

Jorn got up. *"Thanks for your help, Idris. This is not a Gift I want to have; it's terrible to see things at a distance and to know you can't do anything about them."*

"Sadly true, but we do not choose our Gifts," replied the shian mage.

Braidart had said nothing since the shattering news, governing his emotions with rigid discipline. Jorn watched as he shoved a few items into his pockets with controlled intensity.

"I can't say anything to make it better, Braid," he said quietly. "I wish I could. I did see people escaping; hold on to that."

The young nobleman nodded, his face strained. "But many did not. I have seen the results of fire, Jorn. It's terrible; one of the worst ways to die. I just need to know what happened, and if my kin are safe."

The team watched tensely as Rolf wove the portal. They emerged into the courtyard at Mage Hall to find it busy with hurrying people. Braidart was so anxious about his family that he hardly felt the usual nausea. Rolf came last with Tricky. He handed her to a groom, who uncovered her head, and then they all went quickly into the Hall.

An elderly human servant, his livery scorched and a livid burn across his cheek, hurried past.

"Trevor, wait!" called Braidart. The man turned and recognised the young nobleman.

"M'sar, I am so very sorry for your loss," he said with a respectful bow of his head.

"What has happened? I only just got back," demanded Braidart tensely.

The servant straightened to the rigidly formal posture of a soldier giving an emotionless report. "M'sar, I wish I did not have to give you such ill tidings. I have to tell you that your noble father, Arnori Barrass, died in the raash attack. Philip was able to make a portal and the rest of the family are safe except for one. Your brother, Sar Brendan, was badly burned, and it is feared that he cannot survive. Forgive me, M'sar, but I have an urgent errand to run." He bowed again and left quickly.

Braidart took a shuddering breath, and sagged against the wall for a moment, his eyes closed and his face strained, fighting to retain his control. The others gave him space and avoided trite comments, but looked at each other in deep dismay.

"This disaster hits us all," sent Rolf. *"Barrass was our staunchest ally."*

"Poor Braid; I know only too well what he feels right now," responded Jorn.

After a moment, Braidart straightened, like a soldier returning to duty, ignoring his own wounds. "What is, is. The time for mourning will come later. I must find my family, and see Brendan."

"Braid, Oh thanks be! We have such need of you!" A lovely, dark-haired, young woman ran down the stairs into his arms, looking distraught. She searched his face. "You know about father?"

He nodded grimly. "What about the others?"

"Borodin and Brogan got away through the portal. Philip was wonderful, he saved our lives. Our other brothers were not at home. But Brendan got caught in a blast of that awful fire. Brogan carried him through the portal." Tears welled in her dark eyes. "Oh, Braid, he's so badly hurt. The healers and the dwarran medics can't help him; they don't think he will live."

"Where is he, Bea?"

"Upstairs. They've turned the big conference room into a hospital. The mages have been opening portals and getting the injured away as quickly as possible. Borodin and Brogan are back at Darnell Hold now, organising the evacuation and salvage operation. The whole place is a ruin."

"I need to know exactly what happened. But first, I must see Brendan."

She nodded. "Be prepared, he is in a terrible state. Forgive me if I do not come with you, but looking at him tears me apart. He's in so much pain and there is so little anyone can do."

"You must excuse us, Braidart, but Mordant and I have to report to Kayman," said Rolf. *"I must see if there is news of the Wand,"* he added silently to Jorn. They hurried off and Clarriss followed them. Braidart went quickly upstairs, Jorn beside him, the horn in his hand.

"Was that your sister?"

"Yes, Beatrice. Brendan is the youngest. Hell, Jorn he's my kid brother, and I am so fond of him. I can't bear to think of him suffering."

They reached the conference room. The floor was covered by beds and mattresses, occupied by bandaged figures. Part of the room was hidden by screens covered in fabric. A neatly-uniformed dwar came over.

"Are you hurt?"

"No Mistress," responded Jorn. "This is Sar Braidart Darnell; he is looking for his brother, Sar Brendan."

"He is over there behind the screens. But I must warn you that he is not an easy sight. He has very severe burns over more than 80 per cent of his body. We cannot apply dressings."

"I need the truth. Will he live?"

The slim dwar looked up at the tall man, her dark face calmly professional, but her eyes full of sympathy.

"It is very unlikely. His injuries are too severe for the Mage-Healers to deal with. They are already tired, and must keep their strength for those who can best be helped. Our dwarran medics can offer little, except fluids and some slight relief from pain. On the whole, we must hope that he does not linger long, he is already dehydrated, but there is no fever yet. He is young and very strong. It may take some days. I am truly sorry, M'sar."

Braidart compressed his lips grimly, braced himself, and walked to the screens. Somehow, his voice managed to be almost normal as he said, "Bren, It's me. Death's blood, but you're a mess lad. You look like my worst attempt at a hog-roast. That must hurt like hell. Don't try to speak; I'll stay with you for a while."

Jorn placed the horn safely on the floor and poked his head around the screen. He rapidly withdrew, feeling totally appalled. *By the Nine, this looks bad. Braid must be gutted.* He had never imagined that anyone could be so terribly hurt and still live. Then he braced himself and went to kneel beside the injured man.

Brendan lay with the careful stillness of someone whose least movement causes unendurable agony. A light sheet covered his torso, lifted on a frame so that it did not touch his body. What could be seen of the rest of him was a mess of charred, split skin, oozing blisters and red-raw sores. His right hand was a blackened claw, charred to the bone. Only his dark hair and upper face and his feet were unburnt. Jorn felt that made the ruin of the rest somehow worse. *I guess he was wearing a helmet and stout boots,* Jorn thought, his mind grappling to find a way past the horror.

Brendan looked up at his brother with mute appeal. His cracked, swollen lips moved in an attempt at speech, but failed. He gave a low moan of pain and frustration.

Braidart turned to Jorn, his blue eyes filled with shared pain. He murmured, "He's trying to tell me something, but I can't understand. It's so upsetting. Is there anything you can do?"

"I'll try." The young mage moved round to lay a hand very lightly on Brendan's head. "I'm going to touch your mind. It will feel a bit strange." He reached out a delicate pink thread, seeking connection and communication. He recoiled as he encountered a searing wall of pain. "Sorry, just a moment, let me do something about that." He withdrew the contact and brought the red of Disjunct into the working, aiming to sever the awareness of the agony, and followed it up with a strong, cooling flood of indigo and turquoise. He projected that and saw the injured man's eyes clear a little as the pain eased. He re-established the connection and said gently. *"My name is Jorn. I'm a mage, a friend of Braidart. Braid knows you want to tell him something. Just say the words in your mind, I can hear you."*

"Please, please, just ask him to kill me. The pain is too much and I'm dying anyway. Please, I want at least to keep my honour. I don't want to hang on and end up raving in a few days' time."

Jorn shook his head in shocked denial. Brendan's eyes entreated and his lips tried to form the word 'please. *"Please ask him,"* he begged.

Jorn took a deep breath and looked at Braidart. "He wants you to end it for him," he said flatly. "He's in a lot of pain. He knows he's dying. He wants to do so with honour."

Braidart closed his eyes for a moment as the weight of that hit him, and then looked at his brother with anguished tenderness. "I thought it might be that. If I were you, I'd want the same. But I'm just not sure if I can do it."

"Are you still here, Jorn?"

"Yes."

"Tell Braid he's my only way out. Borodin pretended not to understand. Brogan refused point-blank. Braid has done it before, after battle, he won't make a mess of it. Please ask him to do it now."

Jorn repeated the dying man's words, and added, "He is truly not afraid. And he loves you very much." The feelings had been so strong and near the surface that he felt it was right to share them.

Braidart took a deep breath, bracing himself to meet his brother's final demand, and free him from his unbearable pain. "Bren, are you sure?" he asked. Brendan gave a minute nod and breathed "esss". Braidart reached out a hand and caressed Brendan's dark hair, his eyes never leaving his brother's.

"Jorn, leave us alone for a while. And try and keep those nurses away for a few moments."

Jorn swallowed hard to check the tears. *Oh Powers, I see the need, but Braid will have to live with this for the rest of his life.* He felt a deep compassion for both brothers, closely followed by welling anger and a sudden fierce determination.

He said quietly. "Braid, wait. There may be something I can do. It's an outside chance, but let me try. If it doesn't work, you can do as he asks."

Braid looked at his brother and then back at Jorn. His voice was tight with emotion. "Be quick then. I can't bear to see him like this, but if I wait too long, I won't be able to manage it."

"I just need the horn."

He fetched it and came back to stand beside Brendan. *"Horn, can you help me heal him?"* The horn warmed decisively. Jorn took a deep breath. "Brendan, I am going to try to heal you. Will you let me?"

Brendan looked uncertainly at his brother. "Give it a try, eh? I'll be here," Braidart encouraged. Brendan managed a tiny gesture of assent.

"It will take me a few minutes to create the working," Jorn told them, trying to sound totally confident. *Adjunct; the healing Sector; and yellow to bind; green to renew.* With a focussed intensity of will and Power that he had never felt before, he entered his workroom, engaged with the Quincunx, and began to work the colours, using sheer instinct to guide his construct. Finally, he came back to awareness. "All set." He smiled reassuringly at Brendan who gave a small nod.

Jorn picked up the horn. *Now for the hard bit. We have to heal these burns, make his flesh whole, grow him new skin. I'll start at the top and work down.* He extended the horn and let its tip rest lightly on the young man's head. He aimed to encase the damaged flesh in a fine, healing mesh, woven from head to toe like a tightly-fitting garment. He drew out his construct and began to apply it, closing his eyes in total concentration.

It seemed to take forever; time stood still. The drain of physical and mental energy was dreadful, but somehow, wonderfully, the horn did not let him tire. He heard Braidart give a low gasp and opened his eyes. The terrible ruin of burnt skin and split, weeping flesh was being wiped away. It was like watching a candle reverse the melting of its wax.

Borrowed energy surged through him. Somewhere, underneath, he knew that he was overextended, burning himself out. His heart galloped unevenly and a searing pain grasped his chest. Faintness threatened to overwhelm him but he would not give up now. Obstinately, he poured out healing until, at last, the blackness rushed up to meet him.

*

When Jorn awoke, he was lying in bed. He felt drowsy and thirsty, but comfortable and very disinclined to move. After a few moments, he heard Mordant say, "Welcome back Wonder-Boy! And don't lie there pretending to be asleep. I can see your eyes moving under your lids."

He opened his eyes and found himself in his own room. Mordant was sitting by his bed, a book on her lap. Late afternoon sun slanted through the window. Memory returned in an urgent flood.

"How is he?"

"Recovering nicely. And so, finally, are you. You've been dead to the world for three days. Indeed, you very nearly died. We fetched Idris back to heal you. Your body was exhausted and your heart overstrained, but Idris healed that. Only you failed to recover as you should. And then Idris realised that your shian essence was also on the point of death. He took you to your oak tree and Mara and Kern helped you to shift your *shi* into the tree. You were there for more than a half a day. They wrapped your sleeping body and kept you warm. They knew it was a great risk, for your essence might not be able to return to you in time, but in the end, it did. Rolf has been worried sick, and so has Braid and Brendan. They have been taking turns to sit with you, and so has Beatrice."

"I don't remember anything. The last thing I knew Brendan was being healed." Jorn tried to sit up and promptly felt dizzy. Mordant helped him to prop up against the pillows and gave him a glass of water. His hand trembled as he took it. "Oh my, I'm as wobbly as a week-old kitten!"

Mordant gave her thin smile. "That's what you get for attempting the impossible! I'll go and tell them you are back with us."

"I could not have done it without the horn." He looked round for it and saw it near the bed, but out of reach. "Let me have it by me, please. I need to say thank you." She passed it over and left to find the others. Jorn stroked the shining spiral.

"Thank you for helping me to save Brendan. And for keeping me alive." The horn warmed under his hand and a gentle strength oozed into him.

A few moments later, Rolf rushed into the room. "Jorn, how do you feel? By all the Powers, you damned fool, I thought I'd lost you!" he said in tones of mixed relief, frustration and affection. He plumped down on the bed.

"So that's your way of not drawing attention to yourself! Every mage, student and servant in the place has talked about nothing else for the past three days."

Jorn shrugged uncomfortably. "I couldn't just stand by and watch Braid have to kill his brother."

Rolf patted his arm. "Of course you couldn't. You did the right thing. But you do know you are lucky to be alive? The Power drain should have stopped your heart." His hand closed on his guard-child's arm in a tight squeeze.

Jorn winced. "Ease up, Rolf. I'm fine, just a bit wobbly."

"I'm not surprised. No one can understand how you did it."

"I don't know myself. But Brendan really is all right?"

"He is fine. And…"

"Visitors!" announced Braidart from the door. Jorn grinned delightedly as Braid came in with Brendan and Beatrice. Brendan was the living image of Braidart but some five years younger. He came over quickly and reached out and took Jorn's hand in his own, giving it a quick, firm shake. There was not a mark or a scar to be seen.

"Thank you. It's a stupidly small thing to say to someone when he just saved your life, but it will have to do." His smile was Braidart's too. "I owe you one."

"And so do I," said Braidart.

"And me!" Bea went round to the other side of the bed, climbed onto it and planted a loud kiss on his cheek. He felt himself grow slightly pink. "You were wonderful!" she said warmly.

"But do not try that again in a hurry!" said Idris from the doorway. "Not, at least, until I have had time to teach you how to work a healing without killing yourself in the process. Now then, all of you, out of here. I need to check over my patient, and then he needs to rest."

Rolf smiled. "I'll get supper sent up at six." The small mage left the room, his relief obvious.

Jorn

Jorn watched as his friend came over. "Thank you, Idris. Mordant said you got me to my tree. You saved my life, *tantar*."

"It takes a shian to understand a shian." The healer spent a few moments looking at Jorn's eyes, feeling his forehead and taking his pulse. The young Master's aura was still faint, but quite intact.

Idris smiled in relief. "All is well, *tantar-issa*. I can see you are feeling better because you have a whole batch of questions queuing up to be answered, but you will have to wait. We will bring you up to date over the next few days. Now you must rest."

Jorn held up his hand, remembering the one question that could not wait. "Just one thing. Did the raash get the Wand?"

"Yes Jorn, I am afraid they did. Kayman searched the deep vaults beneath the ruined Keep, but there was no trace of it. Which means that we are fast running out of time. Kayman blames himself, but he did all that any Warden could have done."

*

The following day, Jorn felt well enough to get up. Brendan insisted on helping him downstairs. He had the tact to stay quiet, understanding that Jorn needed time to himself. The young mage got himself a warm cloak and they went slowly into the frosty garden. After a rest, and with Brendan's support, he made it into the Grove. His essence hungered and he knew he would feel much stronger when he had absorbed the sweet nourishment from his oak tree.

He turned to Brendan. "Can you do something for me?"

"Need you ask? After what you did for me, I'd walk barefoot to the Bitter Sea and back!"

"It's nothing so dramatic; I just need a body-sitter."

Brendan looked totally confused. Jorn grinned at his bewilderment. "Has Braid explained about me? I mean, about me being half shian?"

"He tried to explain but I don't think I really understand how this shian business works. Since I recovered, I have discovered that there are worlds and people I never knew existed. I'm still in a bit of a daze!"

"I know the feeling!" Jorn told him. "You can imagine how I felt when I suddenly found out that I am only half human, and a mage as well! But anyway, there is a part of me that is shian, and that part needs to go inside a tree every so often in order to absorb nourishment. I've become very weak, and I need to do that now to get my strength back. I'm just going to sit down by this oak tree; it will look as if I'm asleep, but actually, part of me is in the tree. It's very important that my body is not disturbed or moved when I am out of it, so I need someone to watch me until I get back. Pretty boring I'm afraid, and cold, but I'll only be half an hour." He paused. "If I am absent any longer, just go and find Idris, or Rolf; they'll know what to do."

Jorn settled down and slid joyfully into the oak. He was famished. When he came back to himself, he felt amazingly well. He stretched and got easily to his feet. Brendan looked at him in amazement. "You look different."

"I feel different! Almost back to what passes for normal! And now I really want to know what's been happening?" The pair walked back towards the garden. Jorn was delighted to find that he could stride out with his usual vigour, almost.

"Not sure I can tell you much. I'm not exactly in Kayman's confidence."

"Well, let's start with what happened at Darnell Hold. I am so very sorry about your father, Brendan, I knew that he had died in the fire, but Idris refused to give me any more details until I'd rested." He looked at the young nobleman. "But it must have been terrible; if you'd rather not talk about it, I quite understand."

"I've seen things that will probably give me nightmares for the rest of my life," responded Brendan grimly, "but Braid says it will help to talk about it. Not that I can remember that much; it all happened very fast, and after I got burned, I passed out."

They sat beside the pool and he continued his story in a quiet voice. "The attack came just after the noon meal. One moment we were sitting round the table, and the next, there was the alarm call, signalling an attack. Father rushed off to see was happening. The rest of us went to grab whatever arms we could. I went up to the top of the barbican. We only had a small garrison; no real war for years so no need of one. When I looked out, I saw all these weird soldiers just marching out of nowhere through some kind of gateway. Braid says they had another gateway — portal, you call them — on the south.

"Our men had shut the outer gates in good time and got the drawbridge up. Darnell Hold was built in the days when they knew how to prepare for attack and siege. The walls are huge and thick, and we have a steep moat. It had only fallen once in 500 years, and that was the fault of an incompetent holder. Father was not incompetent. He always kept us well supplied. Once the drawbridge was up, our relatively small force could

Jorn

hold out for a long time. We sent pigeons off to the nearest army post, and to the Transit Point, requesting urgent backup. We thought we just had to sit it out." He sighed and shook his head. "It took them about half an hour."

Jorn winced in sympathy. "I know; they melted the walls. I saw that."

"You saw it? How?"

"A far-seeing — a kind of vision."

"Well then, yes. The water simply boiled out of the moat. The next thing we knew, they had crossed and broken through the main gate into the outer circle. There was one raash in command outside. I saw him point at the gateway and wall beneath me. There was heat like a smelting furnace, and the stone just started to melt. I ran down into the inner bailey, and then raash soldiers were inside there as well, coming out of another portal with tubes that threw out a flaming gel, which stuck to everything it touched. It was chaos; people were running around on fire, screaming. A blast of the sticky fire caught me. Oddly enough, it didn't hurt that much at the time; shock, I suppose. Then, in the nick of time, Philip, the mage from the Transit Point, portalled in. He had received our message and realised it was an emergency, so he came straight over. He did something to keep the raash at bay, and formed a new portal and managed to hold the gateway open long enough for the family to get out. Luckily, Brogan saw me and picked me up before I passed out. I don't remember anything after that until I came round in the ward here. As far as we can tell from what we pieced together later, the raash rushed straight for the Round Tower and broke in. Father had gone there to get something. We have not been able to identify his body. Then they set the whole place ablaze. The Tower flamed like a great burning chimney. And then they left. The Hold is a charred ruin."

Jorn shook his head, uncertain what to say in the face of such disaster. "So your eldest brother is Arnori now?"

"Yes, that's Borodin. We are having a wake for Father and a feast for our new Lord this evening. You will come, I hope?"

"Of course, M'sar, I will be honoured to join you."

Brendan smiled, clapped Jorn on the shoulder and got up. "See you later; you'll be feted as a hero! Philip too, and you both deserve it. Thank you once again, Master. Our Clan is forever at your service." He gave an elegant bow.

Jorn didn't feel like a hero right now. He watched Brendan walk away, glad that he had been able to heal him, but also deeply anxious. *The raash are so very strong, and Darric won't stop now that he has the Wand. It's only a matter of time before we hear about a major attack. I must get back to the others and find out what we do next.*

Jorn left the grove and was about to go back into the Hall when he saw Beatrice coming towards him from the direction of the yew close. She smiled as she saw him and came quickly over.

"Jorn! How good to see you up and about. Are you feeling better?"

"Much better, thank you M'sarra. You look a lot like Brendan," he told her as they walked towards the formal rose garden.

"So people say. Our family have strong features. Mother and father were cousins, so 'the Darnell look' comes out true in all the family: dark hair, blue eyes, big nose!" she laughed.

"But yours isn't large... I mean, you are beautiful M'sarra," Jorn stammered awkwardly.

She laughed again and dropped a small curtsey. "I thank you, kind sir. But for heaven's sake, drop the title and call me Bea. I was just looking at the statue through there. Who was Myron?" she enquired as they strolled side by side, doing a circuit of the central pond.

"The original Master of Nine," responded Jorn, happy to move to safer ground. "He founded the first Mage School and did all kinds of other amazing things. Of course, the sculptor did the statue from his imagination, making him look like a great, wise, old mage and human lord. For all we know, he was a nonentity who had thin hair, bad teeth and a weak chin!"

"I doubt that very much! In my experience, really important men usually have the looks to match. I don't mean handsome, necessarily — present company excepted — but strong and attractive, or ugly but charming." Jorn recognised the delicate compliment and felt himself go pink. *Perhaps it's time to leave before things go any further. She is gorgeous, but I can't afford that kind of complication right now.*

"Bea, I fear I can't play the invalid and milk sympathy any longer. I'll see you this evening. Now I must find Rolf and see what's going to happen next." He gave her a small bow and left.

He found his guardian in his study, with maps spread around him and worry lines creasing his forehead. The small mage beamed as Jorn came in.

"Well, I don't have to ask how you are; I can see for myself that you have recovered. That is good news, and I could surely do with some."

"What's been happening?" asked Jorn, sitting down in his usual chair. "Any more attacks from the raash?"

Jorn

"Not yet, thank the Powers. But if they can produce multiple portals and overwhelm a fortress in less than half an hour, then it won't be long before they strike again. Especially now that they have the Wand as well. With three Tools working in unison, Darric's Power is almost equal to your own Jorn, and he has years of experience as a War-Mage. We can only guess at what that may mean, but I have a fair idea. You saw what happened to the Hold with Darric using both the Knife and Chain. Aim that at a human city and just imagine what the consequences could be; with the Wand in use as well, it could be even more damaging. Darric can probably make a portal 10 ems wide and march a regiment through it. He can level any army sent against him, and protect himself and the raash War-Mages with wards that even you will find it hard to break."

Jorn felt utterly useless. "Rolf, I can't match that kind of Power, even if I learn every fighting construct Mordant can teach me. I just don't know enough yet. I have the Nine, and I'll do my best, but what can one Master do against someone who can call up Power like that?"

"Don't underestimate yourself, Jorn." said Rolf, reaching to give his hand a reassuring squeeze. "Look what you did for Brendan. No one here could manage anything like that. We don't know what you can do yet. And Kayman won't give up. The High Council will have to take notice of this now, no matter what Turner says. But we need the Juncture. It's a faint hope, but right now it's the best we have."

"Yes," agreed Jorn glumly. "So what now? I assume we will soon be off on the next stage of the quest?"

"Yes, though perhaps not soon. We still have to find the answer to another verse of the Riddle Rhyme. And it is the Longest Night in seven days."

"Oh my! It is really? I've quite lost track. Though to be honest, I don't feel like celebrating as usual, not with everything that has happened in the past few months. But I could use the time to get my strength back to normal and I need to get some workings prepared and hung ready for action. And Rolf, I must attempt to form a portal. Idris has shown me the basics, but we haven't had time to construct one. I have a strong feeling I will need to be able to do that on my own one day soon."

*

That evening, Jorn dressed in his apprentice suit, which was the smartest thing he had, and went to attend the Darnell Clan's feast, which was held at

Mage Hall. He was well aware that eyes and silent speculation followed him down the corridors. *So much for keeping a low profile.*

The private dining room had been set out with a long table and sideboards loaded with food. The rooms blazed with candles. The Darnell emblem, featuring black swords crossed on a red ground, was much in evidence on banners and shields around the walls.

He immediately felt like the poor relation. The family were mostly arrayed in brightly-coloured court clothes, although everyone wore black armbands in memory of Barrass. Servants in the black and red Darnell livery circulated with wine and savouries.

Braidart was in a mulberry damask dress suit with a high collar and lace-trimmed cuffs. It was a little loose on him but he still looked very fine. His beard was freshly-trimmed in the latest style, a narrow band that followed the contour of his jaw. He looked so unlike his usual scruffy self that Jorn did a double-take, and offered a respectful bow.

"My word, M'sar, you look very smart."

He grinned. "Borrowed from Brand. I can do the court stuff too, when I must. My clients don't all require their hired help to be rough, tough and dirty. I act as bodyguard sometimes, for young, rich women whose parents assume that any man in sight is either bound on ravishing them or making off with the family jewels, or both. I dance well, I can prattle scandal, fuss over my lady's lapdog, and even serve her dainties at the table. A little charm and polish goes a long way."

Jorn raised his eyebrows in amused speculation. "A job with a few perks on the side, I assume?"

"Oh no, my clients are firmly out of bounds; I never mix business with pleasure," Braid responded, with perfect seriousness. And then he winked. "But of course, there are other opportunities. Now let me introduce you to Arnori Borodin."

The eldest brother was fast shaping into the image of his father — tall, thickset, with a full beard, now touched with grey. He greeted Jorn warmly, introduced his wife, Arnora Margaret, and said all the expected conventional things about Jorn having the undying thanks of the whole Darnell Clan for having saved Brendan's life. Jorn nodded and made polite responses as he was towed round the room for more introductions, and smiled until his cheeks felt stiff. He wished he was anywhere but here in this hot, crowded room.

Brogan was a quieter, older version of Braidart and had an attractive wife named Judith, who turned heads in a stunning, low-cut ruby red dress. Boris was so like Brogan that he could be his twin, and, as Jorn later discovered, was. Brett looked well into middle-age, but still very slim and fit; he was dressed less elaborately, in muted browns, and stood quietly on one side with his young wife, Anna.

Brand turned out to be the odd one out; a solid, almost plump, young man, dressed in high style. Jorn studied the man from across the room, and really couldn't credit that he was a Darnell, apart, of course, from the nose. He took in the peacock blue frock coat with its lavishly pleated skirt, featuring a tight collar that came up past Brand's ears at the back, and left him straining over it to sip his wine. Lace fountained out of the sleeves, and his skin-tight blue satin britches were buckled over white silk stockings. He glittered with jewelled buttons and shoe ornaments, his fingers loaded with many rings, and a diamond stud pierced his nose. Jorn stared at this apparition from a fashion-plate, and remembered his manners just in time to hide his amusement with a neat bow when the nobleman glanced across and caught his eye. Brand returned a flourishing salutation.

Beatrice and Brendan came in together. Beatrice had her glossy black hair dressed in ringlets and wore a turquoise gown made from a fine satin, which Jorn knew would have cost a small fortune. Other guests arrived, including Philip, Kayman, Clarriss, Rolf and Mordant. The halfer wore a black dress, which, for once, revealed her figure, and had woven a light glamour to disguise her raash features. Jorn thought it was tactful of her in the circumstances.

Bea made a point of coming over to talk to him. After a few light remarks, Jorn enquired, "Why do all your names begin with B?"

"Ah, that is a long-standing family tradition. It can get quite confusing!"

Beatrice chattered merrily and made sure that she was seated beside him during the long meal. Philip took his place across the table from them, and was plainly enjoying his own role as hero. Jorn soon discovered, to his well-concealed dismay, that Bea was intent on pumping him for information that he was unable or unwilling to provide.

"I want to know all about you!" she told him. "How long have you been a mage? You are young to be so skilled."

"Not long, and I'm still learning."

"But you healed Brendan when no one else could. Everyone says it was quite remarkable."

He made a throwaway gesture. "Beginners' luck."

"I don't think I believe that! You are far too modest. And what is this quest you are all on? I've tried asking Braid but he clams up on me."

"And so must I," Jorn responded.

"Grrr! I hate secrets!" she pouted prettily, and gave him a well-practised, wheedling look. When that produced no further response, she tried another tack. "So where do you get your gorgeous dark red hair and emerald eyes? Is that from your father or your mother?"

Jorn was on the brink of answering when a sharp tweak of warning from his sense reminded him that this too would lead into dangerous territory. "Oh, I never knew my real parents," he prevaricated. "I was fostered as a baby."

"So where did you live?"

He decided that this was probably safe enough, and took his time, between mouthfuls, to explain about his life. Bea listened attentively as he described his home and family, and the weaving trade, and the final tragedy of the raash attack that left him bereft of his foster kin.

"Then we have much in common," she said, gravely.

"Yes. Only you still have your brothers, and I have lost mine, and my baby sister too. They were not blood-kin, but we were really close. I played with them, shared things, fought with them — like any kids do — but we always made up in the end. The last day we had together, I took the boys to the fair. They were so happy. It's worse because I don't know what happened to them, so I can't help imagining dreadful things. I was so looking forward to seeing Rob and Red, and little Polly, grow up, and to having them as friends when they were older. Now I have no one who is family, except for my guardian, Rolf, who's always been like an uncle. But this is no time for me to be loading you with my sad memories when you have enough of your own. Let's talk of other things. I love the colour you are wearing. Where did you get the satin?"

Fortunately, Bea was easily diverted into a discussion of current fashion and fabrics, and after the main course, the speeches started, easing the pressure of keeping up a polite, innocuous conversation.

Borodin began by making a rather long speech about his father, cleverly mixing amusing family memories, and a resume of the Arnori's life and achievements. "To Barrass!" he ended, raising his goblet for a formal toast.

After dessert, Brett made a shorter speech, welcoming Borodin as the new Clan-Lord and High Governor of Dart, at which point everyone rose, cheering and clapping.

Finally, as the cheeses and fruits arrived, Borodin rose to propose yet another toast, this time to Jorn and Philip, "The saviours of our Clan." Everyone rose to offer their salutations and there was another round of spontaneous applause. Jorn went pink and found it all very embarrassing, but Philip beamed and soaked up the admiration.

As soon as the meal had ended, Jorn pleaded tiredness, which was not entirely untrue, and left with as much haste as etiquette permitted. He felt oppressed by the closeness of the huge Darnell Clan, which made his own isolation more apparent, and keeping up social appearances and making the right responses to Bea had been hard work, although it was flattering to be the centre of her attention for the evening.

Chapter 15

The attack on Darnell Hold had marked a new phase in the war with the raash, and every mage in the Hall knew it. Darric had regained the Wand and that was a devastating blow. He had already demonstrated that he had the Power and desire to launch a serious attack on Earth. The place was abuzz with rumours and anxious discussion, as mages and students speculated about what would happen next, and what Kayman might do about it.

The High Master himself was wondering that as well. He paced his study, a frown stitching his eyebrows together, wearing an expression of angry frustration. The theft of the Wand was a disaster. He couldn't understand how Darric had known to target the Hold, but he was sure the whole attack was a deliberate attempt to take the Tool. Both he and Barrass had underestimated the danger, and the Darnells had paid a heavy price, for which he was in part to blame.

The only gleam in the gloom was that the attack had finally provided evidence of Darric's lethal capabilities. The other Council Members could no longer deny it. He had informed the High Council about the firestorm in graphic terms, asking Turner to convene for an urgent meeting. He couldn't see how Turner could refuse, and his past lobbying and the imminent danger might sway enough of the doubters, but whatever action the Council took, it would be too little and too late.

He snorted angrily. *Which won't stop me trying to do something on my own! There are rulers who might sit up and take notice now that one of their own kind has been attacked. Emperor Malchious might finally be persuaded to get his armies onto full alert.*

He gave up on his restless patrol and sat in his chair, considering. It was the problem of the spy that concerned him right now. There had to be one, and far too close for comfort. His sense was tweaking urgently. He called Rolf to join him.

"Rolf, I can't get it out of my mind that we have a raash spy in our midst. I know that Idris Read every person in the Hall, and we weeded out a couple students, and a domestic, but they were small fry. There is someone clever out there, in deep cover, who knows exactly what is going on here and is in a position to get sensitive information and pass it on to Darric.

The raash got a hook for Arden; don't tell me that was just luck. The envoy knew J'Louth by name. He was certain that the Cup is in Arden, even though he did not know that Idris is the Warden and, apart from the High Council, no one knows that. In this last raid, the raash portalled direct to Darnell Hold, and even into the inner bailey, so again, they had the hooks. And I don't believe for a moment that finding the Wand was just a lucky accident. Darric knew, or at least had made a very good guess, that it would be there. Yet only Barrass and I knew that I had left it in the deep vaults under the Round Tower. Am I wrong in my suspicions?"

Rolf paused, ran his fingers through his beard, and sighed. "I've been thinking of little else ever since the attack on the Hold. I think you are right; there has to be a spy. If I was Darric, I'd want a constant flow of reliable information about everything that happens here. You are the pivot point for all the efforts to prevent the invasion. This is the most powerful centre for our craft in three universes, whatever our colleagues at the University of Errington might claim. And you are right that this spy, or spies, must have been here for a long time, in deep cover. Mordant has told us that the raash breeding programme succeeded in producing a few mage-spies who look completely human, but have raash minds and skills. We would never notice such a person. They are so familiar and so well-trusted that we don't give them a second glance."

"Well, you are a spy. Where would you choose to be?"

"Not here at the Hall, but somewhere closely connected with it. A place where I could monitor all the comings and goings. Somewhere that has records that I could analyse, correspondence I could intercept. People I could chat to, casually, just passing the time of day in a friendly fashion, picking up gossip and sifting it. Maybe the chance to pick up a stray, unshielded thought. You've already pointed out how the raash have gained hooks to places they could not reach by simple trial and error. There is one very obvious location for all of that. A Transit Point."

Kayman thumped his fist on his desk, making the inkwell jump. "Powers, Rolf you are right! But all our Transit-Masters and the other mages who staff the Points have been there for years and are totally trustworthy."

"Precisely," agreed Rolf. "That's exactly the kind of person we are looking for."

"But surely Idris would have spotted whoever it is by now? He would immediately see if an aura was hidden."

"Idris always uses the Dolphin Transit Point, because of the fountain, so the mages there are likely to be in the clear. But remember, he has only recently returned to Mage Hall, so he has not used the other Points much, if at all, for many years. The Point most regularly used by myself and the rest of our team is the Horse."

"But that's Philip's. He's been there for years. Probably the most efficient Transit-Master we have. And he rescued the Darnells."

"Yes, he did, and they think he's a hero. But can you think of a better way to get himself accepted and included in our counsels? He has been at the Hall frequently since the attack, and the Darnells trust him completely. Who knows what else he may have picked up? I'm afraid he is my best candidate. The fastest way to find out if I'm right is to get Idris to take a look at him. I'll bet a hundred in gold that he'll find that Philip conceals his aura."

"I sincerely hope you are wrong, but yes, we must do that, and quickly. Once we know who it is, we can start to use him. I have some secret plans in hand, which require a false trail to be laid. Being able to feed information direct to one of Darric's top spies would be ideal."

"So what's your next move?"

"I am going to call a Conclave of my Inner Council, and a few carefully chosen guests. That way, I can involve the people I want to be there, chair the meeting, and keep Turner well out of it. That will provide me with the platform that I need for my other schemes. I'll ensure that Philip is there, and Idris. We'll know the truth by the end of the meeting."

"Clearly you are not going to discuss the quest. But what about our Master of Nine? Are you going to tell them we have one?"

"Not yet. Having a Nine in residence runs counter to the deception that I'm planning. I am sorry to be so mysterious, old friend, but it is better that even you do not know the whole of my strategy at this stage."

*

The ruined city stretched in all directions; a mess of fallen masonry, twisted metal and charred timbers, yet enough still stood, one or even two storeys high, to show its lost glory. Sand and dust had mounded in the corners. No encroaching weeds or vines threw soft drapes to mask the devastation. There was scarcely a blade of green in this arid landscape. The sun glared out of a brazen sky.

A portal opened. Darric stepped through, followed by Ajina and a minimal escort of their honour guard; two carrying folding chairs, and one, a box. Darric strode a few steps across the cracked paving and looked around, his eyes narrowed in consideration.

Ajina gazed around her and spoke regretfully. "This was a beautiful city once, 400 years ago. Filled with spires and towers, joined by walkways, hung across dizzying voids. There were squares and fountains, gardens and pillared cloisters. All gone. We could not build the like in this age. It makes me sad to see it."

"You imagination gilds it, sister. For all you know, the drains stank. And if we wish to build such another, we will do so, not here on Vard, but on Earth. Humans are fine masons. I too have no love of places such as this, which speak of what we have long lost, but we need somewhere to experiment. Enough stands to provide us with a target. Let us see how well we can wreck it."

He clicked his fingers and the guard captain brought him a steel box. The Mage-Lord opened it and brought out the Knife, Chain and Wand. Darric took the Knife in his right hand and hung the Chain around his neck. Ajina took the Wand.

"We will engage with the Tools, as we have done before when we made the war-hammer. This time, we add the Wand. Earth, Air and Fire should be a powerful combination. I have in mind a War-Wind, combined with Wild-Fire, and perhaps an Earth-Shaker. It will take some time to do the working. We may as well be seated.

Some quarter of a glass later, they both had a construct hung ready to deploy. Between them, they were able to use all nine colours. They stood, and ordered the guards to retreat to a safer distance. They had triple-warded themselves.

Darric took the heavy Chain from his neck, wound it around his left hand, and turned his will upon it. He felt the thin rising hum of Power as a vibration in his fingers. He focussed on the Knife and it glowed with a ruby flame. The hilt quivered. Ajina had engaged with the Wand. Colours rose and twisted, red, ether, yellow, and alongside them, thin tendrils of a darkness so deep it defied sight. The humming rose in pitch.

"Now," Darric commanded, and deployed his construct. Ajina released her own at the same time. The two intricate webs linked and merged, sucking the conflicting energies of the Tools into their meshes. Brother and sister strained to retain control as the dark energy twined and buffeted the strands of light. Finally, they stretched out their arms in a thrusting motion and let the constructs release, arrowing towards the ruins, pointing the Tools to direct the forces away from themselves.

The construct reached the nearest structures. The ground shook beneath their feet. There was an instant of total stillness and then a crack zigzagged across the square, the tremors almost throwing them off their feet, and an enormous shockwave of wind and fire blasted across the city, levelling everything in its path in a tumult of destruction. When the force-field dissipated, there was nothing in front of them but a plain of fine rubble.

Darric and Ajina sagged with the release of tension and the backlash of Power, and slumped back unto their chairs. Finally, Darric straightened and let out a deep breath of satisfaction.

"That will serve, I think. That will do very well indeed."

*

Kayman's invitations were sent out, and two days later, his visitors arrived at Mage Hall for the Conclave. Rolf had explained that this was a formal meeting of Kayman's closest advisors, allies and some invited guests. Jorn satisfied his curiosity by watching the courtyard from his bedroom window, hidden by a never-mind.

Arnori Borodin was early. He came through a portal with apparent discomfort, followed by Braidart, and Philip, who must have worked the translocation. The Darnells both sat on a bench and took time to recover. Braidart was dressed in a scarlet and black uniform; on duty as his father's honour guard, he was armed with his sword and a pair of daggers.

A clatter of hooves through the gatehouse arch heralded the appearance of the dwarran queen's carriage, and Kayman hurried out to greet her in person. Jorn was very curious to see Eldessa Maria. Rolf had told him she was a force to be reckoned with, and had a reputation for being shrewd and highly competent.

The elderly dwar was accompanied by four hefty dwarran guards, wearing black-lacquered mail, who lined up to salute as she carefully alighted down the steps provided by her footman. Commander Clarriss followed her out in full dress uniform. The Eldessa was short, even by dwarran standards, and somewhat plump, her white hair coiffured with many braids, pinned with gems. She permitted Kayman to touch his lips to the tips of her white-gloved and ringed fingers, and smiled with gracious acknowledgement before sweeping into the building, her green and gold robe billowing behind her.

She certainly does looks formidable. Another dwarran carriage arrived. Two mages that Jorn did not know portalled in soon after. He reluctantly left the window. *Well, much though I'd love to be a fly on the wall in the Conference Room, that is all I'm going to see for now.* Jorn turned away from his window and resolved to get all the details later.

*

The Conclave began at noon. The Eldessa Maria was ushered in by Kayman, with Clarriss two paces behind. The Eldessa had also brought her Chief Minister with her, who sat tight-lipped and silent at her side, her eyes evaluating everyone in the room.

Idris, Mordant and Rolf arrived, together with Maeve and Rome, Kayman's senior Adepts. Two strangers introduced themselves as representatives from the University of Erren, Doctors Martin and Edwards.

"The one called Edwards is a powerful Eight and he is hiding something," Idris told Rolf. *"The other seems a quite ordinary Seven."*

Arnori Borodin strode in with Braidart, followed by Philip.

Rolf waited tensely for Idris to read Philip's aura. *"You are right. He hides his aura. He is certainly not to be trusted."*

"Powers! I hoped I was wrong. He is well-placed to do us a great deal of damage."

"I was right. Philip has no aura. Idris does not trust him at all," Rolf told Kayman.

The High Master made no response, but bent his head in discussion with the Eldessa on his right and then Arnori Borodin on his left.

The Eldessa looked pointedly at the clock on the far wall, which showed two minutes past the hour, and said in a carrying voice, "We will begin."

Kayman nodded. If he had thought he was taking the meeting, he found himself mistaken. The Eldessa cleared her throat quite softly and an instant hush fell.

"We are gathered, as I have been informed by High Master Kayman, to hear of a threat posed to our Realm by the raash. Kayman, be so good as to explain the situation briefly to the Conclave." The emphasis on the word 'briefly' was subtle but explicit.

The High Master rose, inclining his head courteously to the Eldessa on one side and Borodin on the other. "Honoured Madam, Arnori, mages; briefly then," the emphasis was equally pointed, "we face a most serious situation. Darnell Hold has been attacked. In the course of that, the Wand has been stolen." There were muted gasps from those to whom this was news. Kayman gave a terse account of the horrific use of fire and magecraft. "In the past, the High Council of Mages have demanded evidence that the threat from Darric is real and immediate. I would a thousand times rather have no evidence than anything so shocking, but it is plain for all to see. I have informed Professor Turner, but so far, I have had no response. Mordant, you know the raash Lord better than most of us. He will attack Earth, won't he?"

"He will attack. With the Wand, Chain and Knife, his Power of Eight is hugely augmented. Between them, Darric and Ajina effectively Master the Nine. The raash army is ready, and there is a limit to how long he can keep it standing by. Like any War-Lord, Darric will likely wait until spring before launching his invasion, but attack he will, we can be sure of that, and as we all know, now that he has three Tools, there is very little we can do to stop him."

There was more anxious murmuring. Kayman looked grim.

"Winter is our friend at the moment, but Darric will want to keep the pressure on us. I believe that Mage Hall itself may be his next target."

"That would be logical," agreed Clarriss. "He has much to gain by eliminating his most able and active opponents."

"I have been aware of that for some considerable time," responded Kayman. "We have many treasures here that they would no doubt wish to get their hands on, but of course, more than that, they wish to eliminate our power base. And they still seek the Cup."

"But it is not here, surely?" asked Doctor Martin.

"With the greatest respect, Doctor, you do not seriously expect me to answer that question?" said Kayman. "Some of you know that the raash tried to terrorise the shians into giving it to them. Since then, we have taken what measures we could to ensure its safety. I will leave it at that. But whether it is here or not, if the raash think it might be, it will give them an added reason to assault the Hall."

"But are you not well-defended?" demanded the Eldessa.

"Of course. With as much art as our Adepts can manage. But having seen what happened at the Hold, I fear that may not be enough."

"And I can only support that view," affirmed Borodin. "Our Hold had not been entered by an enemy for over 500 years. The walls are six ems thick and they breached them in less than 30 minutes. The firestorm was terrifying."

"Exactly; so the Hall is undoubtedly at risk. Arnori, you and your families cannot find sanctuary here much longer."

"But the Hold will take many moons to repair; where can we find safety?"

"I suggest Errington. I have a good relationship with the President and he owes me a favour. If you agree, I will acquire a suitable residence for you and Philip can portal you all out as soon as I have the arrangements in place."

"But if Mage Hall is to be attacked, won't the School at Errington soon follow?"

"We believe that it will not, at least, not soon. It would be a costly battle and if Darric attacks Errington, the President will call on his allies and Darric will have a human army to contend with. He will hope to postpone that event until after he has secured some strongholds elsewhere."

"Your analysis is correct High Master," agreed Doctor Martin, "and we have little to interest him. Errington is as safe as anywhere can be in these dangerous times."

"Then we gratefully accept, and we are in your debt again, High Master." Borodin paused; he looked round at the assembled company and spoke with frustrated anger. "Kayman, we Darnells all want the same thing. We want revenge for our murdered Sire, and the ruin of our home."

"I sympathise, but for the moment, there is no way to achieve that. We have to concentrate on defending Mage Hall and what it contains."

"Perhaps a small deception?" suggested Eldessa Maria. "We can assume that the raash have spies. Let us appear to convey your treasures into the deepest vaults in my Realm, and secure them with many strong wardweaves and an armed guard. Then, if they seek a target to attack, they have one."

"But you are using yourselves as bait," objected Borodin. "I have seen what these demons can do."

"I too know what they can do, Arnori. But we are not totally defenceless," responded the Eldessa tartly. "We dwarrans are capable of a few surprises that may yet cause some furrowed brows on the enemy side."

"Ma'am, you are mistaken." Mordant's assertion raised the royal eyebrows to new heights. "Raash lack the ability to produce a furrowed brow. I doubt if any subterfuge we can think of will furrow anything, either literally or metaphorically. All our options for securing the Hall and its contents are bad. All we can do is choose the least unappealing. A deception may draw off some of their forces, but it is a serious risk to your troops."

Clarriss looked doubtful. "It's a high risk strategy, but we must protect the Hall."

"High risk seems to be the only kind we have left," said Braidart.

The Errenish mages had been engaged in silent communication. Dr Martin looked at Kayman.

"If you do have some *'treasure'* here," he loaded the word with meaning, "would it not be safer with us in the University?"

Kayman was saved from a reply by the Eldessa, who felt no need to be tactful. "My dear man, if the mages at Errington could not keep hold of the Wand when Turner had it, why do you suppose that Kayman would trust you with anything else — assuming of course that he might have such a thing."

"Well, the Warden of the Wand has not done much of a job keeping it safe subsequently," snapped Edwards. "And those of us with longer memories will recall that the Warden of the Chain did no better with his charge."

"All the more reason to see that no other 'treasures' are taken," retorted the Eldessa. "And we must trust that the Warden of the Cup, whoever that may be, is more efficient. In any case, what better way to ensure that Darric will next target the University?"

There was a long, uncomfortable, silence.

"Ahem." Dr Edwards cleared his throat rather theatrically. "While we are here, we wish to raise another matter. It has come to our attention that one of your close associates, and his talented apprentice," he stared pointedly at Rolf and Jorn, "are looking for something. Would the High Master be prepared to confirm that, and to enlighten us as to what it may be?"

"The High Master would not," responded Kayman firmly.

There was another half an hour of tense and somewhat acrimonious argument, which resulted in little agreement other than a grim acknowledgement that the danger of invasion was real and imminent, and the Hall must be protected. The general state of readiness of the dwarran army would also be raised to Condition Red.

Finally, Kayman said firmly, "I do not think that continuing our debate will be productive. If there is no further business, I will close the meeting and thank you for your attendance."

There was a general scraping of chairs as people rose to go.

"Could have done without the last half hour," remarked Rolf.

"Yes, and without Dr Edward's not very innocent question about the quest. But it was bound to come up. I've said all along that it's impossible to keep all our affairs secret. Well, I set the trap. Whether Philip will take the bait remains to be seen."

"I'll refrain from asking exactly what trap you set, old friend. And you are assuming it is Philip. We cannot yet be certain. And if he is a spy, it doesn't mean that he is the only one," cautioned Rolf.

"It is as well that there was no other Reader of auras in the room High Master," said Idris, "Yours was flickering with deceit."

"Yes; you were distinctly economical with the truth."

Kayman grinned. "Forgive me, my friends. Allow an old mage to have a few secrets! You'll find out in good time. But that comment of Borodin's about wanting to attack Darric has set me thinking. We need to do something to delay Darric. An attack on Vard might be just the thing, but we have to time it carefully. I must talk to Mordant."

"And I must get on with the next stage of our mission. I've asked the team to meet me in an hour."

"I'll join you. They need to know about Philip."

*

The team had gathered in the small meeting room, where an atmosphere of tense expectation lay heavy. Everyone wanted to get on with the quest, and were aware that time for its completion was fast running out. Darric would attack as soon as winter lifted.

Jorn smiled at Braid as he came in. "Full uniform today, I see?"

"Well, Borodin's a ruler in his own right, he wasn't about to let the Eldessa steal all the pomp!"

"So what happened at the meeting?"

Braid shrugged. "On the surface, it was all about the need to defend Mage Hall from the raash, which in my view won't be easy, but there were all kinds of undercurrents I didn't quite understand. At one point, Kayman seemed to be dropping hints that a Cup might be hidden here.

And then there was a bit of a dog fight between him and the Errenish. Kayman is playing some kind of devious game, but I'm not too sure what it is. He certainly isn't going to tell us until he is good and ready, if he ever is. Oh, and he's going to arrange for our family to move to Errington; he thinks it will be safer."

At that point, the High Master bustled in. Kayman sat down and surveyed the company with a grim expression. "Well, my friends, I have to begin with a somewhat shattering revelation. As of two hours ago, Rolf and I are reasonably certain that we have discovered the identity of the main raash agent. We think it's Philip, the Transit-Master at the Horse."

The team all winced at the disastrous implications. Jorn felt a jolt of dismay as he realised that Philip had been perfectly placed to overhear his conversation with Bea at the wake. He could so easily have responded casually to her innocent curiosity and said too much, revealing the nature of the quest or his own Power.

Braidart shook his head in shocked disbelief. "But he can't be a spy!" he exclaimed. "He rescued my kin, and he's been so helpful ever since. And he looks completely normal... erm, human, I mean," he corrected hastily.

"Darric has been trying to breed halfer mages like that for years," Mordant told him crisply. "I'll bet that Philip is one of his 'successes'."

"And being trusted and relied upon is precisely what a good agent would aim for," agreed Clarriss.

"Well, we had our suspicions, if only by a process of elimination. Idris has just confirmed them."

"The man conceals his aura. No one does that unless he has a great deal to hide."

"Can we use him?" asked Clarriss.

"I intend to, for a while," Kayman told them. "But he must be eliminated before too long. However, I need more proof, and I have taken steps to obtain it."

"We must avoid using that Transit Point," warned Mordant. "At least for anything sensitive. We can't stop using it altogether; it would indicate suspicion."

"You are right. But Philip will shortly be fully occupied for several days, translocating the Darnell Clan to a new home in Errington. Anyway, you now know."

"I must tell my kin at once," said Braid, who still sounded stunned. "They can't have a spy in the house."

"Braid, I'm afraid that's just what you can't do. We mustn't alarm him, and if we either send him away, or he's there with the Darnells all giving him the bad eye, he'll know at once that we are suspicious. We have to keep this quiet until we are certain one way or another. And a known spy has his uses."

"I still find it hard to believe. I mean, how could he have known about the Wand being hidden at the Hold?" asked Jorn.

"I agree that's a puzzle. It's been safely hidden there for almost 20 years. No one except Arnori Barrass, Kayman and I knew that. We knew the raash would consider the Hold an important target because Barrass and his clan have been planting thorns in their hides for years, but we both thought the Hold was impregnable, which was plainly a serious miscalculation. Well, 'hindsight is the wisdom of fools'. It could just be an unfortunate coincidence that they discovered the Wand in the course of the raid, but I suspect they knew exactly what they were doing. Perhaps Philip made an educated guess?"

"Or maybe he is a far-seer, or as good at dowsing for hidden objects as Jorn is," suggested Mordant.

"Be that as it may," said Kayman, "done is done. Philip is a separate problem."

Braid gave an angry snort. "If I find that he is responsible for the destruction of the Hold and the death of my father, I demand the right to kill him myself. It is a matter of family honour."

Kayman nodded. "I understand M'sar. But we'll have to deal with that as circumstances permit. Now, back to the mission plan. What's the next move?"

"It would help if we actually knew where we have to go next," said Rolf. "And I confess that I'm stuck. Has anyone else got any ideas?"

"Well, I've been doing some more research in the last few days, and I just might have a tenuous lead on the 'dry kings lie sleeping' line," responded Mordant. "It may possibly refer to the Mausoleums of Karth. Long ago, the Karthians took their dead kings out into the desert where they buried them in hot, dry sand so that natural mummification took place. Then they were dug up and interred in huge Mausoleums. If I remember rightly, four were still standing in Myron's time, although the old Karthian civilisation had ceased to exist by then. They once occupied the area to the south of the Inner Sea, across the Narrows, now known as Kardash."

Kayman beamed. "That does sound promising! Surely even after a thousand years, monumental tombs should not be too difficult to find?"

"Unfortunately, you are wrong," responded Rolf. "I know that area. For a start, the desert is very remote and difficult to reach. The sands have extended steadily over the centuries and now form huge, constantly moving, dune systems. If the Mausoleums do stand, they could be buried under mountains of sand. And needless to say, it is furnace-hot for most of the year."

Jorn saw Idris shift uncomfortably. The shian took a long drink of water and refilled his glass. Kayman had again provided a large bath of water for him to dangle his feet in, so he didn't have to leave too soon. He sensed Jorn's eyes on him.

"Deserts and shians of the water do not mix," he sent.

"Of course, I'd have to do some more research to see if the ruins still exist and what is known about them," Mordant said, a bit deflated.

"Well, it's a lead, so thank you Mordant. At this stage, we have to follow up anything that looks remotely promising. What does your sense tell you Jorn?" asked Kayman.

"Nothing definite yet, but I'm not getting any negatives. If you can find a map, or an image, I'll dowse it and see what the horn has to tell me."

"I assume there is nothing in the Library here on the mausoleums?" asked Clarriss.

"No. Which means that we probably need to go to the University of Errington," responded Mordant.

"By the Powers! Turner won't allow us within a hundred kays of the place after what happened at the last meeting of the High Council. Especially now he blames me for losing the Wand," exclaimed Kayman.

Rolf sighed. "I know. It's an added problem we could well do without. Mordant, you have an identity that will allow you into the Library of the Mage School, don't you?"

"Yes, I do. But I don't think that a secret trawl will be enough this time. I fear we must swallow our pride and seek the help of Professor Sturminster. She may not be the easiest person to get along with, but she is very knowledgeable, and she is as committed to the fight against the raash as you are, Kayman. And she doesn't like Turner. She may be a professor now, but that's not enough for her. She keeps hoping he'll retire and give her a chance to be head of department, and of course, High Mistress of the Errington Mage School as well. If we make it seem to her advantage, she may agree to help, or at least not get in the way."

"Can we be sure of that?" asked Clarriss "We have one spy, but there may be more at Errington. It might be Sturminster herself."

"There undoubtedly are spies at Errington," agreed Rolf, "and Professor Sturminster may or may not be aware of them, though I doubt if she is one of them. My chief suspects there are Martin and Edwards. I've had them under surveillance for several years, which is why I asked Kayman to invite them. Now that Idris has seen a block across Edward's aura, my money is on him. But despite that, we need to find information about the mausoleums, and if the best place is Errington, then that is where we will have to go."

"And you may be able to ask about something else while you are there. You remember the line about 'burning ice and freezing fire'?" said Kayman. "I have been mulling that over. It might just refer to The Burning Coast."

"Isn't that somewhere in the far North, up on the edge of the Great Ice?" asked Mordant.

"Yes it is. It's long coastline of a big, largely unexplored country, most of which is still beneath the Ice. Very unstable area with active volcanoes, glaciers, hot steam gushing out of the ground. We need to know if there is anything in the region that might possibly be described as 'Earth's opposites'."

Rolf pulled a face. "Well, Errington it is. I'll just have to eat a large helping of humble pie. And if worst comes to worst, we'll have to use glamours and sneak in and hope no one notices."

Kayman grinned. "Cheer up, old friend. The fact that I too have failed to safeguard the Wand may encourage some fellow-feeling from her. Now, we come to the piece of the Juncture we have already found. I don't like keeping it at Mage Hall; we can't just let Jorn hide it under his bed."

"I'm not quite doing that," Jorn responded with a smile. "I am not letting it out of my sight. Would you like to see it?"

He rummaged in a bag hung from his belt and pulled out a rusty caltrop. Then he reached into his purse and fished out a faintly blue pebble. The mages looked at the object with great interest.

"A subtle disguise," Mordant approved. "I can't even sense it is there."

"Which is the whole idea. I have chosen forms that are as close as possible to the reality, and I have used the finest possible thread of glamour. I have removed the sapphire: the copper clasp is quite easy to bend apart. I thought it was safer to keep the jewel separate from the metalwork. I doubt if anyone will look twice at these boyhood curiosities carried by a mage apprentice."

"Good. I think you are wise to keep it close to you. So, that's settled then. Next stage, Errington, to do our research, and try to get Angela

Sturminster on our side. After that, we hope, the Mausoleums of Karth. Winter is the best time to go to Kadesh; the heat will be more bearable."

"Agreed," said Kayman. "So, Rolf, who is going to the University?"

"Me and Jorn for a start." He looked across at Clarriss and raised enquiring eyebrows, but the dwar shook her head. "I have already been away from my desk for too long. Reports will be piling up, and they may hold points of interest. I'll join you on the next leg in Karth, if you want me, but I'll opt out of the research phase."

"Pity, but I understand. What about you, Idris?"

The shian shook his head. "It's all too dry for me, both literally and metaphorically. I will sit this one out. We can talk about the next stage when you have decided for certain where you are going."

"I'd like to be involved," said Braidart, "and I'll be right on the doorstep anyway if we all move to Errington."

Kayman looked enquiringly at Mordant but the halfer shook her head. "If you need me, I'll join you later, but I too have to catch up with my own spy network. In any case, initially, I had better keep out of Angela Sturminster's way. If I wear a glamour, she'll be suspicious, and if I don't, she'll wonder what the hell a raash halfer is doing mixed up in all this. If you need me to do some more research in the archives, I'll go back to my disguise as old Doctor Barnes."

"Right, that's settled," said Kayman decisively. "You should leave straight after the Longest Night. We could all do with a short break, but apart from wanting to get on with the quest as fast as possible, there are good reasons not to have you here at the Hall much longer."

Jorn let the last cryptic comment pass. He had taken little part in the discussion, but he was glad to know that they would soon be on the move again. "Idris, could you supervise me while I construct a portal? I've been practicing hard for the Dolphin Transit Point. I really need to do that before we leave."

The shian mage gave him a considering stare. "You are right. It is time you put theory into practice. I would have done it before, but we have had other things to deal with. I will need to run through the construct with you first, in some detail. No time like the present. Come to the Yew Close and we will see what you can do."

Jorn followed, feeling nervous. Even Rolf and Mordant had to concentrate hard each time they worked a translocation, and Idris had already warned Jorn that the first attempt could occasionally be fatal. But it had to be done. If he could not manage that working, he had little hope of being the Master that they all expected him to be. And Idris had made it clear that the horn could not help him here.

They had been through the construct before, but Idris insisted on Jorn describing it again, one stage at a time.

He nodded in approval. "Excellent. So, all you have to do now is make the working. Just concentrate and focus. I know you can do that. When you have opened the portal, I will look through and check it opens where it should do. I have every confidence in your abilities, but I believe in belts and braces, so I will fix a tether for myself. It will pull me straight back if there is any problem."

Jon nodded. "Then I'm ready when you are." He engaged with his Quincunx, binding yellow, orange, green and violet into the tightly-twisted ropes that would form the structure of the gate. He began the portal carefully, making sure that the doorway was a good size with straight sides and a level top. It formed before him on the grass and, after a moment, looked solid. At present, however, it simply showed the grassy stretch of lawn extending through it and the Close beyond. He projected his tightly-focussed will through the doorway, sensing pressing darkness ahead on both sides, but in between, he found the smallest chink of light. There was a moment of resistance, and then a kind of pop as he passed the dangerous pinch point between the Chaos Zones. The familiar swirling fog now obscured the way through.

He had his second construct — the tightly-braided 'fishing line' — hung ready. He imagined his hook, the ornate dolphin fountain. He projected the twisted braid through the portal, sending his focussed will along the thick thread until felt it catch the hook. He pulled his awareness back into his body, leaving the trail of woven braid extending through the portal like a guide rope.

"Good to cross?"

Jorn nodded, feeling the drain on his power as he supported the framework and maintained the connection. Idris went to the portal, pushed his head forward, and then drew it back, beaming broadly.

"Well done, Jorn. Right on target. You can close it down now."

Jorn let the portal collapse. He felt tired, but not exhausted, and very pleased with his effort. But the energy drain from the working had shown him just how hard it would be to keep a portal open for more than a short time.

"Thanks, Idris. I feel a bit more like a Master now that I can manage that."

Chapter 16

The Winter Festival was just a week away and, rather to Jorn's surprise, it seemed that Kayman intended to celebrate in traditional style.

"Why?" he asked Rolf. "The Darnells are still in mourning for their father and the others who were killed at the Hold. And we have Darric gearing up for an attack at any moment. It doesn't seem a good time to have a party when we ought to be getting on with the quest."

"The University of Errington closes down for the whole week, along with most of the City, so we can't go there right now. We don't keep up the whole Festival, but it's a tradition at the Hall to celebrate Longest Night in the human style. And we have the Darnell children to consider; they need cheering up. Kayman says we should not allow Darric to take all the joy out of life. We have to hang onto the good things; it's what we are fighting for after all. We have earned a night off."

"I suppose so. But I can't say I feel very festive myself. It won't feel right without my foster family. I'm going to be thinking about all the fun we used to have, with the kids running wild with excitement. I can't bear the thought that, if they are still alive, Rob and Red might be hacking away at some mine under an overseer's lash."

"I understand. But perhaps it is time to start some new, good memories?"

"Maybe. I guess I'd better do some shopping for Long Night gifts. Only…"

"You need coin," completed Rolf with a grin. "Not a problem, but remember, just one gift per person, and nothing too expensive."

*

On Long Night, people started to gather in the refectory, which had been cleared for the occasion. The High Master had certainly done his best, bringing in garlands of holly berries and ivy, and branches of fir and pine, and a tree decked with candles and gilded ornaments. There were extra lamps, blazing fires, and traditional sweets and savouries that the Mage Hall cooks had spent days preparing.

Mages and students mixed with staff and servants. The resident Darnells were there, with several excited children. Mordant had come, and stayed close to Braidart, again wearing a tactful glamour to hide her looks. Bea was in scarlet with a low-cut bodice that drew Jorn's eyes; he looked away quickly, but not before she had seen his interest.

He noticed with a grin that Clarriss had also arrived and was keeping near to Rolf. It was much too dry an event to suit Idris and, anyway, shians did not celebrate the four seasonal festivals in the same way as humans did. Philip was making himself quietly useful.

There was a round of applause when Kayman came in with Mara, both dressed all in white as Old Man Winter and his Daughter, wearing wreaths of holly and real icicles. They each carried a bag of gifts to distribute to everyone. These were all the traditional, tiny things, such as gingerbread animals in pairs, puzzle-toys, sweets, riddles, and good-luck-cookies containing charms, which caused a lot of laughter.

After all that, people exchanged presents with close friends and family, one gift per person. Rolf had somehow managed to get a fine pair of walking boots made for Jorn, which were, amazingly, an exact fit. Jorn gave his guardian a new belt with a gold buckle.

Brendan came over to Jorn with a big grin, holding something behind his back. "Braid tells me that he is teaching you to use a sword?"

Jorn nodded. "If we ever find the time."

"Well here is something that may help." Brendan produced a tooled leather sheath and drew out a lethal-looking blade. "It's my own, from a good maker. I'd like you to have it. I found it a new scabbard; the old one was badly charred."

Jorn looked at the fine weapon with appreciation. "Thank you very much M'sar, and a very merry Long Night to you."

Bea came over to find him and playfully pulled him over to stand under the Winter Ring so that she could give him a lingering Long Night kiss.

"Look what I found in my good-luck-cookie!" she told him. She wagged her little finger, showing him a tin ring, and glanced up at him flirtatiously from under her long eyelashes. "And you know what that means! I marry a pauper! What did you get?"

Jorn smiled, trying to ignore his rising interest in her, and took a tiny charm in the shape of a gilded horseshoe out of his pocket. "Good fortune," he told her, "and something tells me I am going to need it!"

She looked at him anxiously. "Is your quest very dangerous?"

"It may be. I really can't talk about it. I'll just be very, very glad when it's all over."

Mordant watched with some amusement; Bea was certainly trying, but not getting very far. The evening had filled her with memories of her first experience of a Long Night party at the Darnell Hold with Brett. The lack of her former lover made her feel lonely. She had friends, but no one to hold her close and share himself with her, and make her feel special.

Idris stirred her feelings at a deep level. He was entirely beautiful, and also a complex and caring person. During the quest to the Caves, she had often imagined being folded into his strong arms, but he was shian, and ultimately alien. After that strange moment of contact in the Cave, she'd tried to get close again, but he'd refused to take her hints. In fact, he almost seemed to be avoiding her. He certainly hadn't allowed her near enough to touch him again, never mind anything more intimate. When he'd heard that the team were going to Errington, he'd almost seemed relieved that he had a solid reason not to come with them.

She sighed and sipped her wine, aware that she had drunk more than she should, and watched Braidart, who was standing by the fire a few steps away, drinking and joking with Brendan. The attractive young nobleman made her laugh, and he expertly roused her desire. He'd made it very plain that he wanted her in his bed.

Tonight, whether it was the wine, or the memories, her need to find out if Braid really was like his brother in more than just looks had grown too strong to ignore. She knew full well that on both sides it was just good, plain lust, seasoned with the spice of curiosity, but it would do. *Maybe a rival would help to rouse Idris' interest?* In any case, one could not have all work and no play, and there was a gap between missions. She drained her glass and put it down, sighed again, and succumbed.

She went over, caught Braid's arm, and said gaily, "Our turn!" She tugged him to stand under the Winter Ring and gave him a long kiss. "You haven't given me a present yet," she chided in mock reproof.

"I know what I want to give you," he told her, "but I couldn't put it in a parcel. You'll have to come up to my room to find it."

She looked at him with amused interest in her violet eyes and purred, "Well, now, Blue Eyes, I do so love a surprise gift. I simply can't imagine what it will be."

She hooked her arm possessively through his and they slipped out together. Rolf noticed, gave a quietly cynical snort, and wondered where that was going to lead, and whether it would affect the mission. Mordant was a professional, but even the best spies could get tangled up in their emotions.

As the party broke up, Kayman, now restored to his usual appearance, came to find Jorn.

"Back to business tomorrow. The sooner you find a hook for the Mausoleum, the better."

"And we are fast running out of time to find the Juncture," said Jorn. "Darric is breathing down our necks. What happens if he arrives before we've found it? I'm still learning the basics. I may have Power, but I'm a long way from knowing how to use it. You need a War-Mage who's as good as Darric, and preferably a lot better. Right now, that isn't me, and I'm not totally sure it ever will be. We need time more than anything. Is there any way we can slow him down?"

"I'm thinking about that. Next year will bring the ending, one way or another, I'm sure of that, but my foresight isn't telling me anything about which way it will go. It will be a race to the finish. Meanwhile, just keep learning as fast as you can. Mordant is the expert on war-hammers and so forth, and Rolf has some nasty tricks. You'll just have to skip the conventional stuff and go straight to the advanced attacking constructs."

"I'll do my best."

"No man or mage can do more."

*

It was not comfortable in the raash Earth Base. The primitive technology available had made lighting and ventilating an underground complex a challenge. The air was fouled with fumes from oil lamps and candles, which covered the walls and ceilings with soot, and it was too hot on the lower levels. Sanitation was basic. The second level down, where Darric and Ajina had their state apartments, had the superficial appearance of elegance and luxury, but they both knew it was a pale imitation of what they were used to, and the less time they had to stay there, the better.

The Mage-Lord of the raash and his Sister Consort sat in a panelled room where a long shaft from the surface gave light to augment the candles, and permitted some freshness in the air. Their Council of War had been brief and to the point. Darric was, for once, fairly satisfied.

"It's a confounded nuisance that the raids on Arden had to be abandoned. Darrison went to much trouble to obtain the hook for the Shian Realm from the Transit-Master at the Dolphin without her realising that he had entered her mind and memory, and I had high hopes. It's a total mystery how the shians are defeating our raids, but plainly they are."

"Well, we can manage without the Cup. The raid on the Darnell Hold went exactly to plan."

"Yes, and that was thanks to Darrison again. His analysis of the Transit Point log books around the time the Wand vanished gave him the clue that Kayman might have taken it to the Hold. It is a source of considerable amusement to me that Kayman has no idea that 'Philip' is in fact my halfer-son. I hope he is able to remain at his post a while longer, but now we have the three Tools, I am ready."

"Yes, and things are ready here too. The humans have no idea that this Base exists. I have 5,000 elite troops in timber barracks in the surrounding forest. We can attack in full force as soon as winter is over." She paused. "But there is one thing bothering me. I have been re-reading one of Darrison's recent reports and my sense is tweaking."

Darric looked at his sister with acute attention. "You have a strong sense. I have learnt to trust it. What troubles you?"

"What, I wonder, is this artefact that Kayman and his odd team are so keen to pursue?"

"Darrison is unsure. It can hardly matter. I will launch the invasion long before they have a chance to find it."

"They are putting in a lot of time and effort; the thing must have some value. I think we ought to eliminate the team to prevent them from finding it. We know the raash-halfer mage can be dangerous. Rolf is a spy. The dwar commander is an unknown. The young Darnell is as bothersome as all his Clan, but he is merely a mercenary. The shian mage has no great power. But the young one, the odd halfer, he is a mystery. Why include a mere apprentice in an important mission? Darrison believes that he has unusual Power, and he observes that Kayman and Rolf treat him with respect. I'd be more comfortable if he was out of the way."

"Well, see that Darrison and our other agents keep a close watch on them. We need to know where they are going next, and what exactly they are looking for. If possible, it would be useful to get a tag onto one of them. Then, we could send in a force and wipe them out."

"I think that would be a good precaution. I don't like loose ends or secret missions that I do not fully understand."

"We will eliminate them. In any case, we have Wand, Knife and Chain. Between us, we Master the Nine. We have 50 years of campaigning experience behind us. Once we launch the invasion, the blob-faces won't have a chance. It won't be long before we can move out of this vile hole in the ground and build that summer palace you fancy so much."

Brother and sister touched hands in a gesture of mutual trust and understanding. Together, they were going to be very hard to beat.

Chapter 17

Darrison, chief spy for his father, Darric, Lord of All Vard, sat in his private sitting room in the Transit Point lodgings, enjoying a good fire as he considered the situation. He munched hungrily on some ham and egg pie. He was bone-weary and his Power was drained, having spent much of the day translocating the last of the Darnell Clan and their servants and baggage to their luxurious, new mansion in the Embassy Quarter of Errington.

His long mission was now reaching a critical stage. His alias as Philip, the Transit Master at the Horse, was wearing thin, but that was to be expected. They were reaching the end game, which was always the time of greatest risk. Now he just had a few final moves to plan.

He reviewed the events of the past six moons, making notes in his neat hand, sipping his ale, and referring to his carefully kept log of all the comings and goings at the Transit Point, and his record of letters and messages, confirming the patterns, looking for anything he might have missed.

Over the period, Kayman's closest associates had portalled in and out of Mage Hall with increasing frequency, intent on urgent business. It had begun last summer, when Rolf had passed through with a newcomer, Jorn, an exceptionally tall, young man with unusual auburn hair and green eyes, who had apparently escaped from a raash raid. It had seemed highly unlikely at the time but he had looked as if he could be a shian halfer. That had been later confirmed by general gossip at the Hall.

After that, it had gone quiet for a bit. He had picked up snippets. Mordant had been busy. Idris, the shian mage, had returned to the Hall after many years of absence. Kayman and his friends were taking a great interest in Jorn.

Then there had been the raash attack on Arden. That had caused considerable dismay and distress, just as his father intended. Members of the High Council of Mages had visited soon after that. Darrison smiled again. He refilled his mug and reached for some apple cake. Apparently, Kayman had been in a simmering fury for days after they left, so whatever he wanted from that meeting had clearly not transpired.

Then, two moons ago, he had twice translocated Rolf to Andrea. The dwarran halfer had come back to the Hall in a hurry soon after the second trip, summoned by the cryptic instruction: 'Found it. Return at once'. Mordant had also returned. So, what did all that signify? Something had been found, but what? Mordant had sent out a coded letter to Brett Darnell.

Unfortunately, this had defied his attempts to decrypt it, but soon afterwards, Mordant had received a reply and then met Braidart, one of the young Darnells, and they had both gone to the Hall, so he had concluded that the message had simply been a summons. Days later, the pair had left again, but as Mordant had formed the onward portal herself, he was not sure of the destination.

His discreet inquiries at the Hall suggested that Rolf and Jorn had also left around the same time. Other fragments had been picked up from chatting with his mage clients as they recovered from portalling in, or rested before preparing to translocate out again. It was meagre pickings, but it added up. Kayman was excited about something. He had set up a team – Rolf, Jorn, Mordant, Idris, Clarriss and Braidart – to look for some hidden object.

And then, of course, he had enjoyed his own carefully contrived moment of glory as he rescued some of the Darnells from their burning Hold. Darrison smiled at the memory. It had worked perfectly. Lord Barrass, the head of his Clan, had been killed, removing one of their most active enemies. His patient detective work in the Transit Point archive had paid off; his deduction was right, the Wand had been recovered. And 'Philip' was now officially a hero, and the Darnell's most trusted confidant and advisor. Which would be useful if only they knew anything worth confiding. Braidart was as tight-lipped as a mussel, even with his brothers and sister.

He looked back at his notes and frowned. There had been that extraordinary matter of Jorn's healing of Brendan's terrible burns. The whole Hall had been discussing it, astonished that such a thing was possible. It was a strong indication that Jorn had unusual Power. The young mage had been greatly praised at the Darnell Wake. Sitting opposite Jorn and Beatrice at the feast, listening to their chatter, should have been useful, but Jorn was cautious and said nothing that he did not already know. The young mage had implicitly confirmed that he and Braidart were on a quest, but refused to say more.

Jorn

The Long Night party had been more productive – a word here, a hint there. And now, Rolf and Jorn had gone to Errington. He had reported all that to Darric and Ajina. The spy stared at the charred remnants of paper in his hearth, evaluating the contents of his aunt's recent reply, and considering what he should do about it.

His most urgent task was to discover what this oddly assorted team was looking for, and where they were going. Ajina wanted him to put a spell-tag on one of them, so that they could be located. Easier said than done. The ideal target was Jorn. The shian halfer was an enigma. He was still in training. There was no reason for him to be sent out on any important mission, no reason for Kayman and Rolf to be treating him with far more respect than an apprentice would merit. He definitely had an unusual Gift. What exactly was he? He had heard whispered speculation that he might even be a Nine, but that was incredibly rare.

Darrison shifted uneasily in his chair. It was rare, but not impossible; he would keep it in mind. A Nine would present serious problems. And that was not the only thing; his sense was twitching, and yet he couldn't put his finger on what was bothering him. He had been Darric's top agent for 20 years, and he had learnt to trust his intuition.

The recent meeting at Mage Hall had been a little too obviously stage-managed. There was clearly a lot going on that Kayman was anxious to hide, apart from this odd quest. Was the artful and ever-suspicious Master of Mage Hall onto him? His own luck as a spy had to run out at some point, and in three moons, when his Lord Father launched his invasion, his job would be over in any case. Meanwhile, he must be doubly careful.

So what next? He needed to keep his finger on the pulse. That meant another visit to the Darnell mansion in Errington. The male Darnells were extremely careful about what they said, but chatter among the guards or servants was always useful, and he could pick up the general atmosphere. His sense would soon alert him if there were hidden tensions and expectations. His best source of information was Beatrice. The young noblewoman trusted him and considered him a friend. She had developed the habit of inviting him for tea, and in between the usual dross of inanities, the odd gem was unconsciously revealed.

So, tea with Bea. And a visit to Mage Hall, as soon the circumstances were right, in order to place a tag on something belonging to Jorn. Although, of course, there were more direct ways of eliminating a threat. Simple murder was often as effective as any complicated plan. Maybe he would try that for a start. But not in person, at least not yet. There were plenty of blades for hire in the back streets of Errington's Old Quarter.

*

The team were acutely aware that, at best, they had three moons in which to complete the quest for the Juncture before Darric launched his spring invasion. Unless they got lucky, it didn't look anything like enough time to find another four pieces of the Juncture, but all they could do was deal with each stage as fast as they could, and at least they had a destination for the next search. But to reach the ruins of Karth, they needed a Hook, and that meant a visit to the library at the University of Errington. That was Jorn and Rolf's task. Mordant was to portal into the city separately and wait in reserve, but Idris remained at the Hall, unable to help at this stage, and Clarriss had business of her own.

The two mages translocated four days after the end of the Winter Festival, arriving in a secluded area of one of the extensive city parks. Despite having now confirmed Philip's identity as a spy, Rolf had deliberately used the Horse Transit Point because the raash agent would rapidly find out that they were in Errington so there was no need for subterfuge. It was all part of their new game of cat and mouse. The fact that both he and Philip considered themselves to be the 'cats' added spice to the layers of deception.

The large stone houses, broad thoroughfares and tree-lined avenues impressed Jorn. The streets were relatively clean and traffic moved smoothly, the sound of hooves and carriages echoing back from high, stone walls.

'This all looks so smart and new,' he said in wonder. 'But what do they do with their waste? I don't see any open sewer runnels.'

'The Errenish have constructed a network of underground sewers,' Rolf explained. 'They even have piped water. Very modern.'

Jorn looked round thoughtfully. His own experience of towns and cities was very limited, having grown up in the countryside, but this one seemed to have something missing.

'They may have got their sanitation sorted, but I don't see any signs of defence. Are there walls or bastions?'

'No. The Island of Erren has not been invaded for centuries,' Rolf explained. 'Thanks to their ports, the Errenish are a prosperous nation, and some five presidents back, after a major fire, it was decided to demolish the city centre and build an entirely new capital. As you can see, it is quite impressive. They have worked fast, although parts of it are still a building site. But you are right, peace breeds complacency, and defence was not a priority. The Errenish rely on a superb navy and an expert diplomatic corps. They have a network of allies on the mainland. Nevertheless, the Assembly must be seriously worried about the rumours of an alien force that can materialise out of thin air and attack at will. I suppose we can at least thank Darric for having forced a few more governments to pay attention, following his attack on Darnell Hold.'

As they walked, Rolf explained the complex politics of Erren, but Jorn found it hard to understand. He was used to autocratic rule. Having an elected president and assembly, and all this voting and devious plotting between factions seemed a strange way to run a country.

The mages' safe house was a rambling, run-down, nondescript building, tucked away in a narrow side street in a seedy part of the Old Quarter. Jorn would have walked straight past it until Rolf grabbed his arm.

'In here; there's a 'pass-by-me' in place.'

The house was larger than it looked from the front and in better repair, and they were soon comfortably settled. After lunch, Rolf took Jorn to the Darnell mansion to find Braidart. It was a fine stone building facing a pleasant garden square. Two Darnell soldiers in smart uniforms guarded the steps to the front door. Rolf and Jorn were ushered by a liveried servant into a long hall with a black and white tiled floor and elaborately gilded mirrors, and from thence, into a beautifully appointed drawing room.

Jorn looked round with considerable interest. *'My, Rolf but this is very grand! The walls are hung with watered silk. The fabric on these chairs costs five crowns an em, and just look at this huge tapestry rug in Empire style. That's worth at least 2,000 in gold. If this is how the very rich live, I can see where the money goes!'*

'Spoken like a true trader! This is a house designed to impress. It's usually leased by one of the foreign ambassadors. Errington may seem to be a small island on the periphery of civilisation, but it's an important trading and banking centre, and acts as a neutral meeting point for many central powers, so it attracts high status diplomats who demand the best and seek to impress. This property happened to be vacant. The Darnells are very lucky, the President has let them have it for fraction of the usual rent.'

At that point, Braidart came in looking relaxed and well-groomed in a fashionable suit of fine navy brocade. It was a marked contrast with his usual rough appearance and Rolf grinned.

'I see you are dressing to match the mansion! Well settled in, I hope?'

'Indeed.' The young nobleman glanced around with wry appreciation. 'The President seems to think that my brother, Borodin, as Lord Governor of Dart, deserves a home befitting his status. He should see how we used to live at the draughty, old Hold, with stone-flagged floors and furniture 200 years out of fashion, and hounds lolling in front of every fire; he'd be appalled! It's going to take a long time to rebuild the Hold so the whole family can move back, and meanwhile, it's fun living like princes, even if half of the hired servants are probably Errenish spies. But we'll soon have our own people back. Philip keeps hanging around like a bad smell and calling to take tea with Bea, who is, of course, totally unaware that she entertains a raash spy. I hate knowing that he's watching and listening. It's all I can do not to cut his lying throat. Do sit, though I fear this fine room offers little comfort.'

'Well, I'm glad you are settled.' Rolf and Jorn perched gingerly on carved and gilded chairs, which looked likely to break under any serious weight. 'And just keep clear of Philip. He'll have to get back to his regular duties soon. We need to visit the university.' Rolf told him. 'Kayman has written to Professor Sturminster, making a formal request for her assistance, and she has agreed to see us tomorrow afternoon.'

'But if we ask the Professor about Karth and the Burning Coast, that is pretty much telling her about our quest, isn't it?' asked Jorn.

Rolf pulled a face and ran his fingers through his beard. 'Something of a dilemma, I agree. It is a risk, but I will tell her as little as I can. If we play it carefully, we gain more than we lose, and in fact, we have little choice because the library is one of the most comprehensive in the western world. If it fails to provide us with the information, we can be sure that it is unlikely to be found elsewhere. And no one knows about the Riddle Rhyme, or the exact nature of our quest, and I certainly won't mention that. Anyway, we'll need a simple cover story in case anyone asks our business on the way in. We'll be there for some hours and a disguise is less tiring than a never-mind. I thought Jorn could be a wealthy, young man seeking to enrol, I'm his tutor and you, Braid, his servant and bodyguard. Perhaps you could find Jorn some appropriately smart clothes in your wardrobe? His apprentice suit just won't do.'

Jorn

'Can't help, I'm afraid. I'm wearing my best. I don't have much left after the fire, and this young giant is getting too big to fit my stuff! I need to do some shopping myself.'

'Well, why don't we all go together? You could do with a couple of new suits, Jorn.'

'But won't that take too long? The meeting is tomorrow.'

'Not in Errington. Show the tailor enough coin and he'll have a suit finished in 12 hours if you need it.'

Jorn suddenly saw himself taking tea with Beatrice, looking as stylish as Braid, and he grinned at the thought. He could do with some new things. 'Fine. One smart suit, and one for every day.' He looked at Braid and grinned. 'But I'm not having one of those high collars that are all the fashion; I feel choked just looking at you!'

'I'm sure that can I satisfy sir's requirements,' said Rolf, using his smoothest trader's voice. 'If sir would care to follow me?'

Braid took his sword and cloak and the three left in high spirits, with Braid and Rolf taking it in turns to suggest improbable combinations of materials, colours and styles for Jorn's new suit.

The shopping trip took a good deal longer than he expected. Left to himself, he wouldn't have had a clue where to go or what to ask for, but with Braid at hand to give advice on fashion, and Rolf to drive the bargains, he quite enjoyed being towed round Errington's best outfitters. Rolf was generous and happy to indulge Jorn, like a rich uncle with nothing better to do than spend coin on a favoured nephew.

'We can count this as your birthday present,' he said when Jorn protested at the mounting bill.

'Heavens, I'd quite forgotten! I've lost track of the date.'

'Thirtieth of Winter,' Rolf told him. 'So just five days to your nineteenth.'

'My word. I can't quite believe that. I guess I'll be celebrating in the middle of the desert.'

'We'll have to take you out before we leave.' Braid slapped him on the back. 'Brendan and I know all the best places!'

'I'd like that.'

'I suspect that Braid's definition of "best" isn't quite the same as yours or mine!' Rolf told him. 'Anyway, now for the shoes to match and then we can go home.'

By the time all the measuring and fitting was completed, it was evening. The street lamps glowed pleasantly. The smart streets were emptying as people went home, but the alleys of the Old Quarter were busier than ever, torches flaming, the shabby stalls, chophouses and taverns doing brisk trade, and the night shift of whores, thieves and beggars lurking in corners. Jorn was glad that Braid had stayed with them; Rolf wanted him to be able to find the mage safe house if he needed to.

Once they left the trading area, there were no streetlights, and the occasional hanging lamp left dark pools of shadow in between. It felt a very different place from the one they had walked through in daylight. The old, jettied buildings leaned out across the narrow lanes, so close that neighbours could shake hands from facing garrets. The slimy cobbles had unexpected potholes, and there was a whiff of garbage and worse. Errington's modernisation certainly hadn't penetrated this far. The few passers-by hurried, heads down against a suddenly keen wind.

Jorn's sense tweaked a bare second before he heard the metallic hiss as Braid drew steel and warned urgently, 'Followers.'

Almost as he spoke, two large men loomed out of the darkness ahead and Jorn heard the sound of running boots from behind. Braid whirled to meet that attack. One of the men in front dropped as Rolf felled him with a stunner, but the other came straight for Jorn. He couldn't see the weapon, but he was unarmed and had no time to wait until it was visible. He reached for Disjunct and aimed it hard. The assailant was propelled backwards as if punched by a giant fist and collapsed in a silent heap.

Jorn caught a shuddering breath. All was quiet. No lights appeared in the adjacent houses, no shutters creaked open.

Braid said, 'I finished mine. Are the others dead?'

'I stunned mine.' Rolf responded. 'May be useful to keep him until we find out who paid him.'

'Huh, if he knows, which I doubt,' grunted Braid. The big man went to investigate the fourth body. 'This one is dead.'

'Powers, I only meant to throw him off,' said Jorn, feeling shaken. 'I never meant to kill him.'

'Well, you overdid the force,' Rolf told him. 'But from the size of the blade he was holding, he was out to kill you, so you can save your pity. Someone has made a serious effort to get rid of us. Which is significant. We were lucky that they simply used hired muscle. If it had been a raash assassin, we might not have fared so well. We'll have to be far more wary from now on.'

'What do we do with the bodies?' asked Jorn, feeling slightly sick, but trying not to show it.

'Pull them into a corner and leave them,' said Rolf tersely. 'Cover it all with a pass-me-by, please, which will do for now. I'll get them moved later. I doubt if anyone saw anything, and if they did, they will probably keep quiet. No one in this area wants to attract the attentions of the City Watch. Give Braid a hand with our guest, Jorn.'

'Will you kill him?'

'No, I just want to question him, and then I'll ensure he wakes up tomorrow with nothing but a bad headache and no idea how he got it.'

They dragged the unconscious man into the safe house, and then Braidart went home. When the would-be assassin came round, Rolf had no trouble in terrorising him into volubility, but as predicted, the ruffian was no help, apart from confirming what they already guessed, that an unknown man had found him in a tavern and paid over the going rate to have them killed. Rolf wiped his recent memory and got Jorn to carry him out and dump him in a heap outside a nearby drinking cellar.

'I'm afraid that puts paid to the idea of you and the Darnell boys going out on the town for your birthday, Jorn. The sooner we leave Errington, the better. When we next go shopping, we'll have to take an armed escort. And I'd better go through some more attacking constructs with you, and check the strength of your mind-ward and body-shield.'

Jorn was actually relieved that he was not obliged to go out to celebrate, because he was sure that Braid's idea of a good night out would have involved a great deal of alcohol, and quite possibly a visit to some of the local working girls. To avoid offending his well-meaning friends, he would probably have had to resort to using a mind-altering glamour to convince them that he was thoroughly enjoying all the amenities on offer.

He was, however, far from happy at the thought that someone, very probably Philip, was out to kill him, or that he would very likely have to kill again himself before the mission was over.

*

It was a pleasant, crisp winter afternoon when Rolf, Jorn and Braid walked briskly across the city, enjoying the exercise on their way to the university to meet Professor Sturminster. Jorn's new suit was a perfect fit, and Bea had smiled in open admiration when they met on the stairs.

When they arrived at the campus, Jorn stared in amazement. The university was by far the largest building he had ever seen; an ornate confection of spires, slim turrets, long roofs and tall, mullioned windows, making Mage Hall seem like a cottage in comparison. It sprawled across vast stretches of lawn, sprinkled with cedar trees and some unfamiliar species; he felt his shian side twitch with curiosity, but there was no hope of exploring.

Rolf was very conscious of the need to avoid Turner, who would immediately prevent them getting any further. Fortunately, the professor was away for a few days. At least Angela Sturminster had agreed to meet him, but he had to tread a fine line between satisfying her curiosity and retaining her goodwill, while not actually telling her anything of much use.

He made for one wing of the building and entered through a massive oak door, past a sign reading 'Darsius Wing. Department of Ancient Studies'. They entered a long, wide hall with a patterned marble floor. Severe stone busts stared down superciliously from high alcoves. Jorn and Braidart followed Rolf up a vast staircase with carved banisters, lit by a stained glass window decorated with heraldic shields.

'My, but I'm glad I'm not really applying to be a student here,' he told Rolf, *'I'd feel a real country bumpkin in all this grandeur!'*

'That's the idea of it. But don't be fooled by all this architectural snobbery. The man who founded this made his money by selling lamp oil.'

They finally reached an oak door with a neat label bearing the name 'Professor A. Sturminster'.

'Leave the talking to me,' instructed the mage.

He gave the door a light tap and a woman's voice replied tersely, 'Come.'

Rolf opened the door. An attractive, middle-aged woman with her greying, fair hair drawn back in a severe bun was working at her desk. She glanced up and then stood to greet them.

The tone of her welcome was somewhat acid. 'Ah, Master Rolf. It has been a while since you visited the university. Over 18 years to be precise, not that we met on that occasion. Be so good as to introduce your companions.'

'Sar Braidart Darnell, my bodyguard, and my apprentice, Jorn. It is good of you to spare us some time, Professor.'

She nodded curtly in acknowledgement. 'I am sure I can let you have half an hour or so.'

'I'm here seeking information.'

'So I gather. I will do my best to help. But I am forgetting my manners. Do please be seated and I will send a servant for refreshments. Lemon balm tea, as I remember, is it not?' She reached for a bell-pull and tugged it decisively.

'Yes, please, and some fruit juice for my apprentice.'

They sat down, but Braid remained standing in bodyguard role, wearing his best *'don't mess with me'* expression. Clearly, the Professor was going to play the meeting in her own way and in her own time. A servant in an olive-drab uniform came in and took her order.

Rolf gave their hostess a meaningful stare. 'Are you aware of what we've been doing?'

'Kayman has only told me it's a secret and highly sensitive matter. You need information about ancient Karth?'

'Yes, Professor, and also the Burning Coast, the Outer Barrens, and the Mountains of the Moon in Lind.'

She smiled thinly. 'I can make some educated guesses about the reason, but I'll refrain from embarrassing you with questions you will be unwilling to answer. When it comes to defeating the raash, petty rivalries and past events must be put aside. The recent news is very disturbing.' She turned to Braidart. 'My condolences for your loss, M'sar. Unlike Turner, I am not blinkered to the truth when it's in plain sight. The attack on your Hold leaves me in no doubt that, improbable as it may seem, the raash do have designs on Earth, and the capability to act to achieve them. I'm not about to sit at my desk and do nothing to stop them, whatever Turner may say. He would undoubtedly bar your access to our records out of sheer spite; however, as you no doubt planned, you have timed your visit well. The Professor is away. It is essential that he does not discover that you were here, so I'd appreciate maximum discretion, and, where necessary, deception. Is that understood?'

'Of course, Professor. We fully understand your delicate situation. We are more than grateful for your assistance.'

'Well, I'm not sure I can do much. I know very little about the places you have mentioned, but there is very probably something in the library. I will provide you with a pass. Is there anything else that you require?'

'It would be an enormous help if there is anyone on the university staff who has been to the Burning Coast and might be able to describe it to us; I doubt if there is much written about it.'

'I know the very man. I'll ask him to join us. He is not a mage, so I suggest that you adopt a suitable glamour, Rolf, and your apprentice also; your appearances are somewhat too distinctive.'

Rolf was not about to let Angela Sturminster know that he lacked enough colours to work a glamour. *'Can you do that for me, Jorn?'* he sent.

'Of course, will a mask do, or do you want a whole body change?'

'A mask will be quite enough. Just make my face paler, age me a bit, and turn my hair and beard white. That will do fine. A slight impression of added height, also, if you can manage that?'

A quiet rap on the door heralded the return of the servant, bearing a tray loaded with tea, juice and small cakes.

'Ah, good! Tea. Briggs, be so good as to go to the Department of Mineralogy and Mining, present my compliments to Professor Maples and ask him to join me for tea. Please explain that I need his advice.'

The servant left and Professor Sturminster served tea and made small talk for a while. Braidart stood near the door, apparently at ease, but watchful. Jorn entered his mental workroom, rapidly made the web-shaped glamour, and hung it ready for use. He made another for himself, changing his own hair and eyes to nondescript shades, and added a thread of never-mind to both to make them utterly forgettable. Then he helped himself to cake. He unobtrusively watched their host, taking in her neat grey dress and the way her hands and face betrayed no emotion. Is she really on our side now, he wondered. Only Idris would be able to tell for certain.

After some 10 minutes, there was a loud knock. Jorn rapidly deployed his disguising constructs on both himself and Rolf. Braidart managed to hide his surprise as his friends' appearances instantly changed.

Sturminster said, 'Come.'

A large, untidily-bearded, youngish man burst in. He had the appearance of someone who would be far happier hill-walking in wild country. 'You wanted me, Professor?' he enquired. His eyes lit as he spotted the cakes. He took two and devoured them as if he had not eaten for some time, scattering crumbs, whilst at the same time shaking hands with the visitors. He plonked himself sideways into a leather armchair, long legs dangling over the arm, and beamed enquiringly.

'Andrew, you have been to the Burning Coast, have you not?'

'Oh yes, spent last summer up there doing a geological survey. Amazing place. Ice meets fire. Why?'

'Our visitors are planning an expedition there. It would help them to gain a picture of the place. Major landmarks, notable natural features, that sort of thing.'

'Natural features? Where to start? Place is full of 'em!'

Professor Maples launched into a staccato seminar on glaciers, geysers, boiling mud pools, volcanoes and other natural wonders, which, while interesting, contained a great deal more detail than his listeners required. When he finally reached a pause, Professor Sturminster slid smoothly into it.

'Fascinating, Andrew, simply fascinating, and most informative, but unfortunately, our guests have other appointments so we lack time to hear more. Unless you have any further questions?' she asked, turning to Rolf.

'Well, we did hear of a place described as having fundamental "opposites". Have you seen anything that would fit that?'

'Mmmm… there's the ice and fire, I suppose, or…' Andrew paused and then chuckled. 'There is one place. Steggles in Anthropology is the man to ask, only he's off somewhere in the wilds. Ancient ritual site. Big stone column on one side. Other side is a smaller stone inside two oval earthworks, and a hot pool. Symbolic, d'you see?'

He peered at Rolf, Braidart and Jorn with the encouraging stare of a tutor hoping that some rather dim students had got the point.

'Male and female, eh? Opposites?' he added, seeing their incomprehension. 'Anyway, Steggles is your man. Wrote his thesis on it. In the Library'. He rose. 'Must dash. Tutorial.'

'Thank you Andrew, you have been most helpful.' The tall man rushed from the room. 'I do so enjoy enthusiasm,' said Angela Sturminster, dryly. 'Well, then, the library will provide what you need. Rolf, I think you know where it is?'

It was an obvious dismissal. They all stood to leave and Rolf said suitable words of appreciation.

On their way to the Library, Jorn sent, *'I noticed that you told her as little as you could, and added in two false locations as a distraction?'*

'Good observation, I'll make a spy of you yet. I have no particular reason to suspect the Professor; after all, she is the Deputy Head of the Mage School. We needed her help, and she seems prepared to give it, but I'm not going to trust anyone other than Kayman until this mission is over,

unless I absolutely have to. Can you sustain our glamours for a bit longer? We can probably drop them after we have dealt with the Librarian, but keep them in store; we may need them again later.'

'Fine, no problem. I'm not at all tired.'

The Librarian checked their passes, explained the complex system for removing and returning items to the Library, all of which required documentation, and pointed them in the right direction. After some time consulting the extensive library index, Rolf discovered an old book of traveller's tales. He requested that, and the Librarian produced it, along with a few other items that he thought might be relevant.

The book contained an engraving of a ruined wall, and some palm trees. In the background, the top of a huge, slab-sided stone structure topped by an obelisk could be seen, encroaching sands mounding high around it. The caption read 'Remnant of a mausoleum near Karth, uncovered by a recent sandstorm'. Unfortunately, a handwritten annotation dated 30 years ago recorded cryptically 'no sign'.

'So, lost again. Damn, that's not much help,' huffed Braidart in frustration.

'The sands shift continually. It may be uncovered again by now,' responded Rolf, trying to be optimistic. 'At least it gives us some idea what to look for. If we can find something else showing the ruins of Karth, that would help'.

Eventually, as they ploughed through the other material, they did find another engraving, this time showing a distinctive ruined archway, covered with panels carved in relief with armed figures driving chariots and men on horseback. After a quick look round to ensure that no one was near, Rolf stuffed the small book into his pocket.

'Better than nothing. Now we have to make show of looking for the other locations I gave her, which is tedious, but necessary, in case anyone checks what we have been looking at.'

After another lengthy consultation, he returned and told them, 'That stuff is in another room.'

'You can give the glamours a rest once we get there, Jorn.'

Jorn spent the next hour finding out a lot more than he had ever wished to know about the exceedingly boring wastes of the northern Barrens, and then the slightly more interesting Mountains of the Moon, which lay on the eastern edge of the Inner Sea. It was strange to think that no one had been able to cross the huge ranges, or knew what might lie beyond. It all brought home to him that Earth was a very much larger and more mysterious planet than he had ever imagined.

Finally, Rolf sighed wearily. 'Enough is enough! Let's try the Anthropology section and see if we can find Doctor Steggles' thesis.'

'*Masks again, please, Jorn.*'

With the help of the Librarian, they soon had a copy, and at once found the answer to their question. Steggles had drawn several careful sketches of the 'Sharfane', as the ritual site was called, showing the monument from several angles. As Jorn saw it, realisation dawned.

'Is that what I think it is?' he asked in some astonishment as he looked at the towering stone phallus.

Braidart grinned. 'The builders obviously felt that size does matter.'

'But what is the other part with the curved mounds and the small standing stone supposed to be?'

Braidart's eyebrows shot up in surprise. 'Blood's death, Jorn, but you must have led a very sheltered life! It's a representation of female anatomy. Hasn't anyone told you about sex?'

'Of course they have. But, er, no one really went into any details about… well, you know… about what women have… errm, down there,' admitted Jorn, awkwardly.

Braidart cast eyes to heaven in mock horror. 'I had that information by the time I was eight!'

The young soldier drew Jorn into a quiet corner and whispered earnestly for about five minutes, providing an explicit account of exactly how a woman was constructed, and what a man was supposed to do about it. Rolf pocketed one sketch and then looked on in some amusement as Jorn's face reflected a series of emotions, and finally went a little pink.

'Well, we have all learnt enough for now,' commented the mage, with a touch of irony, as the pair rejoined him. 'That was profitable. We may have enough of a visual to form a Hook to Karth, and to the Burning Coast.'

Braidart returned to the Darnell mansion. Jorn had been working and was hungry, despite the cake, and he was very relieved when Rolf stopped off at a pie-house to buy them both an early supper.

'I can hear your stomach rumbling from six paces away,' he laughed, 'and I have to say, mine is as empty as a gambler's purse! The safe house is comfortable enough but the catering leaves a lot to be desired. Anyway, I'm not sure we should stay there after what happened last night.'

The steak and kidney pies were hot and tasty, and came with gravy and a generous supply of vegetables. For a while, the pair remained happily silent. Once their plates were cleared, Rolf ordered plum tart and cream and sat back with a contented sigh.

'Well, that feels better.' The mage reverted to mind speech.

'I meant what I said about not trusting anyone, even mages at the safe house. I don't want to say anything about where we are going next or when. That's another reason for not staying there.'

'I understand. But I assume we are off to Karth?'

'As soon as we can. But first, I have to make the Hook for the mausoleum catch; it may take a while. I'll ask Braidart if we can move in with him until we are ready to leave.'

'But Philip is still nosing around there. We don't want to move out of the frying pan and onto the griddle.'

'No, we don't, but we haven't got much choice. We'll just have to hide when he's coming to tea.'

They moved into the Darnell mansion the following afternoon. Lord Borodin had happily agreed to have them stay there. It was a great deal more comfortable, and better guarded than the house in the Old Quarter, but it was simply a luxurious prison as far as Jorn was concerned. He itched for a long walk in deep forest. Luckily, there was a big plane tree in the garden, so he could let his *shi* feed, but being unable to explore the city on his own as he would have liked, he was quickly bored. There was a limit to how long one could spend practicing constructs. At least Braid had started daily fencing tuition. Spurred on by the need to learn how to defend himself, Jorn thoroughly enjoyed the challenge, and the exercise.

Today, they had finished, and the young mage wandered into the rear garden to cool off, noting with pleasure that the shoots of daffodils were bursting through the frosty ground and there were snowdrops out, and a cluster of primroses in a sheltered corner. That made him miss the woods even more, nevertheless, it was pleasant to sit in a gleam of winter sunshine and dream of spring. There would be no such pleasant, cool burgeoning in Karth, which, Rolf had warned, would be very hot, even in mid-winter.

After a while, he saw Beatrice coming down the path towards him. He rose to meet her and gave a bow. She responded with a smile and a bobbed curtsey. She tucked her arm possessively through his own and said persuasively, 'Come on, I must show you the rest of the garden. It's more extensive than you might expect for a town house. I must say, Errington is delightfully cultured, and the shops are a dream. My gowns were ruined in the fire, and now I have the perfect excuse to buy the latest fashions. One could be exiled to far worse places!'

She prattled merrily as she guided him to a wrought iron gate in a wall that led through to another, very private, garden, surrounded by high stone walls. Some violets were out, and more snowdrops. She steered him towards a secluded summerhouse, where the bare stems of roses and honeysuckle draped over the roof, opened the door and drew Jorn inside, pulling him down to sit beside her on a well-cushioned sofa. He did so, suddenly acutely aware of her closeness, of being alone with her.

She is so beautiful. And her hair... Almost without meaning to, he found his hand reaching up to touch it, smoothing a stray raven curl back from her forehead. She did not move away. Her eyes held an unmistakeable message of desire. She smiled. He voice was low and enticing.

'Braid tells me you will be leaving soon. And he says it's nearly your birthday. I wanted to give you a keepsake. Perhaps something like this?' She kissed him on his lips for a long slow moment. Jorn was now acutely aware of his rising need. He pulled her towards him and kissed her with urgent intensity. Her hand slipped down to find him.

His sense tweaked sharply. He was suddenly conscious of a bitter chill penetrating his side. He reached automatically to locate the source, and found that the top of the wooden wand, which he always carried at his belt, was icy cold. The disguised unicorn horn was giving an unmistakeably urgent warning. He suddenly remembered Mordant telling him the legends; he had not believed them at the time, but it seemed that one, at least, was true. He pulled away from Bea and stammered, 'Forgive me, M'sarra, I forget myself. I must not.'

She reached out to pull him close again. 'But you must! I know you want to. And I want you. Don't stop now.'

'I want you too, very much, but...' He faltered into embarrassed silence.

Bea looked at him searchingly. 'Oh, I never thought. Is it your first time? But it's not mine! Are you very shocked? We highborn ladies start loving early. It's an accepted thing. I may take any man as my lover until the time that I'm promised in marriage. There's no need to be shy. I will guide you.'

'No. You don't understand.' Jorn tried to find words to explain. 'Bea, you are the most beautiful woman I have ever known. I'd be honoured to join with you, but I simply can't. Not with you, not with anyone.'

Jorn drew the wooden 'wand' from his belt and quickly removed the glamour. The horn lay there in all its wonderful, iridescent beauty. Bea gasped. He picked it up and gently caressed the twisted spiral.

'This is the horn from a unicorn… It warns me of danger and helps us on our quest. It helps me to focus my power and makes it even stronger. But to use it, I have to remain a virgin.'

'Then you can't make love? Not ever? How terrible.' Bea's eyes brimmed with tears and she quickly dabbed them with her handkerchief.

'I'm sorry to disappoint you,' he muttered awkwardly.

'I'm not crying for me. That's so very difficult for you. You miss so much.'

Jorn stood, in urgent need of being somewhere else before his instincts took over again. 'M'sarra, if the horn and I should ever part company, you shall be the first to know about it.'

Bea smiled. 'Then my dear, I'll keep my offer open. Best that I return to the house alone.' She rose and glided gracefully away down the gravel path.

Jorn sat again and watched her go with very mixed emotions. He touched the spiral and it warmed comfortingly under his hand.

'Thanks for the warning. This is going to be a lot more difficult than I ever imagined. I just hope she doesn't try that again because I am not sure I'll be able to stop next time.'

Chapter 18

Mordant had decided it was time to move to Errington, ready for the next stage in the mission, when she would need to attend meetings with Rolf and the others, but she fancied treating herself to some comfort before facing the rigours of the desert, so she had booked into the best inn in Errington, disguising her raash features with a human mask. She also wanted to continue the pleasantly diverting affair with Braidart, which had started on Longest Night, and the spare days between now and their mission to Karth were too good an opportunity to miss.

She therefore prepared with some care for her afternoon assignation. She looked in the mirror, and her glamorous reflection smiled merrily. Braid loved her ability to put on different faces, bodies and personalities. It had become a sexy game between them. She enjoyed that too, even though it was quite tiring, and pointed out another difference between him and Brett; the older Darnell had loved her exactly as she was, 'funny face' and all.

Never the less, she was happy to play up to Braidart's fantasies and today, she had developed a rather fine disguise to cover her visit to the mansion. Her gown was in the latest style, her fur-trimmed cloak and hood enhanced the carefully worked mask of a woman slightly past her youth, but still very attractive. *Coin well-spent.* She patted the curls of her dark wig, and went to find her hired coach.

She stepped out of it a few doors down from her destination, paid off the driver, and proceeded down the square past the fine houses, walking briskly towards the entrance, enjoying the crisp weather and her impersonation of a smart woman-about-town. She realised, with a kick of dismay, that Philip was coming straight towards her. She swore silently. It was far too late to avoid him; a confrontation with the spy was inevitable. She had no choice but to brazen it out. She assumed an expression of polite civility and went to meet him, her mind rapidly assessing the implications, and working out what to say.

Philip came briskly up the street and gave the stranger a respectful nod of greeting as they met outside the gateway. 'Good afternoon, Mistress. A fine day, is it not? Do you visit here?'

'Indeed. I met Arnori Barrass' wife, Isabella, some years ago. I have only recently heard of his death, and discovered that the Darnells are staying here. I came to pay my respects to the family, and now return to renew my acquaintance.'

Philip nodded gravely. 'A sad business indeed. Most disturbing.' He held out his right hand with easy charm. 'My name is Master Philip.'

She gave an appropriate smile, briefly held his fingers, and responded, 'Mistress Margaret.'

He had his cloak thrown back. He was smartly dressed in shades of grey and plum. The widely cuffed sleeves of his jacket and shirt had ridden up as he extended his arm and Mordant saw something she had never noticed before. There was a tattoo just above the underside of Philip's wrist, of a kind that she knew intimately. She only caught a quick glimpse, and could not read the letters and numbers, but it was enough. She felt a sharp jolt of surprise, although her face did not change.

The spy made a courteous gesture towards the entrance. 'After you, Mistress.'

The guards gave a smartly rigid acknowledgement that both were recognised as welcome visitors. The pair walked up the wide staircase to the front door and a uniformed footman opened it before they had need to knock. Mordant swept up the grand staircase to her own meeting, fuming inwardly, and Philip was ushered down the mirrored hall towards the small salon, where he was to meet Bea for tea, wondering who the hell the visiting mage was and what she was doing here; the mask was subtle but he was used to spotting glamours. He knew something was not right but couldn't quite work out what.

When Braidart joined her, Mordant rapidly described the incident. 'In one way, it was a damned nuisance, but in another, a lucky accident,' she ended. 'I saw something I have never noticed before. He has a slave tattoo on his right arm, above his wrist. It looks a lot like mine, but I had no time to read it. If we could somehow get a good look at it, the number might be revealing; it would confirm if he is a product of Project Star.'

Braidart looked puzzled, so she had to explain about the breeding programme on Vard, mating slave women with raash adepts in the hope of producing mage spies who looked outwardly human but inwardly had the minds of raash.

'Maybe we could get a message to Bea so she could somehow contrive to see the tattoo?'

Braid shook his head. 'My sister is incapable of that kind of deception. Leave it to me.'

He left the room. Mordant sighed crossly and sat brooding about the consequences of the chance meeting. *If he spotted my glamour, he'll know I'm a mage and hiding something, although he has no reason to know who I really am. I'd better not use this face and dress here again. Pig shit! I wonder what the number will show.*

Braidart went downstairs, ambled into the salon as if expecting it to be empty, and came to a surprised halt. 'Forgive me, Bea! I had no idea you were entertaining.'

She smiled. 'Do join us. I have hot rosehip tea and iced fancies, and your favourite fruit cake.'

The young nobleman sat with elegant ease, surveying the table with casual interest, as if relishing the spread. 'Good afternoon, Philip. Good to see you. Keeping busy?'

'I am indeed,' beamed the mage. 'Back to my usual duties now that you are all safely moved here. I do trust you are settling in well?'

'We are. This is probably the most comfortable and luxuriously appointed house I'll ever have the chance to live in!' Braid reached across for the teapot, caught his sleeve against the tall cake stand, tried awkwardly to catch it, and sent the teapot flying in a calculated trajectory. The hot liquid drenched Philip's coat and right sleeve.

Braid reacted with acute embarrassment and at once went to help the sodden spy, while Bea rang for servants to come and sort out the mess.

'Oh, by heaven, I am so sorry Philip, how clumsy; here man, let me have that coat, my manservant will soon set it to rights.' He burbled on, assisted the mage to remove the coat, handed it to a servant with instructions to take it to his valet, and fussed around Philip, mopping up with a napkin. 'Dear me, your shirt has caught it too!' He took hold of Philip's arm and blotted industriously, leaving the spy no option but to sit and let him do it, while making polite comments about it not mattering at all. Braidart finally ceased his attentions and turned to his sister. 'I am so sorry, Bea, I have ruined your party.'

She pouted. 'Yes, you have, you clumsy, great lummox! But never mind, accidents happen, and see,' she waved at the table, which was already immaculately re-laid, 'there was no real harm done. You did not break the tea-pot, thank heavens, and we will soon have new dainties and a fresh brew.'

'I'll go and see to your coat, Master,' said Braid and left rapidly. Back in the upper room, he rejoined Mordant with a broad smile on his face. 'Got it!' he told her, and explained his trick. 'It gave me great satisfaction to give him a good dousing in hot tea! Anyway, the number is 455/HR/27 followed by three small stars.'

Mordant felt the room blur, she swayed dizzily and had to grip the arm of her chair. Her glamour snapped as her colours flared and she lost concentration.

Braidart came to put an anxious arm around her. 'Whatever's the matter, my love; you've changed, and gone ashen?'

She made a huge effort to regain her composure. 'I'll be all right; I have just had a considerable shock.'

He pulled up a chair and sat beside her, gently holding her hand, watching her face with concern.

After a moment, she peeled off her long kid glove and revealed her own tattoo. The last numbers matched the ones that Braidart had just repeated. She said flatly, 'There is something about me that you do not know. When I first came from Vard, I told Rolf and Kayman that my mother was human and my father a raash Mage-Adept. What I did not tell them, for obvious reasons at the time, was that my father was Darric himself.' Braidart gasped softly. 'They still don't know; it never seemed the right time to tell them. Three stars stands for Darric. Twenty-seven was my mother's identity number. She had four other children. Two of the boys, she said, looked human. We never knew what happened to any of them. Now we do. Philip is my older brother.'

'Blood's death, Mordant, what a burden to have to bear! The Mage-Lord of Vard for a father and that bastard spy for a brother.' He drew her to her feet and enveloped her in a strong, loving embrace, and then kissed her gently. 'My dear lass, you need not worry. I'm gutted for you, but it makes no difference to us. I think you need some comfort right now. And then you must tell Rolf and Kayman all about it. You'll feel better after that.' She nodded dumbly and let him steer her towards his bedroom.

*

The following day, Rolf finally gave up on forming a good Hook to the mausoleum and portalled back to Mage Hall to make a progress report to Kayman. He returned, bringing Clarriss, Kayman and Idris. They slipped into the Darnell mansion under cover of a never-mind and gathered in the comfortable parlour, safe in the knowledge that Philip had returned to his duties at the Horse Transit Point. Rolf hung a spy-ward in any case.

'We dare not delay any longer,' he told them. 'I don't want to risk another attack here in Errington. I'd hoped we could have left before now, but as you know, I've tried weaving a portal based on the images we found in the Library until I am halfway to over-extending myself, and either the Hook doesn't catch or it doesn't feel right. I'm not going to risk bringing us out underneath a sand dune, so we'll have to do the journey the hard way. We can leave tomorrow.' He pulled a map towards him and pointed as he continued. 'I can portal you to Trader Town in Tamor on Lake Vyle and then we'll pick up a caravan to Karth from there,' he told them. 'I'm sorry, Idris. It means a long trek over the desert. I know you want to come, my friend, but I don't see the point in you putting yourself through such misery and danger when there's no need.'

Idris pulled a wry face. 'I will not argue with that. Much though I want to stay with the team, I am not going to commit suicide. I cannot survive in such a dry environment for more than a few minutes before I dehydrate. I will have to stay behind.'

Mordant nodded. 'A very good decision.' Which it was, but she was acutely aware that it meant that she would not see him for the duration of this mission.

'I will miss you, Idris,' Jorn told him, *'but if you came, I'd be worried sick about you the whole way. Now I only have to worry about me. I hate the heat!'*

'All shians do, tantar issa.'

'Rolf, are there any trees in the desert?'

'No, Jorn. Just a few date palms when you find an oasis. Is that going to be a problem for you?'

'Maybe. I'll top up well before I go. It depends how hard I have to work. If my *shi* starts to hunger and there are no trees, I may have to portal back and take a refreshment break.'

'Fine. Now, as you know, we need special kit for the desert. I have bought a few essentials but there is a lot of stuff we can only get when we reach Trader Town; for example, good desert shoes, wide-brimmed hats, and thin, long–sleeved, cotton tunics are a must. The desert can be chilly at night, so we may need cloaks. I can hire the tents and pack animals there if we need them. First, I'll have to find us a group to travel with. As I just said, we have a difficult journey ahead of us.' He showed the rather basic map again. 'Between Tamor and Kardash, there's a range of mountains. Not the kind with peaks, more like a ground-down, flattened ridge called the Plateau of the Winds, but it's a considerable obstacle. To reach the ruins of Karth, we have to get to the other side. If we are lucky, we can find a mule train that will make it across in about seven days. If we are unlucky, we'll have to join a caravan to reach the desert the long way round. That means camels. It can take over 30 days. I have done it only once, long ago, and I vowed never to do it again!'

'Why does anyone want to go to the Great Sand?' asked Braidart. 'You've told us there is nothing there, except what it says on the box: sand, sand, and still more sand.'

'The usual reason that men do anything wearying and unpleasant: profit. There's a trade route on the far side of the Plateau that connects to one that leads to the coast, and eventually, to Far Tarsind, which is where the ships from the distant east bring their spices silks and other exotic trade goods. Some of them are literally worth their weight in gold.'

Braidart grinned. 'I always wanted to see remote places! I can't wait!'

'I suspect you will change your tune when you hit the heat,' Mordant told him. 'I was born on Vard where it gets furnace-hot in summer, so I'm used to it, and raash have a much better tolerance of heat than humans do. You, my friend, are going to melt! For once, I'll even leave my longsword behind; we must carry as little as possible.'

'Yes, but you must still be well-armed. You must be even more vigilant this time,' warned Kayman. 'I'm sure that Philip has kept Darric well-informed of our plans. That attack in the alley was just the start. You can expect more of the same from now onwards.'

Mordant shifted uneasily and said quietly, 'You are right, Kayman. I have something else to tell you all.' She recounted her chance meeting with Philip and the outcome. There were sharp intakes of hissed breath as she revealed the identity of her father.

'By the Powers, Mordant, I see why you did not want to tell us before,' said Kayman with complete sympathy. 'And what a terrible shock it must have been when you recognised that number. I feel for you, I really do.'

'And it explains some things that have long puzzled me,' added Rolf kindly. 'We have total trust in you. Your parentage was no more in your control than it was for any one of us. It does not change any part of our esteem for you and your abilities. I can't say "forget it" because that would be stupid, but you know what I mean.'

Jorn

'But it makes getting rid of Philip even more urgent,' said Clarriss. 'If he's that close to Darric, he's doubly dangerous.'

'I agree,' said Kayman. 'But now is not the right time. Get Karth out of the way and then we'll see. I'll keep a close eye on him from now on, be sure of that.'

When the meeting broke up, Idris drew Jorn to one side. 'I am sorry I cannot come with you. I came here with Rolf mainly because I wanted to give you some advice before you leave. You will find the heat difficult. Drink as much as you can, and use every tree you see, whether your *shi* feels hungry or not. A mesh of blue to form a cloak across your body may help to cool you down, but of course, the working will also tire you. Now, what I say next may not make much sense to you, Jorn, but I want you to remember it. You told me how, when you first entered a tree, you tethered your *shi* by using a mirror in which you saw your inner self?'

Jorn nodded. 'Yes, I did. I haven't bothered to check the tether recently because I don't feel so worried about not getting back into my body.'

'I don't know what will happen in Karth, but my sense is tweaking. If you should run into dangers or difficulties and you do not know what to do, go and talk to your essence.'

'Talk to my essence? But Idris, that's just speaking to myself! Why should I want to do that?'

Idris looked steadily at Jorn. 'Have I ever given you bad advice?'

'No, no, I guess not.'

'Then trust me now. You shian self is stronger than you know. Just remember what I have told you. I look forward to your safe return, with the next part of the Juncture. May the Powers be with you, *tantar*-issa *ovrassedea*.'

'And with you Idris, *ovrassedea, tantar*,' Jorn responded, and watched his friend walk away, with a sudden pang of loneliness. The shian mage understood him better than any of the others, even Rolf, and he was going to miss him.

*

Shortly after dawn on his nineteenth birthday, Jorn walked through Rolf's portal and found himself standing amid sand dunes by an ancient well and a cracked cistern containing a pool of stagnant water around, which swarmed a small cloud of flies. It felt like a bake-house, and it was hard to imagine that it could get even hotter, yet the sun had not really got to work yet. He wondered what it would be like in high summer.

The team picked up their packs. Mordant hung a mask. They followed Rolf, who seemed to know exactly where he was. As they came round a dune, they joined a well-worn track.

'Death's blood, what the hell is that?' exclaimed Braid as a long string of tall, heavily-loaded beasts swayed past.

'Camels,' Rolf told him. 'And if you think a horse is difficult, just try managing one of those!'

'I'd heard about them, but I didn't believe it. Now I've seen them, and I still don't!'

Trader Town spread out before them, already half-hidden by a shimmering heat haze. The place was like nothing Jorn had even seen before. A long, circular canal had been dug out in a loop from the lake and back again, creating a large, artificial island, across which sprawled a higgledy-piggledy conglomeration of multi-coloured huts, tents and trading booths. Rows of covered wagons, mule pickets and camel trains made straighter lines across the seeming chaos. Nothing seemed permanent. Beside the lake, an oasis of palms and citrus fruits made a lush green border for a short way until the desert took over.

Entry to and exit from Trader Town was over two bridges opposite to each other on each side of the circular canal. There was a booth on each to collect tolls. Rolf spent a while haggling heatedly with the collector. Jorn noted that his guardian was fluent in the foreign language.

'Rogue!' he said crossly, as they were finally allowed in. 'One expects to pay a bribe in addition to the toll, but that was ridiculous!'

'I see that you pay to go in and again to go out,' said Mordant. 'They get you both ways and in the middle!'

Rolf looked around with acute appraisal. He guided them to the main trading area. Several merchants had finely-worked rugs for sale. Some had inscriptions in the centre in a curled script. Braidart paused to look at one stall and ran his hand over a rug in soft shades of ochre and red. The merchant instantly spotted his interest and came over.

'Fine work, very fine. My Lord will buy?'

Rolf fixed the man with a steely gaze and said something sharp in the local language. The trader looked extremely uncomfortable. The mage hustled Braidart and the others away before the man could make any further attempts at a sale.

'What did you say to him?' asked Mordant curiously.

Rolf grinned. 'Well, the polite version is that "my Lord" would not buy, and he knew what he could do with his inferior merchandise.' He looked at Braidart with cynical amusement. 'I suppose you have no idea what the squiggles on that pretty rug actually said?' Braid shook his head. 'They translate as "your mother mated with a camel"!' Rolf told him. 'That was one of the less vulgar. The nomads who make these have a mischievous sense of humour. They do in fact make excellent rugs, but it amuses them to create these especially for the unwary visitor. I have seen many a fine house with an extremely obscene message lying on the parlour floor!' Even Clarriss laughed. 'Clarriss and I will go and find a mule train or caravan going south. The rest of you, stay together. Buy nothing, especially not anything to eat or drink that you do not recognise. Or even if you do, come to that. If you walk to the end, you will come to the exit bridge. I'll meet you there.'

'And avoid the brothels and gambling dens, and above all, watch out for thieves,' added Clarriss.

'Yes nanny,' muttered Mordant under her breath as the pair bustled off. 'Let's explore. Coming, Braid?'

'Sure. You'd better stick with us, Jorn.'

The young mage was glad to tag along. The whole place was overwhelming. The stinks, cooking smells, noises, babble of different languages, strange garments, protesting camels, and screaming vendors and porters made him stare around in amazement. The heat was an assault, swarms of small biting flies tormented, and his pack soon seemed far heavier than it was. He mopped the sweat from his face and sipped frequently from his water bottle. *Thank the powers Idris stayed behind. Though I suppose he would have gone straight into the lake. What I wouldn't give for a grove of fine, shady trees and a cool breeze! Maybe I can go and explore the oasis later on. Still, this is certainly a birthday I'm unlikely to forget! I'm going to enjoy myself before the hard work starts.*

They threaded a way through the jostling crowds in the main bazaar, lined with stalls and temporary booths. Mordant fingered vivid gossamer silks with surprising interest. Braidart lingered over knives and throwing stars. Jorn spotted some intricately-woven braids in designs he had never seen before and stopped to examine them, totally absorbed by his analysis of the weave.

A sudden tug at his belt focussed his attention and he gave a startled yelp. He patted the place where the leather bag should have been and looked around in a real panic 'My purse! The Juncture is in there!' Luckily, Mordant had seen the snatch and sprinted off in hot pursuit. Braid took off after her. Jorn stood and fretted, feeling like a total idiot.

Mordant chased the culprit down a narrow alley between the booths. The pick-thief could not have been more than eight and he clearly knew Trader Town inside out. He sprinted between two tents and kicked a basket of dates into the path of his pursuer. Mordant jumped that and ran on, her raash stamina carrying her easily. The lad dodged and weaved through the market like a hare, but he couldn't shake her. She had no desire to hurt him, but he had to be stopped. She brought out a stumble-stop, and aimed it with full force. The boy tripped and fell and she was onto him before he could move. Which was fine, except that he did not have the purse. She guessed that he had thrown it away, or stashed it. She hauled him to his feet.

'Where is it?' she demanded crossly. The lad stared at her, not nearly as scared as he should have been, pretending dumb stupidity. His eyes were looking past her. She dropped him and whirled round to find herself confronted by two large locals. One had a hefty cudgel, the other a knife. Small feet scampered rapidly away behind her.

She dropped the cudgel man with a stunner and went straight for the other. He was plainly not expecting a woman to do anything but run away, but his knife came up in a reflex born of long habit. She had him on his back with her own knife at his throat in two simple moves. Braid came puffing up, sword at the ready. The gathering onlookers melted away.

'Have you got it?'

'No, damn it. I had the boy, and then these pig-shits turned up and he got away. But he didn't have the purse on him. It has to be back there somewhere. We'll have to search.'

Braid patted down the stunned man just in case and repeated the process with Mordant's captive. He shook his head. 'Maybe our knife-happy bastard here knows.'

'Where is the bag?' asked Mordant, speaking with careful clarity, in the hope that the heavy spoke Basic. The man glared and made no reply, but Mordant thought he had understood. Her sense tweaked. She exerted enough pressure on her knife for him to feel that a fraction more would cut. 'You know where it is.' She dropped her glamour. The man's eyes widened in sudden terror at the alien features. She regarded him with icy intent. 'The bag has nothing of value in it; I don't much care if we get it back or not. You can tell me where it is, or I can cut your throat. Your choice.'

He knew a killer when he saw one. 'I show,' he whispered.

'Good. Then get up, very slowly. And don't try anything clever. My friend here has even less patience than I do.'

He took them a few paces back to the rear of a cook stall where there was a barrel full of filthy slops and greasy leftovers. 'In there.'

'Well don't just stand there, sunshine, fish it out,' said Braid, who was looming with calculated menace.

The man pulled a face, hitched up his loose sleeve, and dredged around in the disgusting, stinking gloop and finally pulled out Jorn's bag. Braid moved round behind to block his escape. Mordant grabbed the pouch and checked the contents. She gave a huff of relief. 'It's there.'

Braid grinned. He punched the man hard in his kidney, grabbed him, and dunked him head down into the barrel and held him there for a count of 10. He let go and his struggling victim surfaced and collapsed, gasping and puking. Mordant and Braidart left him to it.

They found Jorn still waiting by the stall, looking thoroughly worried. Mordant had replaced her glamour. She smiled and handed back the greasy, dripping bag, fastidiously held at arm's length between finger and thumb.

'I rather think you'll have to buy a new one. This stinks and it's going to get rapidly worse.' Jorn let out a sigh of relief as he gingerly accepted it.

'Thank you. I'm sorry to be so careless.'

'And so you should be, birthday boy! You may be in holiday mode, but this isn't a day at the fair. The way you're wandering around and gawping, you're shouting "easy mark" to every dip-thief and cut-pocket in the area. I spotted this one because he was just an apprentice. If a professional targets you, you'll never know until you reach for your purse 20 minutes later and find it's gone.' She offered Braid her fist for a knuckle touch. 'Nice work, partner.' She sniffed. 'Yuk, your hand stinks too!'

Braidart mopped his forehead. 'I'm melting after all that exercise!' he complained. 'Let's finish with sight-seeing and find some shade, if there is such a thing.'

After his fright, Jorn ceased to take interest in anything much except the people near him. He stuck to the others like a burr and kept his hand resting lightly on the horn, which was once more disguised as a wooden wand in a sheath at his belt. He was, in any case, now far too hot and uncomfortable to be bothered to look at goods.

Rolf and Clarriss found them near the bridge, sitting under the shade of an awning by a watermelon stall, tucking into the sweet, juicy flesh.

'I thought I said no food?' he said crossly. 'You can pick up every kind of stomach ailment here, even from fruit.'

'We earned it,' said Mordant, '*and* we got our hands thoroughly washed first. We needed to!' She explained what had happened. Rolf looked suitably appalled, impressed and relieved by turns.

'For pity's sake, don't tell Clarriss,' Jorn pleaded. 'I'll not hear the last of it for days!'

'Have you found our transport?' enquired Braidart.

'Yes, we're in luck. A mule train is heading south at dawn tomorrow. We can join their camp now. Clarriss is already there, sorting out a pitch for the night. I've fixed riding mules for us, and an extra baggage mule for the water and our camping gear. We can get the other things this afternoon. The trek over the desert and across the Plateau of the Winds and down again to the ruins of Karth will take about seven days.'

'Why the Plateau of the Winds? Jorn inquired.

'Because, at certain seasons, it is scoured by the Sarle, a hot, sand-laden wind that can blow unceasingly for weeks. It is said to drive men mad.'

'Thank you so much for cheering me up,' said Braidart bitterly. 'Death's blood, it can't get much hotter surely?' He removed his hat and mopped his flushed and dripping face for the hundredth time, before replacing the headgear with the brim tipped as far down as it would go.

'Fortunately, this is not the season for it. The Plateau should be relatively cooler, but it will be very hot as we cross the Sands. You'll feel a little better when you've changed into light robes like the locals wear.'

Rolf led them back to the muleteers' camp where he had rented a tent for the night. The area reeked of mule and an acrid smoke from the cooking fire that burnt dried droppings. He left Jorn, Mordant and Braidart to guard their belongings and went off with Clarriss to complete their purchases. The dwarrans seemed to cope well with the heat and Mordant looked as cool as always, but Jorn and Braidart were soaked with sweat. Changing into the loose, cotton robes did help, but not much.

Finally, Jorn gave up, retreated to his inner space, and experimented with making the cooling cloak of blue, which Idris had suggested. It seemed to work when he applied it, so he made one for Braid as well.

'Probably only last for half an hour or so, but it's better than nothing,' Braid sighed with relief. 'Even five minutes is a blessing.'

'Can you do a body-watch for me later, Braid? I want to try one of those orange trees. I'll cover us with a never-mind so we don't have to pay the toll on the way out.'

'Sure. Be good to take a walk by the lake when the sun goes down.'

'Hope the flies like a good night's sleep, or we won't get one.'

*

The following eight days were ones that Jorn was mostly very glad to forget. After a fiercely hot ride across the barren, rocky land to the south of Lake Vyle, they began to climb up to the top of the Plateau, which blocked their way like a gigantic table-tomb with sheer sides and a flat top. The mule ride to the top was a jolting misery, and it was little better as they crossed the high Plateau. Sand got into their clothes, their hair, and unexpected parts of their bodies, and made their food crunch. Mordant and Braidart made no attempt to continue their love-making; it was not just too public, it was simply far too uncomfortable.

On the fifth day, they reached the far side and everyone halted to look at the view. A wide plain stretched below them, rippling like an endless beach waiting for a tide that would never return. In the foreground, a few humps of rock and a small clump of palms emerged from the dunes. The further distance was masked by a shimmering heat haze.

'Is that it?' asked Braidart, irritably wiping a runnel of sweat out of his eye.

'I certainly hope so,' responded Rolf, 'but the way the sands shift, we can't be certain until we get closer.'

'Can't see anything that looks remotely like a mausoleum,' said Clarriss.

'It's there,' Jorn told them, as the horn warmed in response his question. 'I'd no idea we are so high up. Judging by the heat haze, it is going to be seriously hot down there.'

'It's a deal further down than it looks,' said Braidart. 'It will take us at least half a day to get to desert level.'

At the foot of the escarpment, the muleteers called a halt at an obviously familiar campsite, which was slightly shaded by an outcrop of rock. They erected canopies for shelter, but it was just as hot under them as it was outside. A bit of thorny scrub struggled to maintain a grip between the barren rocks. The merciless sun blazed from the burnished sky and the stone was hot enough to fry an egg.

They set off again as the red sun dipped suddenly below the horizon. It took them another day to reach the pinkish rocks they had seen from the top of the Plateau, and when they did, they could see that these were not rocks at all but the battered remnants of ancient stone and mud brick buildings, poking out of the sands at intervals across a wide area.

'At least we've found the ruins of ancient Karth,' said Rolf tiredly, 'but anything else will have to wait until dawn.'

They made camp by an ancient cistern in the shade of a clump of straggling palms. In the last of the sunset, the ruins stretched improbably long purple shadows across the red and ochre sands. They were all silent as they munched their dried fruits and flat bread, and sipped at tepid water. It was too much effort to make further plans when they knew that they could do nothing more until they found the mausoleum. Jorn grabbed his opportunity to enter a tree again, and was intrigued by the strange sweet flavour and huge exotic leaves.

*

They started the hunt at first light. Without the horn, they would never have located the right place. When they did, it was unimpressive. Jorn halted beside the stump end of a greenish, heavily carved obelisk of stone projecting from a dune. It was about twice the height of a man and wider than the four of them could compass as they stretched out their arms to ring the base.

'Are you sure this is the place?' asked Clarriss doubtfully. 'There's no trace of a building.'

Rolf gave a short, humourless snort of disgust. 'No, there isn't. And do you know why? We are standing on it! The whole thing has been buried under the sand. Do you remember the engraving? This is the top of the ceremonial pillar on the roof.'

Mordant examined it with interest. 'Powers! I believe this is sheathed in jade. It must be worth a fortune.'

'Death's blood! Do you expect us to start digging?' asked Braidart, regarding the mounded sand in horror.

Jorn smiled. 'I suspect there is a better way.'

'So what are we going to do?' asked Braid.

'You are all going to move away to a safe distance. I'm going to raise a sandstorm,' Jorn told him. He went into his mental workshop and engaged with the Quincunx. He could already sense the apport weave, and soon had a spiral band of ether and gold winding itself into a tornado-shaped coil of Power, itching to be released.

The others retreated back into the ruins and Jorn climbed to the top of a thick wall where he could get a good view. *I need somewhere to dump all that sand; it has to be kept under very careful control or I could uncover the tomb and bury us a hundred ems deep under sand in the process.* He earmarked a clear patch of desert some distance away. *A new sand dune there, I think.*

He looked at the others. 'There may be sand in the wind. Shield your faces.' He summoned the construct and sent it to spiral around the big pillar. He let the energy of the spin build until a powerful vortex of sand was sweeping around it. 'Watch out! Here it goes.'

The spiral became a whirlwind, which sucked up sand and small rocks and swept them into the air to form a tightly-spinning column. An enormous, dish-shaped depression began to form, in the centre of which the top of a vast black, slab-sided stone structure was revealed.

Jorn controlled the spinning sandstorm as it lifted several hundred ems into the air and waited until the removal operation was completed. He then turned the spiral towards his chosen dumping place. Several thousand tons of sand and small stones cascaded from the sky as if coming from a giant invisible hourglass, and formed a vast, neat pyramid. He let his working end. His companions offered a small round of applause and he took an ironic bow. He was amazed that he still felt quite fresh, and was secretly delighted with his exhibition.

The mausoleum lay on a clear paved area in the centre of a deep, steep-sided, round valley in the sand. It was a forbidding two-storey, oblong structure, some 30 ems long on each side and about the same in height from the paving to the upper roof. The shining black marble walls sloped slightly inward. The second tier was a smaller version of the first, guarded by a set of giant statues, clad in ancient armour. The carved obelisk on the flat roof now thrust up for a clear 10 ems. On the lowest level on the side facing them, gigantic bronze doors, flanked on each side by more guardian figures, stood firmly shut.

Jorn grinned. 'Well, that was the easy part. Now we have to find the Juncture.'

The team kitted themselves out with dwarran wind-up torches and two flasks apiece. Braidart carried a coil of rope. They descended the steep slope with slow caution, the loose sand shifting under their feet, acutely conscious of the danger of a slide.

At the bottom, the shiny black bulk of the mausoleum towered above them, and the massive bronze doors drew them like a magnet. The lower panels had a central knob on each side. Braidart pushed experimentally and then shoved harder. The doors did not budge. He stepped back and regarded the barrier with frustration.

'Ahem!' coughed Mordant discreetly. She moved past him, grasped a knob and pulled. The door opened smoothly outwards. Beyond was intense darkness.

'Why wasn't it locked?' asked Clarriss suspiciously.

Rolf shrugged. 'I don't know. Be cautious.'

They wedged the outer doors securely, switched on their torches, and entered. As their eyes adjusted to the gloom, they could see a plain square hallway, lined with the ubiquitous black marble. There was a glint of gold from the high, coffered ceiling. In front of them, a wide white marble staircase swept downwards.

Drawn by an irresistible urge to explore, they descended into the cooler, dry darkness, the thin beams from their torches lost in the immensity of the stairwell. Jorn was suddenly acutely aware that they were entering a tomb. The thought of dead kings lying in wait for them was not reassuring.

At the foot of the staircase, they found a plain, octagonal chamber, lined in white marble. A pair of immense, thick, gilded metal doors stood open. Two tall marble figures, their mourning faces hidden beneath carved veils, kept vigil in niches on each side of the entrance. Braidart and Mordant took the lead. Jorn heard Braid give a gasp of wonder.

'You have to see this! It's quite unbelievable!' Rolf, Jorn and Clarriss entered the tomb chamber. Their feet raised small puffs of dry dust. The air tasted stale but not foul.

Down the centre of the room ran a line of six raised, sculpted black tables bearing recumbent figures. The probing torchlight picked up gleams of gold. As they stood still, swinging their lights in wide arcs, they could see that the veined marble walls were decorated with enormous mosaics that depicted processions of solemn, robed figures in rich colours set again a golden background, studded with the glint of gems.

Jorn shone his torch on the nearest table and shuddered slightly. Brown parchment skin pulled tightly against the crowned skull. Sightless sockets searched the gilded ceiling and bared teeth grimaced from between withered lips. The remains of rich fabric draped across hollow ribs and skeletal hands still clutched the hilt of a richly-jewelled sword.

Braidart and Mordant had gone further into the vault and Braid went towards one of the mummies, drawn by the macabre sight and the glint of gold. Jorn took hold of the horn, which was back in its disguise in the sheath at his belt, intending to scan the chamber with it. To his dismay, it was icy cold to his touch. Just as he was about to warn the others, Braid said excitedly, 'Wow, I spy loot! This crown must be worth 50,000. That'd pay for the repairs on the Hold and leave change.' He took a step forward.

Rolf shouted, 'Braid NO!' It was too late.

The young nobleman looked down at his foot where a marble slab at the head end of the tomb had just given a loud click. Hidden machinery whirred and the heavy doors slammed shut with appalling swiftness. There was no sign of any way to open them.

'Oh, by the Powers!' whispered Jorn as he stared in horror at the thick bronze barrier. After a frozen moment of shock, the group tried everything they could think of, from brute force to constructs for opening, to no effect.

'There are three of us. Can we join our powers and blast our way out?' asked Jorn hopefully.

'No chance,' said Rolf grimly. 'All that will happen is that the ceiling will come down and we'll be buried alive.'

They all wound up their torches and made a rapid but thorough search of the entire vault, being careful not to go towards the centre of the room in case of more booby-traps. Finally, the grim truth was all too evident.

Braidart looked at the others in appalled distress. 'We are trapped, and it is all my fault. I am so very, very sorry. I should have been more careful. I fear I have doomed you all!'

'The fault is as much mine as yours,' Rolf told him, his voice cross with self-reproach. 'I should have thought to warn you before we entered. Royal tombs are renowned for having traps and protective devices. That was probably not the only one. Any one of us might have set something off.'

'But it was I who did so. And now I've condemned us all to a terrible death in the darkness.'

Rolf looked grim. 'I'm afraid Braidart is right. The torches will only run for another six hours before the bulbs give out, and without food or water, we will not last more than a day or two.' Clarriss moved to his side.

Mordant said nothing but stared round the chamber with rising terror. Her worst nightmare, being trapped in a closed place with no hope of escape, was coming true.

Chapter 19

Braidart went to the halfer mage and drew her close. He could feel her tremble. He was gutted by the result of his greedy impulse and could think of nothing useful to do. As a last resort, there was always his knife, but he wasn't ready to admit the need for that just yet. Clarriss gave a sudden, stifled sob, and Rolf took the little dwar into his arms and held her tenderly as she buried her face against his broad chest.

Jorn was trying hard to subdue his own panic. He refused to accept that there was no way out. He withdrew the wand and swiftly turned it back into the unicorn horn. *'Please help us,'* he begged urgently, *'there must be something we can do? I don't want us all to die in this terrible place.'* The horn remained inert. He realised that he wasn't asking a yes/no question. He tried again. *'Horn, is there any way out of this?'* The spiral warmed.

Jorn did a slow circle of the room, seeking for another exit, but there was no response until he came back to the main doors. The horn warmed again, decisively. *'Through there? But we have tried everything. Is there something else we could do?'*

There was no reaction and Jorn racked his brains for a more specific question. *'Something one of us could do? Is it me?'* The horn warmed. *'But what? By the Nine, I don't understand. I don't even know what questions to ask.'*

He fought back his rising desperation. The horn began to pulse with shifting colours, throbbing with pent power. He could feel it vibrate under his hand, as if it was striving to make him understand what he had to do.

'Oh blood's death! If only you could talk!' And as he said that, Jorn could hear Idris' voice in his mind as clearly as if he was be-speaking.

'Talk to your essence.'

The young mage sat cross-legged on the floor, his hands on the horn in his lap, and went into his workroom. He walked swiftly across to his store and went straight to the long mirror, which still stood with its back to the room. He turned it round and gave a soft gasp. The mirror did not reflect the storeroom. It showed a green forest glade. Standing close up and watching him, shian-naked, was his inner self. *'Oh, thank the Powers! I thought you were never going to come!'* His double bespoke urgently.

'Jorn, I've got so much to tell you, but there is no time now. I can get you all out of there, but first I have to leave your body.'

Jorn was stunned. Had the danger driven him mad? How could this inner self be talking to him as if it had a separate existence? 'But you can't,' he whispered. 'You can't leave me. You are part of me. Anyway, I tethered you.'

The mirror-Jorn hissed out his breath in frustration. He held up his left arm. *'Blood's death! I broke that tether ages ago. You know I leave you when we go into a tree together. Well, all I need to do now is to leave without you coming with me. If you go to sleep, I can do it. Please, Jorn, you must trust me. I'll open the door and get us out, and then I'll come back to you, I promise. By the Nine, you must believe me, or we are both going to die, and so will the others.'*

Jorn stared at his double, still too bewildered to respond, trying desperately to understand. Finally, he forced himself to ask the obvious question. *'I thought you were my shian essence. If you're not that, then what are you?'*

'Not what, Jorn, who. My name is Jan-Keb. You can call me Jan. I'm your twin, your shian brother. I want so much to meet you properly, in my solid form, but that must wait. Let me deal with that door first.'

Jorn was way beyond stunned. He stared at the mirror image in total disbelief. *'My twin brother? It's not possible!'*

Jan sighed and realised that Jorn needed a jolt to get him past his shock. *'So, I'm a lying figment of your imagination, am I?'* he snapped. *'Powers, Jorn, we don't have time for this right now. If you want to get yourself and your friends out of the tomb alive, you have to believe me, however weird it seems. Are you going to trust me to get you out, or do you just want to sit down in the dark and die of thirst?'*

'Out sounds good.'

'Right decision. Look, I'll explain everything later. You must go back and tell the others. They are all frightened and worried sick. Get Mordant to send you to sleep.'

'Yes, yes, all right. I'm going.' Jorn went towards the door, and then turned back, still unable to believe what had just happened, but his brother made a 'hurry up' movement with his hands.

'Quickly Jorn.'

Jorn

He came back to awareness of the dimly-lit tomb and found the others standing in a silent huddle watching him. Their fear was palpable, and the need to deal with the emergency steadied him at once.

He pushed all his emotions and questions aside and spoke with quiet urgency. 'Mordant, I need you to send me to sleep, right now. My inner self is going to leave my body, and unlock the door. Don't ask me how, because I don't know. Just do it.' He settled himself down as best as he could on the dusty floor.

Mordant came over to him. She closed her eyes for a moment, and then he felt a gently soothing thread of orange and pink slide into his mind. He relaxed at once, and was deeply asleep a moment later. The raash halfer stepped back.

There was a shimmering of released energy. Rolf and Mordant watched in disbelief as an almost invisible entity slipped from Jorn's sleeping body and flew across to the door. It paused and then slid down to the floor, flattened, and slipped underneath, through a gap no wider than a knife-blade. Rolf held Clarriss a bit tighter, hardly daring to breath. She and Braidart had seen nothing.

'What the hell's happening?' Braid demanded.

'Jorn's *shi* just left his body. Wait,' responded Mordant.

There was an interminable pause, a loud clank, and then the big doors moved slowly inward. 'Oh, Powers be praised!' whispered Rolf.

Braidart scooped up Jorn's sleeping body, Mordant took the horn, and the four ran out of the doors as if the ghosts of the dead kings were at their heels. Mordant indicated the stairs with an urgent gesture. 'Rolf, you get Clarriss out of here. We'll be with you in a moment.'

Braid set Jorn down again and Mordant saw, as he could not, the nebulous stream of energy pass smoothly back into the young mage. She snapped her sleep spell. Jorn opened his eyes and realised they were out. He gave a shuddering gasp of relief and sat up.

'Let's move!' said Braid.

He and Mordant helped Jorn to his feet, but he felt fine. He joined them in their rapid ascent of the stairs. They came out, black-dazzled by the blinding sunshine, and Jorn sagged to the hot sand and knelt there for a moment, trying to deal with the fact that he was not only alive, but had his twin brother to thank for that. *'Jan, you were amazing! You and I must go somewhere quiet and private right now.'*

There was no reply.

266

Rolf and Clarriss were hugging each other; the short couple turned, still holding hands. Rolf gave Jorn a huge, relieved smile. 'I'm not sure what happened there, but thank you. I had all but given up hope. Even the desert air tastes sweet!'

Jorn got up and nodded happily. 'It surely does. I can't explain right now. I have to portal out. I need to do something in private. It's urgent and it can't be done here. Finding the Juncture will just have to wait. Don't worry, the mausoleum is a strong Hook. I'm only working an Earth transition. Go back to camp and take a rest. I'll meet you in an hour or so. Look after the horn for me, Mordant.'

The others watched him in silence as he quickly formed a portal and vanished through it.

'What the hell was all that about?' asked Braidart. 'Can one of you mages explain what just happened in there?'

'We know as much as you do,' said Mordant. She kissed him and took his arm. 'Come on, Blue Eyes. I always find that a near-death experience gives one an appetite, don't you?'

*

Jorn emerged from his portal into the well-remembered glade in the forest near his old home, in a remote rural area of Dart. He had formed the Hook to it as easily as if he'd been doing so for years. In the depths of winter, the great beech stood proudly bare. The freezing air made him shiver in his thin robe, but he didn't care, anything was better than that frightful desert heat.

He settled comfortably on the debris of bronze leaves and old beechmast, and readied himself for what he must do next. Then he went back into his inner space, entered the store and went over to the mirror.

Jan was waiting for him. *'Thank you for bringing us here. I can't think of a better place for us to meet properly for the first time. Will you let me out, brother? I want so desperately to be free.'*

Jorn made the only possible reply. *'What do you want me to do?'*

'Leave your workshop, but don't shut the doors. Open your eyes. Then relax as you do when you let me out to enter a tree, only remain awake. Just want to let me out. I can do the rest.'

Jorn walked out of his store and through the workroom, leaving the doors wide open, and returned to awareness. He got up and stood with his back to the beech tree. It was very quiet, this safe childhood space, and deeply comforting. Somewhere, a robin trilled its thin winter song.

Jorn took a deep breath, relaxed all his defences and said silently, and with all his heart, *'Come out, Jan. Come now.'*

He felt, for the first time, the tingling change as his shian essence slipped out of him. There was a sudden, achingly hollow emptiness at the heart of his being. The air near him shimmered. A moment later, his twin took form beside him. Jorn simply stared in wonder, quite unable to find any words.

His double came to him and gave him a long, wordless hug, and then stepped back, leaving his hands on his brother's shoulders, and regarded Jorn with a joyful smile.

'I can't tell you how many times I've imagined this moment!'

Jorn was still trying to grasp the fact that he was looking at his own identical twin brother. He knew he was gawping like a fool. 'Jan, my mind is spinning! Let me look at you, it feels so weird to see someone who is so much like me, and yet isn't!'

Jan obligingly did a twirl. His hair was as rich and glossy as a freshly husked horse chestnut. He looked strong and fit, slim and muscular, and, Jorn realised with a genuine shock, his body was extremely handsome. *Which means I must be too! Oh my, I've never seen the whole of myself naked like this, and I never really thought about how other people see me!*

His twin grinned, as if he knew exactly what Jorn was thinking. 'Well, come on, say something, or I'll say it for you! "Oh wow!" would do for a start. And yes, we are exactly the same!'

'Well, almost,' said Jorn. His shian twin had the usual decorous, small *kiri*.

'I think we both need to sit down. I'm still not used to being in form. I get a bit wobbly.'

Jorn settled by the tree, feeling decidedly shaky himself, his colours flaring, his emotions in turmoil, halfway between amazement and overwhelming joy. Jan sat neatly cross-legged facing him. He seemed uncertain how to begin.

Jorn's voice was rough with emotion. 'I can't imagine what it was like for you, being trapped alone inside me all those years.'

'It wasn't easy.'

'But why didn't I know about you before? How could you be there, inside me, and I couldn't hear you or feel you?'

'You did feel me. Often, if you stop to think about it. You eventually recognised what you knew as your "shian essence". But you couldn't hear me. Idris explained it to me. The human mind is not constructed to tolerate two identities in one body. You walled me off for your own survival.'

'Oh my! I never meant to do that!' Jorn looked at his twin in distress, and then what he had just heard registered in a different way. 'Hey, did you just say that Idris told you? How did he know about you?'

'He and J'Louth both knew as soon as they met you that your shian essence was very strong. At that point, I don't think I really knew exactly who or what I was. I had to rely on human nourishment so I wasn't growing the way I should have done. I'd never met another shian. When J'Louth first touched you with their essence, it was amazing, wonderful. I wanted to shoot straight out of you, to go and meet them, but they didn't understand. J'Louth thought that I was part of your inner self and it would hurt you if I left you. They were right in one way, and quite wrong in another. They blocked me from emerging. But I suddenly understood everything. I knew I'm not part of you, but a separate individual. I knew I'm shian, just as you are human. It was astonishing.'

Jorn tried to take all this in. For the second time in his life, his fundamental beliefs about who and what he was had suddenly been turned upside down. 'But I am shian in my essence,' he said in soft distress.

His brother put his hand on his shoulder and gave a quick squeeze. 'No, Jorn, I am. But you can be also, at least in part, when I am in-dwelling, just as I can be, almost, human.'

'Oh my.'

Jan's face twitched in a sympathetic grimace. 'Oh my, indeed!'

'I'm still not quite sure how we both came to exist in one body.'

'I'm not sure either. Your body is human; mine is shian. Normally a shian child remains in the home-tree from the moment of conception, a simple *sut* or nucleus of essence, growing very slowly. The tree is like a womb, and later, a nursery. I had no tree, so I used your body instead. It was my home, my whole world, I inhabited it just as you do. I touched what you touched, saw what you saw, and understood what you learnt. And then you began to sense your Power, and you had this chaos of colours swirling in your mind. And I had some too; it was horribly confusing. But you found a way to control them, so I copied you. And then Rolf told you about being a mage, so everything made sense.'

'But then it all went wrong. You starved, and that made me ill, and Idris told me you were close to death, because you couldn't get out to feed.'

'Yes. It was horrible. I really don't want to talk about it.'

'You don't have to. I know exactly how it felt, I had nightmares about it. But I don't understand why you couldn't leave?'

'It would have hurt you too much if I'd had to force my way out. Like ripping away a part of you. You might even have died of the shock. I couldn't do that to you, even to save my life. And then in the end, I was just too weak to try.'

Jorn squeezed his twin's hand. 'But finally you did escape, when I let your *shi* out to enter the tree. But I was right there with you. I felt as if it was me inside the tree.'

'I know. Our minds and essences are so closely bonded, you just came with me. I was happy about that. Only I knew we couldn't go on like that forever. As I got stronger, I needed to eat more often. I couldn't keep waiting for you. And I wanted so much to be free. I thought perhaps I could slip out of you at night when you were asleep. I was very frightened. Afraid of hurting you, afraid of leaving without you, terrified I might not be able to get back. But in the end, I managed it.'

'You must have been really scared; I'm sure I would have been.'

'I was. It felt so strange.'

'When was that?'

'It was when we were in the forest, on the way to the Cave. I went straight to Idris, because I knew he'd understand. He was a great comfort. He helped me to take form for the first time.'

'He began to call me *tantar-issa*. It was you he meant.'

'Yes. But he meant us both, of course.' Jan hesitated and then went on in a rush. 'Jorn, there's something else you need to know. I am also a Mage of Nine.'

'But that's wonderful!'

'I've been trying to help you. I have some Gifts you lack. I can find things, and I sometimes sense danger before it gets too near. Since our quest began, I've guided you, and pushed you in the right direction, and helped you with your workings.'

'But it's been the horn that guided me – us. It channelled Power to me, went hot and cold to show me what to do, or give me warnings.'

Jan sighed, his eyes reflecting the pain he knew his next words must cause. 'Jorn, it wasn't the unicorn horn. That was me. I'm sorry, but you need to know the truth.'

'You! But how, Jan, how?' Jorn was battling to find at least some certainty to hang onto as, strand by strand, his whole understanding of recent events was cut away.

'The horn doesn't have powers of its own. It helps the user to focus his own Power. I discovered I could use the horn as a channel so that I could communicate with you at last and use my mage-sense to guide you. I helped you to find the Riddle Rhyme. I guided you to the Cave and found the first part of the Juncture. It nearly drove me mad with frustration that you still couldn't hear me, wouldn't listen, never asked the right questions. When you healed Brendan, you used my strength, and nearly killed both of us in the process! Even with Mastery of Nine, no human mage could have completed that working unaided.'

Jorn thought about that for a moment and went cold to the core of his being at the implications. Irrationally, he exploded with a sudden surge of angry resentment. 'But that means that it was you who wouldn't let me make love to Bea! I wanted to so much! Why the hell did you stop me?' He was surprised to find that it had mattered so much.

'Merciful heavens, Jorn! I had to! How could I possibly let you do that most private human thing with me inside you, having to watch and feel it all?'

'Oh my! I see, of course, no, of course you couldn't.' Jorn squirmed inwardly at the thought.

'And anyway, Bea is gorgeous, but she's older than you think, and an incurable flirt, just like Braidart. She wanted to know what it would be like with a shian halfer. We were barely 19, about to leave on a vital quest, which couldn't wait. There was no time for you to fall in love, and if you had – and you would have done – it would have been a terrible distraction, and in the end, you would have been hurt.'

Jorn could see both caring and embarrassment in his twin's expression, but he was still coping with the shock, as the full impact of Jan's words hit home. He exploded in anguished denial and confusion. 'But Jan, that means it's all you and not me at all. You've been doing the magic; you are the Master of Nine. So what am I? I don't understand.'

Jan gave him a gentle thump. 'Don't be daft! Of course you're a Master of Nine as well. But you're a human mage and I'm a shian one. We do things differently. I may have more natural ability with some types of workings than you do, and I'm much stronger physically, but your will is unshakeable. Acting together as Masters of Nine, we'll be totally formidable, and Darric had better watch out! But we have to be independent; we both have one hell of a lot to learn, and we have so much to do in the next few moons.'

'When I mastered the Nine, my storeroom filled up with colours, so many shades I can't count them all. Have you got those too?'

'No, Jorn I haven't. I think that may be your own special Gift. Maybe it comes from your training as a weaver.'

'I guess it might. I just wish I knew how I'm supposed to use them. Nine is hard enough to manage.'

'Well, they are safe enough where they are, and you'll have years for experiments once we finish the quest.'

'If we ever do. And if we manage to stay alive. I wouldn't be now if it wasn't for you. I haven't even thanked you properly.'

'You don't need to. I was just so frightened that you wouldn't come to me in time.'

Jorn was getting cold. He felt the empty, aching, lonely space inside him and could not help a shiver. 'It hurts,' he said softly. 'Jan, it really hurts, inside. There's a horrible gap where you ought to be. I don't think I can manage without you.'

Jan's eyes winced in sympathy. He said tightly, 'Do you suppose I don't miss being inside your body? I feel like a snail without a shell. I don't mean that we can never be together again. We will, much of the time. And now we'll be able to talk. We'll be closer than ordinary brothers ever can be. But in between that, we have to be able to spend some time apart.'

He laid his hand gently on Jorn's shoulder again. 'It'll be all right. You'll see. We have to go back and tell the others soon, but before we do, why don't we slip into this tree together? It will be just the way it always is for you, except that this time, you'll be able to bespeak me. But you feel icy. Let me do something about that, or your body will be thoroughly chilled before we get back. I'm coming inside you now.'

His twin shed form and the tingling sensation came again. The empty space at the heart of Jorn's being was suddenly filled. He was complete, and totally at peace. He heard Jan sigh with pleasure. *'Oh, that feels better.'*

Jorn felt a comforting warmth suffuse him. '*Jan, I can hear you*! *And yes, that feels so good.*'

'*Lie down by the tree as you always do.*'

Jorn lay down, still feeling warm and deeply comforted. He closed his eyes and let his awareness of his body cease. He experienced the blissful moment of release; the atoms of his inner being streamed into the tree, and this time, for the first time, he knew that his own human consciousness and spirit were being carried out with Jan's *shi*, leaving his body as an empty husk. It should have been terrifying, but it wasn't. Together, they surged up the great trunk, and he knew that the joy he felt was not his own, but Jan's. It was Jan who fed, Jan who explored, and took Jorn with him to share the wonder of being shian.

'Oh Jan, I understand now! I'm you, bound to your tree-self!'

'*Yes, just as I'm you, when I'm in-dwelling. Do you see, Jorn? We are separate, and yet we are one. Now we won't ever be lonely again. It's a great wonder. Come on, I'm going to feed a little, and then I want to reach the top. I've always longed to look out over the forest from the summit of this beech tree.*'

Finally, and with his usual reluctance, Jan ended his exploration and carried his twin safely back to the haven of their shared body. He settled back into the place he had made for himself. It was his own version of Jorn's inner workroom, except that it was, of course, a forest glade. It enabled him to shield himself from Jorn's thoughts and emotions, and hide his own, and he had his Quincunx set out on the leafy floor.

'We must go back to the others.'

'Yes we must. I can't wait to see their faces when they meet you!'

'*To be honest Jorn, I'm not looking forward to that. Apart from Idris, I haven't met other people in my own form. I feel really shy and awkward.*'

'Relax, Jan, they're going to be delighted! I think the biggest problem is going to be getting them to understand that, however much alike we may look, you are not me, and that's going to be really confusing for them. But they're all my friends, and they will want to be yours too. If it all gets too much to handle, just come back inside and we'll deal with it together.'

Jorn formed the return portal to Karth with careful precision. He was aware of Jan watching his working. He threw his line, caught the unmistakeable Hook of the mausoleum, and stepped back into the bright, hot sunlight. He walked back to the campsite and found the others sitting in the shade of the date palms. They got up with obvious relief as he came into view.

'Well, Wonder-Boy, are you going to tell us what in the name of the Powers has been going on?' demanded Mordant. 'We've done nothing but talk about it for the past hour.'

Jorn gave them his best infuriating grin. 'I'll explain. But first, there's someone you have to meet.'

'*Go on, Jan. Time to give them the surprise of their lives!*' He could feel the effort of will that Jan had to make to leave the shelter of his body under the pressure of four pairs of acutely interested eyes, but then his twin shot out him in a surge of energy. A moment later, his form shimmered into view. Braid swore loudly and the others gasped in unison. Their faces were pictures of incredulous wonder and incomprehension. Even Mordant looked stunned.

Jorn put a steadying arm round his brother's shoulders. 'Meet Jan. He's my shian twin. We've only just been able to meet properly for the first time. It was the emergency in the tomb that broke through the barrier. This is going to take a long time to explain, and he isn't yet used to taking form for long stretches, so say hello, and then we'll get back together again and we'll do our best to tell you about it all.'

Rolf went straight to Jan with a huge smile splitting his dark face and stared up at him with his hands on his hips and joyful amazement in his eyes. 'I never even suspected! By the Powers, Jan, having not just one guard-child but two is going to take a lot of getting used to, but you are so very welcome.'

'That you are, Jan,' said Mordant.

Braidart grinned, and came to shake Jan's hand. The shian winced a bit at the powerful grip.

'Just testing your reality! Blood's death, I was just about getting used to the first one, and now there are two of you!'

Clariss gave the newcomer an acute evaluation from head to toe and finally allowed herself to smile. 'We have you to thank for saving our lives, Jan, don't we?'

Jan smiled back, but his shy unease was obvious. 'Yes, erm, yes, I guess you do. I... er... forgive me but I need to go back now.' He lost form and disappeared.

Rolf shook his head, still stunned by the idea that two identities shared one body. 'Are you back together again?'

'Yes, we are. Jan uses me like a home-tree.'. He mopped his forehead. 'My, I'm starting to melt again, and my mouth feels as dry the buried kings. I must have some water. Let's get into what passes for shade and I'll explain the whole thing, at least as far as I understand it myself, and Jan can fill in the gaps. You can still talk to him. At least you mages can, you can bespeak him, just as you do me. But I'd better get the other really important bit of news out of the way first. Jan is not just like me to look at. He is also a Mage of Nine, and he might even be rather better than me!'

He was rewarded by another round of amazement. He could sense Rolf and Mordant exchanging urgent and excited silent messages.

It really did take a long time to explain, and he took it slowly, beginning with the moment he had been prompted to speak to his inner self. The mages were full of questions and fundamental incomprehension. It was hard work trying to answer them, but it also helped him to understand things better himself. Jan chipped in from time to time. Jorn felt that his twin would have liked to be able to go somewhere really quiet in the deep forest and just settle himself properly, and get used to this new stage in their relationship. Jorn wished he could do that too, but there was no time right now.

When the questions finally began to run out, he said firmly, 'That's enough for now. We still have a mission to complete. The sooner we all get out of this horrible desert, the better. We have to find the Juncture. I guess that means going back to that dreadful vault; we never did do a proper search.'

'Well you can do it without me,' declared Mordant. 'Nothing in the entire multiverse is going to persuade me to go down there again!'

'Tell her she doesn't need to!' Jan told him. *'If you had only bothered to stop and consult the horn before you all dashed in, I would have told you it isn't there.'*

'Not there... Hang on a minute...'

'Just need to talk to Jan for a moment,' Jorn explained aloud.

'You indicated that we had the right mausoleum. If the Juncture is not inside, then where the hell is it? The Rhyme says "seek me where dry kings lie sleeping"; that couldn't be plainer.'

'Plain on the surface, but deceiving. Just like the last time, when it sounded as if we ought to go through that stone maze to find the hiding place. Think what it says in the third line of that verse. "I am not within

death's keeping." The Juncture is hidden here, but outside the tomb. As soon as we go back, I'll be able to use my sense to locate it.'

'Oh, by the Nine! Then that horrible ordeal in the tomb was totally unnecessary?'

'Well, yes, although it did bring us together. You had to be in very serious danger to force yourself past all those barriers you'd erected between us.'

The others had been watching Jorn's inner dialogue with rising impatience. He sighed and said, 'It seems I owe you all an apology for what happened in the tomb.'

'Why?' asked Braidart. 'Blood's death, I got us all into that mess, and you and Jan got us out of it. I owe you both my life.'

Jorn sighed and shook his head. 'It's my fault because I should have checked with the horn before we went in. We were so obsessed by wanting to see inside the tomb, and so sure that the Juncture must be there, that we headed straight inside. Jan knew the answer, but I didn't give him a chance to tell me. It's all in the wretched Riddle Rhyme. It does direct us to "where dry kings lie sleeping", but it does not say that the Juncture is inside the tomb. In fact, it says the exact opposite; "I am *not* within death's keeping". Jan says that the Juncture is here, but somewhere outside the tomb. We are going to find it.'

'But not alone,' said Braid. 'After all our trouble, I want to be in at the kill!' Rolf also rose to come with him, but Mordant shook her head.

'Even if it's outside, I'm giving this one a miss.'

'Me too,' agreed Clarriss. 'If I never see that ghastly heap of black stone again, it will be too soon!'

'Good decisions,' agreed Jorn. 'You two pack up and we'll all portal out as soon as we get back.'

A short while later, he stared across at the black bulk of the mausoleum. '*So, where is the dratted thing?*'

'*Halfway up the column,*' Jan told him after a short pause.

'*Well isn't that just typical!*' Jorn exploded angrily. He turned to his friends.

'Jan says it is hidden on the obelisk,' he said crossly. 'If I'd known that yesterday, I needn't have moved half the desert to reveal the whole tomb. We only had to clear away the sand round the bit that was sticking out.'

'And now you've made it extremely hard to get up there,' said Braid in frustration. 'Those marble-clad walls are as sheer and smooth as polished steel. You're not doing that climb on your own,' he added in a stubborn tone.

Jan sent, *'We can cross-step up there.'*

'Are you sure that's a good idea?'

'Do you have a better one?'

'I guess not. I'll do the working.'

'Then I'll leave you and go up the pillar in my shi. I can find the Juncture and apport it down to roof level, and then we just cross-step down again.'

Jorn looked doubtfully at the roof some 30 ems above him. It was a long way to levitate but his twin sounded very certain. 'No need for a climb, Braid. We'll do it the easy way.'

'Ready?'

'I guess so.'

Jorn fixed his will on the obelisk on the roof and cast a braid at the Hook. There was a dislocating wrench and he was at once standing on the roof, feeling very dizzy and disorientated. After a moment, he told Jan shakily, *'Well it's fast, but I don't want to do that too often.'*

'I didn't feel a thing!'

Jan's essence emerged onto the burning hot roof with a quiet *'Ow!'* and Jorn sensed rather than saw his brother ascend the obelisk.

'I've found it! It's in that dark gap between the winged lion and the eagle. I'll send it down to you.'

The triangular object drifted gently down into Jorn's outstretched hand. He looked at it curiously. It was much the same as the first part, except that it was made from bronze, and had a red gem. He felt Jan slide back into him.

'Phew, that's better. It's far too hot up here. Let's go down and portal back to Errington before we all fry!'

'I'd rather take an apport down again. Can you work that for me?'

Jan worked the levitation. Jorn did his best to hold his nerve as he drifted over the edge of the roof and watched the steady descent downwards. He landed with a soft thump back on the sand.

'I can see why people don't use a cross-step unless they have to,' he told his waiting friends. 'Never mind. Jan found it. Let's go home!'

'Good teamwork brother,' he added silently.

'Well done, the pair of you!' congratulated Rolf warmly. 'But I suppose you'd better leave things as you found them, Jorn. We don't want any other unsuspecting treasure seeker getting shut into that horrible vault.'

Jorn nodded. 'I'll see to it. You two go back and let the others know that we have succeeded.' They climbed back up the sand slope and the young mage found a vantage point where he could see both the pyramid of sand he had removed the previous day, and the dark bulk of the mausoleum. He wove the same spiral apport as before, this time shifting the sand back to cover the entire building including the top of the obelisk.

'Nice work,' approved Jan. *'Though, if you are honest, you'll admit that you were showing off, just a tad, when you did it the first time.'*

The young mage went back to join the others who had packed up and were ready to leave. 'Let sleeping kings lie,' he told them wearily.

Rolf managed the portal back to Mage Hall with his usual competence. The team were all too hot, tired and dusty to want to anything but go straight to their rooms for long baths, cold drinks and a good rest. Jorn was every bit as hot and exhausted, but he had something to do first. He went to the waterfall.

'Idris, are you there? We're back.'

The shian mage took form at once. 'I can tell from the excitement in your aura that you succeeded in your quest. But something else has changed as well. What has happened, Jorn?'

'This!' he said happily, and Jan left him and took form on cue.

Idris looked from one twin to the other and was out of the pool in three long strides. He gave Jan a hug and followed that up with one for Jorn, which left him breathless. 'Powers be praised! You finally found each other! I cannot tell you how delighted I am for you both. Tell me all about it!'

'It's mostly thanks to you,' Jorn told him. 'If you had not told me to talk to my essence if I got into trouble, the whole team would be dead by now.'

'So you got into trouble, did you?'

'And then some! Jan saved our lives!'

Jorn and Jan settled down by the pool, ignoring the cold and their weariness, eager to tell their story, knowing that Idris was the one person who really would understand.

Chapter 20

Rolf had told Kayman they were back and had the second part of the Juncture, and as soon as the team had rested and refreshed themselves and, with the exception of Jorn, drunk rather more wine than usual, they went to tell Kayman the news in detail.

The High Master took the new piece from Jorn to examine it with a nod of delighted satisfaction. 'So, two down and three to go. Tell me what happened in Karth and then we must decide what you are to do next.'

Jorn was getting rather used to the inevitable introduction. This time, he added a twist of drama. 'Kayman, before we go any further, I'd like you to meet the second person for a thousand years to be Master of Nine; my twin brother, Jan.'

Jan obediently took form and Kayman's face went through the now familiar repertoire of expressions of stunned amazement and disbelief. 'By the Powers! A *second* Master of Nine? Jorn, are you serious? How on earth is this possible?' The High Master made an effort to recover his manners and his professional aplomb. 'I am more than pleased to meet you, Jan. I see there's more than one story to be told this evening.'

Rolf beamed. 'Indeed there is, old friend. And now, at last, we fully understand those strange foretelling dreams you had so many years ago, where two "Louth lookalikes" seemed to merge as one. If it was not for these two, the mausoleum would now hold five more bodies. I think Jorn has told this story often enough for one day, and he is very tired, so I'll do my best to give you the bones of it.' Braid winced at the unintended pun.

Jorn knew the mage was a born storyteller and he was certainly glad of the rest, so he listened with rising amusement as Rolf turned their adventure into an epic. Jan was once more in residence.

'It sounds even more unbelievable the way he tells it,' he chuckled. 'But Kayman's only half listening; he's too busy thinking about how to make use of two mages with the Power of Nine!'

Finally, Rolf drew his tale to an end, and Kayman leant back in his chair and steepled his fingers over his rotund stomach.

'Well, that is all quite astonishing. The Riddle Rhyme is plainly even more devious than we thought. We must beware of more hidden twists. But that brings me back to our task. We have to find a new destination; is it to be the Burning Coast, or one of the others?'

'The Burning Coast sounds promising,' said Clarriss, 'but it's still early in winter. There's no way that we can travel so far north until the Great Ice retreats again.'

'Clarriss is right,' agreed Rolf. 'Although we do have a potential Hook in the form of that ridiculously vulgar standing stone, that won't work if the Sharfane is buried under drifts. Even if we knew exactly where the next part of the Juncture is, which we don't, we couldn't locate it under several ems of snow. I suspect we may have to wait at least two moons before we can attempt it. We'd better try to crack one of the other two verses.'

'I agree. We can't go so far north at this time of year. But I think I may have an idea about the "eagles" one, although it is a long shot.' Everyone looked inquiringly at Mordant. 'The clue says, "where eagles dare not fly", so one has to ask what they are afraid of. There are not many creatures that eagles have cause to fear, but there is one – the gryphon. It has a huge wingspan and it can fly well over short distances. Gryphon pairs are highly territorial and they can easily take down an eagle.'

'You are not seriously expecting me to believe that a mythical creature with the top half of a bird and the rear end of a big cat actually exists, are you?' demanded Braidart.

'Well, actually, yes. Anyway, you've already seen one such "mythical" monster, the blind-wyrm. And Jorn has a unicorn horn. Those are not supposed to exist either.'

'But how can such impossible creatures as gryphons be real?' persisted Braidart sceptically.

'Ah, now, Blue Eyes, you have got me onto my hobby!' answered Mordant. 'I've spent many years researching chimeras in my spare time. Most people assume the beasts were made by magic, although there's no good explanation for how or why, but I've never found that convincing. I can't imagine any construct that would achieve it. It's my personal belief that they were created by the Old Ones.'

'How?' asked Braidart and Jorn together, in shared astonishment. 'And anyway, I thought the Old Ones were just a myth themselves. You can't have a myth making a myth,' objected Braid.

'The Old Ones are no myth, but they lived millennia ago in the remote past, before the world was changed. Humans have somehow lost all but the most distorted memory of them, but you can still find their traces if you know where to look. It's plain from these remains that they had a vast amount of knowledge and abilities that we have long lost and simply do not understand. They were far more advanced than the raash, or even the dwar techs. Who knows what they may have been capable of doing? Anyway, however the chimeras came into being, some do exist. The more outlandish ones, such as the manticore and wyvern are almost certainly myths, but I've seen gryphons at a distance, and a unicorn. I once stood in a hidden valley in the Mountains of the Moon and watched a herd of flying horses, no bigger than swans. But enough of that; back to the quest.'

She reached for a map and unrolled it. 'This is Daunce. Here is the Cave. If we continue to trek northeast back up into the mountains, we'll reach this place, which is known as Gryphon Heights. It will take us at least five days to get to the foot of the mountain, maybe longer; hard to tell from this map exactly what the terrain will be like.'

Rolf had been peering at the map. 'That certainly sounds promising; we ought to check it out.'

'It fits the rhyme,' agreed Braidart. 'At least we must eliminate it before we look elsewhere. From the sound of it, we'll have to climb. That means good equipment and more to carry.'

'It is still three moons to spring; if this is at high altitude, we must prepare for snow and ice,' warned Clarriss.

'The weather in Daunce is comparatively mild,' said Braidart, plainly keen to minimise the problems and get the team going again. The thought of a climb had brought a gleam to his eyes.

'It may still delay us,' cautioned Clarriss. 'We have no Hook, so we'll have to start from our old campsite near the Cave of the Damned. We can take Tricky as a baggage pony, but Idris had to release the horses when he was portalled back in a hurry to heal Jorn. They'll be long gone and we can't get new mounts to such a remote area, so this will have to be a foot-slog. We'll need to know more about the weather conditions in that part of Daunce before we decide when to go. Will the gryphons pose any threat?'

'Hard to say,' responded Mordant. 'They are said to be highly territorial, and they are meat eaters. They have fearsome talons and wicked beaks, so they could do some damage if they attack.'

'A high-powered crossbow would soon sort them out,' said Brett.

'Yes, it would, but these are very rare animals. I'd hate to have to kill them.'

'Well, at least you have a destination,' said Kayman, 'and if the fourth part is hidden in the Burning Coast, we only have one more verse to solve.'

'Don't count your peaches before they ripen,' Mordant retorted. 'And remember, we still have the problem of Philip to deal with. What's he been up to while we were away?'

'Not much, as far as I can tell,' replied Kayman. 'He's back on duty at the Horse Transit Point and carrying on just as usual. We'll have to get rid of him at some stage, but not right now. I have various stews on the boil, and I need to get those well and truly cooked before we tackle him. And there is the looming problem of Darric and his invasion. The window of time to complete your quest is shrinking fast. You have three parts left to find. Given the delays caused by the weather and the fact that we have no idea where the fifth part might be, that could take, at best, four moons; it could be much longer. Of course, winter will hold Darric up as well, but he is likely to attack as soon as the weather eases, and that will be long before we complete the mission. If we can delay him, it would help enormously.'

'What did you have in mind?' asked Mordant sceptically.

'I was thinking of an attack on Vard. Something significant that will really slow Darric down. We'll have to work on the details.' Kayman regarded her with a tight smile. 'I thought you and the Darnells might enjoy that.'

Braidart was at once alert and interested. 'We most certainly would! But is it remotely possible?'

'Oh, it's possible. But highly dangerous.' Mordant's memories had brought a gleam to her eyes.

'But what could we possibly do on Vard that would cause Darric serious problems? We can't send in an army, even if we had one,' objected Clarriss.

'I'm not thinking about an army. I'm thinking about our Master of Nine,' said Kayman.

Jorn looked worried. *'I don't much like the sound of that,'* Jan told him silently.

Rolf shook his head. 'I am not certain that we can risk this; we have to keep Jorn safe. And don't we need to keep his identity secret?'

Kayman replied with grim certainty. 'We must have more time. If we can hold Darric up for even a moon, it could make a vital difference. Look, Philip has been passing information direct to Darric. He already knows that Jorn worked an unusual healing for Brendan. Every mage and student in the Hall is wondering about Jorn's powers and speculating wildly. As the quest progresses, it will become obvious that Jorn is taking a leading role in it. We can't keep him hidden much longer. I believe it's time for Jorn to show Darric what he's capable of working, and let the War-Lord realise that he's not the most powerful mage in two universes.'

'Mmm. I suppose you are right,' said Rolf, still sounding doubtful. 'So, Jorn, how would you like to become a War-Mage?'

'Powers, I don't know! I'm still learning. I have no idea what I could do that would terrify Darric into delaying his invasion, not that I wouldn't like to try. He's had too much of his own way. But if I can learn, of course I will. And Jan will too. Anything we can do to strike against the raash is good by me.'

'Speak for yourself,' Jan told him rather crisply. *'I'm all for defeating Darric, but I'm not at all sure that I've got the right Gifts to be a War-Mage. But I'll help you if I can.'*

Kayman smiled, unaware of Jan's objections. 'I hoped you'd say that. I've been looking forward to imagining what a Nine can achieve by way of destruction! However, I'm still not totally certain about the timing. That's always the problem when you're juggling with more than one interlinked scheme. Nevertheless, it might be a good idea if you could both learn how to make a war-hammer. Could you teach them, Mordant? From the sound of it, the team may not be able to leave for Daunce for several days. You could take the opportunity and do it now.'

'Yes, I could. We'd have to go somewhere pretty remote where they can let rip without being noticed. I know just the place.'

Kayman grinned, 'That's settled then. You and the twins can do that, and the others can get ready for the trip to Daunce. And I'll carry on stirring my stew-pots!'

Rolf snorted. 'Three steps ahead of us all, and as secretive as ever, old friend!'

*

The following day, Mordant found Jorn in his room after lunch. The young mage sat in his armchair by his fire, looking very pensive. He'd been having a long internal debate with Jan over the next stage in their quest and the development of Power. He knew he'd need the skills of a War-Mage sooner or later, but he wasn't looking forward to it, or even certain that he was capable of it, and Jan had made it clear that he wasn't able, or willing, to help much with that.

Mordant could sense his uncertainty and knew she must do something about it, and fast. No Master could function unless he had total confidence in his own abilities. Which meant a compelling demonstration.

'Right, Wonder Boy, get some warm clothes and good, strong boots,' she said cheerfully. 'You and I are going to do some serious work, and we can't do it here.'

Jorn grinned at her business-like tone and got to his feet. He extinguished his fire with a quick gesture and went to get his boots and thick travel cloak. 'Where are we going?' he enquired as he tugged the snug, fleece-lined leather up past his socks with the usual struggle.

'Earth, and a long way away from anywhere. You need to be able to practice your war-hammer where it can't do any damage. Or rather, where it can do a lot of damage but it won't matter.'

'That sounds good. Can I take the horn?'

'Of course. Not on show though, I'll have to use a Transit Point.'

'Right.'

The pair left to find the duty Transit Master, who duly formed an Earth portal to bring them out in the Oak Transit Point. Mordant created the next portal with brisk efficiency. Jorn watched, wondering what she intended to show him what was so powerful that he couldn't try it at home. The thought of that kind of working was both exciting and alarming, but he knew he had to get used to it. The gateway formed and Mordant gestured for Jorn to pass through. He entered the swirling mist wondering what he would see on the far side. It was mainly rock and mountains, and very cold.

'Welcome to the Mountains of the Moon!' she told him with a flourish. 'We are in the wilds on the far eastern side of the Inner Sea, and a very, very long way from other people. Which, as I hope you will soon see, is just what we need. The weather isn't too bad, considering the time of year.'

'How did you find a Hook for this place?'

'Long story. Mostly, I sight-stepped. I was hunting for chimeras. There are none near here, it was a false lead, though I did find them later. Those little flying horses. Delightful creatures. Must show you one day. But now you need to work. I hope you had a good lunch?'

He nodded. 'As usual.'

'And I went to my tree this morning,' added Jan.

'Right. Find a rock and sit down while I explain.'

They settled as comfortably as they could in a sheltered corner. It was dry but cold, with a cutting wind that made odd noises against the bare stone. Sheer walls and buttresses soared upwards towards ice-crowned, craggy peaks. Giant boulders and chunks of rock littered the ground.

'Now, you will both remember, all too well, the devastation that Darric caused to the glade where your parents lived. He used a construct called a war-hammer, and powered it with the added focus of the Knife and the Chain.'

Jorn winced slightly. 'I'm not likely to forget that. It was appalling.'

'So how would you like to do the same to somewhere on Vard?'

'That sounds interesting,' he responded cautiously.

'Mordant, I'm going to watch Jorn first time around. I don't think my Gift is much use for something like this, but I'll give it a try later.'

'Fine, Jan. Now, I know the construct, and I'll give you a demonstration first. Then I'll explain how it works and you can try. While I'm doing the working, deploy a body-shield, I don't want any accidents.'

Mordant retreated to her inner space, engaged with her Quincunx and spent several minutes creating the complex, tightly-woven, round braid. She opened her eyes and pointed to a small rock about a hundred ems away. 'Are you ready?' Jorn nodded. 'Now, watch.'

The rock split with a loud crack, sending shards in all directions.

'That was just a small one. I suspect that you can do a great deal better, but I have no idea how much force you can put into it, and of course, neither do you. We are going to find out. Now, this is how you work it. The hammer has to pack a punch, so it needs to be a rigid construct, like a round plait. The skill lies in how you blend the colours. Many mages make the mistake of believing that red is the strongest destructive force because it's the main Primary in Disjunct, but it's not. The effect is comparatively weak unless combined with other colours. Violet is far stronger, and so, oddly, is blue; I can't use that, of course, but you can. We may have to experiment, but I suggest you begin by twisting nine strands, which you should make by weaving red, blue, violet and gold. Then you need to knot them into ropes using three twists at a time. Do you follow me so far?'

Jorn nodded; he was starting to get interested. 'Yes. And my colours are already excited. This working will not be easy to control, I think.'

'Probably not. The effort to master it will add to the force behind it.'

'So I have three ropes now. Is that all I need?'

Jorn

'In your case, I'd aim for nine, so just repeat what you have just done two more times. And then you need to braid them all into a tight nine-fold construct that can be aimed like a thrown spear. At that point, you may want to add your other colours so you have all Nine in the weave. She looked around. 'See that big, square boulder over there, about the size of a garden shed? Smash it, Jorn.'

Jorn looked at the laughing challenge in her eyes and grinned. His Quincunx already throbbed with pent Power. 'My pleasure. Just give me a moment or two.'

The Master of Nine retreated to his mental workshop, engaged with his Quincunx and began to work the colours. He fed his knotted ropes with controlled anger, using the remembered images of raash destruction to fuel his working. The final braid was complex; working with nine stiff cords and maintaining a tight, round plait was difficult, but that was where his weaving skill was so useful. It took him some 10 minutes of fierce concentration before he had the thing hung ready.

'Can you deploy a really strong shield for me, Jan? Then I won't have to divide my concentration by maintain two constructs. I think this thing is going to pack a big kick!'

'Right. No problem.'

'It might be a good idea to ward yourself and find a place to shelter,' he warned Mordant. He felt Jan hang the shield and prepare to feed him added Power.

Mordant scrambled a short way up a slope and slid into a handy crack between two large chunks of rock. She watched with acute interest as Jorn faced up to his task. He grasped the unicorn horn and pointed it at the boulder. *'Ready, Jan?'* He closed his eyes for a moment, opened them, and aimed his construct.

The result was more than impressive. There was a thunderous crack of pure Power. The huge boulder disintegrated into a lethal spray of fast-moving fragments, which shot off in all directions, and clattered and splattered against the mountainside, causing further chaos. Dull percussions echoed back. Finally, the dust settled.

Mordant provided a slow handclap.

Jorn was amazed, and slightly scared. 'Wow. I, erm, I think I overdid that a tad.'

Mordant gave her pupil her best smile. 'Not from where I was standing. That looked about right. I was busy imagining what the result of that would be when it hit a raash barrack block. Well done, Wonder Boy! I rather think you are going to give Darric a very unpleasant surprise. How do you both feel?'

'Fine. Not tired.'

'Do you want to give it a go Jan?

'I don't think I can manage anything as powerful as that, but I'll try. Don't help me, Jorn, we need to know what I can produce on my own.' Jan took form and sat on a rock to work his construct.

Jorn could sense his brother's uncertainty, and knew he hadn't really got his heart in it. He worked a shield ready to hang over both of them, but it was hardly necessary. He could sense that Jan's braid was not as strong as his own. He handed to horn to his twin and waited. The result was not impressive. Jan knocked chips off his boulder, but did not explode it.

Mordant shrugged. 'Never mind. That might improve with practice. Anyway, Jorn packs all the punch we need.'

Jan shed form and slid back into his brother, glad to have got that out of the way. He had known from the start that he was not going to be good at this sort of thing. *'See what I mean?'* he sent, ruefully. *'I can't seem to summon enough mental energy to work it properly. I think this is something we'll have to leave to you, Jorn.'*

Mordant was looking unusually cheerful. 'Let's go and tell the others that we have a War-Mage in the making! I'll sort out a few more constructs for you, Jorn. I think that attack on Vard has just become a distinct possibility!'

*

Darrison had translocated to the Earth Base to report to Ajina. His father, Darric, was busy on Vard, putting the final touches to his invasion plans. His aunt listened to his report with close attention; Darrison was always ahead of the game.

'I tried to have Jorn, Rolf and Braidart killed, but the thugs were incompetent, so it's back to the other plan. The team have returned from their last mission. I think they went to Karth as we expected. I'm pretty certain they found whatever they were looking for, but I'm still not sure what it is. I didn't get a chance to attach a tag before they left, but I have now. I managed to slip into Mage Hall while they were all away. I've left a small spell-tag on Jorn's new sword, and another on his hat, so the next time they leave, we should be able to track them.'

'Excellent! I'll organise an assault team. We can use the war-hounds to find them.'

Darrison handed over a closed bag. 'This has some clothes belonging to Jorn and Rolf. That will give the hounds their scent. Make sure you use experienced soldiers, and plenty of them. These people are all tricky to deal with, and Mordant and Braidart are expert Sword-Masters. Will you send mages as well?'

'No, I don't think so; we don't need more than one, just to form the portal, and send the hounds to sleep so we can translocate them. I think one surprise attack at night in full force may be more effective. I'll try that first, anyway. If that fails, then we can try to pick them off one by one, starting with the boy. Maybe you could do that? Or will it destroy your cover?'

'I think Kayman is getting suspicious. My usefulness is becoming limited, so I'll have to drop the "Philip" identity soon anyway. And I'm aching for some action after all these years of playing the long game.'

'I know. And I hope to give you the chance to show your other skills in the near future. But we could not have managed without you. Your intelligence has been invaluable. Anyway, your task will soon be over. Darric is making the final preparations as we speak. And I'm all but ready to organise the attack on Mage Hall. If we can eliminate Kayman and his power-base, and kill the whole nest of mages and students, it will make things a lot easier. We might even find the Cup there.'

'It's possible. Good luck with that. Let me know when you are ready for me to help. I know the Hall like the back of my hand now, and I can work all the Hooks you need. I can't wait to get rid of that smug mage and his cronies.

*

Jorn was looking forward to his first quest with Jan. He was getting on well with his inner twin, although from time to time, Jan made it very clear that he had a mind of his own.

The young mage was brooding over his packing list for their next mission and making experimental piles of things on his bed, muttering as he did so. He was well aware that he needed to be selective as he was going to carry all this stuff on the trek, but it was so hard to leave things behind, and the 'must have' pile kept growing instead of shrinking. It wasn't going to fit into his pack. But he really *needed* that warm fleece, and the extra socks, and his favourite treacle toffee.

He put the horn beside the pile and added his new sword and scabbard, then stood wondering what he could possibly do without.

'Why are you taking those?' demanded Jan, sounding surprised. *'You don't need the horn, you have me now. If you think you have to rely on it to get full use of your Power, it could actually hold you back. There's going to come a time when you haven't got it to hand.'*

'I know all that. But I'm still taking it with me. I'll keep it in its compact form, it won't be in the way.

'And why the sword?'

'I want to carry on fencing with Braid.'

'You didn't bother to take it to Karth.'

'I thought it would be far too hot for practise, and we wouldn't have time, and I was right. But according to Mordant, this time we've got at least a five-day trek. It gets boring in the evenings. And after that attack, I'll feel safer with a blade close to hand.'

'I've never understood why you want to learn at all. I mean, you're a Master of Nine. Rolf and Mordant have taught you a heap of new constructs. You can form a shield that no blade can pierce. You can wrench a weapon out of the hand of anyone who attacks you, turn the hilt too hot to hold, bind them in a net, suspend them in mid-air three or four ems off the ground, and that's all without having to get seriously unpleasant or inventive with the killing constructs such as Mordant is teaching you. Why would the sword and knife work? Do you want to stab people?'

'No, at least, not unless I absolutely have to.'

'So you are carrying nearly an em of heavy steel as an ornament?'

'No, of course not. It's good exercise, and it's fun. And Mordant and Braidart do it.'

'Well, just remember, you have to carry the things.'

Jorn huffed and went back to his vain attempt to cut down his luggage.

*

Once they were ready, the team translocated back to their old campsite in Daunce, which was the nearest Hook they had. There was no snow, but it was bitterly cold. Idris and Rolf had cached the tents and some other equipment, so they sorted it through to see what was needed.

'You don't need to provide a tent for me; I'm going to share with Braidart. Lightens the load,' Mordant told Clarriss brightly. The dwar's eyebrows shot up. She compressed her lips and, with an obvious effort, said nothing. Rolf shrugged, unsurprised; the couple had not troubled to conceal their developing liaison.

'*It seems an odd pairing,*' commented Jorn as he hitched his heavy pack over his shoulders and tried to find a way of carrying his sword so that it didn't keep hitting him at every step.

'*Why odd? Because he's human and she's half raash?*'

'*Well, I suppose that is a bit weird, though it doesn't seem to bother Braid, he's been chasing her ever since we started the mission. But I thought Mordant really fancies Idris. She watches him all the time, and tries to send out signals, but he doesn't seem to notice.*'

'*He notices, but he knows he can't respond, although he'd really like to. He's more than fond of Mordant. It's really sad for both of them.*'

'*But why?*'

'*One of those shian things.*'

'*I wish you wouldn't say that. It reminds me that I'm not shian.*'

'*Sorry, but it's private, and I promised I wouldn't talk about it, even to you. It's... well, it's to do with the way shians make love.*'

Jorn could tell that Jan wasn't going to explain, and the team was ready to set off, so he let it pass.

The hike into the Carthians was as tough and monotonous as expected. Tricky had come with them, but they could have done with a second baggage pony as they all had heavy packs to tote. It was bleak, hard walking and climbing, cold and cheerless, with a relentless northeast headwind that had them hunched down under their hoods.

Jan walked beside his twin for several hours a day, getting used to being in form and building his stamina. Jorn still suffered from a persistent hollow ache in his inner being when his brother was absent, but he did his best to ignore it. They bespoke, but not much. Most of the time, each knew what the other was thinking and feeling. They both understood the need for space, privacy and silence.

Everyone did what they could to lighten things up in the evenings when they rested. Jan had taken a liking to Gambit and he and Rolf spent at least an hour every night bent over the board. At times, the young shian disappeared with Idris, and they spent a lot of time together in silent conversation. Jorn had to squash a pang of jealousy. Jan sensed that, and explained that they were talking about 'shian things', which only made it worse.

Rolf was an expert storyteller, and usually offered at least one tale. Clarriss never took her eyes from him when he was speaking. Jorn was much amused to see that the dwar was always at Rolf's side these days, industriously mending his socks and washing his shirts, and giving him extra helpings.

Mordant and Braidart were careful not to take their intimate relationship too far in front of the team, though they sat close together, and Mordant listened to Braid telling tall stories about his exploits as a mercenary with amazing patience. The others did their best to ignore the suppressed giggles and breathy gasps that came from their tent at night.

Jorn watched in awe when the halfer went through her nightly exercise ritual with her longsword. He could tell that Braidart was deeply impressed.

'I've only ever seen one person who moved like that, and that is my brother, Brett, who is a Sword-Master,' he told Jorn. 'He tried to teach me, but I never had the patience to master the Warriors' Way. I'm good, but not that good. And my time as a Tullish mercenary ruined what little style I had. I can kill, no problem, but it's not pretty.'

'Well, you know enough to show me how to fight, and that's all I need,' Jorn told him. 'I'm not bothered about style!' He shadow-fenced with Braidart most evenings while supper was cooking. He would have loved to try some real contact, sword on sword, but Braid had explained that the sound of clashing steel could carry for a long distance and might attract unwelcome attention.

'We can't take the risk, even though there may not be another person within a thousand kays. And anyway, we don't want any accidents!' The tall soldier grinned, looking more like a brigand than ever now his full dark beard was growing back again. 'Though I must say, you have a natural skill with the blade, and your height and strength are assets. It would be fun to give you a proper taste of combat. I must teach you some knife skills also, for close quarters.'

After one practice bout, Rolf drew Jorn to the side, away from the others. 'Why are you doing this, Jorn?'

'Well, partly for the exercise, and to keep warm. And because it's a challenge, and I enjoy it. Braid says every man should know how to defend himself.'

'And you think you need to do that with a sword?'

'Oh, don't you start!' exclaimed Jorn, irritably. 'Jan can't understand why I want to learn either. I just do.'

Rolf looked hard at the young mage. 'I simply want you to think a bit more carefully about the consequences of having a blade. Steel attracts attention, and usually from the wrong sort of person. If you are going to carry it, you must be very good with it. If you are good with it, eventually, you will kill someone. If you are not good enough, someone will kill you. That is the way of the blade. If that is what you want then fine, practice as if your life depends on it, because it very likely will.'

'I hadn't thought about it quite like that.'

'Well, I suggest you do,' the mage told him brusquely. 'And remember that if you get into a sword fight, it will take every part of your concentration, and magic will go out of the window. Which is likely to be the most effective weapon, mage-craft or metal?'

'Mordant manages to use both.'

'Mordant likes to stretch the rules, in this, as in many things. And she is a Sword-Master of unusual skill. Think hard before you seek to copy her.'

Jorn talked to Jan about that. *'I see what Rolf means, and of course, I won't ever be anywhere like as good as Mordant or Braid. But I think there may be unexpected attacks when you simply can't find time to project a working, like when those heavies were waiting for us, and a blade might be very handy. It's really hard to focus on throwing constructs when people are trying to kill you. It all happens so fast, and if there are a lot of enemies, it's all too easy to use up everything you've hung ready, and then there's no time to work more. So, as he says, I'd better get reasonably good at using it.'*

'Your choice, not mine. I'll stick to mage-craft. Not that I want to kill anyone using that either. So far, I'm not much good at working attacking constructs of any kind. Mordant says I don't have your aggressive killer instinct.'

'She thinks I have one of those? Powers, I doubt it! But Jan, you must at least hang some defensive constructs; we simply don't know what we'll meet on this trip. A stunner or a blinder won't kill, but they'll drop your attacker very effectively. And we need wards and body-shields.'

'Yes, we do, or at least you do, and I'm happy to help with that. I need to look after you! Your body is my refuge too.'

'Yes, when you are indwelling. But what if you are out, in form?'

'Then I'll shed it. It's really hard to attack a shi – it's too nebulous – even a construct can't find anything to stick to. And Idris has been explaining what shians do when they really have to fight. It's a closely guarded secret, but I can tell you, it's remarkably effective and very impressive!'

'Oh I give up!' said Jorn crossly.

Chapter 21

The team made good time and, after four days, they had got over the high ground and descended into thick pine forest. Braid and Mordant pored over the map and estimated that they were only two days away from their target. It was a relief to be sheltered from the cutting upland wind.

They made camp and had their usual quiet evening huddled around the fire. The moon was rising and owls hooted in the distance. The wind gusted in the branches and the fire crackled and popped with a pleasant scent of pine. Tricky stamped and blew and shifted. Rolf grumbled quietly as usual about the cold, and the hard ground and the lack of baths, but they all knew that this had been the easier part of the journey, and the terrain was going to get a lot more challenging very soon.

'Time to turn in.' Braidart got up and stretched. Mordant got up too. She had already decided that this relationship was probably a mistake, but now was not the time to call a halt. Braidart was certainly a lot of fun, and a considerate and inventive lover. But not Brett. Very much not Brett. And not Idris either. Mordant felt the shian's eyes follow them, which was, after all, part of the point of what she was doing, but yet again, Idris totally failed to react. He lost form and drifted off to find water. She repressed a frustrated sigh and went to join Braid.

Jorn smothered a smile at Clarriss' prim expression as she watched the couple go off together. *'She's probably jealous!'* he told Jan. *'Clarriss can hardly bear to let Rolf out of her sight, but he's never going to ask her to share a tent!'*

It was bitterly cold at night and Jorn was glad of his down-filled sleeping bag. He was tired but somehow couldn't settle. He tossed restlessly, trying to find a comfortable position. He finally went to sleep. Jan slipped out and took form, and walked off to find a tree. He was looking forward to his first taste of a really big evergreen, but the tall spruce had a strong, resinous flavour, sustaining, but not nearly as enjoyable as his favourite oak. He didn't much care for the tight, prickly leaves either, and cut short his usual curious exploration of any new kind of tree, happy to shift back into the comforting security of his brother's body. As he got near the camp, his danger sense tweaked sharply, and he shed form at once. They were not alone.

Jorn was abruptly woken by Jan calling his name with loud urgency. *'Jorn, wake up. I can sense danger. There is something out there and it's getting closer, fast.'*

A thrill of alarm ran through him and he sat up, straining his ears for any possible threat. He eased out of the warm cocoon and emerged cautiously from the tent, his sword in his hand. Across the embers of the fire, he saw that Mordant had roused also.

'What is it?' he asked tensely. 'Jan senses danger.'

'Not sure. Something's moving out there.' Mordant stood with her hand poised on her sword hilt. In the weak moonlight, the trees were black and the shadows impenetrable. A twig cracked. Tricky whinnied uneasily. On the other side of the campsite, something large rustled.

'Better wake—' Her words were cut short. Huge, snarling shapes, darker shadows against the darkness, launched from the trees on three sides at once, followed by the all-too-familiar sight of armed raash. A lot of them.

The long, steel blade swept from her scabbard and she was instantly in the zone, oblivious to anything except the dance of death, a whirl of precisely controlled, totally lethal action, taking on more than one enemy as they entered her killing circle.

Braidart erupted from the tent a second later and charged into the battle in his long underpants and shirt, with a lethal ferocity in which style came second to sheer brute force. He fought with every part of his powerful body, selecting a target, felling it, and moving on without a pause.

Everything started to happen much too fast in a fury of yells, barks and snarls, which rapidly turned into screams and yelps. Jorn felt Jan slam a defensive shield around him as three raash and two enormous hounds came straight for him. Jan mind-shouted *'LOOK OUT'* and dropped the three raash with a stun-strike, which sent them six ems backwards, as if hit by a giant fist. Jorn summoned the heart-stopping shafts that he had kept in his mental workroom ready for an emergency, and felled the dogs in mid-spring. He got a second killing shaft ready. He used that on the next raash but a new soldier attacked and he engaged him with his sword. The raash fell, but he wasn't sure that he had killed him.

Jorn felt a sword-blade clash against his ward-shield and be deflected. He threw a blinder and the advancing raash stumbled away into the path of Mordant, who neatly removed his head.

Even Clarriss was fighting, her sword moving with skill and speed. She dispatched a hound that was as tall as she was and readied to meet the next snarling brute. Rolf had got there first and aimed a shaft that dropped like a stone. Braidart finished his opponent. Jorn span in a defensive circle, seeking his next target, but there were none left standing. He stood still, tensely prepared for further action, and trying not to look at the results of Mordant's lethal butchery.

The Sword-Master had turned to check that no more enemies were in sight. As she did so, a giant hound launched itself from the darkness towards her back. Before anyone had time to react, a thick coil of mist took the beast in mid-air, wrapped around it and dragged it down. The huge dog writhed, struggling and howling horribly. Then it went limp and its body collapsed like a shaggy rug. Idris materialised.

Mordant saluted him with her sword, cleaned her blade, kissed the hilt, and sheathed it. She drew her dagger and methodically made her way round the bodies with Braidart to check they were all dead, finishing the job as necessary.

Rolf went to calm Tricky. Braidart, Idris and Jorn began the grim task of dragging the corpses a short distance away. The campsite was slick with blood and the stench of recent killing. Mordant completed her round of the corpses and came over to help with the clearing-up operation. She prodded at the body of the hound that Idris had killed.

'What did you do to it, Idris? The thing is all shrivelled up to rags of skin and bone. I've never seen anything like it. What working did you use?'

'It was not mage-craft. I simply sucked all the water from its body. It is a shian defence, but we keep it secret. I try not to use it except in extreme emergency. I would appreciate your discretion in not speaking of this.'

Jorn shuddered, as much from discovering that Idris was capable of killing in such a fashion, as at the realisation of the grim fate of the hound.

Mordant looked at the big shian; his handsome face was unreadable. She gave him her best smile and went closer. 'Saving my life certainly qualified as an emergency. Thank you, my friend. You have surprised me yet again.'

He took a step back and shrugged uncomfortably. 'Is anyone hurt?' Amazingly, everyone shook their heads. 'Well, if all the excitement is over, I am going back to soak in my nice, quiet stream.' He strode swiftly away and Mordant's eyes followed him.

'Pig-shit!' she spat under her breath. *He could at least have let me kiss him.*

Clarriss had got the fire going again. Rolf returned and passed round his flask of liquor. Jorn wished he could have a few sips. They were all shaken.

'Thanks for taking out those raash, Jan,' he sent. *'Mordant is wrong about the lack of aggression; you just have to have a really good reason to make you fight.'*

'That was fun,' said Braidart, hunkering down by the fire with his cloak wrapped round him, 'but not good news. They headed straight at us.'

'Actually, straight at Jorn,' said Mordant. 'And they've been using those giant war-hounds to track us. They are killers. They never leave a scent once they're onto it. Ideal for this kind of terrain.'

'But you are all missing the significant point. They found us. They had our scent. What does that suggest to you?' asked Clarriss.

'Philip's work again, no doubt. Or another spy somewhere far too close for comfort.'

'But only Kayman knew our exact plans,' objected Braidart. 'If Philip did tell Darric we were heading off again, the raash couldn't possibly locate us so precisely. Even hounds would have trouble finding someone in the middle of hundreds of square kays of wilderness.'

'A far-seeing?' wondered Clarriss.

'Perhaps. But I suspect it's more likely that Philip has planted a spell-tag on one of us, or on our belongings,' said Rolf grimly. 'We must find it.'

'More likely to be on something one of us owns,' said Mordant. 'I have a construct that will find it, but it may take a while if we have to go through all the gear. Has anyone got any suggestions?'

'I suggest we start with Jorn,' said Clarriss. 'He was their first target.'

'I'm afraid that you may be right,' agreed Rolf. 'Jorn, what could have a tag attached to it? Something you keep close to you?'

Jorn shook his head. 'Well, it won't be on the horn. I never leave it where anyone could find it. What else? Me? My clothes? I think Jan might spot that. My saddle and tack?'

'And the sword Brendan gave you,' said Mordant suddenly. 'Better check that first, Jorn.' He went to fetch it, convinced that Mordant must be wrong. He drew it from the scabbard and she span a thin web of pink threads around the blade. She shook her head. 'No response, but wait a minute, let me try the belt and scabbard.' She repeated the seeking, and this time, a bright red and yellow spot lit up halfway down the sheath. 'A dab of Fire and Earth to seal it!' she said, grimly.

Jorn

'Can we get rid of it?' asked Jorn anxiously.

'I will destroy it,' answered Mordant, 'but I am afraid that means your blade will lack a scabbard for a time. Lay it here beside the fire.' A moment later, the scabbard and belt glowed briefly with white heat, blazed, and in few moments, were entirely consumed. Once that was over, she methodically checked all their belongings and found another tag, which had been planted on Jorn's hat. As that too vanished in mage-fire, he reflected grimly that he was going to miss it if the weather turned and it started to snow. But it was the thought that Philip had secretly sneaked into his room at the Hall and messed with his possessions that was really chilling.

No one felt like sleep but they could not move until daybreak, so Clarriss and Rolf went back to their tents to get what rest they could. Jorn stayed on watch with Braidart and Mordant. He sat with his back to a tree, taking comfort from its strength, and listening jumpily to every slight sound. He was uncomfortably aware of the pile of dead raash a short way off. His breath made clouds in the frosty air and distant stars glittered above the trees. He shivered.

'Powers, Jan, I was glad to have a sword in my hand and some idea of how to use it, but I'd never really considered the results. Mordant and Braidart reduced the raash to pieces. Seeing heads and limbs go flying is the stuff of nightmares. The blood is everywhere, I can't wait to leave.'

Jan responded with a gentle warmth and a sense of comforting closeness. *'Me too. But you did really well.'*

'I wasn't frightened at the time, I was too busy, but now I do feel scared. Jan, I've never had so many enemies all trying to kill me at the same time!'

'But they didn't succeed. You fought back, and so did I. I surprised myself. If any of the raash got away, they will report that we are a pretty lethal bunch. It may make them think twice before they try again.'

'Or it just might make them send in a much larger force, with a lot of War-Mages in support. I hate the idea that we are being watched and stalked like this.'

'Well, I can tell you that they're not anywhere close right now, so you can relax.'

'You're joking! I'm going to spend the remainder of the quest continually waiting for raash to jump out of a portal at us. Or expecting hired assassins to be lurking around every corner. Speaking of which, I'd better

get back into my workroom and hang some more attacking constructs and wards.'

'You do that. I'll keep watch.'

Nothing further happened, and they left the place as soon as there was a glimmer of grey dawn, tired and tense, and all anxious to move on quickly. After four hours, they finally came out of the rapidly thinning trees and saw the mountains ahead clearly for the first time. Jan gave a soft *'Wow'* as the snow-topped high peaks came into view.

Rolf paused, referring to his map to check their location, and nodded in satisfaction. 'We are right on track. The big peak is Mount Freya. Just look at the heavy snow on the top; we can be thankful we don't have to climb it.'

Braidart gave an unexpected chuckle of laughter. 'The peak is well-named! Freya was a queen of Daunce who was famous for her implacable virginity. No one "climbed" her, and I'll bet that no one has ever climbed that beauty either! Just look at those sheer faces, hardly a crack to get a fingernail into; my, what I wouldn't give to have a try at mounting that maiden!'

Clarriss sniffed and narrowed her lips in disapproval. Jorn smothered a grin. He knew that Braid thoroughly enjoyed offending the dwar's over-developed sense of propriety.

'Thank the Powers we don't have to attempt anything so severe,' said Rolf. 'Gryphon Heights lies between those two mountains, somewhere up the lower col you see there. With the snow cover and ice, that is going to be quite challenging enough for me.'

'And before we go any further, I'd better see what Jan thinks,' said Jorn, scanning the icy mountainside with misgivings. *'Is it up there Jan?'*

'Yes it is. But it's dangerous. I can't tell you how, though, I just have a really bad feeling about us going up there.'

'Great! Thanks for cheering me up!'

'Jan confirms that we are in the right place. The Juncture is somewhere up the mountain. But he says there is danger of some kind.'

'Everything just as usual then,' said Braidart with broad grin.

They moved off again in search of a site for their base camp. Clarriss was as hard to please as usual and, when they did agree on a location, the dwar bustled about organising everything in sight.

'Be sure to stack those supplies under some rocks,' she told Braidart. 'Don't want any predators rummaging through them at night. It's too early for bears but no telling what else is up here.'

Braid said, 'Yes, ma'am,' in a neutral voice, and continued to get on with his job with professional efficiency.

Jorn sighed. Clarriss was an excellent soldier, but he did just wish she would give people some credit for knowing what they had to do without having to be told. 'How do you put up with it?' he whispered.

The big man shrugged. 'When you have had to serve under as many bloody awkward officers as I have, you get used to letting it all flow over your head. And to give the Commander her due, she is very competent, and brave too. She did very well against those huge hounds. But I really don't know what Rolf sees in her. He must go for the dominant type. Talk about bossy! Are all male dwarves stupid, or are they too hen-pecked to answer back?'

'Thank your lucky stars that she doesn't know anything about climbing,' Jorn muttered, 'or she'd be telling you precisely how to knot a rope!' Braidart cast his eyes to heaven.

Mordant's keen hearing had picked up the end of that. She came over. 'Has Rolf told you the story of how the dwars took over the governance of the Dwarran Realm?' she enquired in a low voice. Jorn shook his head. She checked that Clarriss was out of earshot and started the tale in a confidential murmur.

'Well, it was this way. At that time, the dwarrys ruled in Terrea, just as men did on Earth, and there was a High King named Marcus, who was not, by most accounts, the sharpest arrow in the quiver. Things were going from bad to worse and finally, he did something truly stupid. His wife, Queen Miriam, was a forceful dwar, and she swept into court and gave her husband a public roasting. He lost his temper. He pulled off his crown and threw it across the room in a childish gesture, shouting that if the Queen thought she could do a better job of being King than he could, she was welcome to try, and he would be happy to give her complete authority to do exactly as she wanted. Then he stormed out of the room.

'Of course, he assumed that she would at once panic and apologise. Needless to say, she did not. Queen Miriam picked up the crown and placed it on her own head, telling the assembled councillors and courtiers that she would, of course, obey her husband's command, and she hoped that they would give her their total obedience. Within a moon, she had replaced the entire government with dwars. A year later, she had taken over the army, totally re-organised the country, and made it impossible for her husband to do anything but abdicate.'

Jorn hastily clamped his hand over his mouth to suppress a loud hoot of laughter, and Braidart looked across at the busy dwar with a wide grin.

'I can see Clarriss doing exactly that! But didn't the dwarrys object?'

'Well, that's the odd thing. It seems they did not. Now that they didn't have to bother about running the country, they could concentrate on trade and making money, and they had much more time to go hunting and fishing, and playing sports, and gardening, and making fine things, all of which they greatly enjoyed. The dwars were quite happy taking decisions and organising everything in sight, and doing all the boring administration and paperwork, and all the skilled scientific and technical things that took a long time to learn, so in fact, everyone was satisfied. The Dwarran Realm prospered as never before, and the arrangement has continued to this day.'

Braid raised his eyebrows. 'Sounds as if you approve of females being in charge?'

Mordant flashed him a look under her lashes. 'Perhaps I do. Any objections, Blue Eyes?'

'I'll tell you later tonight.'

After setting camp and eating a hurried meal, it was around two hours after noon and Braid decided there was enough time left for them to make an exploratory climb. Idris took refuge in a small stream and Clarriss stayed behind to deal with supper. Jorn felt she was glad of an excuse not to climb until she had to.

The other four took light packs and some basic climbing gear and ropes. With Braidart in the lead, they began to ascend. Jorn soon stopped, looking up to see how far they had gone, for the distant ridge never seemed to get much nearer. The icy wind whipped tears from his eyes.

They reached a steep slope of loose ice and scree, which halted them. Mordant suddenly went still and said quietly. 'Don't move. Look up there.' Jorn scanned the sky in the direction she was indicating. Very high up, black against the light clouds, something large soared in a gentle spiral on huge, outspread wings. It was hard to tell the scale of it at that distance. It might be a bird, but it seemed too large.

'Is it a gryphon?' he asked, knowing that the halfer had the best distance vision in the group.

'I think so, though it's hard to tell. But the rear end doesn't look right for a bird, it's too lumpy. Watch where it goes.'

The giant creature made several circles and then began to descend in a long swoop towards the mountainside. It made for a landing site too far away for them to see clearly, and they lost track of it against the jumbled rock.

'It's a gryphon all right,' Jan told him, *'and my sense tells me that it has a nest somewhere further up, beyond that slope.'*

'We have to get over that, Braid. Jan says they have a nest up there.'

Braidart gave the steep scree slope a long, professional appraisal. 'I can traverse that, but the rest of you will have problems. I'll need to rig some ropes for you. We don't want to scare the beasts away. I think it will be best if I go on up and see if I can find where their lair is. We can't do much more today in any case. Rolf, I suggest that you and Mordant go back to camp to explain the situation to Clarriss, and I'll go on up and reconnoitre. Jorn, you stay here and wait for me, just in case something happens and I need a mage in a hurry!'

Jorn huddled into his cloak and watched as Braid expertly navigated the slope, until he emerged from the far side, and began a steep rock climb, by now, looking as tiny as a beetle. He was soon lost to sight. It took another hour of anxious, chilly waiting before he reappeared and descended with care.

'Well, you can have the good news or the bad news,' he said, as he stretched tiredly and flopped down on a low boulder.

'Both.'

'The good news is that I've found a pair of gryphons. Extraordinary animals! The upper part of a gryphon is just like a huge eagle, and it has front legs with bird talons. Then the back end is like a great tawny cat, with another set of powerful legs and a tail. They really shouldn't be able to fly, but somehow they do, though not with the full grace and mastery of an eagle. The bad news is that it's a hard climb to get there. I doubt if Rolf will make it and I'm sure Clarriss won't. And the eyrie is about as awkwardly placed as it gets.'

'Inaccessible?'

'Very. There's a stack of rock a least 200 ems high, separated from the cliff, standing alone like a huge pillar. It looks as if a giant axe blow severed it from the cliff behind. It has absolutely sheer sides. The gryphons have some kind of nest at the top. I'll lay you a hundred in gold that the Juncture is up there.'

'So we'll have to find a way up too. But not today. We'd better get a shift on before it gets dark.'

Coming down proved more difficult than going up. By the time the pair reached base camp, it was already dusk. Braidart explained what he'd seen.

'So, if the weather holds, who is coming with me tomorrow?' he asked. 'It has to be Jorn, because we need Jan's finding sense and, if it's like the last ones, there will be some kind of binding to break. Mordant climbs well, and I may need a partner. You three would be better off staying here.'

'I'm not going to miss out on the next find,' declared Rolf, with determination, 'and I badly want to see a gryphon! I'll manage. It's not the first mountain I've had to climb. But you don't have to come with us Clarry, we need someone to mind the camp.'

'No, you do not. You know I'm not much good with heights, so you seek a reason to keep me away from them. You left me behind at the Cave and once was enough. I want to see a gryphon too. I'm not going to stay here in camp and miss all the excitement, and I'm not letting you out of my sight! And, in any case, given the choice between a mountain and a pack of war-hounds or a hunting party of raash turning up when I am here alone, I think I'll choose the mountain.'

Braidart shook his head but held back from a reply; she had a point about the raash. Now that they had located the team, they might well try again, so sticking together was safer. In any case, they could all see that, despite her fear of high places, the stubborn dwar was determined not to let Rolf go up the mountain without her.

Idris said, 'If you would permit me, I will be happy to carry you, Clarriss, when it gets steep. I sense water above, and you never know when a healer will be needed, especially on a mountain.'

Clarriss hesitated, weighing the damage to her pride against her determination to stay close to Rolf. Finally, she said crisply, 'Thank you, Idris. I would much appreciate that service, if my weight isn't too much of a burden for you. I mustn't hold you all up.'

The dwar had done one of her amazingly good field-kitchen meals, a tasty hash made from dried beef and vegetables, flavoured with herbs and pepper, and the team was in high spirits. Braidart and Mordant discussed the tactics for the following day, but as usual, there were too many unknowns to get far. They set up a guard rota and settled down for an early night.

While Jorn slept, Jan went back down the mountainside to find a large tree. He was troubled. He felt no raash nearby, but his sense was loudly telling him that there was serious danger connected to the gryphons, only he couldn't see what. Were the creatures themselves dangerous, or was it something else? He had given the warning, and there was no point in alarming Jorn or the team without something more definite to tell them. They were going up the mountain tomorrow come what may. He would just have to keep vigilant. He reached the big pines and sighed; the slightly bitter, resinous evergreens were definitely not to his taste, but there was nothing else large enough, and the trees did not sleep in winter, so they were sustaining, and he needed all his strength.

In the morning, a thick, freezing mist blanketed the camp and kept the team all irritably confined until it cleared. Finally, they were able to get kitted up and started off on the ascent. The mountainside was a piebald patchwork of rock, snow and ice. Jorn enjoyed the physical effort of climbing, and looking down did not bother him, but Clarriss soon felt uneasy and was very happy to let Idris carry her. The strong shian made light work of it.

The climb got steadily more challenging after the scree slope was safely passed. Mordant lifted Clarriss and Rolf up over a few vertical places using an apport.

Braid climbed fluently, with considerable skill and calculated daring, usually without a rope, finding the route and carrying a line to rig for the others He seemed able to balance with his toes on the smallest projection, and barely a fingertip on another while his free hand searched for the next hold. There was one point when he had to use both hands to hammer in pitons and he just tucked a knee under an overhang and worked on, paying no attention to the vertical drop below him. Jorn could hardly bear to watch. He didn't mind tackling the verticals himself, and his height and strength were an advantage, but somehow watching another person do it turned his stomach.

Finally, well into the afternoon, they reached a more level area of rocky ground just below the ridge. There had been no further sighting of the gryphons. The team paused for a break, drinking thirstily and eating some high-energy rations. Idris went to look for the mountain waterfall he could sense a short distance away.

'Call if I'm needed, or when you are ready to get to the Juncture,' Idris told them.

After the rest, the others made the final ascent, which was more of a steep scramble than a climb. Clarriss was determined to walk, but stuck close to Rolf, keeping a tight hold of his hand, and managed quite well now that there was no precipitous drop in view. They rounded a bend and Gryphon Heights suddenly loomed above them. The stack that Braidart had described was clearly in view and it certainly looked formidable. Jorn surveyed the tower of rock with a feeling of sudden dread.

'Is it there, Jan?'

'It's right at the top. And tell them that the gryphons are nesting there. They are dangerous in some way. I still can't see it clearly.'

'My sense is tweaking too.'

'Good news or bad?' asked Braidart, seeing the inward consultation between the twins.

'Both. As you guessed, it's right at the top, and so are the gryphons. And we both think the creatures are dangerous in some way.'

Braidart swore softly.

Mordant had been studying the terrain and was looking grim. 'This is not going to be easy. The stack is far too high to send one of us up using an apport, and the gryphons are bound to defend their nest. If there were no gryphons, we might manage a cross-step to the summit of the stack, but the top is very narrow, and you can't maintain a glamour and cross-step at the same time, so the gryphons would attack as soon as you landed. We could possibly cross-step up to the nearest point to the stack, up there, and then apport across?'

Braid shook his head. 'Too risky; the mountainside is still under thick snow, but there's been a recent thaw. It all looks solid, but we could trigger a slide.'

'And again, we'll be sitting targets for the gryphons,' added Rolf. Right on cue, there was a harsh squawk from the eyrie.

'It would be a great deal easier if we just got rid of the beasts,' said Clarriss. 'One of you mages could kill them and then we just have to work out the best way to get up there.'

Mordant hissed her breath in and out. 'I know that's the practical answer, but I really don't want to do that unless we really have to. They're breeding here, and they are so very rare. Killing them is a last resort.'

'This isn't a good time for sentiment,' snapped Clarriss.

'It's not sentiment, it's conservation,' retorted Mordant.

'Then I'll just have to climb,' said Braid, anxious to please Mordant and prevent an argument. 'I need to take a closer look at the stack. If I can make it to the top, I can rig a rope so Jorn can use it to climb up and deal with any binding or concealing weaves. You could cover us with one of those useful thingamajigs so the gryphons don't notice us. That would work, I think?'

'It might. I'm out of other ideas. But that is one hell of a climb. Can you manage it?'

'I'll tell you when I've had a good look round the stack.'

Mordant looked questioningly at the other team members but they were all grimly uninspired. No one was very happy about it, least of all the twins, but there was no obvious alternative.

Braidart reached the base of the huge column and then spent a long time in minute examination of all four faces. When he came back, he didn't even try to make light of the problem. 'Well, the west face is severe and so is the south. North is bloody impossible. It will have to be the east, I think, the one that faces the cliff. The angle is a little less vertical and there are more holds to begin with. There is a nasty traverse halfway up and a bastard of an overhang near the top. I think I can do it, as long as the wind doesn't strengthen, but it will take time. It won't leave us enough daylight to get back down to the camp again.'

'Forget that!' said Mordant. 'We can portal back to camp if we have to. Let's take it one stage at a time. Good luck, Blue Eyes.'

He grinned at Mordant. 'Nothing like a challenge! I think I am going to remember this one!'

She covered him with a never-mind and said, 'There you are; good to go.' Braidart checked his equipment with great care, and set off. He selected his approach and began to climb steadily, checking his position and planning his route with confident expertise.

The team unconsciously moved close to the base of the stack. The mages strained their eyes and senses, trying to keep track of his progress. It was like looking at a faint star; you had to glance just to one side to catch a shadow of movement.

The next things happened very fast, but to Jorn and Jan, they seemed like a series of events frozen in time, a nightmare, slow-motion sequence, which had their mage-senses screaming warnings, but left no scope for action.

A big gryphon swept down from the summit of the stack and dived towards the group, massive wings furled, screeching furiously. They scattered in different directions. Rolf staggered and slipped as he ran downhill to safety. When he got up again, he was hobbling, and it was clear he had twisted his ankle. Clarriss rushed over to him..

As the gryphon veered to swoop at the injured mage, the dwar stood her ground protectively in front of him, waving her arms at the big beast as if frightening crows away from a field. As it scythed past again, Clarriss stooped, picked up a fist-sized stone and hurled it at the creature. It hit the gryphon, which shot upwards with a shrill squawk and flapped awkwardly away.

As it did so, an even larger gryphon dived out of nowhere and struck with deadly swiftness. It picked Clarriss up and swept away, wings labouring under the load, out over the mountainside. Jorn and Jan and the other two mages watched in frozen horror. If they used power to bring the beast down, Clarry would be hurt, but if they did nothing, she could be dead.

Trapped by the dilemma, they hesitated. The dwar struggled, obviously terrified. Light caught on a blade in her hand. Rolf yelled, 'Clarry, NO!' but the dwar struck at one of the clutching talons. Hurt, and unsteadied by the blow, the gryphon squawked, lost height and spilled air. It dropped the dwar with appalling suddenness and flew away with labouring wing beats, slowly gaining height.

Clarriss screamed. She had been dropped only a short distance, but her body hit the ground with a sickening thump, and then she rolled, bouncing down the mountainside for more than 200 ems, hitting rocks as she fell. She finally came to rest by a large boulder. She lay dreadfully still.

Jorn made an urgent mind call to Idris. With frantic haste, Mordant and Jorn climbed down towards the dwar's crumpled body. Rolf sat nursing his injured ankle, looking on helplessly. Braidart began to descend the stack as quickly as he dared.

Mordant was the first to reach Clarriss. Jorn stood feeling useless and desperately worried as the mage cautiously examined her.

'*Is she...*' Jorn could not bring himself to say the word.

Mordant shook her head. *'No, amazingly she is still alive, but only just. She is very badly hurt. Unconscious; broken leg, I think. Her breathing's bad. Powers knows what damage she may have sustained inside.'*

Idris materialised. He knelt and laid a hand on the dwar's forehead. His face grew grave. He immediately went quickly back up the slope and picked up Rolf to bring him to Clarriss. The little mage knelt and tenderly touched her battered face.

'How bad is it, Idris? I want the truth.'

'Her spine is broken, high up. She has also got a shattered shoulder, four fractures in her legs, a smashed pelvis, and a list of internal injuries I had rather not go into. She is haemorrhaging inside. I am sorry, tantar-alta, but there is nothing I can do.'

Rolf looked at Jorn with anguished entreaty, but Jorn already knew the answer. *'We're sorry too Rolf, we can't manage a miracle this time.'*

'I can give you a few moments with her before she goes; just enough time to say goodbye,' said Idris gently, 'but that is all I can do.'

'Not if she will be in pain.'

'She will not. She cannot feel anything from her chest downwards.'

Rolf nodded. Idris carefully moved and straightened her body so that she was propped against the rock. He laid his hands on her forehead and closed his eyes. After a moment or two, her eyelids began to flutter. Idris and the others moved away. Rolf very gently took her hand and stroked her forehead. 'Clarry, dear, Clarry, I'm here.'

Her eyes opened. She gave a weak smile of relief as she saw Rolf. 'Yes, I am quite safe,' he told her with a smile. 'The gryphon has gone. Oh my poor love, that was terrible fall, are you in much pain?'

The little dwar shook her head very slightly. 'Hard to breath,' she whispered, 'can't move right now. I'll be all right in a bit.'

'That's good. Just lie still.' He bent and kissed her, their eyes exchanged messages. After a few moments, Clarriss gave a small shudder. Her eyes were suddenly vacant.

Chapter 22

As Clarriss slipped from the world, Rolf gave himself up to overwhelming grief. Idris stayed kneeling beside him, a comforting arm around his heaving shoulders. The group stood in sad silence, watching the small mage, still stunned by what had just happened and unable to find words of comfort for Rolf or each other.

'We should have taken more care when we waited by the stack. We got much too close and we didn't cover ourselves. The gryphons were bound to see that as a threat,' Jorn told Jan, unhappily.

'This must have been the danger that I sensed, but it just wasn't clear enough for me to give a better warning.' His twin sighed in frustration. *'I wish I'd made more of it before we started up, and then you might all have been more careful.'*

'We can all wish things were done differently, but it's too late. Those must be the saddest words in any language, and the least useful,' agreed Jorn flatly, *'but there it is. I wish we'd been able to prevent her death, and I wish I'd been more respectful and tolerant when she was alive. We can't change the past. She's dead.'*

After a while, Rolf took a deep breath and kissed Clarriss for a final time. Idris helped him to stand.

'Time to heal that ankle,' he said gently. 'But not here. Mordant, please weave us a portal back to camp.'

Braidart had climbed back down the stack as fast as he could, taking desperate risks, but by the time he joined them, he could see it was all over. He scanned the mountainside anxiously but there was no sign of the gryphons.

Mordant shook her head. 'She's gone. Nothing we could do.'

Braidart looked gutted. 'I'll carry her.'

Rolf simply nodded. Jorn went over and gave his guardian a brief embrace.

'We are both so very sorry, Rolf; it happened so very fast, there was nothing we could do to stop her fall and no way to heal such dreadful injuries. We should have foreseen the danger, and used a never-mind so the Gryphon wasn't alarmed.'

'And I should have let you kill them,' said Mordant bitterly. 'It's my fault she's dead.'

'It is not. I understood your reason. I could have argued against it, but I didn't. If anyone is to blame, it's me, for not stopping her from making the climb, but she was adamant that she would go, even though she feared heights. She had such courage.' He looked round at the others. 'My friends, she was a remarkable dwar; I am honoured to have known her, and doubly honoured that a few days ago, she had asked me to be her husband. We were going to tell you at the end of this mission. I have the memory of that, and so much more. But we could never have imagined that our time together would be so short, or have such an ending.'

Mordant wove the portal and Idris carried Rolf through. Jorn picked up a few spare bags of kit. Braidart carried the dwar's body through the mist with respectful care and managed not to stumble on the other side, although Jorn had waited to steady him. Mordant came out and closed the portal behind her.

Braidart placed Clarriss gently on the ground. He looked at Rolf. 'We'll need to build a cairn for her.'

Rolf nodded. 'Yes, please do that. Forgive me, but I can't watch you pile rocks on her.' He slipped off his cloak and said, 'Cover her with that. Tell me when it's done.' Braidart assented silently.

Idris carried Rolf into his tent to tend to his ankle. The others chose a level spot and laid Clarriss there, wrapped in the cloak. There was no shortage of loose stone and the dwar's slim body was soon covered. The finished cairn seemed pitifully small.

Mordant went to light a fire and Jorn fetched water. No one wanted to talk. After a while, Rolf came out of his tent, walking normally. Jorn handed him a mug of sweet lemon-balm tea, and Mordant passed round a cold supper, which simply made the echoing absence of the capable dwar more noticeable. Idris went to rest in the stream, weary from his healing.

As the sun set in a scarlet ball, staining the high peaks, Idris returned. Rolf stood and said quietly, 'Well, it is time to say goodbye to her. Will you each say a few words, and lay a stone?'

They all gathered round the cairn and bowed their heads for a few quiet moments. Then Idris said, '*Ovrassedea*, Clarriss. May your essence journey onwards. I, *Idris-ala-ashalla-accadarramon*, shian of the water, will remember you.' The mage laid a stone upon the cairn and stepped back.

Mordant said, 'Rest well. We return to earth what earth has given. I, Mordant will remember you.' She laid her stone.

Braidart drew himself to attention and gave a crisp salute. 'I bid you farewell, commander, as one soldier to another. You have served well. Rest in peace. I, Braidart Darnell, will remember you.' He laid his stone and stepped back smartly, saluting again.

Jorn felt a choking lump building in his throat and hardly knew what to say. 'Goodbye, Clarriss, you taught me a lot more than I realised. Both of us, Jorn and Jan-Keb, will miss you and remember.' He placed two stones and moved back.

Finally, Rolf spoke in a steady voice. 'Dearest love, you gave your heart to me. You died trying to protect me. For every moment, until my life ends, I, Rolf, will remember you.' He laid his stone at her head and turned to Idris. 'Sing for her, old friend.'

The shian drew himself up, his perfect face serene, lit by the red sunset. He sang in his own language, but they had no need to understand his words, his beautiful voice swept them on a rippling tide of music through grief of loss, into celebration of life, and back to a quiet serenity. Jorn let his tears come, and saw that Mordant had turned to Braidart and buried her face against his shoulder to hide her own.

When the song ended, there was a moment of silence, and then Rolf said quietly, 'Thank you, my friends. No need for more words. Clarriss would not want her death to halt our mission. Let us take some time to ourselves tonight, and tomorrow, we must decide how to make another attempt on the Juncture. I fear that we'll have to begin by eliminating the gryphons.'

Rolf disappeared into his tent. Braidart went to check Tricky. Idris returned to his stream and, after a moment, Mordant followed him. Something deep within her had changed as she listened to him sing. She paused for a moment, suddenly anxious, trying to untangle her emotions, confused and uncharacteristically uncertain. She could not continue to deny how deeply she cared for the shian. Clarriss' sudden death had made her realise that life was just too short for self-deception.

She thought back to Brett, her first lover, trying to see if what she felt for Idris was in any way similar. *Brett and I were very good together, but we both knew from the start that we could never marry. I didn't even want to become 'M'sarra Mordant' – even if that had been possible, which of course it wasn't, with me being a raash halfer. Brett was a dear friend, and we gave each other comfort. I always understood that he'd have to marry at some point, and when he did, it hurt to part from him. I still miss him a lot, but am I in love with him anymore? I'm not sure. Maybe I'm in love with the memory, rather than the reality. And, of course, Braid being so much like Brett brought all that back, so that I couldn't help being attracted to him. Idris wouldn't get any closer, and I was lonely and in need of love, and angry with Idris, in a way. I wanted to make him take notice. But I should have known better. Braid's a lot of fun, but he's not Brett and he's definitely no substitute for Idris. And it has done nothing to make Idris want me; probably put him off, if anything. I can't stop thinking about him, wanting him to be close, imagining what it would be like if he held me or kissed me. He seems so isolated. I'd really like to make him happy. I wish I understood him better. I have to talk to him; I have to know what he wants, what he really feels.*

She waited for a while, summoning her resolve, and then followed the soft noise of water until she found small, icy trickle. '*Idris? I wanted to thank you for your song. I never knew you could sing like that. You never have before.*'

'Not aloud. But my essence sings when we are travelling.'

Mordant sat on a rock and tried to find the courage to say what she had in her heart. Idris watched her, read her aura, and knew with profound distress that he could no longer avoid dealing with this impossible situation. He took form, but stayed at a safe distance.

'Is there something else that you wish to say?'

'You know very well there is.' She changed to open speech, her voice soft with emotion. 'You can read me like a book. You must know how much I want to get closer to you and know you better. I've tried, but you won't let me. Ever since that brief moment in the Cave, you avoid touching me. Look at you now, keeping your distance, showing me nothing of what you think or feel. I even let Braid talk me into his bed in the hope it would make you jealous, much good it has done. It isn't him I want. It's you. Idris, at least tell me why you are avoiding me? Do you dislike me so much?'

'Dislike you? Mordant, you must know that I do not. I have cared for you since I saw you 20 years ago, sitting by my waterfall, dangling your toes in my pond. I do not get close to you because I cannot. I dare not risk touching you, with my form or with my *shi*.'

That sent a wrench of dread, which turned her cold. 'I don't understand.'

'I am a shian. When we get close to someone we care for, it rouses desire, as it does in humans. You can have many lovers. We can have only one. For us, desire has only one ending. We unite our essences, blending two *shis* so that we become one entity. For shians, that is normal and natural, but not between a shian and a human. How can I possibly think of starting a relationship with you that would cause the death of your body?'

'Louth and Jelda made union.'

Idris replied with an intensity of emotion that she had never heard from him before. 'Yes, they did. And the result is precisely why I would never do the same, however much I might want to. Louth was very strong, very passionate. He completely overwhelmed Jelda. I do not think he fully realised what he had done. As J'Louth, he was utterly content. I do not believe that Jelda was unhappy, but then I am not sure that there was enough "her" left to think or feel anything. She could not even bespeak in her own voice. Jorn was shocked when he discovered that. J'Louth could not understand why. I can. I would never do that to you, never. You are a unique and wonderful person and I want you to stay that way. You may not care much for your form, but it is dear to me. I beg you, Mordant, leave me alone. Even now, your closeness is testing my will to its limits.'

Mordant did the only thing she could. Her hopes were in tatters, but the shian's courage demanded respect, and his care for her was intensely moving. She rose and stepped back, her voice schooled to careful formality. 'Then I must do as you wish. Goodnight.'

She walked away through the pines, tears welling in shining trails, despite her rigid control. She couldn't rejoin the others yet; they mustn't suspect, and the last person she wanted right now was Braidart.

Idris followed her with his eyes and sense, Reading her grief and need, his own colours flaring with a mixture of desire and despair. As soon as the quest was ended, he would go back to Arden and be sure never to see Mordant again. It was the only way he could keep her safe and end his own torment at having her so close, and yet so impossibly out of reach.

*

Jorn sat for a while by the dying fire, feeling thoroughly wretched. *'Oh, Jan, what a mess! I just have the strongest feeling that none of this should have happened. Clarriss should never have died like that. We got something totally wrong up there, but I have no idea what it was.'*

'I know. I feel just the same. We both sensed danger from the gryphons, but I wonder if the foreshadowing of the tragedy prevented us from seeing something else? What were they really doing?'

'Protecting their nest, I guess. Trying to drive us off. Like birds mobbing a hawk.'

'That's right. Any creature will attack if it feels threatened. That's why Clarriss threw the stone, trying to keep the hen gryphon away from Rolf.'

'So the big male wanted to get her away from his mate, because she had thrown a stone and hit her.'

'And then Clarriss panicked and hurt his claw, so he dropped her.'

'Oh Powers, Jan, was it all just a terrible, stupid accident'?

'Oh bloody, bloody hell!' Jorn whispered aloud softly.

'I think it may be worse than that. We made a serious mistake. We tried to go in and take the Juncture. We never even thought about asking the gryphons to give it to us.'

'Asking them?'

'Why not? I could tell that they are intelligent creatures. Maybe they would have helped us. We ought at least to have tried that before we resorted to a raid on the nest.'

Jorn thought about this for a while from every possible angle. *'I have a really horrible feeling that you're right. So what can we do next?'*

'I think we have to go back up there ourselves tomorrow and try to communicate with the gryphons. If that works, we don't have a problem. If it doesn't then we may have to resort to force. But I'm really reluctant to do that unless we absolutely have to. They are such amazing creatures.'

'But the others will never let us go on our own.'

'We'll just have to stop them from coming with us.'

By early light, the team had all got up and were grabbing a hasty breakfast while they had a heated discussion over what to do about the gryphons. Braidart was all for sending a mage somewhere to find a high-powered crossbow. Rolf was talking about a killing construct, and Mordant was arguing for stun weaves and nets. Jorn remained silent until he had eaten, waiting also until Idris had rejoined them.

Once the shian mage had arrived, Jorn got up and casually walked a short distance from the group. Then he turned back to face them. 'There is no need to kill the gryphons. What happened yesterday was a terrible, tragic mistake. We made the wrong decision in trying to climb up to their nest.

They were simply trying to defend their territory. All we had to do was ask them to bring us the Juncture. That's exactly what we are going to do, now, on our own.'

Four voices spoke at once. 'Are you insane?' snapped Mordant.

'You can't,' Idris stated flatly.

'I forbid it,' said Rolf.

'Not alone, I'm coming with you,' said Braidart, jumping to his feet.

Jorn and Jan had their constructs ready. They each threw a large containment net over the protesting quartet.

'No, you are not,' Jorn told them firmly. 'Forgive us for doing this, but you are staying right here.' He smiled at their expressions of frustration as the mages tested the binding.

'And don't even think about trying to break out. We have each used a Nine-coloured construct; you will just get tired for nothing. The nets will snap anyway in two hours. But, by that time, we should be safely back with the Juncture. I will cross-step to the stack and back again. Don't look so angry and worried. We're in no danger.'

Jan continued silently, *'Idris, we don't want to keep you from water. We know your shi will find a way out, but don't do it too quickly and please, please, don't follow us. Trust me, I know what I'm doing.'*

'I surely hope so, tantar-issa. Be very careful.'

Braidart was pushing in angry frustration at the invisible barrier. 'Jorn, don't do it! For pity's sake, look what happened to Clarriss.'

Mordant was seething with frustration. 'If you get yourselves killed, I'll never forgive you, or myself.'

Jorn ignored them. He wove a cross-step up to the stack, and the wrenching dislocation carried him instantly to its base. The churning in his stomach was not just due to the transit. He took a steadying breath.

'The piece of Juncture is at the top, near the nest, but I sense a binding,' Jan confirmed.

'I'll break it.' Jorn sent a tendril of Disjunct sweeping across the top of the stack, until he felt a faint snap as a construct broke.

'Good. Let me try to bespeak them.'

Jan extended his thought towards the top of the rocky tower. *'Peace, we do not hunt,'* he sent. *'Come, we need to speak to you.'*

The camouflage of the mottled plumage against the rock was so good that it was only when the gryphon moved that Jorn realised he had been looking straight at it, perched on a ledge near the top of the sheer rock face.

Jorn

The big creature rose, stretched, and stared down at him. It flapped its wings and screamed a challenge.

Jorn bowed towards it. '*Peace,*' he soothed. '*Friends.*'

The gryphon rose from its ledge with heavy flaps and then glided down towards them, its huge wings spanning at least 12 ems. It took all Jorn's willpower to stand still and watch it come. It landed awkwardly on a pile of rocks not far away, settled its neck feathers and wings with a shuffle, sitting back on its tawny haunches with its bird legs straight in front of it. He noticed that one claw was being held up off the ground. The long, tufted tail twitched like an angry cat's.

The beast gave a harsh cry and lifted its scarlet crest in challenge. '*Not friend, hurt us.*' The response was as much emotion as words, but the twins could understand it.

'*Friend,*' Jan repeated firmly.

The bird's head cocked to one side and regarded the intruder with a fierce golden eye, in which there was the gleam of intelligence. '*No!*' A sense of angry rejection. Images formed in their minds; stick-like figures clustering around the base of the tower. On top of the rock, a large nest, with four half-naked hatchlings snuggled in a bed of down. '*Attack nest. Harm young.*'

'*No. Seek thing like this.*' Jorn held out a section of Juncture. The gryphon's head jutted forward and twisted as it looked at the object from both angles. It croaked again, doubtfully. Another image, of a small figure throwing stones; feelings. '*Pain, anger, mate hurt, defend!*' The lion tail thrashed angrily.

Jan tried to find a way of making the beast understand that they had not meant to hurt its mate. He formed a sequence of images and emotions; '*Attack by female gryphon; fear. Man falling, dwar female defending her mate. Dwar caught up by male gryphon. Terror of being prey, strike with her iron talon. Falling; dwar dead; shock, huge grief.*'

'*Arrrk!*' The gryphon shifted uneasily. The crest lowered slightly. '*Not want eat. Take far from nest. Sharp talon hurt leg; could not hold.*'

'*Not meant,*' confirmed Jan reassuringly. '*Not meant; frightened.*'

'*Regret death of female.*'

'*Accepted. Our sorrow for hurts done. Peace between us now?*'

'*Peace. Why come?*'

'*Need this thing.*' Jorn held up the Juncture again and pointed at the top of the stack. '*It is up there.*'

'*Take this thing, go?*' asked the gryphon suspiciously.

'*Go fast. Do not return,*' confirmed Jorn.

With a huge bunching of muscles in its powerful hind legs, the gryphon sprang into the air. The vast wings laboured to achieve lift, making a huge whumping noise, like a giant swan attempting flight. Having gained height, it swept to the top of the stack and alighted.

The hen gryphon rose from her nest and there was an elaborate ceremony of calling, bowing and neck-stretching. The male poked around, grasped something in its beak and flew down to perch on the rock again. With a flick of its head, it tossed the portion of the Juncture to lie at Jorn's feet.

'*Go now?*'

'*Thank you. Go now.*'

Jorn picked up the Juncture, bowed to the gryphon, and stowed it carefully away. Once round the corner of the bluff, he stopped, took a few huge breaths, and waited until his pounding heart rate reduced to something nearer normal. '*We did it!*' he sent jubilantly.

Jan could not feel glad. '*Yes, we did it. But how the hell are we going to tell Rolf that Clarriss' death was just an awful, needless accident?*'

When Jorn walked out of nowhere, back into camp, he found Rolf and Mordant sitting in a chilly huddle round the remains of the fire, having obviously given up trying to break his net, whilst Braidart paced backwards and forwards like a caged wolf, his face set in a frustrated frown. Idris was nowhere to be seen.

Jorn stifled a fit of desperately inappropriate giggles and came forward. He and Jan snapped their bindings, and the others hurried towards him.

'I don't know whether to hug you or thump you!' exclaimed Braidart crossly.

'Don't ever do anything like that to me ever again,' fumed Mordant.

Jorn gave into his release from tension and gave a snort of irrepressible laughter. 'Your faces are a picture!' he told them

Rolf glared. 'If it was not for the fact that you are safe and have obviously got the Juncture, your bottom would be a picture too,' he snapped, with the angry relief of a person who has been worried sick about someone they care for. 'You are not too old for a good hiding!'

'But I am much too big,' laughed Jorn, and lifted the outraged little mage and swung him round, before setting him carefully on the ground.

Idris appeared and gave a short nod of approval when he saw that their mission had succeeded. '*You grow strong, tantar-issa; it took a while for me to escape your net!*'

Everyone crowded round and Jorn showed them the Juncture, which was identical to the first pieces, except that it was made from silver and had a glittering white stone clasped at the tip of the spike.

'So what happened with the gryphons?' Braidart demanded.

'It was fine. I confess to going a bit wobbly round the knees when the big male flew down.'

They all settled down and got the fire going again. Jorn told them about their encounter. As he ended, he looked at his guardian and became serious. 'Rolf, we are both desperately sorry about Clarriss. It's bad enough knowing that she died, but to realise that it was all a tragic mistake makes it far harder to bear. The cock gryphon was sorry, he only meant to take her away from his nest, he never intended to harm her.'

'Nothing will lessen my memory of her courage and her devotion to me. The rest I will have to live with, as will you.'

'Well, mission accomplished,' said Braidart, breaking the uneasy, small silence. 'Now what?'

'Lunch first,' Mordant said briskly, 'and then we must pack up and move out. It's time to go back to Mage Hall and report to Kayman. Come on, Blue Eyes, give me a hand. I can manage some hot soup at least.'

'I'll go back to my stream until you are ready.' Idris moved away and lost form.

Jorn really missed Clarriss at lunchtime. There was no doubt that her camp cooking was second to none; even her 'don't ask' stew was memorable. He sipped his soup and chewed his dry trail biscuit without enthusiasm. He was beginning to feel as if a headache was coming on.

'Anything wrong, Jorn?' Rolf enquired, seeing him staring absently into the distance. 'No, why should there be?' he said crossly. Then he gave a small shiver. 'Sorry, didn't mean to snap. I feel a bit odd suddenly. I think there may be another far-seeing on its way.'

'You need something to scry with.' The mage found a tin bowl and filled it with water. 'Try this. It's a bit small, but it should do. Just relax and let your Gift do the rest.'

Jorn stared at the water until it began to go black, and then closed his eyes and concentrated on the vision. The others peered over his shoulders, trying to see if an image would appear. There was just one, a shocking view of Mage Hall as a smouldering, blackened ruin, which caused everyone to gasp. It faded quickly and Jorn came back to awareness.

'Oh, by the Powers!' whispered Rolf in a shaken voice.

'It's exactly as Kayman feared,' said Mordant grimly. 'The raash have decided to eliminate another of our power bases. And we can only guess at what other havoc they may have caused in the Dwarran Realm.'

'But what about everyone who was there? I didn't see anyone in the ruins.'

'They will have got away, Braid, I'm sure,' said Rolf. 'Kayman had plans for an evacuation in an emergency. And I know he's already removed any valuables. His foresight was accurate; he knew we should not stay there. But it's a terrible loss, none the less.'

Idris returned at the run. 'I sensed a troubling; what has happened?'

I had a sudden far-seeing,' Jorn explained. 'It only lasted a few seconds but it showed Mage Hall in ruins after a great fire.'

'That is truly evil news.'

'But we didn't see anyone; Rolf thinks they may have got away.'

'But where to?' asked Mordant.

'Errington,' said Rolf. 'We must go there at once. If Kayman is safe, that is where he will have gone.'

The team packed up at top speed and translocated to the yard at the Errington safe house as fast as they could, bringing Tricky with them.

Rolf sent out a mind call. *'Kayman, are you here?'*

'In the back room on the top floor. Come straight up. Don't talk to anyone.'

The High Master was waiting by the door and his face filled with huge relief as he saw them. He looked tired and Jorn thought he had lost weight.

'Say nothing! Wait a moment. I will set a spy-shield so that we cannot be either overlooked or overheard.' After a moment, he relaxed, and came over with a big smile. 'I've been worried for you. Did you succeed?'

Rolf simply nodded.

'Well that's a blessing. You know what has happened?'

'Jorn had a brief far-seeing, just enough to show us the devastation. I deduced that you would most likely come here. The mainland is too dangerous right now, not that anywhere is exactly safe of course.'

Kayman ushered the mages into comfortable chairs. 'First, tell me what happened on the quest.' He looked round, his sense tweaking with sudden dread. 'Where are Braid and Clarriss?' he demanded.

'Braid has gone straight to the Darnell mansion. Clarriss is dead, Kayman. There was a dreadful accident.' Mordant tersely explained the circumstances. Kayman was deeply moved when the tragic nature of the misunderstanding with the gryphons was described.

He got up and gave Rolf a hug, and patted his back. 'Curse these enigmatic verses!' he exclaimed in angry frustration. 'How are we supposed to know what to do, given such imprecise clues?'

Rolf sighed. 'It was meant to confuse, and it does. But don't keep me in suspense any longer, old friend. What happened at Mage Hall? Did the raash destroy it?'

Kayman smiled. 'That's what I hope everyone thinks, but they are wrong. I destroyed it myself.'

Rolf said nothing, but Jorn could not help a gasp of shock, and Mordant and Idris both looked startled.

The High Master gave a small shrug. 'Sometimes one must know when to sacrifice one's Queen to save one's King from checkmate. I had thought long and hard, as you may imagine, before taking such a drastic step, but I concluded that it would be for the best in the long run. Mage Hall was well-known as the main centre for training in magic, and for its collection of knowledge, gathered over many centuries. But its very fame was starting to become a problem. It was attracting too much attention. It is dangerous to have all one's eggs in the proverbial single basket. I knew that, at some point, it would be the focus of a raash attack, and its existence was putting the Dwarran Realm in danger. Much though I loved the old pile and all its history, what mattered was the knowledge it held. I decided that it was more important to save that resource, and to protect the mages, than it was to keep the Hall. Three years ago, I started to set up new, smaller bases for our craft, and we have worked hard to keep these absolutely secret. I stopped taking new students some time ago.' Kayman gave Rolf a dry smile. 'I will bet that even your most efficient spy network is not aware of this?'

'No comment,' responded Rolf with a glint in his eyes.

'So, then I began to see that I could use the Hall to bait a trap for the raash, and kill some of their best adepts. Obviously, the hardest part was that life had to seem to be going on as usual. I was determined to have one last celebration for Longest Night. After the Winter Festival, I slowly removed all the most important ancient texts from the library. I've copied others. I've created a new, ultra-secure library to house our most valuable archive. I know you were too busy to notice the last time you were there, but in fact, many of the shelves were already empty; the illusion of them being well-stocked was just a sophisticated glamour. Only my most trusted friends, Maeve, Rome and the librarian knew about this. Finally, I shut the library down for "stocktaking".'

'My word!' exclaimed Mordant in astonishment. 'You've been deceiving us all with great skill!'

'As you know, I summoned the Conclave and made a great play of sending the Darnells to safety, and erecting defensive weaves and readying for any future attack. I hinted that we might have the Cup, ensuring that Philip was there to hear the news. Once he was busy moving the Darnells into their new home in Errington, I finally told everyone to get out, though I refused to say why. There was not that much more to do. I secretly planted explosives in the main rooms.'

'Explosives?' queried Jorn.

'A dwarran product, used in mining and engineering. They are basically chemicals that produce a powerful blast when correctly triggered. It's another of those useful inventions that the dwar techs take great care to keep away from humans. But Eldessa Maria, the Dwarran Queen, was in on my plan and Sarra agreed to help. Usually, the explosive is set off by a lit fuse. However, I substituted some simple fire-lighting constructs. The worst part after that was the waiting.'

'I can imagine,' said Rolf, 'I am delighted by your deviousness!'

'Fortunately, when the attack finally came, it all went pretty much to plan. Ajina was there in person. I think she had the Knife, but she hung back from using it at first, and sent in a large force of raash soldiers and mages. She plainly wanted to take the place intact so she could search it at her leisure. They thought that Rome, Maeve and I were going to stay behind for some heroic last stand, defending the Hall to the bitter end. Maeve and Rome had indeed planned to continue to resist until the last moment. It was very brave of them. Maeve did escape, but Rome was killed. I remained hidden by wards and glamour until I had seen most of the raash go into the Hall to start their search. Then I set off the explosions. The entire Hall was instantly demolished in one huge fireball. I wanted it to look as if there had been an immense clash of Power, fatal to all, so

Darric might assume that he had seriously weakened us. I doubt if many in the building survived, although I was too busy getting away to stay and watch the result.'

'From what I saw of the ruins, it was a very thorough job,' Jorn told him.

'So, as far as anyone here knows, we have suffered a serious setback, although you and some others escaped after this titanic, final struggle?'

'Indeed, Idris.'

'And presumably, that is what Philip also believes?'

'Let us hope so. But the raash attack shows that we must eliminate him as soon as possible.'

Rolf nodded. 'So, at last, I understand your secrecy, old friend. And the reason for delaying the attack on Vard, and keeping Jorn under wraps. If Ajina had thought there was a Nine in residence at the Hall, she would not have attacked.'

'Precisely. And now, she will wonder if there was, which may make her next moves less certain. As I told you, a question of careful timing. Darric's losses will reduce his pleasure in his assumed defeat of me and mine.'

'So, what's the next move, Vard or Philip?'

'Both!' said Kayman with a determined glint in his eyes. 'We can make an attack on Vard, and we should certainly try to eliminate Philip. With luck, those actions should combine to delay Darric until you have completed the quest. You only have two more pieces to find.'

'I think you are being over-optimistic,' cautioned Rolf. 'Even if we succeed, unless we manage to kill Darric and Ajina, we still have enormous problems. We have no real idea how much longer this is going to take, and we still haven't solved the last verses of the Rhyme. Our next trip has to be to The Burning Coast to find the fourth piece, and it's still too early in the year to do that yet. I did try the Hook once before we left, but I couldn't make it stick; too much snow, I should think.'

'We'll keep trying the Hook,' offered Jorn. 'The minute it sticks enough to go through, we can take a quick look and see what we are up against.'

'Thank you. But I suspect it will be many days yet before that is possible. And we have no idea where to find the fifth part.'

'We are working on that too,' Jorn told him.

'Good; hope you come up with something soon. But we don't even know for certain that the Juncture will be any real help when we have it completed. It's supposed to master the Tools, but what does that mean? We don't really understand what the Tools can do. Does it matter that Darric doesn't have the Cup?'

'Oh, come on, Rolf!' said Mordant. 'Lighten up. I'm the resident pessimist, remember?'

The small mage sighed. 'I guess I'm just feeling low right now. It was such a blow to lose Clarriss. Even our successes don't please me the way they should.'

Kayman came and patted the small mage on his shoulder. 'I understand, old friend. But you have done so very well. You have been my anchor for 30 years. We need you now as much, if not more, than ever. Let's finish this journey together, mmm? Clarriss would want that.'

Chapter 23

Mordant had not allowed herself to think too much about the shattering revelation that Philip was her brother. The team had been on the brink of the mission to Karth and she had needed to focus on that. During the journey to the mausoleum, she deliberately blanked it from her mind, and refused to talk to Braidart when he asked her about it. After that, there had been far too much going on. But now she was back in Errington, faced with the imminent need to either kill Philip herself or witness his execution, it started to haunt her, and brought back all the memories of Vard she had tried so hard to forget.

She had chosen their mother's people. Philip had chosen their father's. In raash eyes, she was the traitor and he was the loyal son. Yes, he had conspired ruthlessly to kill humans, but she too was a killer, wasn't she? She had never kept count of the number of raash she had dispatched without mercy, and there were some humans too. Were they so different from each other? It was mainly a question of upbringing. If Philip had known their loving mother, and had her wise advice, who knew how he might have turned out? He was plainly a talented mage and a very able and intelligent spy. In one sense, he was as much a victim of the raash as she was. She couldn't exactly admire him, but she did respect his abilities and his dedicated loyalty, misguided though that was, and it tangled her emotions.

Her scabbarded longsword was in its usual place. It drew her eyes, solid, dependable, real. Mordant picked it up and held it across her lap for a long time, her hand running up and down the worked leather. After a while, she got dressed in her leathers and went downstairs into the untended garden at the rear of the safe house.

For an hour, she pushed herself through her exercises, trying to lose herself in the demanding disciplines of the Warrior's Way. At least by the end of the session, she felt hungry, but the underlying bleakness of spirit persisted. She needed action. The attack on Vard would be something positive to focus on, although it was going to be very difficult, but her sense was nagging her that there was something else she ought to do. *We've got a bit of a gap coming up before we can get on with the quest. I feel I need to use it, but I'm not sure how.*

She retreated to the safe haven of her inner workroom, the potting shed with its neatly stacked tools and earthy smells, and a view down a well-filled vegetable garden. It was a place that never failed to calm her mind, and where she did her best thinking.

I can't do anything about Philip. It's just an unavoidable tragedy, and not his fault or mine that we ended up on different sides. He has to die, there's no way round that. I'm sure he'd kill me without thinking twice if he decided that was the thing to do. So, as Matta would have said, 'Move on, Morda, love, move on.'

But it all looks so bad right now. Darric has three of the four Tools, so he's almost as strong as a Nine. Jorn and Jan are tremendous, but they are still learning. Can they really do much against him and Ajina and the entire raash army? We still have to find the rest of the Juncture and we are up against a wall with the last two bits. We are not even sure that the wretched thing will be useful if we do complete it. What does it do? For that matter, what can the Tools do? Corus implied they were not originally meant as weapons.

She considered that for a while. *We don't know enough about the Tools, but Corus does. We never had the opportunity to really talk about them. If the old mage is still alive, he could help us. I can form a portal to Free Vard, I have a good Hook. And if anyone knows how best to hit Darric, it will be Karan and Tara. I've always found excuses not to go back; to begin with, I couldn't because I hadn't learnt to portal. And then when I had, I just couldn't face it, and the longer I left it, the harder it got. It was easier to do nothing and leave the past as a closed book. But now there is a reason; things have changed. Maybe that's what my sense is trying to tell me?*

She suddenly felt that the black cloud was starting to lift. Her colours flamed out with new purpose. Mordant left her inner space and went briskly to find Rolf. The dwarran halfer looked up with a smile as she strode into the room where he was ploughing through a pile of reports.

'Mordant, it's good to see you. I noticed you back at sword practice this morning.'

'Just getting fit before we launch an attack on Vard.'

'Kayman is really keen on that. I must say, I'd like to see Darric get a taste of Jorn's Power. And we need to get rid of Philip. I know that can't be easy for you now you know who he is.'

'I've thought that through. It has to happen. I don't have any feelings for him. It's just fate that we ended up on opposite sides, but we did, so that's that.'

'Yes, it is. A cruel chance, though I suspect it bothers you a good deal more than it would him if he ever found out.'

'You're probably right.' She hitched up to sit on the table. 'Rolf, I've been thinking. We'll soon have the Juncture completed, and by that time, we simply must know more about the Tools so Jorn and Jan can work out the best way to use it to control them. I don't think we are going to find the answer to that puzzle on Earth, and anyway, we can't afford to just wait and hope. My old friend, the mage Corus, knows more about the Tools than anyone. I want to go to Free Vard to find him. If he is still alive, I will see if he will agree to come back with me. If he's dead, there are others who may help me. And we need to know what's happening on Vard before we can plan our attack.'

'My, your brain has been working overtime! That sounds like a plan to me. Let's go and talk to Kayman.

Rolf and Mordant found the High Master in a towering fury of frustration.

'I was just coming to tell you. The bastard's gone!' he exclaimed crossly. 'Philip has disappeared. I've had my best tails on him, and they've lost him! Jan can't sense him anywhere.'

Mordant wasn't totally certain if she was disappointed or relieved. Rolf huffed and sat down.

'Well, there's nothing we can do about that. He's probably back on Vard if he has any sense. He must have known we were getting suspicious, and I'll bet he spotted your tails. Anyway, look on the bright side. He's out the game and out of our way, which is a blessed relief.'

'Braid won't like it,' said Mordant. 'He's been imagining what he wants to do to him. Most of it takes far too long and is fundamentally impractical!'

'Ah well. We have other things to think about.'

'Such as this raid on Vard you keep dropping heavy hints about,' said Rolf with a smile. 'That will cheer Braid up. Nothing he likes better than the chance of a good fight.'

'Mmm. But the question is, can we really do anything effective, and is it worth the risk? What do you think, Mordant?'

She gave him her thin smile. 'I think I need to go back to Vard.'

'Another reconnaissance?'

'In a way. But not to Main Base. I want to go to Free Vard. There's someone there who might be a lot of help, if he's still alive.' She explained about Corus and the knowledge she hoped to gain.

Kayman looked uncertain. 'Is it risky?'

'No. Free Vard is a safe island. I have a clear Hook. I'm determined to do this, Rolf. It's for myself as much as anything. Finding out that Philip is my brother has disturbed me, I admit it. I have to confront the ghosts of my past and put them to rest before I can move on again. And we need to the have the latest on Darric's war preparations, and where we can strike to do the most damage. The Free Varders have a very good intelligence network.'

'Very well. It's a good idea. You had better go soon. Oh, and by the way, I'm moving out of here into the Darnell mansion now that Philip is out of the way. The older members of the clan and their families have gone home, so there's plenty of room. It will be a lot more comfortable, and at least they have a really good cook.' He patted his shrinking stomach. 'I had to make do when I was waiting at the Hall, and the man who provides the meals here is totally useless. I can't think when I'm empty. Join me there when you return, I'll get your bags moved over. Idris has already taken up residence in the garden pond, though he says it's too full of frogs and goldfish for his liking. Jorn and Jan will come too. I want to have the whole team together for the final stages, and well away from flapping ears. I'm not sure if I can trust everyone here. Good luck with your mission. And take care.'

'I will, old friend.'

Mordant went back to her room. She buckled her kor and kring round her waist. She needed to feel the comforting weight of her blades, even though she didn't expect to use them.

In the chilly garden, the halfer mage found a private corner, went into her workroom, engaged with her Quincunx, and began with intensely focussed care to form the structures she needed. Coming back to awareness, she built the outline of the portal. The rainbow-tinted gateway stood in front of her. She thrust her will through, seeking the way through the mist into the different universe. She found the pinch point, pushed past it. Her Hook was the white sand beach with its familiar nut-palms, as clear in her mind as it had been 20 years ago. She focussed on the image, threw her line, felt it catch the Hook. With intense concentration and total commitment, she walked through the portal.

Mordant felt the taste of Free Vard's air, the bright sunlight and the humid heat. The palms waved above her and the sea washed gently up the coral sands. Small raash children screeched in alarm as they saw her appear out of nowhere, and ran towards the settlement, calling loudly for their mothers. She walked slowly up the beach and stood waiting.

Several adults were coming at the run, two or three bearing weapons. She stood still and raised her arms in a gesture of peace, her eyes scanning the approaching people, hoping for someone she knew. *'It's all right, Karan, you can put the war-shafts away. It's only me.'*

'MORDANT?' Karan's mind-shout was incredulous. The raash mage came to a halt, staring in total disbelief, her companions ranged tensely in a defensive line on either side of her. *'We thought you were dead!'*

'Well, as you can see, I'm not pigswill yet! Please reassure your friends that I am not an enemy. I have so much to tell you.'

Karan turned and spoke decisively in raash. The others lowered their weapons and moved away, some with obviously suspicious reluctance. Karan came over and folded Mordant into a firm embrace. 'Oh, my dear, let me look at you! You've changed.'

'I'm 20 years older. But you look much the same. Is Corus still alive? And Tara?'

'Yes, he is. Tara is dead though, five years ago; humans have such short lives. But Corus lives with us now. His spying days are over, but he's still remarkably hale for one of such a great age.'

'Powers be praised! Can you call him? I want him to hear this.'

Karan made the mind call, and the two mages stood quietly side-by-side, waiting for him to arrive. When Mordant saw the familiar bent figure moving slowly towards them, leaning heavily on a stout stick, she felt a surge of rising tears. He still wore a plain brown tunic.

'Now, now, no tears, this is a time for joy. We thought you had died under torture in some deep cell. There was no trace of you. I am so very, very glad to see you again.'

Mordant went to the old mage and kissed his forehead, and took his arm to lead him to a fallen palm trunk where they could all sit in comfort. His eyes were kind, but also sad. 'Martha is dead, my dear.'

'I know. I killed her.' She saw the shock of that in both their faces and hurriedly explained. 'She had been captured along with Simon and she was facing impalement; it was the only thing I could do to save her from hours of torment. I fulfilled my mission. I reached Earth. I have been there ever since. I thought I would never come back here to Free Vard. To be honest, for all kinds of reasons, I didn't want to. But something happened a few days ago to change my mind.'

Corus looked at her with total understanding. 'I read a recent troubling in your aura as soon as I saw you. Take your time. We are both good listeners.'

'You will need to be. Even leaving out most of the tale, it will take a long time to tell.'

The humidity was already making her thirsty and uncomfortable. Combat leathers had not been such a good idea. Mordant looked towards the nearest palm tree, smiled at the memory, chose a ripe nut, cut it, brought it gently and steadily to her feet, and bored a neat hole in its side. She offered it to Corus and Karan, but they shook their heads. She drank, relishing the sweetly refreshing taste, and said, 'Well, it was this way.'

Finally, she reached the point where she had discovered Philip's identity. 'It was a terrible shock. I thought I had put my old life behind me. I thought the past was buried.' Suddenly unable to continue, she faltered to a halt.

Corus reached across and took her hand in his. His wrinkled skin was paper thin, and she could feel all his bones. 'And you were wrong, of course. We are what we have been, what we have known. If we try to hide from it, we are trying to lose a part of ourselves. It cannot be done. It is an illusion. It was brave of you to return, Mordant, and your sense has led you well. You will be even stronger now. But it wasn't just the past that drew you here, was it?'

She was, as always, astounded by his wisdom and insight. 'No, Corus, it was not. We need your help. Darric has regained the Chain and the Wand. He has long held the Knife. We know that the invasion of Earth is imminent. We have our twin Masters of Nine. We seek the Juncture. But I fear we are fast running out of time. Even if we find it, we have to discover how to use it. We need to understand the nature and power of the Tools. Can you tell us, Corus; you of all people must know? And how much time do we have? Are my fears unfounded?'

'No, Mordant, they are not,' responded Karan, who had listening in silence but with acute attention. 'You're right. Darric and Ajina are on the brink of the invasion. They have a secret base on Earth, with several thousand troops already in place. Did you know that?'

Mordant shook her head grimly. She had not known, but it was no real surprise. Darric was the master of the long game.

Corus nodded. 'They could attack at any time. But concerning the Tools, yes, I do know more about them than most. Possibly more than Darric himself. But I'm not sure how I can help you.'

Mordant fixed the old mage with a gaze of earnest entreaty. 'Come back to Earth with me, Corus. Give us your wisdom. My sense tells me that you have a role to play, something I cannot see clearly, but I know it's important, for Earth, and for Free Vard also. Will you come?'

Corus closed his eyes and was silent for a long time. Finally, he looked at her again. 'I'm old, Mordant. If I told you the true count of my years, you would not believe me; I find it hard to credit it myself. My body grows frail. But something deep within me will not let me die. I still have a task to do. I must complete it. My sense tells me that you are right. I do have knowledge that will be of use to you. I must go with you, though I fear that I may not survive the translocation.'

Mordant's eyes shone. 'I will ensure that you do. And I am so very, very grateful.'

The old raash smiled, his eyes alert with interest. 'One last mission, eh? And I confess, I'm curious to see this Earth of yours, not to mention having the chance to meet a Nine!'

Mordant turned to Karan. 'There's something else. This quest of ours is taking longer than we want, and we're running out of time. We want to delay Darric, if we can. We have in mind some kind of attack on Main Base. We can't send in a big force, but Jorn is capable of a causing a lot of damage. Can you advise us where best to strike?'

Karan shrugged. 'There are only two targets that make any sense, and you probably know what they are as well as I do. We have many rebels now, itching for a chance to revolt. It only needs one push and the whole of the government will fall apart and your problem will be over. It's only Darric and his sister who are holding things together. Kill them.'

'That's a tall order. You must have tried.'

'Yes we have. And lost brave people attempting it. But maybe, if your young Masters of Nine are as good as you say they are, they can succeed. Otherwise, I'd recommend destroying the arsenal and as many barracks as you can. At night, when the troops are sleeping.'

Mordant nodded. 'We'll have to talk it over.'

'If you need our help, just let me know.'

'Be sure I will. Are you ready, Corus? Do you need anything to take with you?'

He smiled and stood. He gestured to his simple clothes and stout staff. 'I always travel light.'

Karan went and kissed him, her eyes brimming with tears. She said, tightly, 'Come back to us, old friend. We need your wisdom also. Mordant, I am so very proud of what you have become. If you can somehow defeat Darric and his sister, Free Vard may yet have a chance.' The raash mage turn abruptly away and walked back up the beach.

Corus watched her go and then turned to Mordant. 'My dear, I was not jesting when I said I might not survive a major translocation. My heart is not as strong as it used to be.'

'I will move you with all the care I can. And my friend, Idris, is a powerful healer. Will you risk it?'

'Of course. For you, and for Vard.'

Mordant had the workings for the return portal hung ready and waiting. She beckoned Corus to her side, wishing she could use a construct to support him, but that would break the moment they translocated. She erected the portal, aiming for the familiar Hook in the garden of the Darnell mansion. Then she put her arms around him, held his frail body close, and with great care, took the old raash through the mist to a new universe.

As soon as they arrived, she felt him sag. He leant heavily on his staff, breathing in short gasps. Mordant made an urgent mind call, desperately hoping that Idris was in residence. He was by her side a moment later. 'His heart,' she said.

Idris laid his hands on the old mage. After a while, his breathing eased and he straightened up and looked around. 'Thank, you, my friend. I fear that my aged frame does not stand up to the stresses of translocation from one universe to another as well as it might once have done. So this is Earth! But it is less green than I imagined, and,' he shivered, 'much colder.'

Mordant said gently, 'It's not yet spring. And you are dressed for high summer. Come, you will soon be warm, and there are friends that you must meet.'

She produced a never-mind to keep the servants from being surprised, and led the old raash slowly indoors, with Idris supporting him on the other side. They took him to the small ground-floor parlour, where a fire was blazing merrily. She eased him into a chair and sent out a mind call to Rolf. *'I'm back, and we have a guest. He needs a warm cloak and a blanket, and a glass of wine and some water. Please call the others. I do so want you all to meet him.'*

She removed Corus' sandals and chafed the old mage's feet. He was looking about him with intense curiosity and interest. His body might be frail, but she knew there was nothing aged about his mind or his Power. Rolf came in and bustled across to greet the visitor.

'Don't get up. You must be Corus. I'm Rolf. If you will permit me?' He draped a warm cloak around the old mage's shoulders and tucked a blanket round his knees.

Braidart followed a few moments later and placed a silver salver beside him, loaded with a glass of wine, a carafe of water with a second glass, and a plate filled with small biscuits. 'Master Mage,' he made his deepest bow, 'I am Braidart Darnell. You are most welcome. Our house is yours. Ask for whatever you need.'

Corus looked at them both, his violet eyes warm with his appreciation. 'My thanks for your kindness. As you see, I am not in my first youth. I had thought my travelling days were over, but Mordant has persuaded me otherwise.'

'It's far too hot in here for you, Idris. I'll get you some water,' said Braid and left to do so, holding the door open as Jorn strode into the room. Corus shed his blanket and rose stiffly to meet him.

'A Mage of Nine,' he said in wonder. 'And two auras! Your twin is indwelling. May I meet him also?'

'Of course, Master.'

Jan took form beside his brother and the raash mage looked from one to the other with keen appraisal. 'Well, well,' he said. 'Like and yet unlike. Your appearances may confuse the eye, but your auras are very different. I am honoured. I did not expect to live to see a Master of Nine, let alone two!'

'And we didn't expect to meet a raash adept, standing on Braidart's hearthrug! Do please sit down. What's this all about? Mordant, this is obviously your doing.'

'Yes it is. We need information about Darric's preparations for invasion, and my sense prompted me that we should also discover more about the Tools. I knew we wouldn't find answers to either of those questions here on Earth, so I translocated to Free Vard. And the person who can answer both those questions is now here, and willing to help. It was Corus who helped me to escape from slavery all those years ago. His knowledge is deep.'

'Deep indeed,' said Idris. 'And I am pleased to meet another Reader.' He paused and then said, as if in answer to a bespoken comment, 'Yes, I understand. We must exchange notes on our techniques later.' He looked at Mordant. 'Our guest is in need of a long rest before we subject him to an arrow-storm of questions! He is putting a good face on it, but he is in pain and his aura flickers like a guttering candle. Braidart, can you find him a room, and see that he has warmer clothes and whatever he wishes to eat? Our curiosity can wait.'

'Thank you, Idris. Your diagnosis is correct. I am indeed very weary. But I am raash, and we recover fast. We can meet again in a few hours and I will be ready to answer your questions, if I can.'

Mordant came to help the old mage to rise He moved to the door, leaning heavily on his stick, and then stopped with a sharp intake of breath. He looked suddenly ill.

Idris went quickly to him, and Mordant helped to give him some support.

'It's nothing,' Corus told them. 'It will soon pass. The translocation strained my heart. It is still objecting.'

'Then we must do something about that, at once,' said Idris.

'You cannot heal extreme old age.'

'No, but I can certainly make sure that your ancient body is as healthy as possible. Come, I will carry you to your room.'

'I can walk,' he protested stubbornly.

'You can, but you are not going to,' Idris told him. 'Healer's orders.' He swept Corus into his arms and lifted him easily. He was scarcely the weight of a child.

'Come, old friend,' sent Mordant gently. *'Let Idris see what he can do. A little healing is better than none at all.'*

*

Jorn

Darric and Ajina sat in their private dining room in Main Base, enjoying a fine supper to celebrate Darrison's safe return and the conclusion of his 20-year mission. The silent slaves came and went with a succession of perfectly prepared courses, and the trio allowed themselves to relax. They had much to celebrate.

Darric let the meal end and dismissed the slaves before he began to discuss business. 'You have done well, my son. Now we begin the end game, and you have a new part to play. Jorn and the team must be eliminated. They are far stronger than I thought. They escaped the ambush.'

'I know where they will go next, but they are held up by the Arctic weather, so we are too. As soon as it clears, Ajina and I will set the trap.'

His aunt gave a tight smile. 'I look forward to questioning them before they die. And I would like some elegance in their ending. Nothing too quick, especially for the Darnell and that renegade halfer.'

'Indeed. But there is still Kayman to deal with. A pity that he escaped the destruction of the Hall.'

Ajina tightened her thin lips in acknowledgement. 'He is slippery. And the Hall cost us more than I would have wished. I knew they would expect an attack at some point, but the power of the defence surprised me. But there, it is over and Kayman has lost his base. It should not be too hard to assassinate him in Errington.'

'And it is time to consider the Mage School at the university,' said Darric. 'Turner's opposition to Kayman has been to our advantage, and he has prevented the High Council from taking action against us, but when we invade, he will become an enemy. War makes people forget their petty rivalries; we must keep weakening the human mages.'

'Would you like me to deal with that?' asked Darrison casually. He was itching to get the pompous professor out of the way.

'Yes, see what you can do. We can't target the whole school just yet. That must wait until we have secured our foothold on Earth, but lopping off the crown will stunt the tree. If you can take out Sturminster and some of their colleagues, and disrupt the school at the same time, it would be a bonus. And the other Darnells must not be ignored; yes, I should be delighted if you could manage to cause them further grief.'

Darrison nodded. 'Might I know where you intend to attack?'

Darric paused for a moment, and decided that Darrison had earned the reward of a revelation. 'We intend to launch four simultaneous attacks, each designed to take out the capital city and centre of government in Norlond, Allond, Panya and Daunce. Once that land-holding is secured, we can deal with the smaller states round the periphery, starting with the Lordships and Erren. Meanwhile, my envoys will commence negotiations with the Emperor. They will persuade him that we have no intention of attacking him and wish to negotiate a formal treaty of mutual benefit. Of course, that is only to keep him off our backs until we have consolidated our gains. Once we hold nearly half of the settled world, we can begin a campaign against the Andrean Empire. That will depend on how much backbone Malchious possesses. If he makes a fight of it, fine, but my spies think he'll crumble, he's an old man now. We will see.'

'That is masterly, my Lord. But, if you will forgive my mentioning it, you still lack the Cup.'

'I have decided that it is irrelevant. My experiments show that three Tools are quite sufficient; their combined Power is ample for our purposes.'

'Then there is nothing to stop us. With three Tools deployed, you can raze their capitals to the ground in days. The army will secure the rest of the strategic targets. We have done our groundwork and know exactly where to strike. It should be quick.'

'We hope so. I have allowed three moons for the first phase. Of course, the invasion is the easy part. Taking land is one thing. Holding and governing it is another. But we have overwhelming force, and once we set up the slave system and get our farms and industries into operation, momentum will quickly build. It is the pattern we have used over the many long years of conflict on Vard and it has not failed us yet.'

Darrison nodded, privately hoping that his father's optimism would be justified by events. His 20 years of living with humans had taught him not to underestimate them.

*

Despite Corus' brave words and Idris' careful healing, it was soon plain that it would take the old raash a day or two to recover.

Kayman and Mordant squashed their impatience and began to talk seriously about the attack on Vard.

'The thought of assassinating Darric and Ajina is highly attractive, but is it feasible? You say that many have tried and failed.'

'Sadly, I doubt we can do it. I'd have tried myself if it was not so difficult. They spend most of their time inside Main Base; it would be really hard to get close enough to kill them. However, I'll give it some serious thought. I need to talk to Braid, and I'd love to get Brett involved too. He is still the best, both as a fighter and a strategist. If we review all the options, they may come up with something I have not considered.'

'Good, do that. I can send a mage to bring Brett over, providing, of course, that he agrees to come out of "retirement".'

'For something as important as this, I believe he will.'

*

Meanwhile, Jan and Jorn had decided that they must concentrate on completing the quest and solving the final clues.

Jan had finally got the Sharfane Hook to stick. They visited the Burning Coast for a few moments, but the snow was more than halfway up the big column and there was a vicious blizzard. There was no way at present to continue the hunt for the fourth corner of the Juncture.

If they only knew where to go, they could move on to the fifth and final part, the cross-shaped central section. But they were getting nowhere with the cryptic verse. Jan's finding sense could produce nothing definite, except a vague image of the Pattern, and an even vaguer impression that someone else might help them, but he could not sense who.

The twins went to find Mordant to share Jan's insights and see if she had any ideas.

She shook her head. 'I'm as foxed as you are. But I go back to what I said at the start. The clue is as much about *when* as it is *where*. We have to get into the minds of mages who lived a thousand years ago. The verse makes it plain from the start that the location is somewhere entirely obvious to them, "somewhere that we know". I think we need an expert historian. Much though I hate to suggest it, I think we have to involve Angela Sturminster. She has made a study of Myron and his times. I have great respect for her intelligence. I know that she and Kayman have a long-standing rivalry, but we're going to need her co-operation at some point, and she will be thoroughly insulted if she thinks she's been kept in the dark until the last moment.'

'But can we trust her? We cannot be sure,' said Jorn, doubtfully.

'Idris will know whether we can trust her or not by reading her aura,' responded Mordant. 'An aura cannot lie. She cannot hide deceit or ill will, and if she tries to do so, Idris will see that at once, and so will Corus. Idris tells me he's a Reader too.'

'Very well. I've got to the stage when my brain just shuts down when I start to think about the wretched Rhyme. Maybe a fresh mind is what we need. I'll tell Kayman what you said and ask him to invite her to a meeting with us and the team. And Corus also, if he's feeling up to it.'

'Let's see what Kayman says.'

Chapter 24

Two days later, Corus was feeling stronger, so Idris brought him downstairs again to the cosy parlour where the team members were waiting in anticipation. Kayman had joined them and the High Master greeted the raash adept with grave and somewhat elaborate ceremony.

The ancient raash gave a single nod in reply and his violet eyes were amused. 'Thank you, Kayman. I appreciate your careful etiquette, but it is unnecessary, and I must apologise for not returning it. I was a slave for many years. Now I choose to serve, but I will call no one Master, nor do I wish that title for myself. I am Corus. It is enough.'

The mage settled into his chair by the fire, gave them all his tight smile and said, 'Well, I am ready. You may begin to fire your arrows!'

'An update on the invasion plans would be an excellent place to start,' said Kayman, 'and Mordant tells me that the raash have an Earth Base, do you have the location?'

'To answer your second question first, no, I do not. But our spies have long known about it. Darric started its construction as soon as the Great War ended.'

'He has hidden it with skill,' said Rolf. 'It must be in some very remote location. But a large base would need workmen to build it, and it would need supplies regularly. There may be some clue that we have missed. I can at least start our agents on the hunt for it.'

Corus nodded. 'But as to your second question, Darric has assembled his army, as you know. He will strike fast, hard and without warning, seeking to overwhelm you humans with terrifying force. He has all the experience gained from his long years of war. He will use his arsenal of explosives and fire-lances. And he will, of course, use mage-craft fuelled by the three Tools of Power. However, only Darric and his closest advisors know where he intends to strike. I suspect it will be in several places at once.'

Kayman winced. 'You are confirming our worst fears. But how can he translocate so many troops to Earth?'

'This is where the Tools are so useful to him. With the Chain of Earth, Darric can bind a portal so that it stays open for as long as he desires. He has used the Knife of Fire for many years as a weapon of war. He can, and will, use it to ignite anyone who stands in his path, and reduce the landscape to ashes. With the Wand, he can summon a war-wind to flatten troops, forests, homes. And if that is not enough, using the three Tools together, he can create a war-hammer that no wall, fortress or army can survive.'

'Blood's Death, you paint a grim picture!' said Braidart. 'Men are brave and will fight hard for what they hold dear, but few will stand to face fire and magic.'

'So, then, he does not need the Cup?' asked Idris quietly.

Corus sighed. 'Darric thinks he does not. But without it, he runs a terrible risk. He has never understood the true nature of the four Tools, or that they were made to be used only as a set. Every universe, and the evolution of life within it, is finely balanced between two opposing forces, the Regular and the Random. The Regular consists of the rules that govern the fundamental physical processes without which the multiverse cannot exist. Things are as they are because they cannot be otherwise. Beyond that essential order, all else is the result of the Random. On each planet, evolution and history are shaped by the Random forces we raash call Chance and Choice. Magic manipulates both the Regular and the Random, which is why it is dangerous. The Random force is intrinsically unstable. During a strong working, it might become dominant, overwhelming the Regular, and the balance that holds the universe together could be broken. The Tools are named after the traditional four elements – Earth, Air, Fire and Water – but these are just simple use-names that hide their true function. Each of the four Tools represent an aspect of the Regular. They are designed to operate within the matrix of the Quincunx and prevent the Random from getting out of control and causing chaos. By using three Tools together, outside the matrix, and with full force, lacking the stabilising influence of the Cup, Darric risks breaking the balance. If he does so, the fabric of this universe may implode.'

'By the Powers!' breathed Jorn. 'Is there anything we can do to stop him? Will the Juncture help?'

'Ah, the Juncture. Mordant has told me about it. Made by a mage called Myron, a thousand years ago. It is an odd story. Do you have any cause to doubt the truth of it?'

'Not really,' said Jorn, 'except that it does not make much sense. Jan and I have spent hours talking about it, but we don't get anywhere. There are so many unanswered questions. Why did he steal the Tools from the raash in the first place? Why did he make the Juncture? What was the purpose of his last great working? Myron was a Master of Nine, and very experienced. Why did he die? Did he overstretch himself, or do something wrong, or was there another reason? Why was the Juncture cut up and hidden? Who wrote the Riddle Rhyme? A whole row of "whys" and no answers. How can we know how to use the Juncture when we have so little to go on?'

Corus looked at the team, his heavily-lined face inscrutable. 'Let me tell you another story. A thousand years ago on Vard, there was a powerful and very ambitious high-raash Mage of Eight. He made a play for total Power, much as Darric has done, but he was less successful. He was feared and distrusted. His political power-base was shaky. In the end, he was rejected, exiled and dishonoured.

'For a high-raash, dishonour is unbearable. He sought ways to vent his spite and gain revenge, and in his own eyes, restore his status and esteem. His special Gift was to master difficult translocations in a way no other mage had done before. The raash adepts knew that, in theory, there were other universes, in different dimensions from their own, but no one had ever reached one. Perhaps no one had dared to try, or even wanted to. This mage did. He worked his passage across space and time to find his way to Earth, and he liked what he saw there. Humans were easier to dominate than his own people. He was determined to build his empire there instead.

'With subtle cunning, he stole the four High Tools of Power from their vault and the Juncture that controls them.' He saw their surprise. 'No, the Juncture was not made by Myron, he lacked the skill to fashion anything so complex. He took his loot to Earth, knowing that he could not be followed, as he was the only one capable of making a portal. The raash mages were distraught. So deep was their hatred of the traitor that they erased his name from memory, which, in our eyes, is the ultimate dishonour. It is unspoken to this day. We call him "No one" and curse the name.'

Corus paused. The team were listening intently and with considerable wonder. 'That much I know for certain. Now I will speculate. The traitor mage introduced himself to a group of human adepts, like himself, ambitious, hungry for knowledge. He could not disguise the fact that he was raash, but he could be charismatic, attractive, totally convincing. He taught the mages much, and they regarded him with enormous respect, believing that he had alien wisdom, and occult secrets of great potency.

'He grew in knowledge, and Power, for with the Tools, he was virtually a Mage of Nine and this he claimed to be. But underneath this carefully maintained façade, his was an evil mind, barren of feeling. He delighted in the distress he had caused on Vard by removing the Tools and, from time to time, returned in secret to observe the outcomes of his vengeance. He intended to use the Juncture to combine and augment the Power of the Tools in one enormous working. For what purpose? Who can say? Not, I am sure, to prevent a raash invasion, although that may be what he told the others. More likely, it was to ensure his domination of Earth. But something went wrong. He failed, and died.' The old raash looked at Mordant. 'What is the raash word for "No one"?'

'Nor-ym.'

'Oh, by the Nine!' breathed Jorn. 'Myron, in reverse!'

Corus nodded. 'It took our mages many hundreds of years before Carlion the Great again managed to master the Earth translocation. He searched in vain for the Tools, and found only one, the Knife of Fire, which he returned to us. As I told Mordant many years ago, it would have been better for my race if he had never done so, for the use of the Knife, unopposed by the other Tools, has warped our minds and spirits, and wrecked our planet. Vard is dying.'

Kayman shook his head in wonder. 'What an amazing story! It turns our entire understanding of the past upside-down.'

'And still leaves many of our questions unanswered,' said Jorn. 'How did Myron die? Why was the Juncture hidden, and what use may it be to us in defeating Darric, or preventing some appalling destruction of the universe?'

'I agree there are questions, but my sense tells me that what Corus speculates is exactly right,' said Jan. 'What he has just told us explains Myron's motives and actions.'

Mordant nodded. 'And it provides a reason for the myths and legends that surround him, and our general lack of hard information. As a historian, I know that when information about a famous person is scant, and stories abound, it is often because there is something about him or her that people were trying to hide. Myron's followers would not have wanted to admit how far they had allowed themselves to be deceived. And Myron had taught them much. They could not tell the world that the revered founder of the first Mage School on Earth was an alien traitor. Far better if he was a wonder-worker who died a heroic death, attempting to save Earth from disaster. They could live on Myron's reputation, bask in his reflected glory, create his legend.'

Kayman nodded. 'Exactly so. Corus, you have given us a great deal to think about. We are truly grateful. We still need to know more about the nature of the Tools, and the Juncture, but I see that you are tired now. We can wait.'

The old mage nodded. 'Yes, I am again tired. And I am not sure that I can tell you any more than I already have. Like your own story of Myron, the facts are garbled. The true purpose of the Juncture and the means of using it have been lost. But I want to say one thing before I go to my room. If I had the four Tools, and the Juncture, old as I am, I believe I could find a way to use them to begin to mend the damage that Darric has inflicted on our planet. Vard could grow green again. I know that is meaningless while Darric still has three of the Tools. But who knows? Chance is a strange force and stronger than we think.'

Braidart helped him from his chair and escorted him from the room. 'What an extraordinary mind,' said Rolf as the door closed.

'And an even more extraordinary spirit,' said Jan. 'But I wish he had brought us better news. And we must get him to tell us more about the Tools.'

'Indeed,' said Kayman. 'We are already in grave danger, but the potential threat to the universe from Darric's unbalanced use of Power is deeply troubling.'

'But first we have to solve the remaining clues, and we're still as stuck as ever,' sighed Jorn in weary frustration. 'I do hope that Professor Sturminster will agree to help.'

Kayman smiled. 'That's the good news, she has, and she will be here tomorrow.'

*

The High Master carefully stage-managed Professor Angela Sturminster's arrival at the Darnell mansion. She was met by a footman who ushered her into the splendour of the formal reception room. Kayman allowed her a few moments to be impressed, and to enable him to get a verdict from Idris, who had been waiting in the hall, covered by a never-mind.

'Her aura shows no malice or untoward deception. She is a Mage of Eight, a woman of strong will, sharp intelligence and great determination. I'll go upstairs and wait with the others.'

Kayman nodded, opened the door and smoothed in with a welcoming smile and an extended hand. 'Professor Sturminster, or may I call you Angela? We are most grateful to you for joining us.'

'I'm pleased you asked me. I've been waiting for an opportunity to express my condolences at the loss of your Hall. I am glad you survived, and there was, as I understand it, little loss of life?'

He nodded. 'Fortunately, our evacuation plan worked well.'

It made Professor Turner look thoughtful. But not for long. 'He remains convinced that the raash pose no real threat to Earth. He is wrong. Anyway, how may I help you?'

'We need your expertise, and it's high time that you knew what's been going on for the past few months.'

She smiled with genuine amusement. 'You mean your mysterious quest? Indeed, Kayman, I would very much like to see if my guess is correct! Angela is fine. And of course, if I can help you, I will.'

Kayman ushered the mage up the sweeping staircase. 'Our team is assembled in here. I think you may be a little surprised to meet some of them.' He opened the panelled door and gestured for her to go inside. The professor went two steps into the room and stopped dead, her amazement plain on her face. 'Surprised is something of an understatement. Do please introduce me.'

'My friends, meet Professor Angela Sturminster.' He waved her to a chair and took the one beside her. 'I think you may wish to be seated for the next part. Rolf you know. You have also met Sar Braidart and Jorn before. However, you have not met his shian twin, Jan.' Jan was, as usual, comfortably shian-naked. 'They are both Masters of Nine.' He heard Angela's sharp intake of breath and smiled. 'And this is Idris, who is, as you can see, a shian of the water. Mordant is a raash-human halfer, born on Vard, one of my most trusted agents for the past 20 years. You have met her also, although not when wearing her own face. And finally, we have Corus, a raash Mage-Adept who has recently come from Vard to help us in our war against Darric.'

Angela Sturminster surveyed the company in silence for a full half-minute, looking each in the eye. 'And I thought I knew what was going on!' she said, with quiet irony. 'I see that I was profoundly mistaken. No wonder you did not wish to share this information. Why do so now?'

'Because, as I told you, we need your help. The events that have taken place over the past few moons are extremely complicated, so I will keep all the details until later, but we have indeed been on a quest. As soon as we realised that Jorn was a potential Master of Nine, we knew that we had to try to find the Juncture. All the old stories agree on that fact: only a Nine can use it.'

Angela allowed herself a small smile. 'Well, least I did guess that correctly! So you found the Riddle Rhyme?'

'Yes; Jan did so. It's enigmatic and designed to deceive, but the team have found three of the five pieces of the Juncture, at no small danger to themselves, I may add.' He looked at Jorn who removed the pass-me-by and revealed the Juncture on the table in front of him, the three pieces reconnected as one.

'Oh, by the Powers!' she murmured.

Braidart rose, brought over a heavy tray, loaded with wine and goblets, placed it on the table in front of the dumbfounded mage and said with grave courtesy, 'I think that a glass of wine might be in order, Professor, despite the early hour? White or red?

'Red, please,' she responded, somewhat faintly. Braid served everyone with wine except the twins and Idris. Angela raised her glass, took a large swallow, and a second, and then lifted the goblet in a toast. 'The company! I'm amazed beyond words at what you have achieved, and deeply honoured that you have confided in me. But how can I help? I see that the Juncture is not yet complete. Is there a problem?'

'There is indeed,' said Rolf. 'We are stuck on the final clues. I've written them down to remind us what they say.' He passed round slips of paper and they all looked at the cryptic couplets.

Seek me somewhere that you know,
I am neither high nor low,
I do not lose or win the race,
The still centre is my place.

Master of Nine, be strong and wise,
Complete the quest and win the prize.
Resolve the verse, perform the task,
Unlock the truth, reveal the mask.

'The only insight we have is very vague. Jan has recently sensed that the fifth part has a connection to the Pattern. Did you bring a copy of that with you, Angela, as I requested?' asked Kayman.

The professor nodded, fished in her document case, and produced a large drawing in full colour, showing the Pattern with the overlay of the Quincunx.

'May I see? This is not something we use on Vard,' Corus asked,

They passed it down the table to him. Idris said, 'Mordant has pointed out that, whilst we do not know *where* the clue refers to, we do know *when*. It was written a thousand years ago, just after Myron's death. The "somewhere that you know" must have been completely understandable to the mages of that time. We are hoping very much that you may be able to tell us where and what it is?'

Angela frowned, her attractive features reflecting puzzled thought. 'I'm not sure; I may have an idea. Give me a moment or two to consider this.'

'Before you do, there's something else that you need to know. Corus has given us crucial information about Myron, which changes everything.' Kayman briefly repeated the story of the traitor mage, and their assumptions about what Myron had really been trying to do.

Angela looked predictably stunned and drained her glass. 'By the Nine, Kayman, you have just undermined my last 20 years of academic research! But I'm a historian and we are used to such surprises! We need more evidence, but it has the ring of truth, and as you say, it answers several pressing questions, though not all. But it doesn't help us with our present conundrum.'

Corus had been studying the Pattern with acute interest. He looked up. 'This is very elegant. Is it, as I assume, a map to show the colours required for translocation from Earth to the Realms?'

'Yes it is'

'Mmmm. And the four circles relate to the dimensions? Above and Below, Ahead and Behind?'

'Yes, they do.'

The old raash nodded. 'Then I think that Jan's sense is absolutely right in directing us to it. Look at the very centre of the Pattern, where the Quincunx forms a cross. What does that remind you of?' He gestured at the Juncture. 'And what does the Rhyme tell us? "I am neither high nor low"; "I do not lose or win the race".'

Jan felt a surge of sudden understanding as his sense tweaked hard. 'Of course! Corus, you are brilliant! The fifth part of the Juncture is hidden at the centre of the Pattern! It's neither low nor high, in other words, not Above or Below. It's not fast or slow, so not Ahead or Behind. It's in the middle, in the centre.'

Kayman huffed and tutted crossly. 'Well, by the Powers! Why couldn't we see that sooner?'

'Like all riddles, the answer is irritatingly obvious once you've worked it out,' responded Corus. 'Sometimes a fresh mind can see what those who are too close to the problem cannot. But my insight has not helped us much. We still have no idea where this Pattern may be.'

'But perhaps I do,' said Angela Sturminster. The entire company gave her their instant attention. 'Many years ago, I went to search for the ruins of the original Mage School that Myron founded. I knew from ancient records that it was somewhere by the Inner Sea, near Samar, in what is now the Andrean Empire on Earth, but the exact location was long lost. It was largely academic curiosity on my part. I didn't expect there would be much left above ground, but I wanted to know how large the building was, and I hoped that a careful study of the remains might provide some evidence of how it was used. I was fortunate. I'll spare you the detective story, but I found it. The following year, I took a party of students there to do an excavation. The building was larger than I expected, typical of a fine house of its period, single storey, with many rooms built around a series of courtyards. And in the central courtyard, the Pattern was laid out in mosaics on the floor. When we left, we recovered the ruins to preserve them. I have the Hook.'

Jorn felt a huge surge of hope. 'That's wonderful! It has to be the right place!' He turned to Jan. 'It is, isn't it?'

'Yes, the fifth section is there. My sense is now sure of it.'

Kayman beamed with satisfaction. 'Then the sooner you can all go and find it, the better.'

The professor smiled. 'Are you doing anything after lunch?'

'Sadly I am, but I'm sure that Rolf and the others can spare an hour or so!'

'We can indeed!' agreed Rolf with enthusiasm. 'Angela, I knew you would help us! We can tell you the whole story over lunch, and then go to Samar and see what we can find.'

'My curiosity will have to wait. Braidart and I have other urgent plans to discuss,' Mordant told them.

'And I'll sit this one out too,' said Idris. 'Samar is too dry for my comfort.'

*

As soon as they had eaten, Mordant and Braidart made their apologies and left to do some serious thinking about the attack on Vard.

'I want a fresh mind on this too, Braid,' she told him wearily. 'Much though I like the idea of assassinating Darric, I just don't think it's possible.'

'Well, let's run it through and see.'

They settled down at the table in the small parlour and Mordant began by describing the Base, doodling the plan with her finger on the tabletop as she spoke. 'There is an enormous underground complex on five levels, with Darric's private quarters, the court and the government offices in the middle, like the jam in a sponge cake. We can forget the two lowest levels because the fourth is full of slaves and soldiers and the lowest has the cells and a lot of other stuff that does not concern us. The main entrance is watched day and night. There are armed guards, a duty mage, and various magic wards, and the side entrances are similar. The kitchen entrance, which is where I've slipped in before, is less heavily guarded, and there is more coming and going but, if you do get in, you then have to work your way down to level three, which is where the fun really begins.'

Braidart held up a hand to cut her short and said briskly, 'Let's analyse that as we go. The task has stages; he pulled over a sheet of paper and his pen and ink, and wrote a neat list as he spoke.

A Get to Vard and reach Base unseen
B Get into underground Base unseen
C Enter level three, still unseen
D Find Darric, and/or his sister, again, unseen
E Kill them
F Get out alive

'Anything else?' She shook her head. 'Right. Now let's review that. A and B are possible because I know you've done both of those things before. But I guess your methods would only work for one or two people, so there's no chance of sending in a large force. That brings us to C. What's level three like?'

'Huge; sumptuously furnished, what little I've see of it, brightly lit. Swarming with Darric's personal honour guard, courtiers, mages, ministers, and their assistants. Plenty of slaves, carefully selected, in smart livery, and each having an armband, which carries a coded identity number, changed daily. Every person who enters or leaves is checked at the staircases. These entry points also have built-in wards to detect anyone sliding past under cover of a glamour. I'm told that Darric's private apartments are the same, but even more strongly warded.'

'Right, so we get through all that somehow, and then have to find exactly where our Lord is, in an unknown complex of state rooms, get past his honour guard, get really close, and kill him. I assume he doesn't just stand there waiting for that to happen?'

Mordant gave her tight smile. 'Darric's survived 50 years of war, plots and treachery, and assassination attempts by poison, infection, blade, and mage-craft. He is a powerful Eight with a wide repertoire of strong wards and unpleasant defences. No, I doubt anyone could get within three ems of him without being stopped, whether using magic or any other method of attack.'

Braidart huffed and sat back in his chair. 'Well, I think that answers the fundamental question. We don't get much past B. And even if we did, we can forget F. It's suicide.'

Mordant nodded grimly. 'That's pretty much the conclusion I reach every time I think about it. I don't mind getting killed if there's a solid chance of taking out Darric first, but it's hopeless. If it was possible, someone else would have managed it by now.'

'So what about when he's not in Main Base? Is he more vulnerable then?'

'Somewhat, but not enough to make it feasible. There are still the guards and the mages, and his own abilities. And Corus tells me he hardly ever leaves the Base these days. He simply goes out of a well-guarded entrance, into a well-defended walled yard, and portals out to wherever he wants to go.'

'Non-starter,' declared Braid. 'So, if we rule out A for assassination, what's plan B?'

Mordant shrugged. 'Do some significant damage elsewhere. The arsenal would be my favourite. It's full of arms and explosives, and that filthy gel they use in their flame-throwers. Then there's the barracks nearby, housing several thousand raash from the elite Foragers. I think that might be the best way to use Jorn's war-hammer.'

'Explosives? You've mentioned them before, but I'm not sure exactly what they are?'

'Ah, I forget that you don't know about these things. The dwar techs use them for mining. It's a mixture of chemicals that can be made to react when a fuse is lit. It packs a big, destructive punch, especially good for demolishing walls and buildings. And the raash pack the stuff into small containers, which you can lob at your enemies.'

'Right. So they are portable. Interesting.'

'So, we could launch a fast in-and-out strike at night, and wreck the arsenal before the raash know what hit them. But whether that would delay the invasion or just put a nasty dent in Darric's honour, I really don't know.'

'Let me mull it all over for a bit. I may come up with something.'

About three hours later, he did. 'Those underground levels in the Base must have some kind of air supply, or they'd get unbearable. How does that work?' he enquired casually.

Mordant paused her supper. 'They have machines that extract the foul air and pump in fresh. No idea of the details but it seems to work.'

'Mmm. So would there be shafts running out to the surface?'

'I suppose there must be. I'll try and find out.'

'Does that mean you'll go to Vard to reconnoitre?' She nodded. His sapphire eyes brightened. 'Can I come?'

'Tomorrow, before dawn, at the third bell.'

'Right, early night?' He contrived to make that an invitation, but she shook her head, and gave him a peck on the cheek. 'Not tonight, Braid. I have to do a lot of complex working. I must go and set up some constructs and then I'll need to have a good rest. I'll be draining my Power on this one.'

*

Meanwhile, the twins and Rolf had left for the ruins of Myron's Mage School in the mid-afternoon. The professor formed her portal with confident ease. Jorn walked through and found himself standing in warm sunshine. Just to his right, a line of crumbling, dry stonewall wandered on a random course, leant on by an ancient tree with sparse tufts of greyish leaves and an immensely thick, twisted trunk. Behind that stretched a large grove of the same trees, obviously much younger. Jan slid out of his twin and took form, unable to resist the lure of a new tree. He touched the bark with reverence.

'This is so very old. What is it, Angela?'

'An olive. And yes, it is ancient. It's possible for these trees to live for many hundreds of years, some are believed to be over a thousand.'

'This one feels old enough to have given Myron shade.' He looked around, scanning with his sense. 'The ruins are over there.'

Angela raised her eyebrows in amazement. 'Yes, they are. How could you possibly know?'

'It's his special Gift,' Jorn told her. 'He finds things.'

'I must include you on my next archaeological expedition.'

They followed her towards the grove and then round it. On the far side, a broad, flat finger of ochre land extended out into a hyacinth sea. It was covered by low bushes and pungently fragrant herbs, humming with bees. There was very little else to see, except for jumbled stone, and two fallen columns. Angela consulted some hand-drawn plans and frowned.

'It's been a long time. We removed the marker pegs. It's hard to remember where things were.'

Jan paced about, his face intent, sense scanning. He stopped. 'Here,' he said. Angela went over looking doubtful and Jorn and Rolf followed.

'You just stand over there while Jorn and I sweep this stuff away.'

The layer of gravelly soil and small plants was not that thick. The mages constructed a wind-warp apiece and proceeded systematically to blast aside the covering. Bright colours came into view.

They worked carefully until the whole mosaic was revealed. The Pattern extended over an area some three ems square, glittering as if it had been laid yesterday.

Angela indicated the various sections. 'This is very skilled work. The craftsman used semi-precious stones: lapis and jade, turquoise and rose-quartz, red jasper and agate, jet, even gold and silver.'

Rolf looked at the twins. 'So now what? How do we find the fifth part?'

Jan went to stand on the violet centre point. He closed his eyes and was silent for a while. 'Jorn, let me have the Juncture, please.' He took the incomplete square frame and carefully orientated it so that the jewels were in the right places, and then set it down across the exact centre of the Pattern, so that the crosspieces lined up with the Quincunx and the jewels rested at the intersections between the chaos zones. It fitted perfectly.

'Yes, I thought so! And the fifth piece is here. That is the good news. The bad news is that we can't reach it yet. I am sorry, but we need to have the four parts of this framework completed first. Can you sense that too, Jorn?'

Jorn went to stand at the centre of the pattern, focussed his sense and concentrated. 'Yes, Jan, right as usual. We've found where it is, but we can't get it.'

The shian mage was still looking thoughtfully at the Juncture and the Pattern. He bent to retrieve the artefact and sighed in frustration. 'But I still have no idea how we are supposed to use it; maybe it won't become clear until we have it completed.'

'Never mind, it's an excellent start,' said Rolf, 'and it's easy to reach.'

'Well, we're not likely to find out what to do next by standing here staring like a herd of cattle,' said Angela decisively. 'I'll cover the Pattern with a pass-me-by, and we can go back to Errington and consider the matter in comfort.'

'You'll stay for tea, I hope, Angela?' said Rolf as Jorn formed the return portal.

'Of course. I should very much like to talk to Corus about Myron and the Tools, if he is not too tired.'

Jan nodded. 'So would we.'

*

Darrison had also been busy. He was working through his list of targets from the softest upwards, and had decided that the easiest mark was Professor Turner, whose belief in his own invulnerability was so total that he took few precautions.

Like the twins, the raash agent had been monitoring the weather on the Burning Coast. He too had managed to get a Hook on the Sharfane, using the sketches by Dr Steggles that the team had found in the Errington library. It had been easy to trace the records of what they had asked the librarian to find for them; Karth and the Coast were obviously their destinations.

They had purchased desert kit, so that meant they had been to Karth. He was reasonably sure the Coast was their next target. The weather was easing a bit, but the snow was still very thick. As soon as there was the first sign of a thaw, he could inform Ajina, and she would set up 24-hour mage surveillance. If Jorn arrived at the Sharfane to test the weather conditions, his guess would be confirmed. The moment the full team arrived, they would be captured. That would take care of Jorn, and that traitor halfer, so once Turner was eliminated, his remaining target was Kayman, and the other Darnells. But first things first. Today, it was the professor's turn to die.

It would be pleasant to make the man sweat with terror, and even more satisfying to make his death slow and unpleasant, but Darrison was too much the professional to allow his feelings to dictate his actions. It had to be fairly quick, and look enough like an accident, to prevent any big over-reaction by the authorities.

He changed his appearance with a careful combination of physical disguise and a light mask, and walked openly into the university in the late afternoon, a bundle of research folders tucked under his arm. Candles and lamps were already being lit in the corridors and lecture rooms.

His research had told him that Turner would be where he wanted him, in his study, on his own. The spy went into the Department of Ancient Studies and entered Turner's outer office, where he spellbound Turner's assistant. He then walked into the study and slammed an eight-colour mind-fetter on the professor before he had time to do much more than blink in annoyance at his unexpected visitor. Darrison followed that up with a major binding and pain-bond.

He stood in front of the immobilised mage and spoke with a polite and pleasant manner. 'Good afternoon, Professor. My name is Darrison. Despite my human appearance, I am raash. I am in fact Lord Darric's son and his most trusted spy.' He smiled and strode round the room, pulling papers out of drawers, books off shelves and candles out of holders, making heaps of combustibles, talking as he went. Turner's eyes followed him with uncomprehending fury and then rising horror.

'Lord Darric has asked me to give you his personal thanks for your assistance to our cause over many years. Both your adamant refusal to believe that we raash are capable of invading Earth, and your masterly manipulation of the High Council of Mages, have ensured that both mages and humans are far less prepared for us than they might have been if Kayman's warnings had been taken more seriously.'

Darrison took up a lamp, extinguished it, and began to sprinkle oil from the reservoir around the room, linking his piles of paper with inflammable trails. 'However, your usefulness has ended, and the sight of hundreds of thousands of raash attacking Earth might move even you to action. So now, you are going to die. It should be fairly fast for you; there will be a lot of smoke. With any luck, you will not feel the flames, although I cannot promise that.'

By now, Turner was making desperate efforts to break the bindings on him, but Darrison's skill and will were very strong, and the old mage was long out of practice.

Darrison opened the folders he had been carrying and revealed some pieces of fabric, coated in a sticky gel. He placed some of these on the pile of papers nearest to Turner, and others round the room, went to the door and turned with a final smile. 'Goodbye, Professor.'

He lit two of the nearest piles with a flick of Power and left rapidly, closing the door. He closed the outer office door as well, and cast a confusion glamour in the passage, designed to make people uncertain what to do. He was well down the stairs before he heard the dim echoes of shouting start behind him. He smiled, and left at an easy pace, glancing back just once to note the rising plume of smoke above the Darsius Wing.

The news reached the Darnell household an hour later. Angela Sturminster had taken tea with the team, and was preparing to go home. The university messenger was in a considerable state of consternation.

'You must return with me at once, Professor, I have a carriage waiting. There's been a terrible fire in your department. Professor Turner was burnt to death in his study.'

'I'll come at once.' She turned to Rolf. 'I'll be amazed if this was an accident.'

'So will I,' agreed the mage grimly. 'If Philip did not have a hand in this, I'll shave my beard. We must all be doubly on our guards.'

'And the sooner we can eliminate Philip, the better,' said Rolf. 'I had no liking for Turner but being burnt alive is not a death I'd wish on anyone.'

Chapter 25

The death of Professor Turner sent Rolf and Kayman into a huddle of urgent discussion. Jorn and Jan realised it was highly significant, but felt they couldn't do much about it, so Jan went to find a tree, telling his brother that he'd portal across to the Burning Coast before returning, just to do another rapid weather check.

Jorn nodded. 'Fine. I'll see if I can get any further with the final verse now we know where to locate part five.'

Inwardly, he was worried. The more he thought about the coming raid on Vard, and his own role in that, the less confident he felt. His sense was tweaking and he wondered why, and what to do about it.

Mordant also ignored the news and ran through the reconnaissance mission with Braid after supper. 'There's a high fence all round Main Base,' she explained, 'and the quickest way to get over that is an apport. I must test that out now, to be sure I can manage both of us, and you need to experience the feeling of the lift, because it takes a bit of getting used to.'

She got him to embrace her, and he took his opportunity to drop a couple of kisses on her forehead. She tutted crossly. 'This is not the time. Now just hold me, but not too tightly, and I'll lift us up.' She held them for a moment, with their heads bumping the ceiling, and then steadily let them down, but it was a considerable effort. She stretched tiredly. 'I'll have to beef that construct up a bit. I must get some rest now. See you at the third hour, down in the garden. Bring a torch. Knives, no swords. We won't be there long enough to need anything else.'

As the pre-dawn light began to spread across the indigo sky, they met up as arranged, and Mordant made her portal and brought them out on Vard behind the cookhouse for the barracks, where the water pump provided a convenient Hook she'd used before. The guards came round here less frequently than in the main square. She covered Braid and herself with strong wards and glamours and waited for him to recover from the translocation. His tolerance was improving, but it still made him feel nauseous and dizzy.

He stood and sniffed the air, and she saw the white flash of his teeth in the dimness. Mordant had explained that she could lip-read, so he mouthed his words, 'Dry, warm, dusty and a hint of pig. Where are the patrols?'

She led him to the corner of the cookhouse where they could peer round the corner and see the barrack square and parade ground. The gas-lamps flared. In front of each three-storey brick building, sentries marched up and down at intervals, making crisp, stamped parade turns. It was otherwise very quiet. The barrack windows showed few lights.

Mordant pointed across to the narrow end of the square, where a two-storey windowless warehouse was more heavily guarded. 'Arsenal,' she whispered. He nodded and continued his surveillance. Finally, he slid back into the shadows at the side of the building. 'Main Base next.' She pointed in the direction and the pair slipped towards their target, invisible and soundless.

Mordant had never attempted to explore the surface of the gigantic complex. It was ring-fenced. The long earth mound that topped it off was kept free from scrub and patrolled by guards. Their first task was to get over the fence and find out more.

Crouching down, they studied the high barrier. The upper section slanted outwards to make climbing impossible. Strong, steel posts were set at two-em intervals, and linked by strands of thick razor wire. They could see the silhouettes of guards on the top of the ridge against the lighter sky. Braid pulled a face, indicating rueful acknowledgement of the tight security.

'Over to you.'

Mordant had the construct hung ready. They embraced and she formed the apport. The pair lifted smoothly, sailed over the fence, and landed noiselessly on the other side. She was relieved; it was a demanding working, but now they were inside, she could make a Hook and portal in and out again.

They both went flat and began to worm up the slope, looking for anything that might be an opening, finding nothing of the slightest interest, and, despite the glamour, freezing every time a guard walked past above. At the top, they rested and took a good look round. Braid gripped her arm and then pointed. Big, square metal structures protruded from the earth at regular intervals in a line along the top of the mound, each covered by a protective, pyramid-shaped cowl.

With extreme care, they crawled towards the nearest one. The strong metal casing was hot to the touch. They could feel a draught of warm, fume-laden air, and hear a faint hum. Braid shook his head and mimed to emphasise his meaning. 'Output. Need intake.'

Mordant nodded her understanding.

They waited for the guard to plod past. The raash paused and they tensed, but he simply put his crossbow down, yawned widely, and took a swig of water from his flask. He sighed, picked up the weapon and moved on, plainly longing for the end of his tedious duty.

They located a vent that felt cool to the touch. It was of the same design. There was just enough room between the cowl and the top of the casing for Braid to slip his head and arm in and shine a torch downwards. When he emerged, he was wearing satisfied grin. He gave a thumbs-up and made the signal for 'let's go'.

They crept back to the base of the fence. Mordant set a small spell-tag to mark a fencepost as her Hook for the next visit and then rapidly formed the Earth portal, and they both went through.

Back in the garden of the mansion, dawn was breaking and they shivered in the sudden chill. Mordant waited while Braid recovered, steadying him, and he soon felt better. He gave a broad smile.

'Wow! I have actually set foot on another planet! That will be something to remember. And we saw exactly what we hoped to see. We have a way into the Base. I can chimney down one of those input vents; there must be a network of ducts down below. I should be able to reach the court level.'

'But to achieve what? You'd still have to find Darric, and attacking him hasn't got any easier.'

'I wasn't thinking of assassination, at least not at close quarters. Come on, let's get indoors and I'll explain, it's too chilly out here after Vard. I need a hot breakfast and some beer to lubricate my wits.'

Mordant could see that he had a plan, so she contained her impatience and followed him into the house. As soon as they'd ordered their refreshments, they settled into the small parlour and she said, 'So, what have you come up with?'

'Two attacks at once, with different targets. First Jorn takes out the arsenal, and a barrack block or two as well, if he can manage it. So, the Arsenal goes "boom", and everyone panics and stops bothering about anything else. Meanwhile, I'll go down a ventilation shaft and place some explosives in level three. We'll need some help from a dwar tech with that. Need some way to delay it going off; I want time to get out. Then we all portal home as fast as we can before they get organised. If we're incredibly lucky, Darric and Ajina will be inside and we'll take them out, but even if that doesn't happen, we'll have destroyed their home and disrupted their government. If those things don't combine to slow them down a bit, I'll give up beer.' He took a long swig to underline the improbability while Mordant considered the plan. It had some drawbacks and it needed work, but it was certainly a fresh idea. She gave him her thin smile, and a warm hug and a peck.

'Genius!' she told him. 'Let's start work. This one is going to take a lot of careful preparation.'

*

Idris was relaxing happily in his favourite fountain in a park near the Darnell mansion. It was a large, vigorous display of gushing water that made him tingle with pleasure. His sense tweaked. The twins were coming in his direction. The shian brought his attention back to the surface and rapidly scanned Jorn's aura, clearly seeing his uncertainty. He had noticed that several times recently, and mostly when the attack on Vard was being discussed. Something was bothering him, and perhaps Jan also.

Jorn sat down on the wide edge of the fountain and sent, *'Are you there, Idris?'*

'I am indeed. You need my advice; something to do with the raid on Vard, I think.'

Jorn shrugged and looked uncomfortable. *'You're right as usual. It's bothering me. Idris, my war-hammer is capable of achieving enormous destruction. I'm not sure if I'm pleased about that, or just plain terrified! Mordant looks at me now with this gleam in her eyes, as if I'm a new-forged blade, all ready to wield against the raash. Power knows, I hate the bloody race, but I'm not a mass murderer. And that is what I'm going to have to become. She wants me to take out the arsenal, which is fine, but she also wants me to hit the barrack blocks round the square, filled with sleeping raash. In a few days, I'll be responsible for killing hundreds, hurting many more. They may be raash but the thought of it makes me feel sick to my essence. And if I feel like that, I won't be able to work with my whole will, and that will be a disaster. I've talked it over with Jan and he hates the idea as well. What the hell am I to do?'*

'I do understand your feelings, Jorn. You are not a killer. People like Brett and Braidart and Mordant see things in simple terms, as warriors

must. Raash are the enemy; they will kill us if they can. Our job is to kill them first. But Mordant and the Darnells have strict limits. They do not kill at random. They will not start a killing spree in a local tavern one night, just for the hell of it, and they would stop anyone who tried. Would you find them battering down the door to a cottage and butchering everyone inside?'

'No. They wouldn't do that. But the raash do. That's what you mean isn't it? There is a difference.'

'Yes, there is. Think it through. Do the raash intend to invade Earth?'

'Yes.'

'And what will they do when they get there?'

'Kill, hurt, enslave.'

'And if you go and stand in front of their army and ask them nicely to go away, are they going to listen?'

'No.'

'So, Jorn, if the raash army was lined up in front of you, on Earth, ready to do their best to wipe out humanity, would you hesitate to use your Power?'

'No. I guess not.'

'And if you had the Power to warp time and prevent that invasion force from ever arriving, would you do that?'

'Of course I would.'

'Very well, think of it like this. When you go to Vard to work against the raash, you are acting at the point ahead of attack, in order to slow them down and make it harder for Darric to do exactly as he wishes. Yes, you will kill, and do so in cold blood, which is against your nature. But every raash soldier you kill now is one less to arrive on Earth later. This is war, Jorn. We did not choose that, Darric did, and his choice limits ours. You have to become a War-Mage, whether you want to or not, because you may be the one thing that stands between Darric and success. Do not fear your Power. And do not relish it either. Respect it, and use it only when you must. And when that time comes, then use it with all your mind, will and essence, as effectively as you can.'

'I'll do my best.'

Idris chose his next words with care. 'Of course you will. And Jan, I understand your own reluctance too. Shians do not make war. But I have told you that even we kill, when all other options fail, and we are faced *with threats to our homes and kin. If you cannot kill raash yourself, you must at least do all you can to help Jorn to do so.'*

'I will. But my sense is tweaking; it's going to be dangerous.'

'Powers! What do you expect? A raid on Vard is not a walk in the park.'

Jorn felt his dark mood lighten a little. 'Thanks Idris. That helps me to sort out my head. It's not going to be easy, I'll be heartily glad when it's over, and I won't like the result, but it has to be done.'

The shian mage watched him walk away, and hoped he had said the right things. Jorn needed certainties right now, not an hour's lecture on the ethics of violence versus non-violence and the need for proportionate responses. The young Masters' extraordinary Power did indeed carry an equivalently high price. And it was dangerous. Even his sense was tweaking.

*

Kayman very much liked Braidart's plan. Mordant's only worry was that a lot of slaves would be killed as well as the raash elite, but she could see no way to avoid that, and Kayman agreed that it was something they would have to live with.

At Mordant's request, he sent urgent letters by mage-messenger to Brett Darnell and to Sarra, Mordant's dwarran friend, asking for their urgent assistance. Sarra was not just a Mage of Eight and Member of High Council; she was also a skilled tech who knew all about explosives.

While they waited for Brett and Sarra to arrive, Mordant, Jorn, Rolf, Braid and Kayman did the initial planning. There would be two teams. Braidart nicknamed the Base team 'Ram' because they were going to 'stuff it up Darric's arse', and the demolition team 'Wallop' for equally obvious reasons. Mordant allowed a small smile at his guardroom humour and reduced that to team R and team W.

Team R was Braidart, Sarra and Rolf. Team W was herself, Brett, and Jorn. 'Who can we get to be backup mage for team W?' she enquired. 'We'll need someone to work the portal, I'll be a tad too busy to concentrate.'

'What about me?' suggested Kayman. He enjoyed the short pause that followed.

'Really, you can't, old friend, it's far too risky,' protested Rolf.

'Nonsense!' he retorted. 'I'm not too old for action yet. Just because I've spent most of the last 20 years sitting at a desk, it doesn't mean I like it. Now I'm not running the Hall, I have time to get involved in the field. I want to set foot on Vard. And I want to see Jorn in action. We'll be in and out in less than five minutes.'

The elderly mage was plainly determined. Mordant shrugged, 'I'll need to take each team on another quick visit to Vard before we go in for the mission. You all need to know the layout, and the mages need to practice making the Earth translocation. The colours are not quite as you might expect.'

'Excellent!' beamed Kayman, rubbing his hands and looking as pleased as a kid promised a trip to a fair. 'I'm looking forward to this!'

*

Brett arrived the following morning, with his longsword strapped to his back and a very business-like manner. He gave Mordant an outwardly brotherly greeting and a small, secret squeeze, after which they both behaved with impeccable correctness.

He grinned at his younger brother. 'This will be just like old times, Mordant and me attacking raash together. I've been itching for a chance to get my revenge for the Hold and father.'

Braidart looked startled. 'I had no idea you two even knew each other. When was that?'

Brett slapped him on the back. 'When you were still chasing Brendan round the battlements with a wooden sword!'

Mordant watched the changes on Braidart's face, and his puzzled frown as the implications hit home, and suppressed a snort of laughter as he realised that she must be at least 20 years older than he had imagined.

Sarra arrived soon afterwards, and Braidart and Mordant spent an intense hour explaining the situation, and bringing the new team members up to speed on the attack plans. Sarra was at once interested in the raash ventilation system and their technology, and asked a lot of questions that Mordant couldn't begin to answer.

'So will they work? The explosives, I mean?' asked Braidart. 'My whole scheme for Ram rather hangs on that. And I'd prefer not to blow myself up in the process!'

'Certainly it will work. I can get you the explosive sticks and also time-delay fuses, although the longest is only 30 minutes. The only tricky part is getting them into the right place so they detonate with maximum effect. Look, I'll explain.' She proceeded to do so at length, making quick sketches to illustrate points about blasts in confined spaces, but her three listeners soon got boggled by it all. The dwar grinned at their bemused expressions. 'Sorry! Getting a bit carried away! Once I've been over there to take a look, I'll be able to decide how you need to do it.'

Mordant did her best to concentrate but she found it hard to be so close to her much-loved 'Beaky Boy' without being able to show her feelings. He might be well past 40, but he still had craggy good looks, a warrior's grace and all the charm she remembered so well. One look from his blue eyes was enough to give her warm sensations in places where she should not be having them. It brought home just how different he was from Braidart, despite their strong family resemblance. She really would have to bring her affair with the young Darnell to a conclusion soon, but a love affair, like war, was easy to start and very hard to end, especially if you wanted to stay friends afterwards.

*

The next round of 'rehearsal' visits to Vard went off without any problem. Sarra worked the translocation for Team R, landing them inside the fence. Everything was just as before. Sarra had spent time with Mordant, finding out everything she could remember about level three and the location of Darric's apartments. The dwar had pinpointed that position in relation to the top of the mound, and led them to the extract vent she had selected as being most likely to lead down to that area.

As Mordant and Rolf kept watch and maintained their concealing glamours, the tech examined the vent, peered down it, and surveyed the top of the base with careful consideration. She suggested cutting through most of the struts supporting the cover of the duct so that it could be quickly removed when the time came, and proceeded to do that with swift efficiency. They had to wait while the guard passed, then Braid and Sarra gave the signal, and they inched back down the mound to the fence where Rolf formed the Earth portal.

Jorn

Team W's visit was equally uneventful. Jorn surveyed his targets and tried to stifle his inner concerns. Brett and Mordant took note of the guards and potential escape routes. Kayman worked the return portal.

The entire team met up again for the usual final briefing session in the snug parlour, and ran through the attack procedures.

Braid said, 'I only have one problem with my end; I can chimney down the duct quite easily, but coming back up that way will be slow and I'll be tired by then. And the fuses don't give me much time. It would be better if I could use a rope, but for that, I need a strong fixing point, and some kind of belay. I'm not too sure that the duct casing can take that. Ideally, I want someone managing the rope, but that person needs to be very strong. Sarra can't do it, and Rolf will be down by the fence, ready to get us out in a hurry.'

Jorn felt Jan shift out of him and was surprised when his twin took form and said quietly, 'I could do that for you, Braid.'

The big man looked at him in doubtfully. 'Are you that strong?'

'I'll show you. Just lie down.' The others watched curiously. 'Hold still and stiff now.'

The shian mage scooped Braid into his arms and stood up with no apparent effort. He then hoisted him and held him above his head, just under the high ceiling, until Braid said, 'Right, you've, proved your point! Can I come down now?'

Brett said a soft 'Wow!' of appreciation.

'Heavens, Jan!' exclaimed Jorn. 'I had no idea you could do that!'

Jan grinned. 'Neither did I. But Idris told me that a shian of the wood has a very strong form, so I've been experimenting to see just what I can do. And, of course, I can always add a tweak of Power if I need it. I'm no War-Mage, but I want to be involved in this mission, not just a passenger.'

'Well, you've got the job!' Braid told him. 'I'll show you how to belay, and maybe we can find somewhere to practise a bit.'

Mordant nodded and looked round at the teams. 'I think we're good to go,' she confirmed.

When she and the others had left the room, Braidart drew Brett one side. 'Exactly how well did you two know each other?' he demanded.

'Ah, you noticed. I thought we'd been careful.'

'You have been. But I'm not blind, or daft. And I do know you both pretty well. I wondered why she's cooled off a bit since you came.'

'We've done nothing.'

'Doesn't mean you don't want to. Erm… She must be a good bit older than I thought?'

'I couldn't possibly comment.' Brett looked hard at his brother. 'Yes, we were lovers. For almost 10 years.'

'Blood's death, Brett, you might have told me!'

'Why?'

'I might have had second thoughts, I mean…' Braid tailed off lamely, aware that he was in a hole, and had better stop digging.

Brett smiled at his brother's obvious embarrassment. 'Mordant is totally amazing, and I'm very fond of her. But I'm married now, and she's lonely. I know she's been sharing your bed. I'm happy for her to have some fun with you. But where's it going, Braid? Have you thought it through?'

Braid shrugged. 'Guess not.'

Brett snorted. 'Typical! Sex first, sense second. Well, it's about time you did start thinking, and considering Mordant's feelings as well as your own. If you do anything to upset her, Braid, you'll answer to me. Understand?'

He nodded, feeling compelled to justify his behaviour. 'I mean, it was just fun to begin with. I didn't expect it to last more than a few nights, only it has; and we're still on mission so that makes it complicated. I've got in deeper than I meant to.'

'I know the feeling. Just remember that I'm keeping an eye on you.'

Braidart watched Brett stride out of the room. The thought that his brother and Mordant had been long-term lovers when he was a small boy was deeply unsettling. His affair with the exotically sexy raash mage had become rather more significant than he'd intended, but they were going into action together and he had to stay professional. He wasn't quite certain what would happen after that, or what he wanted as an outcome.

*

Two days later, teams R and W translocated to Vard in the early hours, bent on creating as much mayhem as they could manage in about 30 minutes. The mission depended on everything going just right with perfect timing. Everyone knew that was a big ask; they just had to hope that luck was with them, and their careful preparations paid off.

Braidart inched his way cautiously down the duct, bracing himself against the smooth sides, using his back and legs. He was acutely aware of the satchel strapped to his chest, containing the packets of explosive sticks with their timers ready to be set. Although Sarra had assured him the stuff was inert until the fuse set it off, the sooner he got rid of it, the happier he'd be.

There was a hum of machinery echoing up the shaft, and the sides vibrated slightly. He knew he had to go down two levels to reach the transverse ducts that Sarra said had to run through the ceiling above the court level. They had no way of knowing how far he could get along those, or if he could do so at all. She had speculated that they might be wide enough to crawl through, as a means of maintenance. If not, he had problems.

He reached some kind of lateral junction at the ceiling of the second level, and wedged himself to take a look with his torch. He smiled in satisfaction. Though not as wide as the main shaft, he could indeed crawl down it. He continued to chimney down the shaft to the target level.

Darric's apartments were to the right. Braid checked his pocket watch, removed the first bundle of explosives, detached his rope from his harness, and tied the satchel to it. Then he crawled on his stomach down the tight, dark duct, pushing the explosive bundle ahead of him, and moving as fast as he could. There were noises filtering in from the floor beneath, movements, people talking. After two minutes, he stopped where a grille opened onto the well-lit passage below, set the fuse and wriggled backwards. At the junction, he checked his watch and repeated the exercise down the left-hand duct.

He returned to the shaft and checked his watch again. Ten minutes gone; twenty to get out and clear. It sounded long enough, but he knew it was going to be close. He set the final fuse, dropped his last lethal bundle down the main shaft on a long, thin line, and swiftly tied if off. He got his rope fixed to his climbing harness and gave a signal tug. He felt the line go taut. He began to thrust upwards, Jan's steady strength assisting the lift and taking the strain. The smooth surface gave little purchase. He tugged the rope twice, signalling his need to rest a moment.

He checked his watch again, doing rapid mental arithmetic. Six to the surface. Four to slide down the mound and get back to Kayman; that took it to around twenty minutes since the first fuse was set. Four more minutes to weave the portal. Maybe five in hand. Any minute now, Jorn would launch his war-hammer. He licked his drying lips, tugged the rope, and pushed upwards as fast as he could, his muscles aching with fatigue.

Outside, by the vent, Sarra was monitoring the guards and maintaining the pass-me-by and wards. Jan stood with the rope wrapped round his waist, taking the strain on a ring slide and heaving steadily.

'I'm in place, prepare for the blast.' Jorn's sending was faint, nearing the limit of telepathic range, but clear enough.

Jan nodded at Sarra. *'Get ready.'*

Even though they were waiting for it, the force of the explosion caused by Jorn's war-hammer, and the massive fireball that followed, took them by surprise. All at once, Jan looked up in acute alarm. *'Jorn's in danger!'* He gave the stop signal to Braid, detached the rope from the clips at his belt and hastily tied it off round the base of the chimney with a binding of Conjunct to seal it.

'What the hell are you doing?' demanded Sarra in alarm. *'Braid is still down there.'*

'I know. I have to go. Jorn's hurt.' The shian shed form and vanished.

Stuck some four ems from the top of the shaft, Braid had felt the distant thud and tremor of the explosion, and realised that the rope had suddenly ceased to move. He gave a tug but there was no response. He braced himself against the slippery metal and swore. Something had gone wrong. He reached out a hand and tested the rope, it held. His imagination counted the ticks from the timers below and created dangers above.

Braid swore again, detached the rope from his harness, gripped it and began to swarm up it, using hands and legs, sailor fashion. Two minutes later, he was out. Sarra heaved a huge sigh of relief. There was no sign of Jan and absolutely no time to hang around waiting for an explanation. The pair got back down the mound as fast as they could, raced over to Kayman, and portalled out.

*

Team Wallop had made a good start. They translocated into the rear of the cookhouse without trouble. Mordant set their wards and concealing glamours. Brett recovered quickly and then both drew their swords. Jorn hung his own body-shield and checked his armoury; all was in place. The three tightly-braided war-hammers quivered with pent Power.

'Good to go? Braid should be nearly done by now.'

Jorn nodded at Mordant. *'All set. Keep out of the way. The first one will be big.'* He moved off, following their cautious progress round the side of the building, acutely conscious of the aching void where his twin ought to be. It was the first time he had gone into action without Jan indwelling, and he did not like the feeling one bit.

They eased round the side of the building. Kayman remained by the pump, ready to work the return portal. The big parade ground stretched ahead; everything was just they expected. Mordant and Brett took cover behind the corner of a building and lay flat under a spell-shield.

Jorn sent Jan a quick warning. He reached for his first construct, grasped the war-hammer and engaged his Power. Mordant had told him that the arsenal was filled with armaments, including explosives, grenades and the fuel used in the flame-throwers. He knew exactly what he wanted to do to that. He let his anger build, imagining the destruction, his will tightly focussed. But he found it harder than usual to engage with the construct. The Power build-up was nothing like as strong as it should have been. He paused, feeding more energy, forcing himself through the barrier. Dark threads seemed to weave between the bright ones, out on the edge of his mage-sense, sapping his strength and blocking the flow of energy. He battled past them. Finally, he was ready. He pointed at the arsenal and let fly.

With a thunderclap of Power, the war-hammer punched a gigantic hole into the building. The arsenal erupted in a massive, ear-numbing explosion that shot a huge fire-ball into the air and scattered debris into the night sky. The shockwave powered back across the square and the glass in every window shattered. A lethal blast of glass shards, metal, and flying bricks scythed outward.

The shock of the explosion was far greater than Jorn had anticipated. It knocked him off his feet. A surge of dazed panic sent his colours into turmoil and, for a fatal second, he lost concentration. His shield-ward snapped. Daggers of flying glass quilled his right arm and shoulder, his senses swam, and he passed out.

Brett saw him fall, and not rise. He raced across the square, vaulting debris, hoisted the injured mage across his shoulders and moved back towards safety as fast as he could. Raash troops erupted from the barracks in all directions, in various stages of undress, but all armed and professional enough to ignore the chaos and look for the cause of it.

Mordant sent an urgent mind call to Kayman. '*Portal NOW!*' She and Braid belted back towards the pump-yard, dragging Jorn with them.

As they reached the pump, Mordant saw that Kayman was constructing the portal with intense concentration, ignoring the shouts and the thump of running feet. Suddenly, she was aware of Jan's *shi* sliding back into Jorn. The young mage stirred and began to rouse.

Raash sprinted round the cookhouse building into the yard, searching for enemies. They could not see them, but they could see the forming portal. They made a bee-line towards it. Brett and Mordant leapt to the attack and fought a fierce rear-guard action as Kayman pushed Jorn through the portal.

In the distance, there was a huge, concussive thud, and the ground shook under their feet.

'Come on, quick now!' shouted Kayman. The Sword-Masters made a final killing apiece and dashed through the misty opening with the High Master close behind. The nearest raash pulled up short as the gateway snapped shut almost in his face.

In the cold dawn light, Jorn sat on a bench, supported by Mordant, while Brett removed the shards of glass and Jan dealt with his healing. He was trembling with reaction. Kayman watched anxiously, still breathing hard with a mixture of relief and exhaustion, and then went to check on Team R.

Finally, Jorn straightened up and gave his helpers a rueful smile. 'Thanks. The blast was so huge, it broke my concentration and snapped my shield. But even without that, I doubt if I could have launched another warhammer. I was having difficulty raising Power. We hadn't realised how dependent I am on Jan's strength to support that working. I won't go into action of that kind again without him indwelling, that's for certain. I can't say I'm sorry; I really wasn't looking forward to attacking the barracks.'

Mordant nodded her understanding. 'But you are all right now?'

'Yes, Jan's healed the wounds. But we're both tired and shaken. We'll need a tree, but not before we know the others are safe and we've heard what happened with Team Ram.'

They all went into the house to get breakfast and swap stories. Team R were already there. It was soon clear that the mission had been a great success, even if Jorn hadn't managed to destroy the barracks.

Braidart had called for wine, despite the early hour, and lifted his glass in an ironic toast. 'To Darric, up yours! And if you are still alive, I hope you're as gutted as all hell!'

Mordant lifted her glass to chink with his. 'Oh, he will be.'

When the impromptu party finally broke up, Brett made a point of waiting for her. 'Thanks for sending for me. Having a mission made me feel young again!'

'You're far from old yet.'

'I miss you, Funny Face.'

'And I miss you too, Beaky Boy, more than I can say.'

'So my kid brother doesn't quite measure up?'

'No. He really doesn't.'

Brett took her in his arms for a long cuddle and she pressed against him, feeling her desire rise in a flood of longing. He bent to caress his lips against her neck in the place that he knew she liked, and felt her stiffen and pull away. 'We can't,' she whispered. 'By the Nine, I want to, but we can't, we daren't. We'd both regret it.' He drew back and looked at her, his blue eyes full of need. 'Is it because of Braid?'

'No, because of us; because I've spent the last few years trying not to remember how good we were together. I don't think I could bear to be reminded.'

Brett sighed and gave a wry smile, and let her go. 'You're right, Funny Face. I'm married, and you have Braid. And once would not be enough for either of us. So how long has this thing with Braid been going on?"

'Since Longest Night. I was bored and lonely, and he was very persistent. To be honest, he reminded me so much of you when we first met that I had a job to keep my hands off him. And I was trying to make someone else jealous, only that didn't work. It was good, for a while. As far as I'm concerned, it's over, it's just that Braid doesn't realise it, and now isn't the time to tell him. I'm trying to think of a way to let him down gently, once this quest is all done and dusted.'

'Who's "someone"?'

'Idris.' Mordant looked so sad that Brett had to hold her again. 'What went wrong?' he asked gently. 'Doesn't he care for you?'

Her response was half-muffled against his shoulder. 'Oh, he cares. You have no idea how much he cares. And so do I. But he's shian and I'm raash. It's simply impossible.'

Brett did not understand what she meant, but he held her as she sobbed out her misery against his warm strength.

*

Darric was alive. He and Ajina had been in the Earth Base when the raid happened. Boarrian, the messenger who had drawn the short straw for the horrible task, was a high-ranking Mage-Adept who was so terrified of delivering his tidings that he could hardly speak.

Eventually, he blurted out the news in halting but graphic terms. 'My Lord, there has been an attack on Main Base. They targeted the court level. The explosions ripped sideways with maximum force in the confined space. The damage was appalling. There was a fire. Many mages and at least half of the government ministers are either dead or badly injured. Scores more are receiving treatment. Our engineers say that the saboteurs must have used a ventilation shaft. They dropped another bomb down it, and that exploded at the bottom, taking out the machinery in that sector. The blasts went back up the shaft and split the mound wide open. The ventilation and lighting systems have been disabled. We've had to abandon most of the Base.' He faltered to a halt.

Darric said nothing. The Lord of All Vard was in a place so far beyond anger that he had no words to describe the feeling. He saw that Boarrian's body language still radiated fear, and finally managed to say, 'There is more?'

Boarrian swallowed, ran his tongue over his dry lips and nodded. 'They sabotaged the arsenal too. It's a total loss.'

'Who did this?' asked Ajina with icy control.

'We don't know. It could be the rebels. But the damage to the arsenal looks and feels more like mage-craft than explosives. And if that is so, he or she is appallingly strong. I've only ever seen Power like it when you have used your Tools.'

Darric's anger deprived him of speech. He waved a dismissive hand, and Boarrian bowed and left the room, glad to be still alive after delivering such devastating news.

The rulers of Vard looked at each other in frank dismay. How was such a thing possible? Ajina reached for her brother's hand and took it in hers, and stroked the back of it gently. After several minutes, Darric said tightly, 'This is Kayman's doing, him and that traitor halfer. It has their stink all over it. Darrison's suspicions were correct as usual; only a Nine could produce a war-hammer of such massive Power and it has to be Jorn. I want them all dead, preferably in slow agony. I'll have to return to Vard at once to review the damage, and re-organise the government. No doubt the fools are running round in circles like headless fowls.'

Jorn

Ajina nodded. 'I'll deal with Jorn and the team. I've doubled the round-the-clock watch on the Sharfane and I've posted four of our best adepts. The moment they arrive, we'll have them, Nine or no Nine, they'll pay for this in blood. But we must not let it delay us or distract us. We have to strike soon and strike hard, before there are any more attacks of this kind. I wish I could get a message to Darrison to tell him of this outrage, but he's in deep cover in Errington at present and out of contact. He plans to strike next at Kayman and the Darnells.'

Chapter 26

Around noon on the day after the attack, Mordant made a quick visit to Vard, covered by her strongest glamour, and stayed in the Main Base just long enough to find out whether or not they had eliminated the raash rulers. She returned to the expectant team and gave them the bad news. 'We missed the pig-shitting bastards!'

Braid swore roundly and the others looked disappointed, though not surprised.

'Darric and Ajina weren't at home,' she continued, 'but in every other respect, we did the job. The Base is seething like a disturbed anthill, and we wiped out a good part of the government. I think we won ourselves some time.'

Jorn shrugged. 'It's as much as we could hope for, and time is not quite such an issue now that we know where to find the fifth part. We'll deal with Darric once we've got the Juncture completed, and we can get on with that right now. Jan's just had a look at the Sharfane. He says the sun is shining and we can see the site clearly, even though it's still under the snow. The weather should hold for a few hours. If we all go through as soon as we can after lunch, Jan will soon pinpoint the spot. We'll be in and out again in 15 minutes. But it's bitterly cold, so wrap up well.'

Within the hour, the warmly-clad team were assembled in the garden. 'You've got the horn,' observed Rolf. 'You haven't used that for a while.'

'We need it as a dowsing focus,' Jorn told him. 'And the ground is frozen solid, so we'll have to use Disjunct to thaw it and cut a hole down to wherever the Juncture is buried, and it's easier to do that with a tool to point with.' He patted the bulging bag at his belt. 'And I've got the other three parts of the Juncture here, so that we can fit the fourth part to them, and then portal straight off to the Pattern to find the fifth. We're determined to get the Juncture completed as fast as we can. Right, off we go. Jan is indwelling, he can help to keep me warm that way, and we can work together to find the thing.'

Jan produced the portal and Rolf, Mordant, Braidart and Idris went through, with Jorn bringing up the rear. The sun was low in the pale sky. The immense, glaring whiteness hurt their eyes, and it was way below freezing, but crisp and dry. The Sharfane was set in a wide, rocky crater, which hid the surrounding country from view. The snow-caked pillar stood to their left, and, on the right, almost invisible under the drifts, they could just make out two humped mounds. A thin trail of steam came from between them.

'It's near,' Jan told him. *'I want you to walk in a straight line, holding the horn like a dowsing rod, with the pillar behind you and that wisp of steam ahead. Go slowly.'*

Jorn crunched across the crisply frozen snow towards the mounds, following Jan's instructions, while the rest of the team watched in tense silence. Halfway across, Jan said *'Stop. It's somewhere below you.'*

Jorn turned back to the others. 'Jan's found it, but I'm going to have to dig. And first, I have to melt the snow. Stay back. It may take a few minutes.'

Idris could see he wasn't needed right now. The lines from the Rhyme echoed in his mind; *"Where freezing fire and burning ice collide."* Drawn irresistibly by his curiosity and the pull of the nearby ocean, he walked quickly to the top of the encircling ridge, and then took a few strides down the other side. He was met by an amazing panorama. He could see a wide crescent of coastline, and distant, snow-shrouded peaks. Plumes of steam and smoke rose into the air from various points in the interior. Nearby, the air above the beach was filled with wheeling, screeching seabirds, already bickering over nesting sites. The distant sea ice gleamed, still hard in the grip of winter. At the end of the long bay, a massive glacier met the ocean, and under its towering leading edge, there was the roiling glint of red and a slow river of fire oozed out, just visible under the ice-dotted water. He watched entranced, trying to comprehend why the sea failed to boil when molten rock was discharging into it.

Meanwhile, Jorn was fully focussed on finding the Juncture. He went into his mental workroom, engaged with the Quincunx, and summoned a powerful construct of pure Disjunct. He grasped it firmly and returned to awareness. The young mage aimed the working down the horn and swept it back and forth over the target area, causing the snow to melt and finally steam. He had soon exposed bare, stony ground. He refocussed his construct and now drove down into the frozen earth, cutting a rough square. He intensified the heating effect in the centre of this until he had produced a pool of hotly bubbling mud.

'Now what?' he asked Jan *'How do we get it out?'*

'You take a rest and I'll try using that spiral apport to suck out the gloop.'

'You'd better move back up the slope,' Jorn told his friends. 'This may get messy!'

It did. Before long, the pristine whiteness was spattered with brown gunk as the hole was emptied. At the bottom, a small metal box came into view. Jorn gave a whoop of satisfaction, and leant down awkwardly, head in the deep excavation, to grab the find. He hauled out the box, opened it and saw the fourth piece of Juncture. 'Got you!' he told it triumphantly.

As he reached to remove it, Jan sent *'DAN...!'* but the word was cut short. Before Jorn had time to react, four powerful, attacking constructs hit his mind from different senders. His head exploded with agonising pain. A second attack brought him to his knees. A moment later, he blacked out.

Captivated by the unusual sight of fire meeting ice, Idris totally missed the moment when the raash soldiers and mages stormed out of three portals and knocked his friends senseless with powerful stunners. His mage-sense felt it, however, and signalled urgent warning. He at once lost form. He surged up to the crest and found, to his horror, that portals had opened not far below him. He watched helplessly as his unconscious friends were bundled through them. With frantic haste, the shian dropped his mist-form to hug the ground, flowed downwards, and slid like an eel through the nearest portal, a second before it snapped shut.

Idris emerged from the portal and rapidly moved to the side. He pressed his nebulous *shi* against the earth, straining all his senses. He was at once aware that the ground was moist. Not Vard then, surely? He scented pine woods nearby. If they were still on Earth, where were they? The soldiers were dragging their captives towards the entrance to what appeared to be a huge, grassy mound. Idris followed until he was certain they had gone inside, and then slipped silently away. He needed water, and a plan.

*

About an hour later, Mordant was roused by a gentle mind-touch. The first thing she saw was Idris bending over her. *'Can you hear me?'* She found herself unable to bespeak or move, but she signalled assent by blinking her eyes, feeling confused and slightly ill, and troubled by his unexpected closeness. Seeing that she could hear his mind-voice, he explained rapidly. *'The raash have captured you and the others. We are in* their Earth Base. They have you in an eight-fold mind-fetter and pain-bond and a body-binding. I cannot break them and neither can you. The only good news I can give you is that I am free. Our friends are in cells nearby, mind-fettered and bound as you are.'

At the word 'cell', she flicked her eyes round the dim room, taking in the bare walls and the thick door with its barred window. Her heart began to thump with panic. Idris lifted her until she was resting more comfortably against him, her head on his shoulder. A huge surge of loving strength, courage as deep as a still lake, flooded into her. His body was cool and yet comforting, and in intimate contact with her own. She realised that she was naked. She relaxed and let herself be supported in his arms, wanting the precious contact to continue.

After a moment, he sent, *'Mordant, I came here to carry out a rescue, but I have spent an hour looking round and trying to see how to do it, and I still have no idea what to do next. I cannot break your bonds and there are far too many raash for any hope of escape, even if I could find a way to get you all out of your cells.'*

Her eyes expressed frustration, and then concern. With a huge effort of will, she mouthed 'water', and winced as the mind-fetter punished her for it.

'I have none to give you,' he said sadly.

'No, you,' she mouthed, suffering another severe stab of pain.

'I have taken the life-water of three raash since I came down to this level, and I have no lack of such "containers" at the moment, distasteful as they are, though it is not easy to kill silently and hide the remains. But they will take you up to the court level, and there it will become much harder to find water.' He tightened his arms around her protectively and continued with fierce intensity. *'But I will try my utmost to get you all out of this alive, and if I can find a way to kill Darric and Ajina, be sure that I will do so. I must leave you now, but I will not be far away, even if you cannot see me. If it comes to the worst, I will do all that I can to see that they do not hurt you, or the others. I have not told our friends that I am here; the hope may be too easily reflected in their faces, and betray my presence.'*

He settled her gently against the wall, making her as comfortable as possible, and lost form. His misty *shi* slipped up to the barred window in the cell door, paused, and then vanished through it.

Mordant tried to come to terms with what he had told her. Their predicament was grim, and the fate that awaited them, unspeakable. She knew full well what the raash did to traitors. *'But Idris held me. And he's there for me. Whatever happens, I know he'll take care of me if he can, I can't ask more than that.'* She hugged the memory of his gentle, cool strength, and tried to rest and regain her wits.

*

An hour later, the guards came to fetch their immobile, naked prisoners. When he was roughly dragged from his cell, Jorn was hugely relieved to see that the others were unhurt. As they were dumped in the bleak and dimly-lit corridor, they looked at each other with grim encouragement. At least they were all still alive, and together, for now.

'No sign of Idris. Let's hope he escaped.'

'It's really hard to capture a shian if he is in his shi,' responded Jan. *'They only got me because I was indwelling, and like you, I was concentrating so hard on finding the Juncture that I sensed the warning too late, and I had no time to leave you before they hit you with the bindings. If Idris had even a split-second more warning, he would have shed form immediately.'*

They shared a small surge of hope. The twins could bespeak to each other, though not send any outgoing messages to others. The bindings on Jorn somehow prevented Jan from leaving him. Unlike Jorn, he could work with his Quincunx, but although he could hang constructs, he could not apply them. Jorn had tried in vain to break his bonds and mind-fetter, but excruciating pain snapped his concentration every time. Not even a Nine could work through a blinding, stabbing headache. They knew that the raash must have taken the Juncture, and Jorn blamed himself bitterly for it. His impatience to get the thing completed had placed it straight into Darric's hands. They were in no doubt of the appalling fate that undoubtedly awaited them, or the apparent impossibility of escape, but neither were prepared to give up trying until the last moment.

'At least they don't seem to know about me. I'll keep quiet here inside my workroom. I'm hanging as many attacking constructs as I can in case I get a chance to use them.'

'Right.'

As the guards grabbed him again, Jorn summoned all his stubborn will and tried not to let his imagination play on what was going to happen next.

Jorn

The thought of facing Darric and Ajina, both pumped with fury over their recent losses and out for vengeance, was terrifying.

The four captives were dragged along the dimly-lit passage and up a flight of stairs, their shins and toes bumping agonisingly on every step. They were thrown in a heap in another corridor. Confident footsteps approached. A tall raash surveyed them dispassionately. He was robed in a richly-embroidered blue tunic, belted with an intricate mesh of silver and white gems, and round his neck, he wore a heavy gold chain.

The Chain of Earth, thought Jorn, with a jolt of recognition. The mage's alien, cat's eyes regarded them intently.

'An interesting group. One human male, one male dwarran halfer, a female raash halfer, and a lad who looks to have some shian in him. And you have brought us interesting gifts. A strange horn. And parts of an artefact of unknown power. We are most grateful.'

Jorn felt sick to the roots of his being. The raash regarded them expressionlessly.

'So now you must have a reward. I trust you will find your last few hours entertaining. I can assure you that we will. As you see, I carry the Chain. I have a binding upon you and you will do exactly as I say. Remain silent, get up and follow me.' Jorn felt the fetter on his will and tried again to challenge it, but once more, extreme pain flared through his head, and he could not stifle a cry. The Chain was too strong. 'There is, as you see, no point in fighting me.'

They stood up and walked stiffly, following the mage. Idris slid after them, his *shi* thinned to no more than a long ribbon of barely visible moistness, creeping along the edge of the floor next to the wall. The air was stuffy, heavy with the fumes from candles and oil-lamps. All the surfaces were dry, and contact steadily robbed him of water. He had not been able to satisfy his thirst for over an hour, and thinning out his *shi* expanded his surface area and meant that he was rapidly dehydrating, but there was nothing he could do about that right now, he had to keep track of where his friends were being taken. He had told Mordant that he would save her, one way or another, and he had meant it, but this was so much harder than he had expected, and it was taking him far too long to move unseen in his mist-form. He was getting steadily weaker. He cursed both his need for water and his inability to form a never-mind to hide himself more effectively and kept moving.

They were now in a wider passage, hung with tapestries and gilded mirrors. Ornaments were displayed on slender columns or in niches. The raash mage halted at a pair of double doors, supported by elaborate hinges, shaped like leaping flames. 'Welcome to the Hall of Light,' he said with an ironic bow.

When the doors were flung open, a long chamber lay before them, bright with golden light from many hanging lamps and immense glass chandeliers. Two rows of tall pillars arranged in delicate clusters ran down each side of the central aisle, supporting a coffered ceiling. At the further end, a row of back-lit, stained-glass windows gave the illusion of daylight, although Jorn realised that the great chamber was probably underground. The air smelled of some kind of spicy fragrance, which failed to mask the underlying reek of burning lamp oil.

Still unseen, Idris slipped in behind them. The Hall was vast and there were many raash. It was going to take him far too long to get to the far end where he needed to be, but the faster he moved, the drier he would get. With urgent haste, he slithered along the side wall, shedding precious moisture as he went. He had few options left now, and all of them were desperate.

'Walk.' The four prisoners had no option. Their spelled feet marched them inexorably towards the raised thrones at the end of the chamber, passing an assembly of raash, dressed in rich colours, plainly members of the court or council. Jorn was acutely conscious of being naked and totally vulnerable in front of the many staring eyes, but he saw how Braidart drew himself up and strode down the Hall as if wearing his finest clothes, and he tried to do the same. It was a tiny victory and it helped to make him feel a little less afraid. Rolf and Mordant followed, both equally determined to show no sign of fear or humiliation.

The raash who sat on the gilded throne had the same gaunt, bone-crested face and sweeping bare skull as the mage who had led them in, but her gorgeously-embroidered gown in shades of gold and amber proclaimed her to be female. Her long tail of pale hair fell over her left shoulder, draped in a net of red jewels. The Knife of Fire hung at her belt, and the Wand was in a loop beside it. Her right hand gripped the unicorn horn. Jorn saw, with a final lurch of sick despair, that the Juncture lay on a cushioned stool at her side. The square was now complete and joined.

'Guests, be welcome. I am Ajina, Sister-Consort of Darric, Lord of All Vard. I give you leave to speak. I have your names, I think, but you will confirm them.' She pointed at Braid. 'Your face speaks for you; you are a Darnell.'

The young nobleman drew himself up and said with formal grace, 'My lady is correct. I am Sar Braidart Darnell.'

Ajina acknowledged that with a nod. 'And you, the halfer female. You are called Mordant.'

'I am, Aunt,' she responded in raash, with deliberate emphasis. Ajina stiffened. She gestured to the nearest guard and said curtly, in the same language, 'She bears a slave mark. Show it to me.'

The soldier grabbed her arm and read out '457HL/27 and three stars, Madam.'

Ajina hissed in her breath. 'Darrison bears those numbers. You had the same mother. The Lord Darric is your father.'

Mordant saw Ajina's knuckles pale as she gripped the arms of her throne. With icy self-control, she resumed her identity parade and spoke again in Basic. 'Master Rolf, greetings. And finally, we have Jorn. Master of Nine, I believe?' he nodded. 'Tell me, Master, what is the nature of this thing that you have taken so much trouble to find?' She pointed at the Juncture.

Jorn had no option but to reply. 'It's called the Juncture. It masters the four High Tools of Power. How it does this, I do not know. We have yet to find the central piece.'

She nodded in satisfaction. 'Then it is just as well that you will not have the opportunity to do so.' She held up the horn. 'And this thing?'

'A unicorn horn. It is a Mage-Focus.'

Her eyes registered interest, and then narrowed, her nostrils pinched with anger. 'So, Master, was it you who destroyed our home?'

'No, hell-bitch, I did that.' Braid told her with considerable satisfaction. 'Jorn destroyed your arsenal.'

Her whole body gave a surge of fury, quickly suppressed. Her voice maintained a tone of icy control. 'Well, no doubt you intended to kill us, but as you see, you failed, though I confess, you have caused us inconvenience. We have been obliged to move the court to our Earth Base rather sooner than we intended. Even now, my brother is on Vard, dealing with the aftermath. He regrets he cannot be here. He would have enjoyed watching your ending. As you see, the Tools are also safe. We thought you would like to see them for one last time before we use them to destroy and dominate your world.' She waved her arm like an actor revealing some stage wonder. 'Let us show our guests what we have prepared for them. Each death is appropriate I think.'

The raash on her left drew back to reveal three peculiar and incongruous items that were placed in the side aisle. Jorn heard Rolf hiss in his breath. Braidart swore. Mordant said nothing, and fought against her terror. There was a tall, door-shaped framework of poles that she recognised as an impaling frame, a kind of bed-shaped implement with ropes and winding wheels at each end, and an iron grid, already glowing red-hot from braziers placed beneath it.

Jorn stared at the instruments of slow death and sought to master his horror. He did not fully understand the uses to which they would be put, but he could tell that his friends knew all too well. Braidart looked proudly straight ahead. Rolf and Mordant also stood steadfast, staring up at Ajina with contempt. She studied their reactions with malicious interest.

'I see you understand the purpose of these toys. You will all die.'

'Stale news. I have known of my coming death since I was some five summers old,' said Braidart coldly.

'But not the manner of it. It will be a long agony. For you, impaling. For the dwarran halfer, the rack, to stretch his height a little.' There was a murmur of amusement. 'For my renegade niece,' she loaded the word with venom, 'a slow roasting.'

She turned towards Jorn. 'Bring him to me,' she ordered sharply. The guards dragged him up the four steps of the dais to stand before her. 'As for you, halfer boy...' Ajina moved closer, still holding the horn, her nostrils now wide with the pleasure of her triumph. 'Darrison told us all about you. I can sense your latent Power, but you lack the skill to use it. And you can be assured we do not intend to give you more time to attain Mastery.'

'Jorn, do you trust me?' Jan's mind-voice was urgent.

'You know I do.'

'I have an idea, but it involves a terrible risk, and it will hurt you dreadfully. She means to use the horn to kill you. You must make her do it now, before she starts on the others. At the exact point of your death, the bindings on us will break. I will kill her and heal you. Then we can fight.'

Jorn felt sick with fear, but if there was the smallest chance that Jan could pull it off, he had to do it. He could only die once. He stared at Ajina, his face a mask of abject terror. 'No, no, please, have pity, please,

please don't hurt me. I don't want to die!' he whimpered. Ajina's eyes gleamed as she saw his total fear.

Braidart winced and looked away as if he could not bear to see his young friend so unmanned.

Rolf spat, 'Take me first, hell-bitch.' She regarded the mage and the big human with interest.

'The young mage is dear to you? You would prefer not to watch as he dies a coward's death? Then he shall be first.'

Both Braidart and Mordant made convulsive efforts to break free but they had no power to move, and the vicious pain punished them again. The mage with the Chain said curtly, 'Stand still. Watch and be silent.'

Ajina gave a nod of her head and two guards hauled Jorn upright and held him fast. He was unable to resist but he made small moaning sounds, continuing his act. Now that it was about to happen, he did not have to fake his fear, his bowels churned, his mouth was dry, and his heart was racing, but he clung desperately to his faint hope.

'Trust me,' Jan told him steadily. *'I'm sorry that I can't stop it from hurting, but it won't be for long, I promise. I must work at speed. Ajina is going to die before she knows what's hit her.'*

Jorn screwed his eyes tight shut and turned his head to one side, as if trying to deny the sight of his approaching death, but in fact, was trying to mask any sign of his deeper intentions. He felt the wickedly sharp tip of the horn locate with careful precision between his ribs, just above his pounding heart. Ajina thrust it a tiny way into him, puncturing his skin and muscle, deliberately pausing, savouring the moment, and letting him feel the small, intense, white-hot hurt. He stiffened and gasped.

'I win!' she said, and laughed, and then screwed the horn viciously and with horrible, deliberate slowness into his chest, twisting it savagely to drive it home. Jorn had prepared for pain, but this was worse than he could possibly have imagined. He gave a shuddering cry, and then the deepening wound took his breath away. He felt his legs buckle but the guards held him straight, bracing him to receive the killing stroke.

He could feel the agony of the horn actually piercing his heart, the damaged organ desperately trying to pump, blood in his mouth, fighting for one last breath. He wanted to tell Jan that he loved him, that it had been worth the try, but words were a long way away now. Everything was spinning, falling into darkness. Ajina gave the horn a final twist and wrenched it out.

There was a distant sense of release as the bindings on his body broke, the mage-power finding nothing left alive to master. The pain was gone. His essence floated free, leaving his ruined body for its final journey. And then Jan's boundless strength reached out and pulled him from the brink of death, tethering his spirit by a bond of Conjunct. His awareness hovered, uncertain, somehow near the ceiling, observing the Hall below him. Jan's *shi* shot out of his sagging twin, and for the first time, Jorn could see him clearly, a shimmering, rainbow-tinted entity who sent a shaft of wild-red-killing rage to strike in swift and fatal revenge, and then whirled to strike again, sweeping a swathe of the nearest raash to the floor like a scythe through corn.

There was an appalling scream of agony, a clatter as the horn fell. Ajina staggered a step, clutching at her heart, as an exact replica of the wound she had just inflicted brought blood blossoming from her breast and darkened her golden satin robes. She fell, sprawling headfirst down the steps. The table crashed over and the Juncture rolled down to land, ringing on the floor beside her. The shocked guards dumped the corpse they were holding and ran.

As Ajina fell, Jorn's spirit was abruptly dragged back into his body. There was one moment of intense pain and then it vanished, and a wonderful sense of warm strength and well-being suffused his being as Jan re-entered him. A powerful tide of loving healing poured through him. The dreadful wound was being sealed. Then he was once again totally alert, fully recovered, and in control of his Power. It had all happened in barely two minutes. There was a moment of stunned silence and then pandemonium broke out as raash shouted, drew weapons and ran towards the doors or the dais.

Jorn bent and grabbed the horn, and then turned to survey the Hall. He could sense that Jan was too exhausted to help him further. He only had a few seconds before he was going to be fighting for his life. His three friends were still held rigidly in thrall and had no means of defending themselves. He targeted the adept with the Chain, intending to kill him next before he had time to recover and react, but he was amazed to see the mage writhing in the grip of a thin swirl of mist. Idris' need was great and he quivered with relief as his thirst was quenched, exultant that he was finally able to kill an enemy. The adept was drained so fast that he folded soundlessly like a cast-off cloak. As he died, his constructs snapped, and Mordant, Rolf and Braidart were finally free.

Mordant leapt into action and was soon armed and fighting with her usual lethal skill. Braid disabled the nearest guard, took his sword and launched himself at the next. Several other raash fell as Rolf used a killing shaft.

Jorn jumped down the steps, past Ajina's body, snatched up the Juncture, wrenched the Chain from the drained and shrivelled mage, and wove a binding with Conjunct that froze every raash in the Hall into statues. Everything stopped. Idris materialised, looking gaunt; the life-water of the raash had been barely enough to rehydrate him sufficiently to take form. He pulled the Knife and the Wand from Ajina's belt.

'We must get out of here,' called Braid urgently. The five pelted down the Hall, past raash, transfixed in attitudes of anger or dismay. Braidart grabbed a cloak. 'My thanks!' he told the owner. Rolf and Jorn quickly copied him and Jorn seized a sword. Mordant had a sword in one hand and a dagger in another, and disregarded her nudity. At the door, they were met by three running guards, but Braidart finished two of them and Mordant killed the next.

'This is Earth Base. We are on the second level down,' called Idris, 'we must get to the surface before we can translocate. This way!'

Rolf was gasping as his short legs pumped, trying to keep up. Idris unceremoniously tossed the mage across his shoulder and ran on. He was terribly aware that his thirst was returning and his strength would not last long. Jorn had no time to form complex constructs, but he could master the raw power of Disjunct to send killing shafts. Jan was silent, still recovering his strength. Raash began to converge on them like hornets from a stirred nest. Jorn felled the nearest ones, tripping others as they crashed into the fallen. Mordant and Braidart killed, and killed again.

Idris changed direction at the next intersection and pounded up stairs two at a time, but pursuit was close behind them. The five ran on down yet another dimly-lit passage, disposing of a group of guards who ran to meet them. They were now in a vast, bare hall with many exits. Raash ran in from several directions, armed and angry. Jorn felt killing shafts being aimed at them and blocked them in the nick of time.

He flung heart-stopping bolts of his own and the advancing raash dropped. The friends ran in the only clear direction, flung open a door, dashed through, and slammed it behind them. Rolf and Mordant both erected strong barrier wards. Braid sagged wearily, gasping for breath. It was pitch dark. Shoulders thudded against the door.

After a moment, Jorn produced a thin glimmer from the end of the horn, looked around, and spotted a lantern with a stub of candle. He set it alight. They were in a windowless storeroom; its corners cluttered with empty barrels and discarded objects. The door rattled on its hinges as a couple of raash mages attempted to break the seals, but failed. It went suddenly quiet. The team pulled their stolen cloaks around them and sat wearily on the floor while they recovered.

After a few moments, Braidart got his breath back, looked about him in the dimly flickering light and sighed in frustration. 'I feared it was all going too well! Now we've found ourselves another perfect trap. No windows, only one door, and hordes of angry raash working out how to get in. Pity. For a while out there, I thought we might actually make it. Now we have little choice but to starve or sell our lives as dearly as we may.' He got up, turned to Jorn and gave him a salute with his sword. 'That was the bravest, most amazing thing I've ever seen! Did you know what would happen?'

'I hoped it did. It was Jan's idea. He worked it all. It seemed a risk worth taking.'

Rolf came and gave him a warm hug. 'You were both astonishing! I too have never seen such courage. Whatever happens next, I want you to know how very, very proud of you I am.'

'And so am I,' said Mordant warmly, as she wrapped herself in a tatty bed cover. 'That was a hard thing to watch. But Idris, couldn't you have got to Ajina first?'

His voice was oddly tight and strained. 'I wanted to, but I was weak with thirst. I could not launch my usual flying attack. I could see that you were all going to die in torment. I was getting ready to drain the nearest raash to give me strength. I hoped that I might drain several of them fast enough to cause some chaos and distract Ajina, and maybe that would give me the chance I needed. But then I sensed that Jorn had a plan. His grovelling fear was so out of character, it had to be an act. So I waited and slid towards the adept with the Chain, using my last strength. I knew that if he died, the rest of you would be free. I'm sorry I could not manage to do more.'

Mordant could sense his distress. 'You did enough. You set us free, and that was all we needed.' She went to give him a comforting touch and was startled when he backed away.

'Don't!' he said, with urgent warning. 'Please, you must not touch me Mordant, not you or any of the others. The life-water of that mage was only enough to revive me for a short while and that last run has depleted me again. I have had to hide and I have not drunk properly for more than an hour. I am fast drying out. If I cannot find more water soon, I will be compelled to seek it, and the only source here is inside your bodies. I will fight this with all my strength, for I will die sooner than take the life-water from any of you, but if I touch you, I will not be able to stop myself from draining you. Please, Jorn, just try to get us out of here.' Idris retreated to a corner and sat down, closing his eyes.

Jorn looked round their new prison and anger welled within him, fuelled by a deep and unshakeable resolve. *'I won't be beaten, Jan. Not now, when we are so close to victory. We didn't cheat death to die here like stags at bay, torn down by hounds. There has to be some way of getting out. But how? We are trapped, and you shifting under the door isn't going to help us this time.'*

'I'm thinking.'

Jorn turned to his friends, speaking with far more confidence than he felt. 'We are going to get you out of here. By the Powers, we are both Masters of Nine and we have three out of the four High Tools of Power, not to mention most of the Juncture and the unicorn horn. If we can't work a way out of here with that lot, we don't deserve to be called mages! Just leave us to think quietly for a few moments. Keep up the door weaves, and see if you can find us any more candle stumps.'

'Mordant, how far are we from the surface?' sent Jan.

'Close; I think we should be on the upper level.'

'Well, that's a help, but we must reach the open air.'

Jorn sat quietly, took himself into his mental workshop, and reviewed their situation with intensely focussed concentration. *We cannot translocate through solid walls. But the surface can't be that far away. If I can drive a way through to the outside, I can take us through to it. Of course, the area may be swarming with raash, but we'll tackle that when we get there. Now, how to do this? I wish I was not so tired and hungry.* He began to get the glimmering of an idea. He stood up.

He walked around, surveying the room, engaged in an urgent internal discussion with his twin. The floor was paved with square flagstones. Working with swift precision, he cleared a space in the centre of the room and marked out an area, five slabs by five. A bundle of old broom handles helped to define the edges of the square. He ripped up some fabric into thin strips to make the cross lines.

The others watched his preparations in intense silence. Idris continued his silent battle against his increasingly desperate thirst; his skin was already beginning to dry and shrivel. His whole form throbbed with dull pain, his essence was screaming for relief. Soon, he would lose form and start to die.

Jorn went and poked around in the pile of junk in the corner and fished out a small wooden bowl with a chipped edge. Next, he took the three Tools of Power and laid each on its corner Nexus, and the battered bowl on the fourth.

Jorn looked at his friends and offered them a tense smile. 'Before any of you tell us that what we are trying to do is impossible, that we cannot translocate from an enclosed space, I know that full well. But we are still going to try and work us out of here. If we get it wrong, we'll very probably be dead. But we'll all die anyway if we stay here. Shall we try it?'

Blows began to pound again on the ward-bound door. Mordant spoke with steady determination. 'If anyone can do it, you can. Be quick, Idris won't last much longer.'

Braid's voice was as light as if he was talking about the weather. 'I wasn't too keen on being impaled. Do it.'

Rolf nodded. 'I didn't fancy being racked to death either.'

Jorn took the Juncture and turned it until the jewelled spikes had the correct orientation, and attempted to balance its cold weight on his head. It was far too big. He found some more cloth and rapidly wound it round to pad his head until he could get it to sit comfortably. He took his position in the centre of his improvised Quincunx, the unicorn horn glimmering softly in his hand.

His mind was calm now; he closed his eyes and focussed on his next working with an intensity, which left no more room for doubt, Jan feeding him steady Power. As soon as the construct was ready, he gave his instructions.

'We are going to bore a pathway through the ceiling and upwards to the open air. Once I can see daylight and the shaft is big enough, we can take you all through. We need your help. The Power drain will be huge and you must each use a Tool to focus the working and feed us with your strength. Rolf, put on the Chain and stand there. Mordant, take the Wand. Idris, take the bowl; I know it's not the real Cup, but I want you to use it exactly as if it is. Use your all your will and focus your need, *tantar*; water awaits outside.' The shian rose with a visible effort and nodded grimly, his face wrinkled and cadaverous with dehydration.

Jorn turned to Braid. 'I know you are no mage, but take the Knife and stand here at this corner. When I begin, I want you to fill your mind with red. Just concentrate on that, excluding everything else, point the Knife and imagine that you are pushing your strength into me along it, forming a fixed red line to the centre, aiming for the ruby. The rest of you, use the primary colour of your Tool and do the same, aiming for the corner gem. Do not relax your focus until we are safely above ground.'

He took his place at the centre point, blanked out everything but his implacable intention to pierce through to freedom, focussed his Nine-coloured construct, gripped the horn in his right hand and said quietly, 'Use the Tools.'

A yellow beam shot from Rolf's corner to link with the jewel on the Juncture. A moment later, a blue ray came from the corner with the bowl and a silver one from that of the Wand. Sustaining energy flowed into him from his friends and he held it and drew more. 'Now Braid, I know you can do it. Use your will. Think red.' All at once, a shaft of red light lanced towards the ruby on the crown, and he felt Braid's steady strength pour into him.

Jorn's entire body tingled with pent Power, but his mind was filled with ice-cold determination and control. He let his Nine-coloured braid focus in a tight spiral, immensely strong, and sent it spinning round the horn, holding it in both hands above his head, and aimed it straight at the ceiling.

For a heart-stopping moment, nothing happened. Then the roof began to vaporise and a hole over an em wide started to open above him. He increased his drain on the Power. The Juncture controlled the flow and fed it into him. Jan was working with him. The hole continued to bore upwards, one em, then two, then three. *How much further? We must get through, we must*! He gave a final desperate thrust, ignoring the punishing drain on his strength. *Yes! I sense the way through. Now! NOW*!

Daylight shafted down the round opening. Unable to wait a moment longer, Idris sent, '*Must find water. I'll portal back.*' He shed form and shot upwards. Jorn was dimly aware that the pounding on the door was getting louder.

'Come as close to me as you can. The shaft is narrow. Hold me, keep the Power flowing. One more effort and we'll be free. Jan will work the apport to lift us.' Jorn felt them link arms around him, warm strength flowed into him. Jan summoned the last of his own strength, cast an apport, and lifted them up through the shaft as fast as he dared to go. Behind them, the doors finally burst open as the ward-weaves broke. The room was empty.

Finding firm ground beneath his feet, Jorn steadied himself, and with one final effort, closed off the shaft. He was exhausted beyond the point of feeling anything very much. He looked around and saw that his friends were all safe, and heaved a long, shuddering sigh of relief. He sank to the ground. 'Must rest,' he whispered, and promptly fainted.

Rolf knelt swiftly to examine him. 'He's not ill, simply totally exhausted. They both are. That drilling through solid rock and earth was almost too much for them, even with all our strengths, and the Tools and the Juncture and the horn to help them.'

Mordant said crisply, 'Rolf, you take the Chain, and the Wand, and the horn. Braid, can you hold onto the Knife and carry Jorn through? You'll have to ditch your sword though. I'll take the Juncture.' The big man nodded. She sighed wearily. 'Darnell mansion. I think I just about have the strength left for a portal.'

There was sudden movement and shouts. Four raash guards were heading for them. They fell like stones before they had gone two paces as Rolf aimed killing shafts with deadly accuracy.

'We have to go now,' said Braidart urgently. He looked round tensely at the thick pine forest that surrounded them, expecting more raash to burst out at any moment, knowing that, encumbered as he was with Jorn, he could do nothing to stop them.

The portal had formed and they went through it as fast as they could. They raced through the garden and into the mansion, far too tired to raise a never-mind and careless of the scandalised amazement of the servants at their state of undress.

Kayman rushed to meet them, plainly deeply relieved; he'd been frantic with worry when they had failed to return. Jorn was quickly carried upstairs and put to bed. The rest of the team hastily washed and dressed, and gathered in the small parlour, consuming everything the servants provided with urgent appetite. It was many hours since they had eaten, and the mages were exhausted and famished from their use of Power.

Rolf sighed wearily. 'I have seldom felt so worn out in body and mind. What an astonishing few hours we have lived through. Truly, I expected to die in agony.'

'And so did I,' said Braid. 'But not only are we still here, we have the Tools and the Juncture, and that hell-bitch queen is dead. I call that a remarkably good day's work, don't you?' He looked at the Knife that lay on the table with the other Tools. 'I can't believe I made that work as it did! I mean, I'm no mage.'

'Mage-power is mainly a matter of will and belief. You had the will, and Jorn made you believe that it was possible,' Rolf told him. 'But where can we put these precious things? They must be guarded and warded.'

'There's a large safe in the basement. We can lock them in there, and I'll set up a guard rota, four men at a time. I'll leave the wards to you.'

'Good. Let's do that, and then I really must rest. They will be safe enough; the raash cannot yet know where we've gone. The wards will have to wait for a few hours. I can't raise enough Power to light a candle right now. I need my bed.'

'And so do I,' agreed Mordant. 'But first, I must make sure that Idris has recovered. He was perilously close to death.' Tired though she was, she grabbed a cloak and went into the garden. Idris portalled in about 20 minutes later, his body taut and refreshed. He smiled to see her waiting for him.

'You should have gone inside to rest,' he scolded gently, 'but I am glad you waited for me.'

'I was worried about you. And I wanted to thank you. You said you would try to get us out and you did,' she told him warmly, 'and you came to me, and held me, and gave me comfort. That must have been difficult for you. I won't forget that, even if it can never happen again, though I do so wish it could.' She planted a kiss on her fingertips, and very lightly brushed them against his cheek, and left rapidly.

Idris watched her go, fighting his desire to follow her, hold her again, make her one with him forever. Difficult was hardly the word. She had no idea how much their intimate physical contact in the cell had strained his control, or what that brief touch had done to him. Right now, he hardly dared to get within two paces of her, and his whole essence ached with need as if he thirsted again and she was water. It was all so totally impossible. He left to find his favourite fountain in a nearby park, hoping that the cold, lively water might bring him a little ease.

*

Darrison was back in Errington, considering his next moves. He had shaved his beard and used a light glamour to age his face and whiten his hair. The stooped, old man who shuffled back and forth between his modest lodgings and the nearest pie shop twice a day attracted no attention at all.

In deep cover and cut off from contact with Vard, the spy was completely unaware of the tumultuous events of the past few days. His last message from Ajina had confirmed that the trap at the Sharfane was set, and his aunt was confident that the team would be eliminated.

Much as Darrison would have liked to witness the slow torment of their final hours, he had other work to do. His prime target was Kayman, but the elderly mage was far more wary than Turner had been, and it would not be easy to get near him.

But the younger Darnells were still in their mansion, enjoying life to the full. The men might be expert swordsmen but he was sure they had no defence against his skills as an assassin, and Bea was a prattling fool. The Darnell Clan were high priority and low risk. He would continue his strategy of picking off the softer targets before giving Kayman his full attention.

Chapter 27

It took Jorn two days to recover. For the first 24 hours, he slept without even dreaming. Twice, Idris carried him down to the plane tree and watched Jan's essence slide from his twin and enter. The young shian was still too weak to take form. *'Take him into the warm again, quickly, Idris. I'll return to him when I've fed and rested.'*

On the second day, Jorn roused a little, sensing that he was safe and cared for. He knew full well that he had seriously overstretched himself when he worked their escape and must simply rest. Jan was indwelling and almost as weary as his twin. They bespoke little; somehow, there was no need. The intensity of the terrible shared torment of Jorn's moment of death was fresh in both their minds, and their bond was even stronger. Jorn ate a small meal and slept again.

When he awoke in the late evening, he found Corus in a chair at his bedside. The raash mage gave his thin smile. 'I won't stay long. Your auras are stronger now, but you still need rest. I simply wanted to thank you both. I will happily call you Masters, for that is what you are. Great in Power and strong in spirit.'

'Oh, Corus, for heaven's sake, we allowed ourselves to be captured by Ajina, and it was sheer chance that we were able to take back the Juncture and the Tools; and Idris, of course, he was amazing.'

'Did I not tell you that Chance is a strong force? And Choice is another. It could have ended in disaster, but it did not. And that is chiefly due to both of you. Thanks to your extraordinary workings, Ajina is dead. You have weakened Darric immeasurably, prevented the invasion and, what is more, your universe is safe from his misuse of Power! I say again, Masters, I salute you! Now sleep, and recover. You still have work to do.'

On the third morning, Jorn felt a great deal better. He got up, still moving a little slowly. He looked at himself in the mirror. He seemed outwardly much the same, except for a small star-shaped scar above his heart, but he knew that he was changed, and so was Jan. Their Powers were closer now, stronger. He washed and dressed, and went downstairs to find breakfast. Braidart greeted him with a big smile and a back-slapping hug. Rolf was already at the table and he too smiled with relief as the young mage came in.

'I can see you're better. You have that "I've got a lot of questions" expression. But you must be famished; perhaps you should have breakfast first?'

Jorn laughed. 'Yes, I'm starving, and Jan wants to go to the plane tree, but the eggs can wait until we've heard the news. Come on, Rolf, don't keep us in suspense any longer, what's been happening?'

Rolf smiled. 'Well, I hate to disappoint you, but I can't give you any details. Mordant has returned to Free Vard to find out what has happened in the aftermath of Ajina's death, so we'll know a great deal more when she gets back. However, with the loss of the Tools, I think we can safely say that the threat of a major invasion of Earth has been ended, for the foreseeable future. You two have saved the planet!'

'Oh Rolf, don't you start! We didn't do it all by ourselves! But what's happened to Darric?'

'We don't know. Mordant may bring us news.'

Jorn poured juice and buttered hot toast, unable to wait a moment longer, and conducted his conversation between mouthfuls. 'But before we deal with him, we must complete the Juncture. Jan and I will go to our tree, and then we can portal out to the ruins and find part five. We can do that on our own, in the next hour. It will only take us a few minutes. Jan says he has a good Hook on that ancient olive tree. And once that's out of the way, we can really focus on the end game.'

Rolf nodded his agreement. 'Yes, I think you should do that, as long as you feel strong enough. Braidart and I will go down to the safe and fetch the rest of the Juncture for you.'

Thoroughly refreshed by his breakfast, Jan managed the transition without difficulty. The Pattern was exactly as they had left it. Jorn took the completed square and carefully orientated it so that the jewels were in the right places, and then set it down across the exact centre of the Pattern, as Jan had done before, so that the severed crosspieces lined up with the Quincunx and the jewels rested at the intersections between the chaos zones.

Jan smiled. 'It fits perfectly. Whatever else this thing is, it was not made to be worn as a crown.'

Jorn

Jorn gave a snort of amusement. 'It certainly wasn't! I had to wind ems of padding round my head to make it fit!' He considered the problem, extending his sense to try to find the required construct. 'What do you think, Jan? A braid of nine to fire the gems and activate the Quincunx?'

'Yes. I'll do that.'

Jorn watched as his twin produced the rainbow-coloured cord and sent it to wind around the base of the Juncture. For a moment, nothing happened, but then Jan engaged his will. The lines and Nexuses of the inlaid Quincunx glowed, as transforming Power travelled from the centre to the periphery, and lit the outer Nexuses like blazing beacons. The four jewels on the Juncture flamed in answer, and the entire structure pulsed brightly, no longer plain metal, but enamelled in its proper colours. An instant later, it was suddenly, wonderfully, complete. The fifth piece appeared from nowhere, slotting into place with a tangible surge of Power, and the central amethyst shot out a starburst of intense violet rays. Then all the brightness faded and the Juncture stood at the still centre, gleaming with colours, but once more inert.

Jorn let out a huge gust of relief. Jan picked it up. 'Oh my. So there you are. Whole at last. But what happens now?' He turned the thing carefully and then handed it to Jorn, who looked thoughtful.

'I'm still not sure. It doesn't feel any different. No sudden surge of enlightenment, I'm afraid.' Then he grinned and held out his clenched hand for a trader's knuckle touch with his brother. 'But we've done it, Jan! The quest is over!'

Jan grinned too and bumped hands. 'Well, this part is. But we still have the Lord of All Vard to deal with. And the matter of the Tools; we must to talk to Corus about them. And ask Idris to release the Cup. I have a feeling that the Juncture will respond when all four Tools are present.'

Jorn looked round at the area where Myron's school had once stood. 'And there are still mysteries to solve. How did Myron die, and who hid the Juncture, and why? I wonder if we'll ever know?'

Jan stood stock still with a sudden expression of extreme concentration furrowing his forehead. 'Jorn, my sense is tweaking urgently. There is something else here. Something that we have to find. What was that final verse? Can you repeat it for me, slowly? And let me have the Juncture again, please.'

'"Master of Nine, be strong and wise,

Complete the quest and win the prize.
Resolve the verse, perform the task,
Unlock the truth; reveal the mask."'

Jorn was watching his twin tensely. He knew the signs by now. Jan was fully engaged in the hunt; his eyes closed, focussing his finding sense. He opened his eyes and began to pace around the Pattern. He went back to the centre point, knelt down, and once again, set the Juncture in place, but to Jorn's total astonishment, upside-down.

Jorn was expecting Jan to use a working, but instead, he firmly but gently pressed down on the square, his large hands placed so as to keep the pressure even on all sides. There was a soft click. Jan rapidly jumped safely off the Pattern. The Juncture sank slowly downwards, the five gem-crowned points locating in concealed holes. When the diagonal straps prevented it from sinking further, there was another, louder click. In total silence, the entire Pattern slid smoothly and silently sideways for two ems and stopped. A flight of stairs stretched down into darkness.

Jorn resorted to Braidart's favourite oath. 'Blood's death, Jan! How in the name of the Nine did you know how to do that? And what the hell have you found?'

Jan returned a mirror image of his own most infuriating grin. 'The answer to your recent questions, I hope! And don't worry, I'm not going to dash down those steps in a hurry. I do remember what happened last time we went into an underground vault. Even though my danger sense is not tweaking, we'll take this slowly. How did I know? Well, as usual, it's in the Riddle. The "prize" is clearly the completed Juncture. We have a "task". We should "unlock" something to reveal a "truth". The bit about resolving the Rhyme is one of those deceptions. It should be written "*re-solve* the rhyme"; in other words, go back to the last solution, which told us to go to the still centre of the Pattern. The rest was just deduction. The Rhyme is always literal. If something is to be unlocked, there must be a key and a keyhole. Since the Juncture is the prize, it is logical to assume that it is also the key. It won't work with its square base flat on the floor. But keys have pointy bits and so…'

Jorn came over and gave him a firm hug. 'I always knew you are much, much cleverer than I am, and you have just proved it! So don't leave me in suspense. What's down there?'

'The Rhyme tells us; "truth", and a "mask". I think we'll find a message from the person who hid the Juncture. I am also unpleasantly certain that we'll find a "mask"; in other words, a skull-headed alien raash masquerading under the name "Myron", or at least whatever is left of him after a thousand years.'

The tall shian went over to the opening and stared down it. 'It's quite safe, Jorn. I am sure of that. Are you coming?'

'You are certainly not going down there without me.'

The stairs were even, the walls flat, and the sunlight illuminated the stairway. 'This doesn't look like anything that people might have built a thousand years ago.' Jorn moved cautiously down. He could see at once that the stairs led to a short passage that was blocked by a sheet of metal, still shiny, and probably thick, with no obvious sign of any way to open it.

'Jorn, you are right, I think this is the work of the Old Ones!' Jan said, excitedly. 'It must be one of those hidden stores that Mordant told us about. And there is something here on the floor. A metal box. That looks more like something from Myron's time.'

'Well, let's take that and get out. There is no way I'm going to even think about going any further, even if we could. This is a job for Professor Sturminster and her team. They will be thrilled!'

The twins went up the stairs, Jorn carrying the box. It was good to be back in the warm, aromatic, bee-busy sunshine. Jan gently pulled the Juncture and it came loose easily. The Pattern closed again.

'I'll portal us back,' he said. 'I can't wait to show the team the Juncture and this box. They must all be there when we open it for the first time.'

The twins ran into the house, pumped with excitement, belted into the hall, straining the astonishment of the usually imperturbably footmen, and mind-shouted, '*WE ARE BACK!*'

Rolf appeared on the landing and peered down at them. 'My, you are excited! I assume you have completed it?'

'Yes we have. And thanks to Jan, we've found something else. But we want to tell the whole team about it.'

'Well, you're in luck. Everyone is already here. Mordant is back, and Corus has asked Kayman for an urgent meeting. We were just waiting for you two. This is splendid, I can't wait to see the Juncture completed.'

The twins followed Rolf up to their usual meeting room, and burst in, still brimming with excitement.

Jan placed the Juncture on the table with a ceremonial flourish, and Jorn planted the bronze chest beside it with equal drama. There was a babble of excited comment and questions. 'Whoa,' Jorn told them. 'You can see that we have news, but it can wait. Mordant has a report to give, and Rolf says Corus has something urgent to say to us.'

Corus nodded in acknowledgement. 'Yes it is urgent. But I rather think you have to open that box before I begin. I do want everyone's full and undivided attention, and so does Mordant!'

Everyone settled down and Jorn gave them a quick account of how they had completed the Juncture and Jan's discoveries. 'So, we hope that there's a message in this box that will clear up all the mysteries. Jan has checked it and he is sure it is safe to open. It's not even locked or warded.'

Kayman nodded. 'Open it then, Jan, don't keep us in suspense.'

Jan lifted the lid, and carefully removed the contents, a small leather folder. Inside that were several sheets of brittle parchment. He passed them over to Jorn. 'You read them to us.'

'Let's hope they are in a language we can understand. Let me see... Well, yes, it's in Basic, but rather old-fashioned, as I suppose one would expect. Nice, clear writing. Here goes.

"My greetings to the reader. If you have found this, you must also have found the Juncture. Therefore, you must be a Master of Nine. Master, I salute you. I foresaw your coming, but dimly, as it might be in many centuries to come. The full story of our times and the grave dangers that so nearly overwhelmed us are locked behind the steel door. There also lies the body of the arch-deceiver, thief, and traitor to the peoples of two worlds.

The four Tools, and the Juncture used to Master them, have been safely hidden. Our world is not ready for such Power, which we barely understand. Maybe you will by now have gained the wisdom needed to work with them aright, or else the wisdom to understand that they must be left alone. The vault contains many wonders left behind by the Old Ones, and a store of ancient knowledge. We also thought those too dangerous for our times. You will make your own judgement. I am most respectfully, your humble servant."

It's not signed.'

Corus gave a long sigh. 'So, at last, the end is known. A bad one, as one might perhaps expect. What will you do now? Will you open the Vault?'

'Yes, of course it has to be opened, but not by us. We thought that Professor Sturminster would be the right person to do that. Apart from finding the full story of Myron's actions and intentions, there is plainly material of enormous importance from the far distant past.'

Corus nodded. 'And I believe that you have the wisdom to know, as our anonymous writer hoped, whether to use it, or refuse it. Chance and Choice have worked their own strange magic yet again. But now we should hear from Mordant.'

'Well, as you might expect, Vard is in chaos. The death of Ajina and the loss of the Tools hit Darric as nothing has ever done before. For many hours, he was half-mad with grief and anger, and quite unable to take control of the situation. The government was disorganised, still reeling from our attack on the Base. The ministers and generals had no idea what to do next; they feared to act without their Lord's consent. The rebels have been waiting for just such a disruptive event, and their plans were well-prepared. The human slaves in the city have revolted and taken up arms, and many of the field-slaves have joined them. Several regiments of halfer soldiers have rebelled and joined the Free Varders. It's far from clear at this stage whether they can win, but one thing is certain, Vard is again in the grips of a full-scale civil war, and there is no way that the raash can invade Earth.'

There were sighs of relief from all round the table. 'That's the best news I have heard in 20 years,' said Kayman. 'But where is Darric, and what is he going to do about all this?'

'We simply don't know. He's disappeared, and his personal guard have gone with him. But I know one thing. He cannot tolerate such a devastating blow to his honour. He will seek revenge.'

'So what do we do now?' asked Jorn.

'That question brings me to my purpose,' said Corus. The old raash looked at the team. 'It has been my privilege to meet you all. You have treated me with a kind courtesy beyond my expectations. My friends, for I will now call you that, if I may, I have one last favour to ask. You may well guess what it is. As we speak, the Free Varders are engaged in a desperate struggle for survival. They have plainly done well, but even without Darric, the odds are stacked against them. There will be terrible bloodshed and loss of life. Our poor world has already had its fill of that.

You can spare us from more. Let me have the Tools and the Juncture. With them, I can not only hasten the end the war, but begin the restoration of our planet. I ask this in the name of all our peoples, human, raash and halfers. What is your answer? I will await outside if you need time to find it.'

Jorn and Jan exchanged looks. Jorn nodded. Jan said quietly, 'I don't think that will be necessary, Corus. Jorn and I are in full agreement, and we hope and believe that our friends will stand by our decision. The Tools do not belong to Earth; they are yours by right, not ours. You must take them back. And as far as the Juncture is concerned, other than its use in opening the entrance to the sealed chamber, we have no need of it either. If it belongs to anyone, it belongs to you. We don't know how to use it, nor do we wish to do so. We are more than happy to let you take it. Heal your planet, Corus. We have no love of war.' He looked round the table with a degree of challenge, but everyone was giving warm assent.

'Of course we agree,' said Kayman, 'and we understand your urgency. Every moment wasted may be a life lost. I suggest that Jan and Jorn return to the Pattern with Professor Sturminster as soon as possible, unlock the entrance, and then bring the Juncture back to us as fast as they can.'

'And I will go and fetch the Cup,' said Idris, who had been sitting apart by the window with his feet in a bath of water, 'and then Mordant can take you home, Corus.'

Corus bowed his head. When he looked up his violet eyes were bright with tears. 'Thank you, my friends. Please, make haste.'

They did. The twins cross-stepped to the university. Professor Sturminster was urgently summoned from a seminar, rushed into the university precincts, and portalled back to the Pattern before she had time to do much more than make a few breathless protests and enquiries.

'No time,' Jorn told her firmly. 'This is an emergency.'

Jan repeated his unlocking routine, and Angela watched the stairway appear with speechless amazement. Jorn thrust the box into her hands. 'We found this outside the steel door. It explains everything – well, at least enough for you to understand what this is about. We will wedge the sliding hatchway in its open position, and then you'll have to portal your own way home. It's safe to go down the stairs, but I wouldn't try to go further just yet. We'll tell you the rest later.'

Jan and Jorn worked apports that lifted a few chunks of pillar into place to ensure that the entrance stayed wedged open. Then Jan removed the Juncture, Jorn formed a portal, and they were gone, leaving the dumbfounded mage staring at the box in her hands with total confusion. She shrugged, sat down, removed the parchment and began to read.

*

The twins returned to the Darnell mansion to find Mordant, Braidart, Kayman, Rolf and Corus waiting for them.

'We are all coming with you to Vard,' Kayman told them. 'This is a moment of huge, historic significance and none of us want to miss it. We thought you'd like to take a last look at the Tools, before we put them back in their boxes.'

Jorn stood by the table and studied the four objects with intense interest. It was the first time that he had seen all four of them close enough to examine them properly. The long, bronze Knife had a flame-like pattern etched down the blade, and the ruby on the moulded hilt glinted with inner life. The Cup was a simple, large, wooden goblet, made of yew, he judged by the colour and grain. The base and rim had been covered with beaten copper, which had turned green, and was decorated with a pattern of leaping fish and waves.

Jan sent, *'These are so very old.'*

'Yes, and they have great Power. I can sense it strongly.' Jorn moved round to examine the Chain more closely. It was formed of heavy gold links; the sun gleamed off the serpent-headed clasp and caught a flash from its emerald eye. 'This is complex,' he looked at Corus, 'it's far more than a simple focus for Earth workings.'

'Yes, it is a powerful Tool,' Corus told him. 'The serpent swallowing its tail represents infinity; each link is a flat, twisted strip, like a figure of eight; if you run your finger along it, you will find it is single-sided. It governs the bindings that hold time and space in conjunction and permit matter to exist. All the Tools have deep purposes and meanings that we barely understand after such a stretch of time.'

'They have changed since they came together. Now they are ready to work.'

Mordant nodded. 'Yes. We noticed it as soon as we put all four on the table. When I held the Wand before, it felt inert. Now it vibrates. If you hold it, you can hear a faint, musical hum. They all do that, but in different notes.'

Jan slipped out of his twin and took form, his sense exploring. 'There is a latent energy here that I have never sensed before. When we work the colours, it's like using light. The Tools have that feeling too, yet underneath that, I can feel a darkness now, a different kind of energy entirely. Have we time for me to try one more thing?'

Kayman looked at Corus, who nodded. He was impressed by Jan's intuition and wanted to see what he would do.

The young shian very carefully took the Juncture and placed it in the centre of the four Tools, turning the gemmed spikes to their proper orientation. The soft hum became a deep, musical chord, the air in the room vibrated with it. The sense of dark energy increased. He hastily shifted the Juncture out of alignment and removed it. 'As I thought; the Juncture augments the dark Power.'

Kayman gave a sharp snort. 'I wish Turner was here to see that! So much for the Tools being "simple focusses"! I think I will gladly leave their use to others.'

'But what is the darkness I can sense?' pondered Jan, half to himself. He looked at the others. 'It has tremendous Power, the kind of bound energy one feels when making a Nine-colour construct. But I have never seen it when working within the Quincunx. Do you know, Corus?'

'I am not sure. I have not heard of dark energy.'

'Nor have I,' said Kayman. 'But, like you, Jan, I sensed its Power. And if that is what happens when the Tools and Juncture come together, no wonder only a Master of Nine can manage them. If you intend to use them, Corus, you must do so with great caution.'

'Of that I am well aware. Let me put them into their boxes where they are safe.' He packed them carefully.

Kayman said, 'Well, we are ready. You take the Juncture, Jorn. And Braidart, you have the Knife. Idris must take the Cup. Kayman will have the Wand, of course, and I will take the Chain.'

The party went into the garden. It was already late afternoon. Mordant worked the portal to Free Vard with her usual expertise. Jan helped the old mage through, and then the entire team followed. The white coral beach gleamed in the sunshine. Seabirds called. Corus stood quite still, leaning on his stick, breathing a little hard, and obviously making an urgent mind call.

A crowd of people came running through the fringe of nut-palms, setting the fallen red blossoms of the gar-bushes swirling around their bare feet. They crowded in a ring, staring in wonder at the weird strangers. The Free

Varders were mostly women, a mixture of humans, raash and halfers, with children of all ages, the smallest hugging knees and keeping close to their mothers.

Karan came forward and bowed in greeting. 'Welcome back, old friend. As you see, our younger males are away at the war. You return with guests?'

'Not guests, gifts.' Corus looked around. 'Karan, Meliand, Teysa, Thorn, come forward.'

The people he had named did so, and all except Karan did so with shy awkwardness, for they were children around the age of 12.

Corus raised his voice. 'My friends have come to return to us the four High Tools of Power, which were stolen so long ago. Accept them, if you will, on behalf of the people of Free Vard, and of all Vard.'

The four came forward, and each solemnly received a Tool, Karan the Knife, Teysa the Wand, Meliand the Chain, and Thorn the Cup. 'Now hold them safe for me for just a little while.'

Jan and Jorn stepped forward and jointly placed the box containing the Juncture in his hands. 'The Powers be with you, Corus,' said Jorn.

'And may Chance and Choice be kind,' added Jan with a smile. 'There is no need for any long speeches. We have done what we came to do, and we will be gone. We still have Darric to deal with.'

Corus and the Free Varders watched in respectful silence as Mordant formed her portal for the return trip to Errington. The team lined up and together gave formal bows, and then rapidly filed through the shimmering mist.

*

That evening, Braidart insisted on hosting a small party for the twins and the rest of the team to celebrate the completion of the quest. The ending, unexpected though it was, seemed entirely right. What happened next on Vard was not in their control, although much in their minds.

Braid produced a wonderful sparkling wine, which popped loudly when the cork was removed. He looked at Jorn. 'This is something very special. Are you sure you won't try it?'

Jorn was about to tell him that he couldn't when Jan said, 'Taste it if you want. I am not indwelling. I'm the one who can't tolerate alcohol, it's poisonous to shians.'

Jorn laughed. 'Well, that's another mystery solved. I'll risk one sip in a toast to our triumphs!'

Idris raised his tumbler of water, and Jan chinked his glass of apple juice against Jorn's wine-flute. The quest had dominated their lives for so many months, it was hard to believe it was over.

The team did their best to maintain the sense of celebration, but the adventure had involved them all in events they would be very happy to forget, as much as ones that they wanted to remember. It was the arrival of Angela Sturminster, included as 'honorary team member', which lifted the party. She was bubbling with uncharacteristic enthusiasm, totally immersed in her plans to explore and excavate the vault, and delighted at the prospect of a stream of academic publications, which would establish her reputation as the leading expert in her field. They all enjoyed joining her in speculating what the vault might contain. It was certain to be extraordinary.

As soon as she left, the party was over. Jan and Jorn were acutely aware that their job was not yet done. They still had Darric to deal with, and in order to do that, they had to find him. Jorn fetched a bowl from the sideboard, emptied it of fruit and filled it with water. 'I'm going to try a far-seeing,' he explained. Jan took form. Their friends gathered round tensely. Jorn stared into the water and let his mind go blank, awaiting a seeing, focussing his mind on the raash Lord. After a moment, the water began to darken. The image formed, wobbled, and cleared.

On a raised dais, Darric stood, dressed all in white, in front of a table draped in cloth of gold. The scene was dimly lit by four tall candles in golden floor sconces, placed at the corners of the table. Darric smoothed the covering, arranged a pillow, then walked down the steps and disappeared from the image. A moment later, he returned, carrying Ajina's limp, white-clad body. He laid it tenderly on the bier, smoothed her long tail of hair across her shoulder, caressed her face, and arranged her hands over her breast. He fetched another golden sheet and laid it across her, draping the folds with care. The Mage-Lord bent to press his lips against his sister's crested forehead, stepped back, stood for a moment with bowed head, and then went to sit on the carved throne beside the bier. The vision grew faint and faded. Jorn took a long breath and closed his eyes, waiting for the unpleasant physical after-effects of the seeing to subside. Jan placed his hands on his brother's shoulders to bring him support and comfort.

Everyone was silent for a long moment, and then Braid said, 'Where is he?'

'I think that was Earth Base,' replied Mordant.

Jan said, 'Yes, it was.'

Jorn raised his head wearily. 'Pity we don't know where it is.'

'Oh, but we do,' Idris told them. 'I tagged it before I left. I can form the portal.'

Jorn nodded. 'So now all we have to do is kill him.'

*

The team met the following afternoon for a briefing. Braidart had assumed command of the final stage with professional competence, and was plainly enjoying the preparations for action.

'He is a soldier from his toes to his fingertips,' sent Jan

'I know. We all long for peace, but he lives for a good fight.'

The young nobleman gave a concise report. 'The repairs to Darnell Hold are going well, and a few rooms and the outer barracks are habitable, so Borodin has decided to move back and we have set up the garrison again. That means we can use the Hold as our base for the attack, which is convenient, because our assault force will come from the Darnell guard. This morning, Idris translocated myself, Mordant and a small team of scouts to Darric's Earth Base. There was no sign of life. The barracks in the surrounding forest seemed abandoned. The only visible entrance, the main gates, stood open. No one entered or left. I've posted watchers.'

Kayman turned to Jan. 'Is Darric still there?' he asked tensely. 'What does your sense tell you?'

'That he is. And that there is great danger.'

'No surprises then,' said Braid. 'Well, we don't have an army, but even if we had, it could achieve little. We are not planning a siege, but an assault. I intend to use a small elite force of highly experienced soldiers from the Darnell guard. These are tough men who know their business. We'll hit hard and suddenly, under the cover of one of those useful never-minds, aiming to penetrate the Base at high speed in order to locate Darric and take him out. I will divide my men into two teams, each having a mage to provide cover and manage the translocations. We have no option but to make our assault through the main gate. There may be other entrances but they are well-hidden. I propose to go in the early hours, tomorrow.'

'I agree that's the only option, but I don't like any part of this,' Mordant told them. 'Darric wants revenge. We have killed his sister and affronted the honour of his name. He cannot let that pass.'

'A rat is always most dangerous when you corner him,' agreed Braidart, 'and his honour matters deeply. What will enable him to keep it at the end, Mordant? You understand how raash see these things.'

'His honour is more important than his life. He wants to kill us all. He will do everything he can to make that happen. He hates us, but especially you, Jorn, and you, Braid, because you are a Darnell. We have destroyed his hopes, his army is useless, and his whole Realm is in chaos. He has lost the Tools but he still has Power. Even if it is abandoned, going into his Base is putting us all in harm's way. He will do everything he can to ensure that we do not get out again alive.'

'I know,' said Rolf, 'but what choice do we have? We can't just leave him there, if indeed he is inside. And if he has left, we need to know; he can still cause us a great deal of trouble. And if he were to return to Vard, he could rally the remains of the army, just when the Free Varders are making progress. He has to be eliminated.'

Jan nodded. 'Jorn's far-seeing was very clear, and my sense tells me he's there. We have to confront him. We are Nines. He is an Eight. Whatever he does, we are strong enough to meet it. Darric must die, and that's the end of it.'

Mordant looked at the twins, her face as impassive as always. 'There's one detail we haven't settled. Who is going to kill him, and how? I know you both want to, and you have good reasons, but even Darric can only die once.'

'And you'd like to be the one to make it happen,' said Idris. 'We all understand that. But we can't predict what we will find. I think we have to let Chance decide. When the time comes, it will be obvious.'

Jorn shook his head decisively. 'I'm not about to leave anything to Chance where Darric is concerned. Where do you think we'll find him, Jan?'

'In the great hall, with Ajina's body.'

'I agree. So what are we going to do when we get there? I suggest we both hit him with death shafts at the same time. That way, we can be sure that at least one of us will succeed.'

'Sounds sensible. But also too simple. I can't see him just sitting there and waiting for us to do that,' objected Jan doubtfully.

Jorn

'Neither can I,' agreed Mordant. 'Darric is old and cunning. He's a powerful adept. He might be able to work a mirror-shield and send the attack back to us; that's a favourite with raash War-Mages – bouncing Power is easier than trying to block it. I think powerful mind-fetters and body-bindings might be a better first choice. In any case, I want him to know who I am before he dies.'

'Is that wise?'

'Probably not. But deeply satisfying,' responded Mordant. 'Once we have him bound, each of us can launch a death-shaft at the same time. That way, we all have justice for what he has done to us.'

The twins shared a long look and then nodded agreement. *'I understand why Mordant wants to kill Darric herself, but if there is no alternative, I'll have to use the shian attack; we know that even a powerful mage has no defence against that,'* Jan told his brother.

Kayman had listened to the plans in silence. His foresight was full of warnings, but he could see nothing clearly. They knew the danger, and they were doing all they could to meet it, so there was no point in making things worse by sharing his forebodings of disaster.

*

Jorn walked out of the portal for yet another dawn raid, with deep misgivings and an even stronger determination that he would see Darric die if it were the last thing he did. He and Jan were fully prepared, Nine-colour bindings hung ready, together with multiple wards and other defensive and offensive constructs. They had both rejected weapons and armour, apart from light cuirasses. Neither of them knew what to expect, except that it would be something dangerous and hard to deal with. Darric was surely going to fight to defend his honour to his last breath.

He looked round at his friends. Braidart was fully armoured in mail and some plate. Mordant was in her fighting leathers with a metal cuirass and helmet. She had her kor and kring drawn at the ready. Even Rolf was mail-clad and armed. Idris had nothing, except for a string of water bottles strung across his broad chest; with no way of portalling out when they were underground, he was taking no chances.

Rolf came over and gave Jorn a grim smile. 'I feel like the fifth wheel. I have no skill for this kind of fight, but I had to come. Darric has so much grief to answer for, I have to see the ending.'

'We feel the same. Take care, Rolf, you are all the family we have left. Just stay well back. Braid and Mordant know what they are doing, and we are as well-prepared as we can be. We'll finish him, come what may.'

Rolf nodded, his dark face full of difficult emotions, and clasped Jorn's hand firmly in both of his own. 'Powers be with you both,' he said, and went to take his place at the rear.

The twins hung some strong wards to give added protection to their friends, and finally covered the entire assault force with a never-mind. They looked at each other with fixed determination. The time for words was past.

Braidart assembled his men. They entered the open gates and began to move down the dark, wide passage, exercising acute vigilance. There was no sound other than their own breathing and soft footfalls. The mages scanned for defensive wards or booby-traps, but they could sense no nearby threat, no living thing at all. When they reached the first level, they stopped, and Braid sent scouts to check the area.

Jan sent, *'There is no life here, and no threat on this level. Darric is below. And I sense extreme danger down there.'*

Jorn reported, 'Jan says Darric is definitely down there.'

'But why? What is he waiting for?' demanded Braid. 'It doesn't make sense and it reeks of a trap.'

'Yes, it does,' agreed Mordant, 'but we have to find him.'

'He wants us to,' said Idris grimly. 'He will be well-prepared.' The shian laved himself with water from his flask and took a few sips.

The scouts returned and confirmed that the upper level seemed to have been abandoned. They moved on, most of the soldiers fanning out ahead, and some keeping rear-guard. They found the stairs and flashed torches downwards, but the same uncanny silence and stillness prevailed.

'Do we go down?' asked Jorn tensely.

Braid shook his head. 'Not until I know what's there. Need the scouts again.'

'I'm going down as well,' said Mordant. 'There may be wards and mage-traps.'

Braid called six men over and gave brisk orders. Mordant took the lead and they went down the stairs like shadows, and disappeared into the gloom. The air below felt warm and stuffy.

The team waited, stretching their senses, tautly alert for any sign of movement or hint of danger. Jorn's sense was tweaking with urgent

Jorn

insistence. He knew as well as Jan did that something evil awaited them. He fought against the sense of foreboding dread. *'I'm scared,'* he confessed.

'I'm plain terrified,' agreed Jan, *'but we have no choice. This must be ended.'*

The scouts slipped back up the stairs. 'We have company below,' Mordant reported quietly. 'Darric's Honour Guard. Some 40 well-armed raash, waiting halfway down the corridor, and guarding the entrance to the great hall. They're his elite troops, sworn to fight to the death to defend their lord. A few lamps are lit. And there are mage-traps at the foot of the stairs. We need to break those first.'

Jorn nodded, hoping he did not look as nervous as he felt, and the twins followed Mordant down into the gloom, never-minds and shields in place. Jan sensed the traps, a simple capture net, and a much more unpleasant wall of fire. Mordant stood guard, kring and kor in hand, and the twins dealt with the delicate task of detaching the constructs and breaking them. The release of Power reverberated like a snapped bow-string.

'If Darric didn't know we were here before, he does now,' sent Jorn.

'Which was probably the point,' agreed Mordant. *'He's making us play his game.'* She took a look down the corridor where the raash were rapidly forming up and ready for action. *'And the next round is with them.'*

'Do you want us to take them out?' asked Jorn tensely.

Mordant gave her tight smile. *'What, and deprive Braid of his chance of a good fight? He'd never forgive us. Anyway, the guards want to die honourably, with their swords in their hands. I'm sure we can help them to achieve the ambition.'*

They went back up the stairs to give the all-clear. Braidart brought his men together. 'Right lads, there's work ahead; this is where you earn your beer. Hit them hard, at the run. No survivors.' He looked at the mages. 'We don't need the never-mind now, this is a straight fight. Stay back, unless some raash mage or Darric starts to interfere. If we're in trouble, I'll yell.'

Mordant moved to his side. Braid nodded. The pair took position at the front of the attack force and descended the stairs at a steady rate. Jorn and the two mages followed more slowly.

As they reached the court level, Jorn glanced round at the rich furnishings and ornaments. Their previous confrontation with Ajina was seared into his memory. The scar above his heart pricked and felt cold. What would the meeting with Darric bring? Jan was silent, supporting his twin with the steady comfort of his presence. His danger sense was screaming at him that they should leave now, before it was too late. He ignored that. It already was.

Mordant, Braid and his assault force went down the corridor at a fast run, as the Honour Guard took up a defensive formation. A few moments later, the yells and clashes of fierce combat commenced. The mages went slowly forward. The area outside the hall was filled with vicious fighting. It was the usual hard-to-follow melee, and they couldn't intervene, even if they'd wanted to, for fear of hitting Braid's men in the confined space.

They did not need to. The raash were eliminated with brutal efficiency in less than 10 minutes, and with remarkably few losses to their own side. Idris went to tend the most seriously wounded men.

Braidart came back, out of breath, blood-spattered, and looking grimly satisfied. 'They had their wish. They are dead, and with their soldiers' honour intact. They fought well, but I don't think their hearts were in it somehow. The last six just threw down their swords and waited for us to kill them.' He nodded towards the closed doors of the hall. I guess we have to go in there again?'

Jorn nodded. 'Yes, at least, we do. This is where sword-work stops and mage-craft begins. You can do nothing against Darric. You and your men must wait here outside the entrance, and keep clear of the doors until we tell you to come in. Start to evacuate the wounded. The rest is up to us now. Rolf and Idris, you had better keep back as well.' He checked his strong triple-Nine body wards and mind-shields for the tenth time. *Are you ready, Jan?*'

Mordant used Disjunct to throw the doors open. The twins ran through, one to each side of the hall, expected to be assaulted by lethal bolts of Power, but nothing came. They had an instant to check that Darric was there, and then their Nine-colour shield-breakers slammed against the Mage-Lord's wards from two sides at once and smashed them. Jorn instantly followed up with a complex and immensely powerful mind-fetter, while Jan's elaborate body-binding slammed down to secure Darric in rigid paralysis on his throne.

'*Why the hell did he let us do that?*' demanded Jan anxiously, as he and Jorn walked very slowly towards their enemy, side-by-side, with Mordant keeping pace, her blades steady, her entire concentration focussed on the still figure on the dais. Idris slipped silently down the left side of the chamber, tense and watchful. The mind-fetter had dulled Darric's aura so that he could not read it, but he could not believe that the Mage-Lord intended to succumb without a fight. Rolf moved a short way down along the right and kept behind a pillar. Braidart peered cautiously around the doorframe, whilst the rest of his men continued with first aid or kept watch.

The room was bright. Candles cast rainbow sparkles in the great glass chandeliers. Torches flamed in cressets. Just as the seeing had shown, Darric was robed in mourning white. His tightly-sculpted face was unreadable, a golden circlet glittered above his high crests. His long tail of flaxen hair flowed down his right shoulder. Beside him, Ajina's body rested on the gold-draped bier.

Jorn walked to the foot of the dais and stopped. 'I give you leave to speak, Lord,' he said curtly.

Darric's violet eyes narrowed and glittered with malice, but his deep voice showed no emotion. 'So, twin Masters of Nine. That explains much. And this must be the renegade halfer, Mordant.'

'Yes, Father,' she replied in raash. 'I am Philip's sister. I have spent many years imagining the moment of your death.'

Darric's eyes widened for an instant, but soon regained his control. He said, also in raash, 'Then I trust you will enjoy it, daughter. I have no reason to live. You have robbed me of kin, and home, and Realm, and thwarted all my plans. I have nothing left but my honour. That I will take unsullied to my grave.'

Mordant understood the threat perfectly and she reacted with lethal speed. Despite his fetters, Darric clearly intended something, and she was not going to give him the chance, or wait for the others to react. With the force of all her years of pent fury, she sent a killing shaft to end the menace. Her father's body jerked and slumped, the bindings on it broken by his death.

Jan had not understood the words, but his warning sense interpreted their threat with graphic clarity and showed him in a split-second exactly what he had to do. He yelled 'TRAP!' threw himself at Jorn with full force, knocking him flat, and pushing him 20 ems away, across the polished wooden floor. Then his own shian defence reflex kicked in, instantly making him lose form and sink his *shi* into the planking.

There was a massive explosion. The entire dais erupted in a mind-numbing roar of destruction. The ceiling above it collapsed in ruin, the chandelier smashed. A hot shockwave loaded with shrapnel, glass, dust and debris punched down the hall, felling everything in its path.

Mordant had taken a moment too long to recover from the surge of emotion that followed the killing, but even if she had started to move, it would have made no difference. She was far too close to the impact, and her wards and armour were no match for this kind of force. Caught squarely by the violent, disruptive blast, her body was torn apart and thrown aside.

Idris had shed form and flattened with reflex speed. With frantic haste, he regained it and began to look for Mordant, knowing even as he did so that she could not possibly have survived. He found her in the semi-darkness, using his sense rather than sight, thrown against a side-wall like a bloody, dismembered doll.

He knelt and gathered her broken body into his arms, torn by helpless grief, his sense scanning urgently. There was enough light from a few flickering lamps and small fires to show him that the cuirass had protected her chest to some extent, although it was dented and crushed inwards. Her helmet had been lost, her head was bloody but intact. With the appalling wounds and traumatic amputations to her lower body, the end was inevitable. But right now, she was, incredibly, still alive. With a surge of desperate hope, Idris poured healing strength into her, heedless of the drain on his Power.

After a few moments, her violet eyes flicked open in dazed incomprehension, then cleared to loving relief as she realised who held her. Oddly, there was no pain, but something was terribly wrong. Then the terrifying awareness of her shocking injuries hit home. Her mage-sense knew full well that this was the end, and Idris would kill himself trying to change that. Her mind-voice was weak but loaded with anxious warning. *'Don't, Idris. Don't try. Can't heal this. I'm dying, love. Just hold me.'*

His voice was vibrant with certainty, his rising passion a running torrent flowing through the words. 'I'm not trying to heal you. You poor body is broken beyond any hope of that. I just want to give you strength for a few more moments. Mordant, you do not have to die. I had a thousand times rather see you whole than in such a state as this, yet cruel Chance has gifted us the thing I most desired and never thought could come. Make union with me, love of my life, come to me, be one with me, live!'

His love was flooding into her, the shocked awareness of her damaged body fading in its path, the fear ebbing, her desire rising to meet his own, her mind and spirit reaching out to him in a great rush of wordless longing and acceptance.

His essence entered her and, for the first time, she truly knew him. He was huge, alien, complex and completely wonderful. It was like being washed in a fresh fountain, tickled by bubbles, rushing headlong down a foaming stream, swimming in a sea of love and joy so deep, she could not fathom it. For the first time in her life, she felt all her barriers and conflicts being melted and swept away. An ecstatic rapture was swelling in her essence. With infinite care, on a tide of pure love, Idris plunged into the depths of her inner being to find her self and soul and meld them with his own.

Chapter 28

After a few moments, in the awful, stunned aftermath, Jan managed somehow to find the strength to emerge and regain form, and go in search of his brother in the dark chaos, terrified of what he might find.

In the corridor, by the twisted doors, Braidart and his men started to pick themselves up, deafened and groggy from the blast, sending shafts of torch beams through the swirling dust and smoke to assess the damage. Braid had been outside, and his helmet and armour had done its job; he was shaken but unharmed. Rolf had been behind the thick pillar, and amazingly, had escaped with no more than dulled ears.

Jan found Jorn huddled against a pillar, unconscious, cut and bruised by flying debris. He engaged Adjunct, scanned his twin with anxious care, and gave a shuddering sigh of relief. Jorn was only stunned. His body-shield had deflected the worst of the blast before his temporary unconsciousness snapped the working.

Jan dealt quickly with the minor injuries, and then helped Jorn to his feet and held him in a long, tight embrace. '*I have never been so frightened. I thought I'd lost you.*'

'*You nearly did.*' Jorn was still feeling dazed. '*What happened?*'

'*A massive explosion of some kind.*'

'*By the Powers, what a mess. Is anyone hurt?*'

'*I don't know.*' Jan looked round at the dimness of the wrecked hall. Yellow flames flickered in a corner. His sense suddenly tweaked with acute foreboding. 'Mordant! She was near you.'

Jan turned, urgently seeking, and raced across the room to where Idris knelt, head bowed, cradling the remains of her blood-soaked body. Braid stood nearby, turned away, his helmet off and his hand covering his face as his shoulders heaved with silent sobs. Rolf stared in shocked disbelief, his torch illuminating the rubble-strewn ground. One sight of Mordant had been enough. Jan had no need to ask if she was dead. It was all too obvious. Jorn came over, still feeling too stunned to move fast, and caught his breath in horror. No one spoke.

Idris kissed Mordant, and set her down with gentle care. The shian mage stood and turned to his distraught friends. His body was drenched with blood but his face showed nothing but transcendent joy, and then he threw his arms wide, and span in a dancing circle, and gave a long, ululating cry of triumphant shian celebration. They stared at him in bewildered incomprehension, wondering if the shock had turned his mind. He became still. His voice was deeply happy.

'You must forgive us. You wonder at such inappropriate elation when Mordant's poor, maimed body lies in pieces. My friends, rejoice with us, and put aside your grief. Mordant is not dead! I reached her in time to make union. It is an overwhelming wonder and delight for both of us.'

Braidart stared at Idris in stunned disbelief. 'I don't understand.'

'Mordant is part of me now.' The shian mage paused and then he smiled. 'I think, maybe, with my help, she can tell you that herself.' There was another short pause and then he spoke again. The voice was unmistakably Mordant's, if a little hesitant.

'I'm here, Braid. That wreck is just a shell. I'm quite safe. Or perhaps I should say we are. I'm still trying to get used to this.'

'Oh blood's death!' exclaimed Braidart in a shaken voice. He looked back at the ruined body, and back again at Idris. 'I don't think I can cope with this right now.' He turned abruptly and went towards the door to reassure his men and see if anyone else was wounded.

'I don't think any of us can,' murmured Jorn. He was still too shocked to feel pleased that Mordant was alive. Everything about the last few minutes seemed unreal.

Rolf recovered faster. He went over to his friend, grabbed his hand and pressed it hard. 'I am so very happy for both of you. Not that I would ever have wanted the awful circumstances, but the result is splendid, simply splendid. And Darric is dead.' As if in answer, a shower of debris crashed from the ceiling.

Jan's danger sense tweaked urgently. 'We'd better get out of here fast. The explosion has weakened the structure; this whole roof could cave in at any minute.'

They all moved rapidly into the corridor. Jorn was about to ask Idris what they should do about Mordant's body, when a reverberating crash made his question redundant. A rush of dust through the doorway made them all cough and cover their eyes. Jan's warning had come just in time.

Jorn looked back at the heap of rubble that now obliterated the hall. 'Father, aunt and daughter, entombed together. Thank the Powers it was not worse. I'm very lucky to be alive. If Jan hadn't pushed me, I'd have caught the force full on, just as Mordant did, and I doubt if my wards could have coped with that. I guess Darric thought explosives were appropriate after what we did to his home. But how did he set them off? We had him immobilised and mind-fettered right to the end.'

Braidart shook his head. 'He let you do that so you'd get close. He wanted to die taking us all with him. It was his idea of honour. I think he used a timer; probably set it just as we reached the door. He only needed a delay of three or four minutes.'

'I should have thought of that, especially as we used the same trick, but we were both so busy triple-warding ourselves and everyone else against mage-craft, we forgot the other options,' admitted Jorn ruefully.

Jan suddenly stiffened in alarm. His danger sense pulsed again with urgent certainty. 'By the Powers, that was not the only trap! Darric wanted to make certain of it. The whole base is set to explode at any moment. RUN!' he yelled. 'Run for your lives!' He saw Jorn hesitate for a second and look at the remaining wounded who were not going to make it out alone. *'No, Jorn, you can't. Run, brother, I'll be right behind you.'*

Jorn took off, knowing his twin was right. There was nothing he could do. Jan grabbed one of Braid's injured men and took off down the passage after Jorn, his long legs and shian strength propelling him like a sprinter, despite his load. Idris scooped Rolf up and followed with equal speed.

Braid yelled, 'Everyone out lads, at the double! If you can run, do it; if you can't, I'm sorry.'

They pelted along the corridor and up the stairs, raced for the entry ramp, reached the open air and kept going, heading for the trees. The whole straggling group had managed a hundred ems into the forest when Jan's sense gave another urgent warning. 'GET DOWN!' he shouted. He set down his casualty, shed form and so did Idris. The humans all threw themselves to the earth, gasping for breath. An almighty concussion shook the ground. The nearby pines lifted on their root plates and settled again, showering needles and cones. Further back, over the base, a giant fireball exploded into the air. Trees crashed and flamed. A wild, hot, disruptive force blasted over them. Then it all went still.

'Sorry about that,' Idris told Mordant. *'The last thing you needed right now was to lose form without warning.'*

'I'm coping,' she told him, shakily, *'but I feel as if I've been dragged through a cross-step 10 times in as many minutes! I don't know where I start and finish anymore.'*

Jorn

'I will take form again in a moment. That will help. I am going to portal us back to Arden. We need rest and quiet and time to really get to know each other.'

'Could we go back to that waterfall? It's the most beautiful place I've ever seen.'

'Ideal.'

Idris took form. The humans were picking themselves up, yet again, and dusting down. Braid had his hands over his ears. 'Head's ringing,' he said crossly. 'I'm half deaf.'

The shian mage formed his portal. 'We'll be back in a few days.' He grinned at Braidart. 'You can think of it as our honeymoon.' He stepped through and the misty gateway closed behind him.

Braidart looked bemused. 'I get the feeling I just lost a game I didn't even know I was playing. You are going to have to explain this shian union thing to me,' he said ruefully to Jan. 'I still have no idea what's happened to them.'

'I think it's called love,' Jan told him. 'Surely you knew?'

'I thought Mordant... I mean we... Blood's death, who understands women?'

Rolf looked at the young nobleman with raised eyebrows. 'Oh come on, stop pretending to be a jilted lover. You went all out to get her into your bed. How did you think that was going to end? You can't really expect much sympathy.'

Jan grinned, lost form and slid back into his brother. 'I don't think us bachelors are best qualified to advise on females, Braid,' Jorn told him. 'And a shian union is a mystery to everyone who isn't shian. Anyway, let's get you and your men home to the Hold. We'll help with the wounded. And then we both need to find a tree.'

'And I'm going straight back to Errington to tell Kayman the extraordinary ending, and reassure the young Darnells that all is well with their brother,' said Rolf briskly.

*

The twins spent the night at the Hold. The place was still a mess, the burnt-out tower stood forlornly abandoned; the family wing and damaged curtain wall were covered in scaffolding and bustling with workmen. Arnori Borodin and his capable wife had furnished a few rooms, but it was far from comfortable. Despite that, Braidart and his men had a considerable, largely liquid, party.

Jorn and Jan did their best to join the celebrations but they were feeling flat. The quest was finally well and truly over. Darric and Ajina were dead. Earth was safe; Vard was working out its own destiny. The young Darnells would soon return home. Idris and Mordant had made union. Now what? But Jorn could not quite shake off the feeling of unfinished business. Darrison was not accounted for, and Vard was not yet at peace.

*

At dawn the next day, the twins decided that they must give the Free Varders the good news about Darric, tell Mordant's old friends about her extraordinary transformation, and catch up with Corus.

Braidart roused enough to watch them portal out, and then returned to the Hold to nurse his considerable hangover. He wanted to ride over to see Brett to break the news about Mordant in person, and he needed to get his own emotions in order. Jan had done his best to explain what had happened but he was still not sure he understood. He *was* sure he didn't like it. He was torn in all directions; glad Mordant was safe, missing her physical presence, angry at her, and deeply jealous of Idris. He was also uncomfortably aware that Rolf had been right. He'd started it, and he hadn't bothered about where that might take him, so if he'd got more involved than he bargained for, he couldn't really blame anyone but himself. He needed some hard work to take his mind off it all.

*

Jorn portalled onto the beach in Free Vard and walked up the soft white sand, accompanied by the usual crowd of small children who had been playing there.

Corus came to meet him, walking slowly, leaning on Karan's arm, and looking, if possible, even older. The two raash took the news of Darric's death with their usual inscrutability, but Jan felt they were pleased, relieved, and, rather like themselves, not quite sure what to do next.

'How's the war?'

Karan spread her hands and rocked them to indicate a fine balance. 'The generals who command the western and northern armies have asked for a truce. They think they can string out the negotiations in the hope that our rebel forces either fall apart or starve, and give them a chance to reorganise and attack again. They forget that many of us were field slaves; we'll be better fed than they are. We slaves are the ones with skills; they are useless without us. And their essential supply lines have been cut. Darric's death might be a tipping point. I don't envy the poor envoys who have to sit through moons of useless argument, but in the end, we'll have peace, or something very close to it. But meanwhile, we have a new country to run, and that is going to be a considerable challenge.'

'What will happen to all the slaves?'

'They have been freed, of course, but they are bewildered and leaderless. Most of the humans want to go home; who can blame them? We may need some help from human mages to arrange that; it will take a long time to sort them out and portal them all back to where they belong. The raash halfers will stay here. They know full well there's no prospect for a home for them on Earth.'

Jorn said quietly, 'I lost two young kinfolk last year to a raash raid. I think they may have been sent to the mines. If they've survived, I want to know. Their names are Rob and Red. They'll be around twelve and seven by now.'

'We'll let you know if they turn up.'

'I guess it will all sort itself out eventually. Have you used the Tools yet?' enquired Jan, who had taken form to ease the flow of conversation

Corus sighed. 'I've tried, but the forces are too great to control. I fear that Kayman is right. The working is far beyond my strength. I so want to stop the civil war and heal Vard, but I cannot master the Tools and the Juncture. I'm not doing something correctly, but I have no idea what that is.'

'Might we see the Tools again?'

The old mage nodded, and Karan went to fetch them. Jan placed the Juncture on the warm sand, with each Tool adjacent to its proper jewel but safely in its box, and set his Gift to scanning and exploring. Jorn watched him, knowing that he couldn't help with this.

After a while, Jan said thoughtfully, 'I believe that, for a start, we need a large copy of the Pattern, just as there was at the ruins. Somehow, the Pattern and the Juncture work together. And the Quincunx too, laid out across it. We need the matrix to control the flow of energies. And then...' His voice trailed away and he stared rather vacantly into space.

Eventually, Jan took a deep breath and smiled. 'I see now why you cannot do the working, Corus. No single mage could do so. Each Tool requires its own Master. Maybe that's where Myron went wrong. We need four mages; ideally, four Nines, but of course, that's impossible.'

'Two will be a help, though, and two strong eights,' said Jorn. 'Corus, I know this is a hard thing to put into words, but what construct were you trying to make?'

Corus waved his hands in uncertain small movements. 'I was trying to form an image of peace and plenty. Remembering Vard as it used to be, a very long time ago, when the weather was kind, and rain fell, and crops flourished, and people did not spend their time killing each other. Oh, I know, I make that sound like an impossible paradise. It was not, of course, but it was right and real, and everything was in balance. Yes, I suppose that is what I want. To put the balance right. But I cannot make the colours work.'

Jorn said quietly, 'Corus, I think I can help you to form that construct. It will take me some time, but when I am ready, I will come again. We'll work together to heal Vard.'

'And meanwhile, make a copy of the Pattern and Quincunx. Out there on the beach above the tide-line will do, but it must be flat, three ems square,' added Jan.

Corus nodded, and smiled. 'Thank you, my friends. I await your next arrival with great hope.'

When Jorn returned to the Darnell mansion, he went to his bedroom, retreated to his inner weaving loft, and started work on a construct so intricate in its complexity that only a skilled master weaver with several thousand colours in his control could have attempted it. He told no one what he was doing, except, of course, Jan.

He set up his imagined tapestry loom, all ready to start the weft. He had the design clear in his imagination, and he worked with intense precision to create it, not needing his hands, but weaving with his mind and will, drawing his colours through the matrix of the Quincunx, focussed to the exclusion of anything else.

The tapestry, which grew on the loom, was a richly-coloured landscape, a composite of sky, mountains, water and woods, fields and sea. It teemed with life. The border contained flowers and fruit, vegetables and leaves. Animals peered from between the vegetation; birds flew and perched.

Jorn

Twigs held butterflies and bugs; ponds were rich with frogs and fish. It was an entire world captured in fine threads in every colour ever seen. He poured into it all his own love of peace and plenty and wild beauty, binding his working with both will and passion.

Jan came from time to time and watched his twin work in awestruck wonder. This was a true Master Work. His only contribution at this stage was to feed Jorn strength at intervals, and nag him into stopping to rest and eat, which he did reluctantly. His commitment was total. He was hardly aware of whether his brother was indwelling or not. Most of the time, Jan left him to it and went to rest in the plane tree at the end of the garden. He wanted to be around when Idris returned; or was it Mordris now?

*

Bea and Brendan were sitting in the warm spring sunshine near the plane tree, enjoying the burgeoning greenery and the bright displays of daffodils and early tulips. None of their oddly assorted houseguests had said anything about what they had been doing, but they had all been wearing a collection of big, cheesy grins for the past few days, so things must be going well, and Kayman had told them that the mission was over and they would soon be going back to the Hold.

Bren was looking forward to some hunting but Bea was not too certain she wanted to return to the bleak austerity of their damaged fortress. She had to make the most of the city before she left, and was telling Bren at some length about her final shopping plans.

Kayman walked down the path, heading in their direction. The elderly mage gave a cheery wave and came to join them. Two strides away, he halted. Bea suddenly found she couldn't move or speak. Brendan was similarly bound. They regarded the mage with surprise and a degree of concern. Kayman was not given to practical jokes, and if this was one, it was decidedly not funny.

Their discomfort turned to total fear when the voice that spoke to them was not the rich tones of the old Master, but the lighter, crisper voice of Philip. 'Just too easy.' He now had a dagger in his hand. 'Of necessity, I must be quick. However, Sar Brendan, you will watch me cut your sister's throat before I render you the same service.' Brendan made a snarling noise and a convulsive effort to rise, and was unable to lift a finger. He watched in helpless horror as the disguised spy advanced on Bea.

Jan's *shi* shot from the plane tree. Darrison's head exploded outwards in a bloody spray of bone and brains as the shian energy form blasted through it. His mask snapped and his body collapsed. The bindings on Bea and Brendan vanished. Bea folded into her brother's arms, sobbing with shock and relief.

Jan took form and regarded the body with acute distaste. That had been extremely unpleasant, but at least he had been in time to prevent another tragedy.

He looked up. Jorn was coming down the garden at a fast run. He ground to a halt, took in the situation at a glance and said, 'I got the call. Congratulations! What happened?'

'I was in the tree. My danger sense tweaked, but when I looked out, I could see no reason for it. Bren and Bea were sitting chatting. Kayman was walking down the path. Only I could still sense that something wasn't right. I left the tree and scanned him. He was warded, as Kayman often is, but the signature on the constructs was all wrong. They were raash triple-wards. I knew at once it was Philip using a whole-body mask. So I called you. And by that time, he had Bea and Brendan bound and was on the point of cutting her throat. I used the shian attack.'

Jorn looked at the smashed remains of the spy's head and pulled a face. 'Highly effective. Come on, Bea, let's get you indoors, you've had a very nasty shock. And you don't need to see this.' He covered the body with a pass-me-by.

Brendan helped his sister to her feet and smiled at Jan. 'We owe you, all over again.'

*

Idris and Mordant were happy beyond the reach of words. Their 'honeymoon' at the lake had been blissful. Mordant had never imagined anything like the feeling of being in pure, clear water without the least fear of drowning. A *shi*, she found, had no need to breathe. The joyous energy of her surroundings was only surpassed by the wonder of having Idris as close to her as it was possible to get. The sheer rapture of shian love-making was indescribable.

Despite all that, she was most comfortable when Idris was in form. She still found it deeply strange to lack the support of a body, and yet have her mind and senses in full use. Idris understood that completely and he was trying hard to help, with rather surprising results.

When it got too much and she needed privacy, she retreated into her mental 'potting shed', which now opened out onto a well-filled vegetable garden that she could wander round. It amused her to create new displays of produce as the days passed.

They still had a lot to learn about each other. It had taken a while to get the balance right between them, and a certain amount of experiment, but they had made progress and they were looking forward to showing Jorn and Jan a new skill.

Idris translocated back to Errington and they settled into the pond in the garden. Mordant made a mind call to the twins. Right now, she could taste the flat, rather muddy, water, and felt the sliding fish and tickling tadpoles. '*I can totally understand why you prefer the fountain in the park, love,*' she told him. '*This pond is pretty disgusting.*'

'*We'll go there soon. But we must tell Jorn and Jan our news.*'

Jan soon came up to the pond, wearing a delighted smile, and sent, '*Hello, Idris; hello, Mordant, great to have you back. Should we be using a combined name now?*'

'*You should indeed, we've decided on Mordris, but we've agreed that you only need to do that, and use the plural, when we lack form. But where is Jorn?*'

'*He's working on something quite extraordinary. He'll be down in a minute, just has to get to a good place to stop and secure his construct.*'

'*That sounds intriguing,*' sent Mordant.

'*I expect he'll tell you about it.*'

'*Anything else been happening?*' she enquired.

'*Philip is dead,*' he told her. She felt the shock of that surge through her essence and Idris at once gave her the loving strength of his presence.

'*Power's, Jan, you might have broken that more gently!*' Idris sent crossly. '*He was her brother, after all. You have upset her.*'

'*Sorry Mordant, that was tactless.*'

'*I'm not upset; it was just unexpected. What happened?*'

'*It was only three days ago; it's still a bit too fresh for comfort,*' Jan explained, and gave them a quick account of it.

'*Well done, Jan. As I told you, not even a warded mage can withstand a shian attack,*' said Idris.

'I'm glad he's gone, and more than glad I did not have to be the one to kill him. Thank the Powers you were on hand to do so. I could not have born it if he'd killed Bea and Brendan. And it would have destroyed Braid,' Mordant told him gratefully.

Jorn had come to join them and greeted the pair with pleasure. 'Come on out, you two, I want to see you and know that you are both well. You had to leave so fast after that dreadful business in the Base. I was still feeling shocked and a bit dazed, I never got a chance to talk to you or congratulate you properly.'

Mordris emerged from the pond and took form. The shian gave a broad smile, looking just as usual, and said, 'We've agreed that you can use "he" when I'm in this form; the whole "they" business just gets too complicated.' Jorn gave his friend a hug and patted his shoulder. 'Good to have you both back. But I'm going to miss your physical presence, Mordant.'

Idris smiled even more broadly. 'No, you won't,' he said, in Mordant's voice. And then his form shivered and flowed and changed, and the halfer mage stood before them, the familiar tight smile on her face, and her human eyes sparkling with delight at their amazement, and the fact that Jorn had gone slightly pink at her nakedness.

'We haven't quite got the hang of forming clothes yet, but we're working on it,' she told them, 'and we can't hold this for long, but it's coming.' Her form wobbled and remodelled as Idris.

Jorn was totally astounded. 'How on earth did you do that? Is it magecraft?'

The shian mage sat on the edge of the pond and trailed his hand in the water. 'Mordant uses the construct for a whole-body mask to help me shape it, but it is rather more than that. Millennia ago, my race were shifters. We could take any shape we chose, and then we met humans, and eventually, we adopted something like the human form and ceased to change. But the ability to shift is still there, buried deep in our essences. I am trying to regain it. Soon there will be two of us again, though, of course, only one can be visible at a time. But I felt it only fair to share.'

'And that is not the only thing we are sharing.' Mordant's voice was full of satisfaction. 'You two are no longer the only Mages of Nine on the planet. We too have Mastery!'

Jan said, 'But how…' and then he smiled and said, 'Of course! Your Spectrums combine to cover the Nine!'

'Exactly so,' said Idris. 'We have formed a shared workplace and a new Quincunx. It will take some time to learn how to make Nine-coloured braids, but we are practising. We may not have the full Power of a natural-born Nine as you two do, but we should be able to give you some powerful support if you ever need it.'

'Well, we soon may. I've been working hard on something important,' said Jorn. 'Now that you are back, I think it's time to tell Rolf and Kayman about it.'

*

The six friends enjoyed a happy reunion, and the solid-forms had lunch. Then Jorn grinned at Rolf and said, 'I expect you and Kayman have been wondering what I've been doing shut away in my bedroom?'

'We have indeed speculated wildly!' agreed the mage. 'To no avail.'

'I'm creating a very complicated construct in the form of a big tapestry. Corus needs it to heal Vard. When it's done, we'll go back and see if we can apply it. It won't be easy; Jan thinks we need four mages to work with the Tools and the Juncture. Preferably Nines.' He turned to Idris. 'Well, we have three, if you will both help us?'

'Of course we will,' responded Idris. 'But, you know, you *do* have four Nines. Corus himself is a Nine, but he has hidden it, by blocking violet, for very many years. I read it as soon as we had met, but he begged me not to reveal it.'

'When Idris told me that, it explained a great deal,' said Mordant. 'I always thought Corus had hidden depths.'

'But why did he hide his Power?' asked Jan. 'I'd have thought he'd have wanted to do all he could to beat Darric.'

'I asked him that,' responded Idris. 'He said that the slide from strong leadership into tyranny is well-greased; he was afraid of the addictive side of Power, of becoming another Darric, another War-Mage who never knew when to stop. He wanted to remain true to his essence, keep his honour in his own way.'

Kayman sighed. 'He has a point. Total Power corrupts. And yet there are times when we must be brave enough to use it.'

'And times when we must resist. A hard choice.'

'But in this case, I choose to act,' said Jorn firmly. 'The four of us should be able to do this. I'll let you know when I'm ready. But Kayman, I've been meaning to ask, what are you going to do now? I mean, the missions are over, and the threat of war is ended. But you no longer have Mage Hall. Will you stay in Errington?'

'No, I won't do that. You remember I told you that I have secretly founded new Mage Schools? Well, there is one in Daunce and another in Dart. Rolf is going to become High Master of that one, and I'll carry on in Daunce. It will be good to get back to the ordinary problems of teaching young mages how to avoid creating chaos through sheer over-enthusiasm and ignorance!'

Rolf chuckled. 'I have to say that I'm not too sure about the mounds of paperwork that go with all that, but I'll give it a try. Angela has taken over as head of department at the university here. Not that she is going to be behind a desk much, she plans to spend most of the next year investigating that vault.'

That night, Jorn sensed that Jan was restless and unsettled. *'What's the matter?'* he sent. *'Something is bothering you. I've felt it all day, ever since Mordris returned.'*

'Seeing how happy they are suddenly made me realise that neither of us is ever likely to have that kind of deep relationship, unless we separate, permanently. That's a very difficult thought to handle.'

'Do you want to make union?'

'Powers, Jorn, no, I simply can't imagine doing so. But you might want to marry one day, and have children. If... if you do, I'll go. I couldn't bear it if you couldn't be happy or fully human because of me.'

Jorn sent his twin a surge of loving reassurance and comfort. *'Jan, I can no more imagine that than you can imagine making union. I don't know what the future will bring, and I'm not going to lose sleep over it right now. If I get into another "Bea situation", you can move out for an hour or two. Whatever comes, we'll find a way to deal with it together.'*

*

It took another two weeks of patient working before Jorn had his huge construct ready. Mordant made the portal to Free Vard, and Idris and the twins, accompanied by Rolf and Kayman, who had insisted on coming to see this extraordinary working, went through. Jorn, Jan and Mordris were in no doubt that what they faced was the most difficult and potentially dangerous working of their lives.

Corus greeted them with a single nod of profound respect that signified his understanding of their courage and commitment. He was totally amazed by the shian's transformation. He spent several minutes reading Idris' new, conjoined aura, making soft exclamations of astonishment. Idris could at once see that the adept's own aura now flamed with the Nine. Corus had unblocked his Power.

The Pattern and Quincunx had been drawn on the beach as Jan had requested. The sand had been wetted and compacted, and then incised and painted with the overlaid designs. Jan nodded in satisfaction. He said, 'We are all quite ready, Corus. Do you feel strong enough to attempt the working?'

'Strong, no, at least not in body, but ready, yes. I have my Nine. And my will is fixed on this.'

'I think it would be safer if no one from the village watches,' warned Jorn. 'We must concentrate, and I'm not sure what would happen if the construct goes wild. We are dealing with unknown forces here. But Karan can watch from a safe distance, and Rolf and Kayman, of course,' Jan told them.

Karan brought the Juncture and the Tools from their warded boxes. Mordant made an apport to convey the Juncture to precisely the centre of the Pattern without disturbing the design.

Corus said, 'Choose the Tool that speaks to your Power.' Idris took the Cup and held it cradled in both hands. He went to the blue Nexus and took up his place behind it.

Jorn said, 'I will take the Knife.' He held it with reverent care and stood behind the red Nexus. Jan reached for the Chain with complete certainty. The old mage nodded and took the Wand. They moved to their appointed stations. Corus drew himself up and seemed to shed his years by sheer force of will.

'So, are we ready? Jorn, what would you have us do?'

'First, we must engage with the Quincunx and activate it. Once it is ready, we must each place our Tool on its Nexus at the same moment. Remember that the key to this working is balance and harmony. We are not totally certain what will happen next, but Jan thinks that the jewels on the Juncture have to flame with Power before I can begin the working. When the Power reaches the critical moment, I will say "lift". I think we'll all know when we reach the climax. Set your Tool down when I say "now".'

Each mage reached for his own Power, and mastered the Sector in front of him, and then drew forth and released the Nine-colour construct Jorn had told them to prepare. Mordant and Idris worked in unison to control their Nine. Responding to the concentrated direction of the four Masters, the diagonals of the Quincunx blazed with sudden fire, and the jewels on the Juncture answered them. The Power spread in glittering sparks down the sides of the matrix from each Nexus and, when the sparks met, those lines also flared into steady brilliance each in their right colour. Finally, the central Nexus, crowned by the amethyst, sent its light skywards in coruscating violet rays. Jorn said "Now", and each mage bent to set his Tool on the Nexus at his feet and straightened once more, waiting for the outcome. The humming thrum of rising power rapidly escalated.

Rolf and Kayman looked at each other with tense concern. This was the critical moment. The four Masters would either control the releasing energies, or fail, with unpredictable, and probably fatal, consequences. As they watched, the hum rose to a painful intensity, and swirling threads of energy began to be visible in all Nine colours and an unexpected black so absolute that it hurt the eyes with its nothingness.

The churning maelstrom intensified and span around the Pattern until the mages were hidden inside a vortex of Power.

'By the Nine, is it supposed to do that?' muttered Kayman in an awed whisper.

Rolf made no reply; his hands were clenched and pressed to his mouth, fingers locked together as he willed his friends to hold on.

Within the dizzying whirl of colour, the four mages battled to maintain the balance, each acutely aware that if the working tipped in any direction, all would be lost. The drain on mind and will was punishing. The strange blackness was deeply worrying. It rose and extended, threatening to overwhelm the glowing Nine.

Jan stretched his sense, urgently seeking to understand this phenomenon. He was sure that the Juncture was the key. *I must balance this, but how?* His mind raced, seeking the solution. He was aware of his friends struggling to hold their Sectors against the assault of the dark. *Nine colours of light; Nine hues of night.* He had no idea where that came from, but he instantly knew it was the answer. The dark Nine needed to be balanced by their partners of light, and that was what the Juncture had been created to do. With his entire will, he engaged with Conjunct through the Chain, directed the dark at the yellow jewel on the Juncture, and willed the joining. Dark threads of energy detached from the spinning vortex and mated with the yellow ones. With intense, draining concentration, he united the other eight colours with their dark twins.

Finally, wonderfully, the spinning ceased. There was a sense of ordered harmony. The Nine colours, mingled with threads of the dark, became fixed above the lines of the Pattern and the Quincunx in rippling curtains of energy, a shimmering aurora throbbing with latent Power that hummed with a deep, complex tone. Karan, Rolf and Kayman exchanged looks of relief as the working stabilised and the mages came back into view.

Jorn heaved a shuddering sigh of released tension, gathered all his will and skill, reached for the tapestry construct and grasped it firmly. He brought it out. The supporting mages felt the drain on his Power and intensified their focus to balance it. With infinite care, Jorn let his weaving expand until the square tapestry lay spread above the Quincunx in a smooth sheet. The aurora continued to dance and shimmer above it. Slowly, the tapestry itself began to glow as it absorbed the energy, and finally burst into radiant life. Jorn took a deep breath and readied himself for the final crucial stage of the working.

'Lift,' he instructed, his voice tight with strain.

Working as one, the mages raised their hands, willing the apport. The watchers gasped as the tapestry became visible, rose, floated, and began to grow. As it soared, it seemed to stretch and warp, expanding into dimensions beyond the scope of sight or sense. Then it vanished. The entire Juncture, Quincunx and Pattern blazed out in a final burst of blinding glory, and went out.

Jorn gasped and sagged to the ground on his hands and knees, head down, utterly spent. Jan rapidly slipped back into his twin to give him comfort, but he was too exhausted from his own struggle to master the dark Nine to manage a healing. On the far side of the Pattern, Idris was tending to Corus, who had collapsed, breathing in shuddering gasps. Karan went to help him, and Rolf and Kayman came to look after the twins.

Eventually, Jorn recovered sufficiently to stare around him. Nothing seemed to have changed. 'Did we do it? I'm too tired to be able to tell.'

Rolf shook his head. 'I don't know. I do know that I have never experienced such a working. I doubt if there has ever been another of such mighty Power in all the history of mage-craft. It must have had an effect.'

'It was totally awesome,' agreed Kayman. 'But the black was unexpected. What was it?'

'Dark energy,' Jan told them. *'Nine hues of night, twinned with the Nine colours of light. The Juncture was designed to balance them, to make them work in harmony. I think that's what Darric risked disrupting by using just three Tools and ignoring the balance. The dark energy would be unopposed and totally destructive.'*

Jorn was about to answer when he heard Idris' urgent mind-voice. *'You must come, quickly! I fear that Corus is dying. The strain on his heart was too great. He wants to speak to you both.'* He went quickly to kneel beside the ancient raash. Corus smiled weakly and reached out to take the young mage's hand. He bespoke with calm certainty.

'The balance is restored. I feel it, in earth and air and fire and water. We mastered both dark and light. Thank you, my friends. You have done everything possible. The future of Vard must lie with others now. My task is done. I am tired and ready for my rest.' His eyelids fluttered and closed and, after a few soft breaths, his chest grew still. Karan sobbed. Idris bowed his head.

After a moment, they all stood and stretched wearily. Mordant said quietly, 'It was as he wished. I will miss him, but he was right. He achieved what he most desired, and it was time for his tired spirit to go onwards.'

'And we must go home and rest,' said Jan. 'I badly need a tree, and you both need a long soak in your fountain.'

Kayman had gone to take care of the Tools and the Juncture. 'I have them back in their boxes,' he told them. 'I wonder if they will ever be taken out and used again?'

Karan shook her head. 'I doubt if any here on Vard can master them, or would dare to try. But we will keep them and guard them well.' She gazed round at the white sands and the lapping sea. 'I wonder how long it will take for Vard to heal? I guess you don't change an entire planet in a few short minutes.'

'No, but you can start the process,' Jan told them. *'Like a pebble tossed in a pond, making the ripples swirl.'*

Jorn smiled. 'We'll be back to see what happens, and help Vard to recover, if you need us. But now we must rest. I want a feast of sweet things, and then bed. Take us back to Earth, please, Kayman. I have no strength left.'

Jorn

The elderly mage nodded and formed the misty gateway to their home universe. They all passed though, and it closed swiftly behind them.

Epilogue

On a bare, recently rain-drenched field, a faint green mist of new grass spread across the ochre earth. Two groups of males and a few females lined up in opposing huddles, staring with suspicious unease at the people opposite and muttering to each other.

One group consisted of humans and halfers, mainly dressed as field and factory slaves; the other was mostly halfers and a few raash, wearing the remnants of military uniform and overseers' tunics. The muttering ceased and silence lengthened.

One of the humans stepped forward. He was a wiry, young man, skinny but well-muscled from his labours. He took a large, round leather ball from his sack and did a few fancy ball control exercises with it.

There was a scattering of applause from his side, and a few catcalls from the other. He looked across at them and grinned. 'So, you bastards, is your team ready for the game then?' he called, casually.

A BRIEF GUIDE TO THE WORLDS

THE MULTIVERSE
The four Realms within this story are clones of our own universe. In each universe there is a galaxy that is a replica of our own, and an Earth type planet in the same location as ours. Each 'earth' is, however, subtly different from our own, having been cloned at a different time in Earth's history, and thence having followed its own pathway of development.

THE PATTERN
Human mages have discovered that it is possible to translocate to another Realm from Earth. The Pattern, (a set diagram of four overlapping circles) acts as a map to guide the use of colours to form the portal.

In relation to Earth, (which lies in the centre of the Pattern in the 'Here and Now') the Realms are separated by minute differences in their locations in space and time.

The Dwarran Realm is Behind (i.e. a fraction of a second in our past) and Below (in a spatial dimension beneath ours).

The Shian Realm is Ahead (i.e. a fraction of a second into our future) and Below.

The Raash Realm is Above and Below.

In theory there is a fourth Realm located Above and Ahead, but this has not been reached.

THE PLANETS
Earth: the Earth inhabited by the humans in this story is our own planet some eighteen thousand years in the future.

A barely remembered natural global catastrophe in the late 22nd century triggered a prolonged Ice Age, which almost wiped out humankind, and created a mass extinction that removed many species of animals and plants. People returned to a primitive Stone Age culture, but enough survived to re-establish a population once the ice retreated. As the ice retreated, the geography changed due to lowered sea levels.

It took many thousands of years to reach a culture resembling that in Europe in the 17th century. At the time of the story, science and technology is limited and much knowledge has been lost. People have resettled in Europe, but much of the remainder of the world is unknown. The lost past before the catastrophe is mythologised, and the distant ancestors are called "the Old Ones". In this new culture magic has emerged, because mages are born survivors and it is a useful mutation, but the Gift is regarded with suspicion.

Terrea in the Dwarran Realm, is very similar in climate and geography to our own world, and like Earth suffered a global catastrophe. The people who survived were a race of short, black-skinned humans who have gone on to develop a new culture, and are more scientifically advanced than people on Earth. Human and Dwarran mages have developed a friendly relationship, and Mage Hall is a multiracial training school.

Arden in the Shian Realm, is a verdant, mainly forested world where humans never evolved. The inhabitants are an intelligent form of quantum energy who were originally shape shifters, but have now adopted humanoid shapes. (This may have been due to contact with human mages at some point before the catastrophe, but the cause is forgotten.) They have two distinct races, the shians of the water, who require water for their survival, and shians of the wood who have a symbiotic relationship with trees. A few shians have the ability to become mages, and these usually travel to Mage Hall on Terrea to train.

Vard is like Earth at the time when it was covered by a single giant continental land mass. The raash are not indigenous, they came to Vard from another planet or dimension, and either eliminated the original inhabitants, or found an empty planet ready to be occupied. There are two species distinguished by the prominence of their bony crests. High-raash long ago defeated and subjugated their low-raash cousins and turned them into a subordinate slave race. Originally a cultured and technologically advanced people, the raash have declined due to centuries of civil war, becoming an exclusively militaristic society over-reliant on slaves for all necessities of life. The majority of high-raash have the ability to work magic. Recent overuse of violent magic has destabilised the climate and turned Vard into a semi-arid wilderness that is rapidly drying.

GLOSSARY

Adept	A mage who has mastered between five and eight colours.
Adjunct	One of the Sectors of the Quincunx, related to the element Water.
Apport	The ability to move and lift objects by means of magic.
Arden	The name of the shian planet, also known as the Shian Realm.
Basic	The language used by all humans as shared means of communication.
Bespeaking	Telepathic communication between mages.
Biddable	A spell construct implanted in the subject's mind that renders him or her obedient. to the mage's will, or compelled to act in a certain way given a cue.
Binding	A spell construct which either binds (i.e. blocks) the Power of a mage or prevents him from acting; the most commonly used form is the mind fetter.
Blinder	An attacking spell construct that renders the enemy blind.
Blob-Faces	A derisory term that raash use to describe humans.
Candrim	A nation of raash, ruled by Peridor, mortal enemy of Daric.
Chain of Earth	One of the Tools of Power, which masters Conjunct.
Colours	The nine colours of magic that are mentally manipulated to construct spells.
Construct	A spell form produced by mentally manipulating the colours into plaits, ribbons, twists, webs, ribbons, knotted cords and other complex structures. Constructs can be stored ready for use.
Conjunct	One of the Sectors of the Quincunx, related to the element Earth.
Cross-step	Instant transfer from one place to another over a relatively short distance, without using a portal.

Cup of Water	One of the Tools of Power that masters Adjunct.
Disjunct	One of the Sectors of the Quincunx, related to the element Fire.
Essence	The term used by shians to describe the dynamic spiritual entity that inhabits a sentient being and is, they believe, released at death.
Far-seeing	A vision of events happening at the current time but at a distance, sometimes experienced as a dream, more usually by means of scrying.
Fore-seeing	Having a vision of the future.
Form	The solid shape adopted by a shian.
Gift	The specific set of Powers that a mage innately possesses.
Glamour	A type of construct that changes the outward appearance of something, or makes an observer react in a particular way.
High raash	The ruling elite who have prominent brow and forehead crests.
Hook	A clear mental image of a feature of the place to which one wishes to translocate. This is essential in order to form a portal. It is not possible to translocate to a place for which one has no hook.
Knife of Fire	One of the Tools of Power that masters Disjunct. The Knife was found and returned to Vard some 500 years before Mordant's time.
Hyakim	A nation of raash ruled by the Mage-Lord Darric and his Sister-Consort, Ajina.
Injunct	One of the Sectors of the Quincunx, related to the element Air.
Juncture	The central nexus of the Quincunx.
Low raash	The slave race of raash, who have lower crests.
Mage	One who can work magic. A mage has mastery of at least four of the nine colours. A Mage is described according to the number of colours,, for example, Master of Five.
Magic	Magic aims to manipulate mind and matter, time and space, for a defined purpose, through the applied use of will and innate power.

Mask 1	A derisory term used by human to describe raash, referring to their rigid skull-like faces.
Mask 2	A construct used to change one's personal appearance. A mask changes only the face, whilst a whole body working changes the entire appearance.
Mastery	The ability of a mage to control his or her colours; this is achieved by willing the colours to remain inside the confines of the Quincunx until brought into use.
Master of Nine	An extremely rare level of ability in which the mage masters all the colours and possesses great Power. The only recorded Master of Nine was Myron who lived a thousand years before the time of Mordant.
Mental Workroom	A space created inside the mind of the mage where the Quincunx is installed. The mage can enter and leave his workroom at will and when there it seems as real to him or her as the outer world. This is the place where Power is brought into use and constructs are created and stored.
Mind-fetter	A construct used by a mage to bind the Power of another. The mind-fetter also prevents any action that is not specifically permitted by the mage.
Nexus	One of the five dots on the Quincunx.
Never-mind	Similar to a Pass-me-by, a glamour that hides or disguises an object.
Numerator	A spell construct that makes it seem as if a group of people is the original number when one or two have been added or removed from it.
Pattern	The Pattern acts as a map to help when forming a portal to another Realm/universe.
Pass-me-by	A construct that makes the user blend into the surroundings so well that they appear to be invisible.
Portal	A gateway through time and space formed by a mage, used to translocate people and objects from

	one Realm to another or from one place to another on a planet. Only adepts can form portals.
Power	Magic.
Quincunx	The matrix that the mage uses to perform magic. It has five dots (nexuses) linked by lines to form an outer square and inner cross. Each line and dots carries one of the nine colours.
Raash	A race of humanoid aliens who inhabit Vard.
Realm	One of four parallel universes known to earth mages in which there is an earth-type planet reached by a portal.
Scrying	Using a bowl of water as a means of inducing a vision.
Sense	The paranormal ability of a mage to be aware of things unseen or magical.
Sigil	A magical symbol.
Shaft	A spell construct using a pure form of a colour without manipulation, often an attacking spell using the red of Disjunct.
Shi	The intangible, almost invisible energy form of a shian.
Shian of the Water	A sentient entity that lives in water. This being must have water at frequent intervals in order to survive. A shian can change shape, transforming his shi either into a mist form, or into a semi-human solid form.
Shian of the Air	Separate, but related race to those of the shians of the water.
Shin of the Wood	Shians of the wood have a symbiotic relationship with trees on which they depend for nourishment and protection. Each shian has a home tree. When out of the tree, a shian can take a near-human form.
Sector of Command	A large triangle, half of the Quincunx. (see Injunct, Adjunct, Conjunct and Disjunct).Working within a Sector focuses Power on specific functions.
Sleep-and-forget	A construct that sends the subject to sleep and removes his memory.

Spectrum	The nine colours of Power.
Sending	A vision.
Spell-tag	A tiny construct that marks a person or object to enable tracking and re-location.
Stunner	A spell construct that knocks out its victim.
Tag	An object with a distinctive pattern painted onto it which acts as a hook for a translocation.
Terrea	The name of the dwarran planet, also known as the Dwarran Realm.
Translocation	The act of using a portal to pass from one universe to another.
Transition	Using a portal to cross a distance within the same planet.
Transit Point	A secure place to which mages can portal in or out when making journeys between universes. Each Point is staffed by mages who can help those who need to travel, but do not have the right colours for their destination. Transit Points also act as 'post offices'.
Triad	A triangular section of the Quincunx, consisting of three Nexuses and their linking lines, also half of a Sector.
Tools of Power	Originally made by raash mages, these embody the Powers of the Sectors of the Quincunx and can be used to augment and sustain the Power of a mage when working. These are subject to much myth and misunderstanding.
Vard	The home planet of the raash.
The Wand of Air	One of the Tools of Power that masters Injunct.
Ward	A spell construct designed to protect the user from attack. This may include a mind shield (which prevents an enemy mage from entering and taking over the user's mind) or a body shield (which acts as armour against weapons), or a combination of both. To increase effectiveness, a mage may be double or triple warded.

Warlock	A man who has limited magical ability, having between one and three colours. He is unable to form or use a mental Quincunx.
War-hammer	An attacking construct of great power with enormous destructive potential. Only used by high-level adepts.
Witch	A woman who has limited magical ability, having between one and three colours. She is unable to form or use a mental Quincunx.
Working	The process of mentally creating a Construct.

SHIAN DICTIONARY

Bibba	Mummy/Daddy; shian child's name for parents
Corun-i-lashulann	Gathering for Music
Do	on
Dol	sun
e	and
fullisarra	may (it) shine
-isse	youngling. An affectionate, diminutive suffix
Jan	oak tree
jan-keb	oak cup
jorn	acorn
kiri	the flap that covers the groin area of the male shian
lorgan	tree
ovrassedea	blessed be your days; shian equivalent of 'farewell' before a journey, or a parting of friends.
Pella	kindly or softly
salla-leashta-te	'may the waters sustain you' a polite greeting used by shians of the water
shi	the energy form of a shian
sut	essence; the immortal core of an individual, a combination of consciousness, personality and soul
Taktata-Deshuka	drumming dance
tantar	dear friend; used between those who have a close relationship
tantar-alta	my dear old friend
tantar-isse	my dear young friend
(tuk)	a click made by the tongue against teeth; signifies a pause
Tuka	the solid form that the shi can adopt
Unmelli-Diakluna	Song of Earth and Sky; a traditional welcome

If you enjoyed *Jorn*, please share your thoughts on Amazon by leaving a review.

For more free and discounted eBooks every week, sign up to the Endeavour Press newsletter.

Follow us on Twitter and Instagram.

Printed in Great Britain
by Amazon